A DIAM
IN HER STOCKING

BY
KANDY SHEPHERD

All rights reserved including the right of reproduction in whole or in part in any form. This edition is published by arrangement with Harlequin Books S.A.

© Kandy Shepherd

MILLS
BOON

Published in Great Britain 2014
by Mills & Boon, an imprint of Harlequin (UK) Limited,
Eton House, 18-24 Paradise Road, Richmond, Surrey, TW9 1SR

© 2014 Kandy Shepherd

ISBN: 978-0-263-91339-2

23-1214

Harlequin (UK) Limited's policy is to use papers that are natural, renewable and recyclable products and made from wood grown in sustainable forests. The logging and manufacturing processes conform to the legal environmental regulations of the country of origin.

Printed and bound in Spain
by CPI, Barcelona

Kandy Shepherd swapped a fast-paced career as a magazine editor for a life writing romance. She lives on a small farm in the Blue Mountains near Sydney, Australia, with her husband, daughter, and a menagerie of animal friends. Kandy believes in love at first sight and real-life romance—they worked for her!

Kandy loves to hear from her readers. Visit her website at: www.kandyshepherd.com.

To the A-team,
Cathleen Ross, Elizabeth Lhuede and Keziah Hill,
with heartfelt thanks for the friendship and support!

CHAPTER ONE

As Lizzie Dumont looked around at the soon-to-open Bay Bites café, her new place of employment, she vowed she would never reveal how she really felt about the way her high-flying career as a chef had crash-landed into a culinary backwater like Dolphin Bay. Not when people here had been so kind to her.

She would put behind her the adrenalin rush of working at star-rated restaurants in the gastronomic capitals of Paris and Lyon. Give up the buzz of being part of the thriving restaurant scene in Sydney. Embrace the comparatively lowly life of a café cook.

Her sigh echoed around the empty café. Who was she kidding? That heady time in France had been the pinnacle of her career. But she'd been sinking in Sydney. Working shift after shift until past midnight in restaurant kitchens—no matter how fashionable the venues— had hardly been compatible with being a good parent to her five-year-old daughter, Amy.

With no family in Sydney to fall back on, and few friends because she'd lived in France for so long before her divorce, she'd struggled to give Amy a reasonable life. Drowning in debt, swimming against the current of erratic babysitter schedules and unreasonable rosters, after less than a year she'd been going under.

By the time her sister Sandy had approached her to manage the new café adjacent to Sandy's bookshop, Lizzie had been on the edge of despair. She'd even been contemplating the unthinkable—letting Amy live permanently with her ex-husband Philippe in France.

Gratefully, she'd grabbed the lifeline Sandy had thrown her.

And here she was. Dolphin Bay was a rapidly growing resort town on the south coast of New South Wales, with a heritage-listed harbour and beautiful beaches. It was also, in her experience, a gastronomic wasteland—the only memorable meal she could ever remember eating was fish and chips straight from the vinegar-soaked wrapping.

But Sandy had offered her sanctuary and a new life with Amy. In return, Lizzie would throw herself wholeheartedly into making Bay Bites the best café on the south coast. Heck, why stop there? She would use her skills and expertise to make Bay Bites the best café in the country.

She let herself get the teeniest bit excited at the thought. After all, she would be in charge. No cranky head chef screaming insults at her. No gritting her teeth at an ill-chosen item on the menu she'd been forced to cook whether she'd liked it or not.

She continued her inspection, her spirits rising by the second. Sandy had done a wonderful job of the fit-out. The décor was sleek and contemporary but with welcome touches of whimsy. In particular, she loved the way the dolphin theme had been incorporated. Hand-painted tiles backed the service area. Carved wooden dolphins supported the wooden countertop and framed the large blackboard on the wall behind it where she would chalk up the daily specials.

There was still work to be done. Lots of it. Boxes were stacked around the perimeter of the café waiting for her to unpack. Large flat packages, wrapped in brown paper, were propped against the walls. She itched to get started.

But someone had started the unpacking. Outsized glass jars were already lined up at the other end of the counter to the cash register, their polished chrome lids glinting in the late afternoon sun that filtered through the plate glass windows that faced the view of the harbour.

She could envisage the jars already filled with her secret recipe cookies. Nearby was the old-fashioned glass-fronted rotating cabinet for cakes and pies she'd asked Sandy to order. The equipment in the kitchen was brand new. It was perfect. *She would make this work.*

Lizzie ran her hand along the wooden countertop, marvelling at the intricacy of the carved dolphins, breathing in the smell of fresh varnish and new beginnings.

'Those dolphins are kinda cool, aren't they?' The deep masculine voice from behind her made her spin around. She recognised it immediately.

But the shock of seeing Jesse Morgan stride through the connecting doorway from Bay Books next door expelled all the breath from her lungs. Her heart started to hammer so hard she had to clutch her hands to her chest to still it.

Jesse Morgan. All six foot three of him: black-haired, blue-eyed, movie-star handsome. Jesse Morgan of the broad shoulders and lean hips; of honed muscles accentuated by white T-shirt and denim jeans. Jesse Morgan, who was meant to be somewhere far, far away from Dolphin Bay.

Why hadn't someone warned her he was in town?

Lizzie's sister was married to Jesse's brother Ben. Six months ago, Jesse had been the best man and she the chief bridesmaid at Ben and Sandy's wedding. Lizzie hoped against hope Jesse might have forgotten what had happened between them at the wedding reception.

One look at the expression in his deep blue eyes told her he had not.

She cringed all the way down to her sneaker-clad feet.

'What are you doing here?' she managed to choke out once she had regained use of her voice. She was aiming for nonchalance but it came out as a wobbly attempt at bravado.

'Hello to you, too, Lizzie,' he said with a Jesse-brand charming smile, standing there in her café as confident and sure of himself as ever. A confidence surely bred from an awareness that since he'd been a teenager he would always be the best-looking man in the room. But she noticed the smile didn't quite warm his eyes.

She tried to backtrack to a more polite greeting. But she didn't know what to say. Not when the last time they'd met she'd been passionately kissing him, wanting him so badly she'd been tempted to throw away all caution and common sense and go much further than kissing.

'You gave me a fright coming in behind me like that,' she said with a rising note of defensiveness to her voice. Darn it. That was a dumb thing to say. She didn't want him to think he had any effect on her at all.

Which, in spite of everything, would be a total lie. Jesse Morgan exuded raw masculine appeal. It triggered a sudden rush of awareness that tingled right through her. Any red-blooded woman would feel it. *Lots* of red-blooded women had felt it, by all accounts, she thought, her lips thinning.

'I didn't mean to scare you,' he said. 'But Sandy told me you were in here. She sent me to give you a hand with the unpacking. I've made a start, as you can see.'

He took a step towards her. She scuttled backwards, right up against the countertop, cursing herself for her total lack of cool. She was so anxious to keep a distance between them she didn't register the discomfort of the dorsal fin of the wooden dolphin pressing into her back.

It wasn't fair a man could be so outrageously handsome. The Black Irish looks he'd inherited from his mother's side gave him the currency he could have chosen to trade for a career as an actor or model. But he'd laughed that off in a self-deprecating way when she'd teased him with it.

Which had only made him seem even more appealing.

How very wrong could she have been about a man?

'I only just got here from Sydney, after a four-hour drive,' she said. 'I...I haven't really thought where to start.'

'Can I get you a drink—some water, a coffee?' he asked.

He sounded so sincere. *All part of the act.*

'No, thank you,' she said, regaining some of her manners now the shock of seeing him had passed. After all, he was her sister's brother-in-law. She couldn't just ask him to leave, the way she'd like to. 'I stopped for a bite to eat on the way down.'

Despite herself she couldn't help scanning his face to see what change six months had brought him. Heaven knew what change he saw in her. She felt all the stress of the last months had aged her way more than her twenty-nine years.

He, about the same age, looked as though a care had never caused his brow to furrow. His tan was deeper than when she'd last seen him, making his eyes seem even bluer. A day away from a shave, dark growth shadowed his jaw. His black hair was longer and curled around his ears. She remembered the way she had fisted her hand in his hair to pull him closer as she'd kissed him.

How could she have been so taken in by him?

She squirmed with regret. She'd known of his reputation. But one champagne had led to one champagne too many and all the tightly held resolutions she'd made after her divorce about having nothing to do with too-handsome, too-charming men had dissolved in the laughter and fun she'd shared with Jesse.

Was he remembering that night? How they'd found the same exhilarating rhythm dancing with each other? How, when the band had taken a break, they'd gone outside on the balcony?

She'd been warned that Jesse was a heartbreaker, a womaniser. But he'd been fun and there hadn't been much fun in her life for a long time. It had seemed the most natural thing in the world to slip into his arms when he had kissed her in a private corner of the balcony lit only by the faintest beams of moonlight. His kiss had been magical—slow, sensuous, thrilling. It had evoked needs and desires long buried and she had given herself to the moment, not caring about consequences.

Then a group of other guests had pushed through the doors to the balcony with a burst of loud chatter, and broken the spell.

It had been the classic wedding cliché—the chief

bridesmaid and the best man getting caught in a passionate clinch.

Lizzie cringed at the memory of those moments. The hoots and catcalls of the other guests as they'd discovered them kissing. 'Jesse's at it again,' someone had called, laughing.

She'd never felt more humiliated. Not because of being caught kissing. They were both single adults who could kiss whomever they darn well pleased. She'd laughed that off. No. The humiliation was caused by the painful awareness she'd been seen as just another in a long line of Jesse's girls. Girls he had kissed and discarded when the next pretty face had come along.

But, despite knowing that, it hadn't stopped her from going back for more with Jesse that night. Why had she imagined he'd be any different with her?

What an idiot she'd been.

Now she cleared her throat, determined to make normal—if stilted—conversation; not to let Jesse know how shaken she was at seeing him again. How compellingly attractive she still found him.

'Aren't you meant to be gallivanting around the world doing good works? I thought you were in India,' she asked. Jesse worked for an international aid organisation that built housing for the victims of natural disasters.

Jesse shook his head. 'The Philippines this time. Rebuilding villages in the aftermath of a gigantic mudslide. Thousands of houses were destroyed.'

'That must have been dangerous,' she said. Jesse was a party guy personified, and yet his job took him to developing countries where he used his skills as an engineer to help strangers in need. She'd found that contradiction fascinating.

Just another way she'd been sucked into his game.

'Dangerous and dirty,' he said simply. 'But that's what we do.'

She shouldn't feel a surge of relief that he had escaped that danger without harm. But she did. Though she told herself that was just because he was part of the extended family now. The black sheep, as far as she was concerned.

'So you're back here because…?'

'The "good works" led to an injured shoulder,' he said. He raised his broad right shoulder to demonstrate and in doing so winced. His so-handsome face contorted in pain and the blood drained, leaving him pale under his tan.

Her first reaction was to rush over and comfort him. To stroke his shoulder to help ease the pain. Or offer to kiss it better…

No! She forced her thoughts away from Crazyville. Gripped her hands tightly together so she wouldn't be tempted. She was furious with herself. Wasn't she meant to now be immune to his appeal?

Getting together with Jesse Morgan at the wedding had been like nibbling on just one square of a bar of fine Belgian dark chocolate and denying herself the rest even though she knew it would be utterly delicious. Quite possibly the best chocolate she had ever tasted.

But she prided herself on her willpower when it came to chocolate. And men who offered her nothing more than a fleeting physical thrill.

Her aim was to build a new life for her and Amy. She didn't want a man around to complicate things. Not now. Maybe not ever. And if she did decide to date again it wouldn't be with someone like Jesse Morgan. She'd been there, done that, with her good-looking charmer of an ex-husband who had let her down so badly.

The next man for her—if she decided to go there—would be steady, reliable, living in the same country as her and average-looking. She wanted a man who only had eyes for her.

Jesse was a player and Lizzie didn't want to play. Her party-girl days were far behind her. It would be work, work, work for her in Dolphin Bay. And being the best mother she could possibly be to her precious daughter.

Not that Jesse was giving her any indication that he had a real interest in her. Not now. Not then. It still stung. *How could she have believed in him?*

After they'd been interrupted on the balcony, she'd rushed away to look in on Amy. When she'd returned, out of breath from her hurry to get back to Jesse, she had found him dancing with a beautiful dark-haired woman, his head too close to hers, his laughter ringing out over the noise of the band. Had he taken her out onto the balcony and kissed her too? Lizzie hadn't hung around to find out. She'd avoided him for the rest of the evening.

'I'm sorry to hear you've been hurt,' she said stiffly. *Boy, had she wanted to hurt him back then.*

'All in the line of duty,' he said. 'My own fault for grappling with a too-large concrete beam without help.'

'So you've come home to recuperate?' she asked. She became aware of the carving pressing into her back and moved from the countertop, being careful not to take a step closer to him. Her reaction to him had unnerved her. She didn't know that she could trust herself not to reach out to him if she got too near.

'That's right,' he said. 'But I'm bored with all the physiotherapy and "taking it easy". I've been helping Ben and Sandy finish off the café.' He looked around him with a proprietorial air that she found disconcerting. 'Impressive, isn't it?'

'Very,' she said. 'I love the dolphin carvings. Every business in this town has to display some kind of dolphin motif, if I remember correctly. These are works of art.'

She kept her tone neutral but inside she was seething. In all their phone calls and Skype discussions about the progress of the café, Sandy had never once mentioned that Jesse was back in town. Her sister, along with everyone else in this gossip-ridden small town, knew she and Jesse had been caught making out on the balcony.

It wouldn't have been a huge deal anywhere else but here it was big news. Jesse was the kind of guy the locals kept odds on. The big bets were on that he would never settle down with one woman.

She found herself nervously glancing out of the plate glass windows that led to the street for fear people walking by might notice her and Jesse alone together.

She didn't want to become part of the Jesse mythology. Be a butt of local jokes. But her indiscretion on the night of the wedding meant, most likely, she'd been added to the list of his conquests. Why hadn't Sandy warned her Jesse had made an unscheduled visit home? That he'd be working on the café? It would be almost impossible to avoid him.

As Jesse reached out to touch the dolphin carvings, she jerked away from him to avoid any possible contact. He raised a dark eyebrow but didn't say anything. Which made her feel even more ill at ease.

'They're by the same Balinese carvers as the fittings next door in Bay Books,' he said, stroking the dolphin. She couldn't look, couldn't let herself remember how good his hands had felt on the bare skin of her back in her strapless bridesmaid dress. 'Sandy had the countertop custom-made and then imported it. I only finished installing it yesterday.'

'So you've completed work on the fit-out now?' She spoke through gritted teeth. *Please, please, please let him be on his way back to his job in the Philippines.*

'Just about.'

She sighed with too-obvious relief. 'So you won't be around much longer.'

Only a tightening of his beautifully chiselled lips betrayed he'd noticed her tone.

'There's the unpacking to do. And I still have to finish off some tiling upstairs in your apartment,' he said.

'You've been working up there?' She regretted the squawk of alarm as soon as it had escaped from her mouth. Jesse in her bathroom; maybe in her bedroom? The thought was disconcerting, to say the least.

But she couldn't let him know she was worried he would invade her private thoughts when she was alone in those rooms. *She mustn't let that happen.*

'Sandy wanted the bathroom remodelled to be as comfortable as possible for you and your little girl,' he said.

'Thank you for your help,' she managed politely. 'It was a big order to get it ready in time for us to move in.'

Her real gratitude was to Sandy. How many other down-on-their-luck chefs had a sister who had offered not only a job but also a place to live, rent-free?

But having Jesse Morgan around hadn't been part of the deal. She didn't want to be reminded of her lack of judgement on the night of the wedding. Of the folly of being in his arms. She should have known better than to fall for that kind of guy again.

Because, no matter how many times over the last six months she'd told herself that Jesse was bad news, seeing him again made her aware she'd be lying if she thought she was immune to him. He was still out-and-out the most attractive man she'd ever met. She would have to fight that attraction every moment she found herself in his company. Dear heaven, let there not be too many of those moments.

She looked purposefully around her again. 'I'd hate for the building work here to delay your recuperation.'

Jesse's deep blue eyes narrowed. 'So I can get the hell out of Dolphin Bay, you mean?'

She struggled to meet his gaze. 'I…I didn't mean it like that,' she lied.

His face set in grim lines. 'You might not like it but you'd better get used to me being around. I'm going to be here for at least another month while my shoulder heals.'

She couldn't help her little gasp of horror. 'What?'

Only the twist of his mouth indicated he'd heard. 'Sandy needs help to get this venture up and running and I intend to give it to her. The Morgan family is grateful to Sandy. Heaven knows where Ben would be if she hadn't come back into his life after all those years.'

'Of course,' she said, suddenly feeling shamefaced that all she was thinking about was herself.

Lizzie and Sandy had first visited Dolphin Bay on a family vacation as teenagers. They'd stayed in the Morgan family's character-filled old guest house. Lizzie remembered Jesse from that time as an arrogant show-off, flexing his well-developed teenage muscles at any opportunity. But Sandy had fallen in love with Ben. They hadn't met again until twelve years later, after Ben had lost his first wife and baby son in the fire that had destroyed the guest house. Together they'd taken a second chance on love.

'I want to make this café a success for Sandy as well,' Lizzie continued. 'And for Ben, too—he's a marvellous brother-in-law. They've both been very good to me.'

Sandy was the only person she felt she could really trust. They'd been allies in the battleground that had been their family, led by their bully of a father. Her older sister had always watched out for her. Just like she was watching out for her and Amy now. Lizzie owed her.

'Then we're on the same page,' Jesse said.

'Right,' she said, unable to keep the anxiety from her voice.

'Bay Bites opens in a week's time. We don't have time to waste bickering,' Jesse said.

He took a few steps towards her until she was back up against that dolphin fin again and she couldn't back away from him any further. She felt breathless at his proximity, the memories of how good it had felt to be in his arms treacherously near the surface.

But this wasn't the fun, charming Jesse she'd known at the wedding bearing down on her. This Jesse looked tough, implacable and she didn't think it was her imagination that he seemed suddenly contemptuous of her.

'So better grit your teeth and bear being in my company for as long as it takes,' he said.

She'd had no idea his voice could sound so harsh.

CHAPTER TWO

JESSE NEARLY LAUGHED out loud at the expression of dismay on Lizzie's face. She so obviously didn't want to work with him any more than he wanted to work with her. Not after her behaviour at Ben and Sandy's wedding.

He could brush off his reputation as a player—but that wasn't to say he liked it. And he hadn't liked being made a fool of by Lizzie in the public arena of his brother's wedding reception. He hadn't appreciated having to make so many gritted teeth responses to his Dolphin Bay friends as they'd asked why Lizzie had left him high and dry when they'd so publicly been having a good time together. That had been difficult when he'd had no idea himself. There had been only so many jokes about whether he needed to change his deodorant that he could take. His banter had run dry long before he'd realised Lizzie wasn't coming back.

He indicated the packages propped up against the wall. 'Right now I'm here to help you get those artworks up on the walls.'

'I'm not sure I need help,' she said, folding her arms in front of her. 'I'm quite capable of placing the artwork myself.'

Lizzie's looks were deceptive. Tall and slender with

a mass of white blonde, finely curled hair, she gave the initial impression of being frail. But he knew there was steel under that fragile appearance. Her arms might be slim but they were firm with lean muscle. At the wedding she'd explained that hauling heavy cooking pans around a restaurant kitchen was a daily weight training regime.

'No,' he said curtly. 'That's my job and I'm here to do it.'

'What about your shoulder? Surely you shouldn't be lifting stuff.'

'Canvas artworks? Not a problem. This phase of my rehab calls for some light lifting.'

'But I need time to sort through them, to decide which paintings I like best.'

Her bottom lip stuck out stubbornly. She was putting up a fight. *Tough.* He'd promised Sandy he'd help out. For the years Ben had been immersed in grief, Jesse felt he had lost his adored older brother. Sandy's love had restored Ben to him. He could never thank her enough. If that meant having to spend too much time with her sister, he'd endure it. Lizzie could put up with it too.

He thought into the future and saw a long procession of family occasions where he and Lizzie would be forced into each other's company, whether they liked it or not. He had to learn to deal with it. So would she. And he would have to forever ignore how attractive he found her.

'That's where we read from the same page,' he said patiently, as if he were talking to a child. 'You choose. I hammer a nail in the wall and hang the picture. Then the artists want the rejects back ASAP.'

She looked startled. 'Rejects? I wouldn't want to offend any artists. Art appreciation is such a personal thing.'

'The artists have supplied these paintings to be sold on consignment,' he explained. 'You sell them through the café and get a commission on each sale. If they don't get hung this time, maybe they'll survive your cull next time.'

Lizzie nodded. It was the first time she'd agreed with him, though he sensed it took an effort. 'True. So I should probably compile an A-list for immediate hanging and a B-list for reserves. The Bs can then be ready to slip into place when the As are sold.'

'In theory a good idea. But keep the grading system to yourself. This is a small community.'

'Point taken,' she said, meeting his gaze square on. 'I'll defer to your small-town wisdom. We city people don't understand such things.'

He didn't miss the subtle edge of sarcasm to her words and again he had to fight a smile. He'd liked that tough core to her.

In fact when he'd met Lizzie at the pre-wedding party in Sydney for Ben and Sandy, he'd been immediately drawn to her. And not just for her good looks.

With her slender body, light blonde hair and cool grey eyes set in the pale oval of her face, she'd seemed ethereally lovely. But when she'd smiled, her eyes had lit up with a warmth and vivacity that had surprised him.

'Let's celebrate these long-lost lovers getting together in style,' she'd said with a big earthy laugh that had been a wholehearted invitation to fun. From then on, the evening had turned out a whole lot better than he'd expected.

Lizzie had made him laugh with her tales of life in

the stressful, volatile world of commercial kitchens. That night had been memorable. So had the wedding reception a few days later. She'd kept him entertained with a game where she made amusing whispered predictions about the favourite foods of the other guests. All based on years of personal research into restaurant guests' tastes, she'd assured him with a straight face.

He hadn't been sure whether she was serious or not. Thing was, she'd been right more often than she'd been wrong. She'd had him watching the wedding guests as they made their choices at the buffet. He'd whooped with her when she'd got it right—his father heading straight for the fillet of beef—and commiserated with her when she'd got it wrong—an ultra-thin friend of the bride loading her plate with desserts. The game was silly, childish even, but he had thoroughly enjoyed every moment of her company. Those moments out on the balcony where she'd come so willingly into his arms had been a bonus.

At that time, he'd been in dire need of some levity and laughter, having just unexpectedly encountered the woman who had broken his heart years before. He'd first met the older, more worldly-wise Camilla when he'd been twenty-five; she'd been a photojournalist documenting his team's rebuilding of a flood-damaged community in Sri Lanka. He'd thought he'd never see her again after their disastrous break-up that had left him shattered and cynical about love, loyalty and trust.

At the wedding, lovely, spirited Lizzie had been both a distraction and a reminder that there could be life after treacherous Camilla.

Until Lizzie had walked out on him at the wedding without warning.

And now he was facing a completely different Lizzie.

A Lizzie where it seemed as if the spark had fizzled right out of her. She was chilly. Standoffish. Hostile, even.

It made him wonder why he had found her appealing. He'd been so wrong about Camilla; seemed as if he'd misjudged Lizzie too.

He hadn't been on top of his game at that time; that was for sure.

And now, by the mere fact her sister was married to his brother, he was stuck with her. Trouble was, he still found her every bit as beautiful as when he'd first met her.

The sooner they got the paintings hung and the boxes unpacked, the sooner he could get out of here and away from her prickly presence. He'd endured some difficult situations in his time. But it looked as if putting up with Lizzie was going to be one of the most difficult of all. Even twenty minutes with her was stretching his patience. But there was work to be done and he'd made a commitment to Sandy.

He'd break his time working with Lizzie into manageable blocks. He reckoned he could endure two hours of forced politeness in her company; manage to ignore how lovely she was. He'd make a strict schedule and stick to it. He looked at his watch. One hour and forty minutes to go. 'Let's get cracking on sorting those paintings. There's an amazing one of dolphins surfing I think you might want to look at first.'

Under her breath, Lizzie let off a string of curse words. She swore fluently in both English and French—it was difficult not to pick up some very colourful language working in the pressure cooker atmosphere of commercial kitchens.

But these days she kept a guard on her tongue. No way did she want Amy picking up any undesirable phrases. So she kept the curse words rolling only in her mind. This particular stream was directed—non-verbally of course—towards her sister. What had Sandy been thinking to trap her in such close confines with Jesse Morgan?

He was insufferable. Talking to her as if she was an idiot. Well, she had been an idiot to have fancied him so much at the wedding. To have let physical attraction overrule good sense. But that was then and this was now.

Like many chefs, during the years she had worked in other peoples' restaurants, she had entertained the idea of running a restaurant of her own. In fact she and Philippe had been working towards just that until she'd unexpectedly fallen pregnant and everything had changed.

For sure, her dream of running her own show hadn't centred on a café in a place like Dolphin Bay but she could make the most of her downgraded dream. She knew what it took to make customers want to come to a restaurant—and to keep them coming. She didn't need Mr Know-It-All Jesse Morgan telling her how to choose the art for the walls. For heaven's sake, was he going to tell her what dishes to put on the menu?

She made a point of looking at her watch too. Two could play at this game. 'Okay, let's unwrap the paintings one at a time and then I'll compare them and decide which ones I like best. Without being so insensitive as to grade them, of course.'

For a moment she thought she saw a smile lurk around the corners of his grimly set mouth. It passed so quickly she could have imagined it. But for a second—just that second—she'd seen again that Jesse from the wedding who had appealed to her so much. Boy, had she got him wrong.

She walked across to the stacks of paintings. 'Shall we start with the largest one first?' she said.

Jesse nodded as he followed her over. 'That's the surfing dolphins one.'

She immediately wished she'd decided to open the smallest ones first. But she couldn't backtrack now.

The painting was bracketed with sheets of cardboard and then wrapped with thick brown paper. She started to open it but the paper was too tough to tear. Silently, Jesse reached into his pocket and pulled out a retractable-blade utility knife. Again without saying a word, he clicked it free of its safety cover and handed it to her.

'Thanks,' she muttered, biting down on the urge to tell him not to keep such a dangerous tool in his pocket. She knew she was being unreasonable, but Jesse seemed to have that effect on her. As much as she hated to admit it, she'd been hurt by his behaviour at the wedding, and she would do whatever it took to protect herself from feeling that way again.

She crouched down and carefully slit the paper across the top of the wrapping. As she went to cut down the side, Jesse reached out a hand to stop her.

She flinched. *Don't touch me*, she wanted to snarl. But that would sound irrational. She gritted her teeth.

'Leave that,' he said. 'If you don't cut the sides the painting will be easier to get back in the wrapping.'

She stilled for the long moment his hand stayed on her wrist. Of course he had beautiful hands, just like the rest of him—she couldn't fail to register that. His fingers were warm and immediately familiar on her bare skin. She closed her eyes tight. *She couldn't deal with this.* But she was just about to shake off his hand when he removed it. She realised she was holding her breath and she let it out in a controlled sigh that she prayed he didn't register.

'Good idea,' she managed to choke out. *Why did he have to stand so close beside her?*

'I'll give you a hand to slide the painting out. It's too heavy for one person.'

She had to acknowledge the truth in that. It would seem churlish not to. 'Thanks,' she said.

She stood at one end of the painting and he at the other and they lifted it free of its wrappings. As the image emerged, she could not help a gasp. The artist had perfectly captured in acrylic, on the underside of a breaking aquamarine wave, a pod of dolphins joyfully surfing towards the beach. 'It's wonderful. No. More than wonderful. Breathtaking.'

Jesse would have been justified in an I-told-you-so smirk. Instead he nodded. 'I thought so too,' he said.

Lizzie reached out a hand to touch the painting then drew it back. 'This artist is so talented. It looks like Big Ray beach, is it?' Big Ray was the local surf beach. It had a different name on the maps. The locals called it Big Ray because of the two enormous dark manta rays that periodically glided their way from one headland to the other. As a kid, visiting Dolphin Bay, she had been both fascinated by and frightened of them.

'Yep. One of the smaller paintings is of the rays.'

'Let's open that one next.' She couldn't keep the excitement from her voice.

'So the big one passes muster?'

'Oh, yes,' she said. 'It gets a triple A. You were absolutely right. It's perfect.' She indicated a central spot on the wall. 'It would look fabulous right there.'

'I agree,' he said. 'The artist will be delighted. She was really hoping you'd choose one of her paintings.'

'*She?*' The word slipped out of her mouth.

Jesse's eyes darkened to the colour of the sea on a stormy day. 'Yes. She. Is that a problem?'

'Of course not. It's just—'

'It's just that you've jumped to the immediate wrong conclusion. The artist is a friend of my mother. A retired art teacher. I know her because she taught me at high school. Not because she's one of the infamous "Jesse's girls".'

'I…I didn't think that for one moment. Of course I didn't.' *Of course she had.*

At the wedding, she had wanted to be with Jesse so much, she had refused to acknowledge his reputation. Until he himself had shown her the truth of it.

She took a step away from him. His physical presence was so powerful she was uncomfortably aware of him. His muscular arms, tan against the white of his T-shirt. The strength of his chest. His flawless face. Stand too close and she could sense his body heat, breathe the spice of his scent that immediately evoked memories she was desperately trying to suppress.

She thought quickly. 'I…I just thought the artist might have been a man because of the sheer size and scale of the painting.'

'Fair enough,' he conceded, though to her eye he didn't look convinced. In fact she had the impression he was struggling to contain a retort. 'If you're sure you want this painting as the hero, let's get it up first so we can then balance the others around it.'

'That could work,' she said. He was right, of course he was right. And she could not let her memories of how he had hurt her hinder her from giving him the courtesy she owed him for his help.

He stood in front of the wall and narrowed his eyes. After a long pause he pointed. 'If we centre it there, I reckon we'll be able to achieve a balanced display.'

'Okay,' she said.

It wasn't a good idea to stand behind him. His rear view was even more appealing than she had remembered. Those broad shoulders, the butt that could sell a million pairs of jeans. She stepped forward so she was beside him. Darn, her shoulders were practically nudging his. Stand in front of him and she'd remember too well how he'd slid his arms around her and nuzzled her neck out on that balcony. *How she'd ached for so much more.* She settled for taking a few steps sidewards, so quickly she nearly tripped.

As it happened, she needn't have bothered with evasive tactics. He headed for a toolbox she hadn't noticed tucked away behind the counter and took out an electric drill, a hammer, a spirit level, a handful of plastic wall plugs and a jar of nails. 'It's a double brick wall with no electrics in the way so we can hang the picture exactly where we want it.'

'I can't wait to see it up,' she said.

She found his continual use of the word 'we' disconcerting. No way did she want to be thought as part of a team with Jesse Morgan. But, she had to admit, she was totally lacking in drilling skills. Sandy knew that. And why pay a handyman when Jesse was volunteering his time?

He pulled a pencil from out of his pocket, marked a spot on the wall and proceeded to drill. It seemed an awkward angle for someone with a shoulder injury but who was she to question him? But he easily drilled a neat hole, with only the finest spray of masonry dust to mar the freshly painted wall. 'Done,' he said in a satisfied tone.

He put down the drill, picked up the hammer and the wall plug. He positioned the wall plug with his left hand and took aim with the hammer in his right. His sudden curse curdled the air and the hammer thudded to the floor.

'Jesse! Are you okay?'

'Just my shoulder,' he groaned, gripping it and doubling over. 'Not a good angle for it.'

'How can I help?' She felt useless in the face of his pain. Disconcerted by her immediate urge to touch him, to comfort him.

He straightened up, wincing. 'You hold the nail and I'll wield the hammer using both hands, it'll take the strain off the shoulder.'

'Or you could let me use the hammer.'

'No,' he said. 'I'll do it.'

Was it masculine pride? Or did he honestly think she couldn't use a hammer? Whatever, she had no intention of getting into an argument over it. 'Okay,' she said.

He handed her the nail and, using her left hand, she positioned it against the wall plug. She was tall, but Jesse was taller. To reach the nail he had to manoeuvre himself around her. Her shoulders were pressed against the solid wall of his chest. *He was too close.* Her heart started to thud so fast she felt giddy; her knees went wobbly. She dropped the nail, twisted to get away from him and found herself staring directly up into his face. For a long, long moment their eyes connected.

'I…I can't do this, Jesse,' she finally stuttered as she pushed away from him.

Three of his large strides took him well away from

her before he turned to face her again. He cleared his throat. 'You're right,' he said. 'We can't just continue to ignore what happened between us at the wedding. Or why you ran away the next day without saying goodbye.'

CHAPTER THREE

THE LIZZIE JESSE had known six months ago hadn't been short of a quick retort or a comment that bordered on the acerbic. Now she struggled to make a response. But he didn't prompt her. He'd waited six months for her excuse. He could wait minutes more.

Instead he tilted back on the heels of his boots, stuck his thumbs into the belt of his jeans and watched her, schooling his face to be free of expression.

She opened her mouth to speak then shut it again. She twisted a flyaway piece of her pale blonde hair that had worked itself free from the plait that fell between her shoulder blades.

'Not ignore. *Forget,*' she said at last.

'Forget us getting together ever happened?'

'Yes,' she said. 'It was a lapse of judgement on my part.'

He snorted. 'I've been insulted before but to be called a "lapse of judgement" is a first.'

She clapped her hand over her mouth. 'I didn't mean it to come out quite like that.'

'I'm tough; I can take it,' he said. He went to shrug his shoulders but it hurt. In spite of his bravado, so had her words.

'But I meant it,' she said. 'It should never have happened. The…the episode on the balcony was a mistake.' She had a soft, sweet mouth but her words twisted it into something bordering on bitter.

'I remember it as being a whole lot of fun,' he said slowly.

She tilted her chin in a movement that was surprisingly combative. 'Seems like our memories of that night are very different.'

'I remember lots of laughter and a warm, beautiful woman by my side,' he said.

By now she had braced herself against the back of the counter as if she wanted to push herself away from him as far as she possibly could. 'You mean you've forgotten the way a rowdy group of your friends came out and…and caught us—'

'Caught us kissing. Yeah. I remember. I've known those people all my life. They were teasing. You didn't seem to be bothered by it at the time.'

'It was embarrassing.'

'You were laughing.'

That piece of hair was getting a workout now between her slender fingers. 'To hide how I really felt.'

He paused. 'Do you often do that?'

She stilled. 'Laugh, you mean?'

He searched her face. 'Hide how you really feel.'

She met his gaze full on with a challenging tilt to her head. 'Doesn't everyone?'

'You laughed it off. Said you had to go check on Amy.'

Her gaze slid away so it didn't meet his. 'Yes.'

'You never came back.'

'I did but…but you were otherwise engaged.'

'Huh? I don't get it. I was waiting for you.' He'd checked his watch time and time again, but she still hadn't shown up. Finally he'd asked someone if they'd seen Lizzie. They'd pointed her out on the other side of the room in conversation with a group of the most gossipy girls in Dolphin Bay. She hadn't come near him again.

Now she met his eyes again, hers direct and shadowed with accusation. 'You were dancing with another woman. When you'd told me all dances for the evening were reserved for me.'

He remembered the running joke they had shared— Jesse with a 'Reserved for Lizzie' sign on his back, Lizzie with a 'Reserved for Jesse' sign. The possessiveness had been in jest but he had meant it.

He frowned. 'After the duty dances for the wedding—including with your delightful little daughter— the only woman I danced with that evening was you. Refresh my memory about the other one?'

She turned her head to the side. Her body language told him loud and clear she'd rather be anywhere else than here with him. In spite of the café and Sandy and family obligations.

'It was nothing,' she said, tight-lipped. 'You had every right to dance with another woman.'

He reached out and cupped her chin to pull her back to face him. 'Let's get this straight. I only wanted to dance with you that night.'

For a long moment he looked deep into her eyes until she tried to wiggle away from him and he released her. 'So describe this mystery woman to me,' he said.

'Black hair, tall, beautiful, wearing a red dress.' It sounded as if the words were being dragged out of her.

He frowned.

'You seemed *very* happy to be with her,' she prompted.

Realisation dawned. 'Red dress? It was my cousin I

was with my cousin Marie. She'd just told me she was pregnant. She and her husband had been trying for years to start a family. I was talking with her while I waited for you to come back.'

'Oh,' Lizzie said in a very small voice, her head bowed.

'I wasn't dancing with her. More like whirling her around in a dance of joy. A baby is everything she's always wanted.'

'I…I'm glad for her,' Lizzie said in an even more diminished voice.

He couldn't keep the edge of anger from his voice. 'You thought I'd moved on to someone else? That I'd kissed you out on the balcony—in front of an audience—and then found another woman while you were out of the room for ten minutes?'

She looked up at him. 'That's what it seemed like from where I was standing. I've never felt so foolish.'

'So why didn't you come over and slap me on the face or whack me with your purse or do whatever jealous women do in such circumstances?'

'I wasn't jealous. Just…disappointed.' Her gaze slid away again.

'I was disappointed when you didn't come back. When you took off to Sydney the next day without saying goodbye. When you didn't return my phone calls.'

'I…I…misunderstood. I'm sorry.'

She turned her back on him and walked around the countertop so it formed a physical barrier between them. When she got to the glass jars she picked one up and put it down. He noticed her hands weren't quite steady.

Even with the counter between them, it would be easy to lean over and touch her again. Even kiss her.

He fought the impulse. She so obviously didn't want to be touched. And he didn't want to start anything he had no intention of continuing. He wanted to clear up a misunderstanding that had festered for six months. That was all. He took a step back to further increase the distance between them.

'I get what happened. You believed my bad publicity,' he said.

'Publicity? I don't know what you mean.' But the flickering of her eyelashes told him she probably had a fair idea of what he meant.

'My reputation. Don't tell me you weren't warned about me. That I'm a player. A ladies' man. That you'd be one of "Jesse's girls" until I tired of you.'

How he'd grown to hate that old song from the nineteen-eighties where the singer wailed over and over that he wanted 'Jessie's girl'. Apparently his parents had played it at his christening party and it had followed him ever since; had become his signature song.

She flushed high on her cheeks. 'No. Of course not.'

'You should know—reports of my love life are greatly exaggerated.'

He used to get a kick out of his reputation for being a guaranteed girl magnet—what free-wheeling guy in his teens and early twenties wouldn't?—though he'd never taken it seriously. But now, as thirty loomed, he was well and truly over living up to the Jesse legend. A legend that had always been more urban myth than fact.

But he'd done nothing to dispel it. In fact it had been a convenient shield against ever having to explain why he'd closed his heart off against a committed relationship. Why he dated fun-for-now, unchallenging girls and always stayed in control of where the relationship went.

Camilla's words haunted him. *'You won't miss me for a minute; a guy as good-looking as you can get any woman you want just by snapping your fingers—there'll always be another one waiting in line.'* It wasn't true, as she herself had proven. He had wanted her. Badly. And she had gutted and filleted his heart as surely as his father did the fish he caught. He would never expose himself to that kind of pain again.

'I didn't need to be warned,' Lizzie said. 'I figured it out for myself. You and Kate Parker, Sandy's other bridesmaid, were the talk of the wedding. How you'd come back from your travels and hooked up with her. How Kate wouldn't have more luck with getting you to commit than any other of the long line of girlfriends before her.'

As he'd suspected, the Dolphin Bay gossips had struck again. Didn't the women in this town have anything better to do with their time? Though for all their poking their noses into other people's business, they'd never come close to ferreting out the reasons why he'd stayed so resolutely single.

Kate had been his childhood friend. There'd been a long-standing joke between their families that if they hadn't met anyone else by the time they were aged thirty they'd settle down with each other.

'Not true. We kissed. Once. To see if there was anything more than friendship between us. There wasn't. We were just friends. Still are friends.'

Lizzie shrugged. 'I realised that. I soon sussed out she only had eyes for the other groomsman, your friend Sam Lancaster.'

'True. It seemed like one minute Kate was organising Ben and Sandy's wedding, the next minute she was planning her own.'

'I heard they eloped and got married at some fabulous Indian palace hotel.'

'You heard right. I was Sam's best man. It turned out great for them,' he said.

He was really happy for his old friends. But if he was honest with himself, there had been an awkward moment when Kate had made it very clear the kiss had been a disaster for her. Coming on top of what had happened with Camilla it had struck a serious blow to his male pride. By the time of the wedding he'd been in a real funk, questioning things about himself he'd never before had cause to question.

Meeting Lizzie had done a lot to help soothe his bruised ego—until she'd walked away without a word of explanation.

But that had been six months ago. He'd moved on. Now his circumstances were very different. He'd come to a real turning point in his career and the path he chose was crucial to his future. The recent encounter with Camilla had made him realise it could be time to move on from his work with the charity. He'd told his boss there was a good chance he wouldn't return after his shoulder healed. He would not turn his back on it completely but would remain involved as a volunteer and as a fund-raiser.

A new direction had opened with the offer of a fast-track job with a multinational construction company based in Houston, Texas. It would be a challenging, demanding role in a ruthlessly competitive commercial environment. But living in the United States would mean he'd rarely make it home to Dolphin Bay.

As far as Lizzie went, he just wanted to clear up a misunderstanding that had left her resentful of him and him disappointed in her. They'd missed their chance to be any kind of couple, even the most casual. Once the misunderstanding was sorted, they could work together without awkwardness. After all, she was part of the family now and would always be around. They had to come to some sort of mutual good terms.

'Weddings have a lot to answer for,' she said. 'All that romance and emotion floating around makes people do things they really shouldn't. Fool around when they shouldn't. Behave in ways they later regret.'

'Just for the record, I wasn't just fooling around with you at the wedding,' he said.

She flushed redder. 'Maybe I was just fooling around with you.'

'Maybe you were.'

'Maybe *I'm* the player,' she said. There was a return of that teasing spirit he'd liked so much, a spark that warmed her cool grey eyes. He found himself wanting her to smile.

Jesse only vaguely remembered Lizzie from her first visit to Dolphin Bay. She'd been sixteen, beanpole-thin and flat-chested. He'd been sixteen, too. But testosterone had well and truly kicked in and he'd considered himself a man.

He wasn't ashamed to admit he hadn't found her attractive then. He'd been a typical teenage boy who'd looked to the more obvious.

That summer, his brother Ben had been busy falling in love with Sandy. Jesse had been busy trying to decide between three curvaceous older girls who'd made their interest in him more than clear. He hadn't chosen any of them. Even then he hadn't valued what came to him too easily.

When he'd met Lizzie again, more than twelve years later, he'd been knocked over at the woman she'd become. Elegant; sensual without being blatantly sexy; classy. Now she wore simple narrow-legged jeans and a plain white shirt with the sleeves rolled up. Her hair was tied back off her face in a plait. She looked sensational without even trying.

'Are you a player?' he asked. 'I somehow doubt that.'

Her eyes dimmed and it was as if that hint of party-girl Lizzie had been extinguished again. 'No. I'm a divorced single mum with a social life on hold indefinitely. I'm here to work hard at making this café a success and to devote myself to Amy.'

'I get that,' he said. 'Being a lone parent must be one of the toughest gigs around.'

'Tougher than I could have imagined,' she said. 'But it's worth it. Amy is the best thing that ever happened to me.'

'You were young when you had her.'

'Becoming a mother at age twenty-three wasn't part of my game plan, I can assure you. But I don't regret it even for a second.'

He frowned. 'Where is Amy? Didn't she drive down with you from Sydney?'

Lizzie's daughter was a cute kid; she'd been the flower girl at the wedding and charmed everyone. He'd been sorry he hadn't had the chance to say goodbye to her too.

'She's spending the school vacation in France with her father and his parents. They love her and want her to grow up French. That's another reason I have to make a success of this café. Philippe would like sole custody and is just waiting for me to fail.'

Sandy had told Jesse a bit of Lizzie's background. The domineering father. The early marriage. The break-up with the French husband. She hadn't had it easy. Just as well nothing more had happened with them at the wedding. He wouldn't want to have added to her burden of hurt. He knew what that felt like.

'You'll have a lot of support here,' he said. 'Sandy's a Morgan now and the Morgans look after their own.'

'I know that. And I'm grateful. But I'll still have to work, work, work.' She took a deep breath, looked directly up at him. 'I'm truly sorry I misread the situation with your cousin. But what happened between us at the wedding can't happen again; you know that, don't you?'

Relief flooded through him that she had no expectations of him. She was lovely, quite possibly the loveliest woman he knew. But right now he didn't want to date anyone either. Not seriously. And Lizzie was the type of person who would expect serious.

'Lizzie, I—' he started, but she spoke over him.

'I told you my social life is on hold. That means no dating. Not you. Not anyone.'

'I get that,' he said.

His life was so far removed from Lizzie's. His job took him to all the points of the earth for extended periods of time. If he ever committed to a woman it would have to be someone without ties. Camilla would have been ideal—a freelance photojournalist with no kids, feisty, independent. But what had happened with Camilla had soured him against getting close to her type of woman.

'Good,' Lizzie said, rather more vehemently than his ego would have liked.

'I hope you can remember what we had at the wedding as no-strings fun that I certainly don't regret,' he said.

She nodded. He didn't know whether he should be insulted, the way she was so eager to agree.

'But it—' he started to say.

'Can't happen again,' she joined in so they chorused the words.

He extended his hand to her over the counter. 'Friends?'

She hesitated and didn't take his hand. 'I'm not sure about "friends"—we hardly know each other. I don't call someone a friend lightly.'

He resisted the urge to roll his eyes. 'Yep.'

Her eyes widened at his abrupt reply. 'I don't mean to be rude,' she said. 'Just honest about what I feel.'

Yeah. She was. But her honesty had a sharp edge. All in all, it made him wonder why he'd want to be friends with her anyway. Especially when he knew she was off-limits to anything more than friendship. It would be difficult to be 'just friends' with someone he found so attractive. That two-hour limit he'd set himself on the time he spent with her might just be two hours too much.

'So "just acquaintances" or "just strangers stuck with each other's company" might be more to the point?' he said.

She gasped. 'That sounds dreadful, doesn't it?' Then she disarmed him with a smile—the kind of open, appealing smile that had drawn him to her in the first place. 'Too honest, even for me. After all, we can *try* to be friends, can't we?'

'We can try to be friends,' he agreed. *Two hours at a time.* Any more time than that with her each day and he might find himself wanting more than either of them was prepared to give. And that was dangerous.

'Okay,' she said, this time taking his hand in hers in a firm grip, shaking it and letting it go after the minimum contact required to seal the deal.

CHAPTER FOUR

LIZZIE LEANED BACK from the last of the artworks they'd rewrapped to send back to the artist, kneading with fisted hands the small of her back where it ached. 'That's it,' she said. 'All done, thank goodness. That was harder work than I'd thought it would be.'

'But worth it,' said Jesse from beside her.

'Absolutely worth it. The paintings add to the atmosphere of the café like nothing else could. I hope the artists come in so I can thank them with a coffee.'

But Lizzie felt exhausted. Not just from the effort of unpacking, holding the paintings up against the wall and then repacking the unwanted pictures. But from the strain of working alongside Jesse.

In theory, learning to be 'just friends' with him should have been easy. He was personable, smart, and seemed determined to put their history behind them. Gentlemanly, too—in spite of his shoulder injury he insisted on doing any heavy lifting.

Trouble was, she found it impossible to relax around him. She had to consider every word before she uttered it, which made her sound stilted and awkward. The odd uncharacteristic nervous giggle kept bubbling into her conversation.

Could you ever be just friends with a man you'd

kissed, wanted, cried over? Especially when that man was so heart-stoppingly attractive. *Could you pretend that time together had never happened?*

She would have to try.

If it were up to her, she would choose never to see Jesse Morgan again. Even though they'd cleared up the misunderstanding about his cousin, it was hard to be around someone she'd fancied, kissed, liked…when nothing would—or could—ever happen between them. But with the family situation being the way it was, she had to make a real effort to nurture a friendship with him—be pals, buddies, good mates. Future family occasions could be incredibly awkward if she didn't.

Right now, Jesse stood beside her as they both surveyed the arrangement of paintings on the wall. He was not so close that their shoulders were in danger of nudging but close enough so she was aware of his scent, an intoxicating blend of spicy sandalwood and fresh male sweat. It was *too* close. Being anywhere within touching distance of Jesse Morgan was too close. Memories of how wonderful it had felt to be in his arms were resurfacing.

She leaned forward to straighten the small painting of the manta rays and used the movement to edge away, hoping he didn't notice.

'They look good,' Jesse said. 'You chose well.'

She thought about a friend-type thing to say. 'To be fair, we both made the final selection.'

'You exercised your power of veto more often than not.'

'Is that another way of saying I'm a control freak?' she said without thinking at all.

'I didn't say that,' he said, a smile lurking at the corners of his mouth. 'But…'

If he was a real friend, she would have punched him lightly on the arm for that and laughed. She wished it could be that way. But there would be no casual jesting and certainly no touching with Jesse. It was too much of a risk.

Instead she made a show of sighing. 'The success or failure of Bay Bites rests on my shoulders and I'm only too aware of that.'

'That's not true,' he said. 'You do have help. Sandy. Ben. The staff she's hired for you. Me.'

She turned to face him. 'You?'

'I can work with you for two hours a day.'

'Two hours?' That seemed an arbitrary amount of time to allocate. Maybe it was all he could manage with his shoulder. But she couldn't help wondering what other commitments Jesse had in Dolphin Bay. And if they were of the female kind.

He nodded. 'Whatever help you need, I'm there for two hours every day.'

That was the trouble with denying attraction when that attraction was an ever-present tension, underlying every word, every glance. The air seemed thick with words better left unspoken. At a different time, in a different life, she could think of some exciting ways to spend two hours alone with Jesse Morgan in her bedroom. *But not now.*

She cleared her throat. *Think neutral, friend-type chat.* 'I appreciate the help with the paintings. Though I'm the one who will be looking at them all day and— call me a control freak—but I really couldn't say yes to the one of the bronze whaler sharks, no matter how skilfully it was done.'

He'd argued hard for the sharks and he continued to argue. 'Sharks are part of the ocean. As a surfer I learned to respect them. They're magnificent creatures. That painting captured them perfectly.'

She shuddered. 'They're predators. And I don't like predators. Also, remember people will be eating in this place. They don't want to look up and see pictures of creatures that might eat *them*.'

Jesse grinned, his perfect teeth white against his tan, those blue, blue eyes glinting with good humour. *A woman could forget all caution and common sense to win a smile like that.*

Again she found herself wishing things could be different, that they could take up from where they'd left off out on that balcony. She had to suppress a sigh at the memory of how exciting his kisses had been.

'Good point,' he said. 'But I still think there are too many wussy pictures of flowers.'

'So we agree to disagree,' she said with an upward tilt of her chin.

'Wussy versus brave?' he challenged, still with that grin hovering on his so-sexy mouth.

'If by brave you mean you want to swim with the sharks, then go for it. I'll stick with dolphins, thanks.'

'I've always liked a challenge,' he said.

The challenge of the chase? Was that what he meant? Lizzie really didn't want to know. Or to think too much about how it would feel to be caught up again in Jesse's arms. She'd just steer clear of him as much as she could. It wasn't that she didn't trust him not to overstep the boundaries of a new friendship—it was herself she didn't trust.

'I do love the painting of the dolphins surfing,' she said. 'If I could afford the price tag, I'd buy it myself.'

He sobered. 'You'll have to make sure you don't get too attached to any of the paintings. You want to sell as many as you can. It's an added revenue stream for the café.'

'You're right. I'll just get heartbroken when that particular one goes.'

'Just think of the commission on the sale,' he said. 'The quicker the café gets in the black, the better it will be for all concerned.'

She was surprised at how hard-headed and business-like he sounded. But of course Jesse would be used to not getting attached to pretty things. And that was when she had to bite down on any smart remarks. Not if they were going to try to be friends.

'Thanks again for your help,' she said. 'I'd offer you some lunch but, as you can see, I'm not set up for food just yet.'

'I hear you're still finalising the menu. I'm looking forward to being an official food taster on Saturday.'

Lizzie stared. 'You're coming to the taste test?'

'Sandy rounded up all the family to help you try out the recipes.'

'Oh,' she said, disconcerted. If she'd thought she'd only be seeing Jesse occasionally during his time back home in Dolphin Bay, she was obviously mistaken. Talking herself out of her attraction to him was going to get even more difficult.

'When it comes to taste-testing good food, I'm your man,' he said.

She remembered the game they'd had such fun playing together at the wedding, predicting the favourite foods of the guests. He'd been such good company she'd forgotten all the worries that plagued her that night. *Good company and something more that had had her aching for him to kiss her out on that balcony.*

'Let me guess,' she said, resting her chin on her hand,

making a play of thinking hard. 'The other volunteers will have to fight you for the slow-roasted lamb with beetroot relish. And maybe the caramelised apple pie with vanilla bean ice cream?'

He folded his arms in front of his chest. 'I'm not going to tell you if you're right or wrong about what I like. You'll have to wait for the taste night to see.'

'Tease,' she said.

'You don't like being made to wait, do you?' he said, that slow smile still playing at the corners of his mouth.

'There are some things that are worth waiting for,' she said, unable to resist a slow smile of her own in return.

For a long moment her eyes met his until she dropped her gaze. *She had to stop this.* It would be only too easy to flirt with Jesse, to fall back into his arms and that way could lead to disaster. She had to keep their conversations purely on a business level.

She glanced through the connecting doorway and into the bookshop. Sandy was due to see her at any time and there was only a small moment of opportunity left with Jesse.

She lowered her voice. 'Can I ask you something in confidence?'

His dark brows rose. 'Sure. Ask away.'

'I'm concerned about the food I've got to work with.'

'Concerned?'

'It…it might not be up to scratch.'

He frowned. 'I'm not sure what you mean. Aren't the food supplies being ordered through the Hotel Harbourside restaurant? Ben's hotel is one of the best places to eat in town.'

Ben had built the modern hotel on the site of the old guest house. Alongside, he'd built a row of shops, including Bay Books and Bay Bites.

She winced at Jesse's understandably defensive tone. But who else could she ask? 'That's the problem. I have to tread carefully. But I have to be blunt. The Harbour-side is good pub grub. Nothing more. Nothing less. And it's not up to the standard I want. Not for Bay Bites.'

Lizzie did tend to be blunt. Jesse had noticed that six months ago. Personally, he appreciated her straightfor-ward manner. But not everyone in Dolphin Bay would. No way could the café succeed if Lizzie was going to look down her straight, narrow little nose at the locals. Could she really fit in here?

'But isn't it just a café?' he said.

'*Just* a café? How can you say that?' Her voice rose with indignation. 'Because it's a café doesn't mean it can't serve the best food I can possibly offer. Whether I'm cooking in a high-end restaurant or a café, my food will be the best.' She gave a proud toss to her head that he doubted she even realised she'd made.

There was a passion and an energy to her that he couldn't help but admire. But he also feared for her. Small country towns could be brutal on newcomers they thought were too big for their boots.

'You're not in France now, Lizzie.'

'More small town wisdom for me?' Her half-smile took the snarkiness out of the comment.

'Some advice—you don't want to make things too fancy. Not a good idea around here to give the impres-sion you think everything is better in France. Or in Sydney.'

Her response was somewhere between a laugh and a snort. 'You seriously think I'm going to transplant fancy French dining to a south coast café and expect it to work? I might have lived in France for years, but

I'm still an Aussie girl and I think I've got a good idea of what my customers will like.'

He knew she had a reputation as a talented chef who had established her credentials at a very young age—he wasn't sure she had the business sense to go with them.

'And that would be?' he asked.

'The very best ingredients served simply.' She gave another toss of her head that sent her blonde plait swishing across her back. 'That's what I learned in France. Not necessarily at the fine-dining establishments in Paris but in the cafés and markets of Lyon and from the home cooking of Amy's French grandparents. You know they say the heart of France is Paris, but its stomach is Lyon?'

'I didn't know that.' He'd raced through a see-Europe-in-two-weeks type backpacker tour when he was a student that had included Paris and Versailles but that was as far as his knowledge of the country went. 'My journeys have mainly been of the have-disaster-will-travel type. And the food…well, you wouldn't want to know about the food.'

'Of course,' she said, nodding. 'I remember now you told me about some of the out-of-the-way places you've been sent to.'

She'd seemed so genuinely interested in the work he was doing to rebuild communities. Not once had she voiced concern that he had veered off the career track to big bucks and business success. Other girls had been more vocal. He hadn't seen the need to explain to them that he'd been fortunate in the land he'd inherited from his grandparents and the investments he'd made. He could afford to work for a charity for as long as it suited him and not have to justify it to anyone.

Though that might be about to change. The Houston company wanted his expertise and their offer came with a salary that had stunned him with the amount of zeroes.

'So what's your problem with ordering through the hotel?' he asked.

'Their suppliers will be fine for the basics and the hotel gives us better buying power. It's the organic and artisan produce I worked with in Sydney I need to source. Farm to plate stuff. I don't know where to get it here.'

'Farm to plate? That sounds expensive. Do you really want expensive for the café?' He looked around at the fresh white décor, the round tables and bentwood chairs, the way the layout had been designed for customers to wander in from the bookshop. It said casual and relaxed to him.

'Actually, farm to plate can be less expensive because you cut out the middle man.'

'That's a point,' he said.

'I know ridiculously high prices would be the kiss of death to a café serving breakfast and lunch,' she said with that combative tilt to her chin that was starting to get familiar in an endearing kind of way.

'It's good we agree on that one,' he said.

'But if Bay Bites is to succeed it has to be so much better than the existing cafés around here. What would you prefer—a cheap burger made with a mass-produced beef patty or pay a dollar or two extra for free-range, hand-ground beef? Frozen fries or hand cut fries with home-made mayo?'

'That's a no-brainer,' he said, his stomach becoming aware it was lunchtime and rumbling at the thought of the burger. Though the slow-roasted lamb might give it some competition. 'So you are talking café food, not fancy-schmantzy stuff?'

'Of course I am,' she said, not hiding her exasperation. 'I know people will expect the basics.'

'Egg and bacon roll?' he said hopefully.

'The best you've ever tasted. But there will be some more creative options too, depending on seasonal ingredients. And wonderful desserts every day, of course. We'll do morning and afternoon tea as well as breakfast and lunch.'

'You mentioned apple pie?' The longing crept into his voice, in spite of himself.

She nodded with a knowing smile. He'd given himself away. There was no dessert he liked better than apple pie. She'd guessed right again.

'What I'm asking you is how I source that produce without offending Sandy and Ben,' she said.

'How long is it since you've spent any time in Dolphin Bay?'

'There was the wedding. And I drove down to see the building when Sandy first approached me about the café.'

'So basically your memories of the food here are based on when you were sixteen?' Back when there'd been a fish and chip shop, a short-lived pizza place and the best food in town had been from his mother's kitchen.

'Well, yes.'

'Better get yourself up to date. This area has become somewhat of a foodie haven.'

'Dolphin Bay?' Disbelief underscored her words.

'Maybe not the actual town,' he conceded. 'But certainly the areas surrounding it. Didn't you look into that when you did your business plan?'

She pulled a face that made him want to smile but she was so serious he kept his expression neutral.

'Sandy and Ben did the business plan,' she said. 'And they're dead certain there's a market for a bookshop café with a harbour view. But I had to finish a work contract in Sydney and didn't have time to do as much research into the local area as I would have liked.'

'If you had, you would have found one of the well-known television chefs opened a restaurant in the next town and others have followed. Every time I come home on leave, there seem to be more restaurants.'

Her fine eyebrows rose in surprise. 'That's good. Hopefully the rising tide will float all our boats. But where are they sourcing the artisan produce? And how do I get it without offending my sister?'

Did he want to get this involved with this woman, helping her beyond what he'd agreed to with Sandy when he'd volunteered to give a hand while he was on leave? He knew the answer before he'd even finished asking himself the question.

He'd promised Sandy to do his best to make the café succeed. If that meant getting Lizzie what she wanted, he didn't have a choice. And it had nothing to do with how lovely she was, he told himself. Or how intriguing he found her.

'Ben and I grew up with people who have established organic farms and orchards in the area, if that's what you're looking for. And the seafood comes fresh from our own father's boats.'

'Really?' Her cool grey eyes lit up. 'Sandy told me about the seafood. But I didn't know about the organic farms.'

He tilted back on his boot heels again and stuck his

thumbs in his belt. 'I suspect all you need is here if you know where to look for it.'

'Trouble is, I don't.' She tilted her head to the side as she looked at him and smiled very sweetly.

Jesse suppressed a groan. He knew what was coming. 'You're going to ask me to introduce you to those places, aren't you?'

'Of course I am.' Again he was struck by how a smile brought such light to her face. She'd been so warm and vivacious at the wedding that he'd found it hard to leave her side for even a minute.

'Okaaay…' He drew out the word in mock reluctance. 'I guess I can do that for you.'

It wouldn't be a hardship to show her around, if he kept his distance from anything too personal. *Trying to be friends—that was all*. It would also be a chance to catch up with people he hadn't seen for ages. His job meant he'd lost touch with more friends from the area than he'd like.

'Does that count in your daily two hours of rationed help?' she asked.

His immediate impulse was to say *of course not*. But then he thought twice.

On meeting Lizzie again, he'd thought he'd only be able to endure two hours of her chilly, stand-offish company. Now the Lizzie he'd first fallen for was starting to reveal herself. Warm. Funny. With a touch of snark that challenged him. He didn't want his initial attraction to her to be reignited. That meant seeing as little of her as possible. Now that two-hour limit would be not because he didn't like her—rather because he didn't want to get to like her too much.

Lizzie could never be a casual encounter. An *it's been nice but I don't want to get serious* type of thing.

No. Anything with Lizzie would be serious with a capital S. She was a mother with a child, making the relationship equation two-plus-one, rather than the one-plus-one he was used to. She was also his brother's sister-in-law. If they started something and it broke up, the repercussions would be endless.

There were many reasons to steer clear—not least that he saw in her the same kind of spirited, challenging personality that had drawn him to Camilla with such disastrous results. His life was on track with the prospect of a new start in America. He didn't want any awkward emotional confrontations to derail him if he again fell for the wrong woman.

Six months ago he'd been very taken with Lizzie, had seen the possibility of something more than a casual hook-up at a wedding. Looking back, he could see he'd been raw from his recent encounter with Camilla. Lovely Lizzie's laughter and passionate kisses had been affirmation of his appeal as a man, balm to his shattered heart and bruised ego. But her inexplicable cold treatment of him had plunged him back into his resolve to stay clear of women with the power to wound him.

Now this job offer had further strengthened his resolve to avoid anything remotely connected to commitment to a woman. He needed to remain unencumbered if he were to move up to this new stage in his career. The CEO of the Houston company had pretty much spelled out it was a job for a single man—travelling, lots of overtime and weekend work.

That two-hour restriction on time with Lizzie would stay—he couldn't let himself get to like her too much. He genuinely wanted to try and become friends, though. After all, she'd be part of his life for as long as her sister was married to his brother and that looked likely to be for ever. Two hours a day was more than enough to develop the kind of superficial friendship that didn't make any demands on him—or, in fact, on her. He couldn't deny his attraction to Lizzie—but he could stop himself from acting on it.

'Yes, two hours is all I can spare,' he said. 'None of the farms we'll be going to is far from here.'

He could tell she was perplexed by the time restriction but he had no intention of explaining it to her.

'Okay,' she said. Starting tomorrow, please. I don't have time to waste.'

Lizzie was grateful that Jesse was able to help her with her dilemma. She was about to tell him so when Sandy swept into the shop, all exclamations of delight at how the café was shaping up.

Lizzie silently implored Jesse with her eyes to please not say anything of their conversation about the supplies. Thankfully, he indicated with a slight incline of his head that he would keep her confidence. Not in a million years would she want to cause offence to Sandy or Ben. At the same time, she had to have the best for the café.

Brown-haired, hazel-eyed Sandy swept her into a big hug and she squeezed her sister back hard. The wonderful thing about being in Dolphin Bay was it meant more time with her.

'I am *so* glad you got here okay,' Sandy said. She then looked to Jesse. 'I'm still pinching myself that I got a chef of my sister's calibre to run Bay Bites for us. Aren't we fortunate?'

'We're very lucky,' he agreed.

Sandy hugged Jesse, too, and it gave Lizzie pleasure to see the depth of affection between her sister and her brother-in-law.

She and Sandy had both been so emotionally damaged by their controlling cheater of a father that for a while it had looked as if neither of them would find happiness with a man. But Sandy was now blissfully married to Ben and had been lovingly welcomed into the close-knit Morgan family.

One out of two sisters sorted with a happy-ever-after wasn't bad, Lizzie thought. Philippe had done such a good job of destroying any trust she'd had left in men she doubted there'd ever be a second chance of happiness for her. And certainly not if she kept getting attracted to gorgeous love-'em-and-leave-'em guys like Jesse. She didn't regret kissing him at the wedding. Could never forget how wonderful her time with him had been. But it would never happen again.

'I'm so glad to be here,' she said to Sandy. 'It's the new start I need.'

'I see you two have reacquainted yourselves,' Sandy said, waving to Jesse.

With an emphasis on *acquaintance* Lizzie wanted to say, but knew it would come out sounding ill-mannered.

'Yes,' she murmured, avoiding Jesse's gaze. He just nodded.

Lizzie did not fail to detect the speculation in her sister's eyes as Sandy looked from her to Jesse and back again.

Guess she'd better get used to seeing that look in other people's eyes, too, when they saw her and Jesse together—until it became obvious the incident at the wedding was all there ever was going to be between them.

Sandy spun around to the wall behind her. 'The paintings look amazing the way you've hung them.'

'I have to give credit where credit is due,' said Lizzie,

indicating Jesse with a sweep of her hand. 'He put them all up.'

'The boss is the one who chose them,' said Jesse.

'The boss?' asked Lizzie.

'That's you,' he said. 'I jump to your command.' His words were light-hearted but his already deep voice dropped an octave or two as he spoke.

She had to disguise her gasp of awareness with a cough. Oh, she could think of lots of commands she could give to beautiful Jesse, alone and behind closed doors. But not when they were 'just friends'. Not when he was her sister's brother-in-law. Not when he was a man who had a reputation for toying with women's hearts.

She was spared making any kind of smart reply by Jesse himself. He glanced at his watch. 'I didn't realise it was that late. Gotta go.'

'Your two hours are up?' she said, still intrigued by the limit he had given her on his time.

'What two hours?' asked Sandy.

'Something to do with his shoulder,' said Lizzie.

'Yeah, my shoulder, that's it,' said Jesse gruffly. 'I'll pick you up at ten tomorrow,' he said to Lizzie. 'Bye, Sandy.'

Lizzie watched in silent admiration as Jesse strode out of Bay Bites with a masculine loping grace. His back view really was something to see. Broad shoulders tapered to a tight behind. Worn denim jeans hugged muscular legs. And those tanned brown arms rippled with muscle. If he were any other gorgeous guy than Jesse Morgan she'd want to give him a wolf whistle. 'No!' said her sister, once Jesse was out of earshot.

'What do you mean "no"?'

'I saw the way you were looking at Jesse.'

'And you weren't too?'

'Of course I wasn't,' Sandy said primly. 'He's my brother-in-law.'

'And that doesn't stop you appreciating what a finely crafted specimen of masculinity he is?'

'Of course it does,' Sandy said. 'I'm a married woman.' But then the giggles she was suppressing pealed out. 'I wouldn't be female if I didn't appreciate how hot Jesse is. And he's a nice guy too. But he's a commitment-phobe of the first order.'

'I know, I know. If you told me once you told me a million times.'

'And at the wedding you totally ignored my warnings.'

'That was different. Cut me a break, Sandy. I was lonely. Starved for male company. Heck, starved for adult company outside of a commercial kitchen. And Jesse was…was irresistible.'

Lizzie swallowed hard against a hitch in her voice when she remembered the magic of those hours with Jesse. It hadn't been just physical—for her, anyway. At the wedding she'd seen a spark of 'what might have been' if circumstances had been different.

'I love Jesse to pieces. But I don't want to see you hurt.' Sandy paused. 'Or, for that matter, see Jesse hurt.'

'What do you mean, "see Jesse hurt"?'

'Were you serious about him at the wedding? Or was he just a fling before you got back to the reality of being a single mum?'

'Of course I wasn't serious—how could I be with all those warnings echoing in my head?' *Though there had been moments when she'd been guilty of daydreaming of something more.* 'Jesse was fun. A diversion. He made me laugh at a time when I didn't have a whole lot to laugh about.'

'That's what I mean. We'd be angry if a guy toyed with a pretty woman just for a diversion. Why would it be different for a woman with a handsome guy?'

'You can't be serious. I wasn't *toying* with Jesse. It's not the same thing at all.'

'Isn't it? Seems to me there's a lot more to Jesse than he lets on. Sometimes I think it might be a disadvantage to be as good-looking as he is. Does he ever wonder if women flock to him because of how he looks or because of who he is?'

'It's not something I've thought about,' Lizzie said.

'People think women are throwing themselves at him all the time and he wouldn't care if someone dumped him like you did. He was gutted when you went home without another word to him, though he tried to hide it.'

'R-really?' was all Lizzie could manage to stutter. Could that be true? She'd only thought of her own hurt feelings. 'There…there was a misunderstanding. But we've sorted that out. It's been six months. I…I'm sure there've been other women for him in the meantime.'

It was ridiculous, but her heart twisted painfully at the thought of Jesse with someone else. Even now, when she'd put him strictly off-limits.

She'd been stabbed by a sharp and unexpected shard of jealousy when she'd rushed back to the wedding reception to find Jesse with the woman she now knew was his cousin. Her jealousy had been disproportionate to the incident, she knew; after all, she'd had no claim on him. Seeing him laughing with the lovely woman had brought its own brand of pain but had also ripped the scab off buried memories of Philippe's behaviour. *Never, never could she allow herself to fall for a man like that again.*

'Jesse hasn't mentioned any girls,' said Sandy slowly. 'Would he tell you?'

Sandy shook her head. 'I guess not. He seems to live by the code "a gentleman doesn't kiss and tell".'

'That's a good point in his favour. But there's no need for you to worry about me and Jesse. We've agreed we're going to try and be friends as we're connected by family, but that's all.' *No-strings fun.* That was how he'd described it and it wouldn't happen again.

'Good,' said Sandy with rather too much emphasis. 'Please keep it that way.'

'What do you mean?'

'Jesse is so not for you.'

Lizzie felt stung by Sandy's assumption. 'I know that. I've figured it out all by myself. I don't need my big sister to tell me,' she said through gritted teeth. 'I am not interested in Jesse as anything other than…than an acquaintance. Someone I have to try to be friends with because you're married to his brother.' *She would keep telling herself that.*

'I'm glad to hear it,' said Sandy with an air of relief that Lizzie found more than a tad insulting.

'By the way,' she said, 'thanks for not telling me Jesse would be here when I arrived in Dolphin Bay.'

Sandy looked shamefaced. 'Yeah. That. I didn't know he was going to injure his shoulder and land home here, did I? He's staying in the converted boathouse where we lived before we built the big house.'

'You could have warned me.'

'I was worried you'd get yourself wound up at the thought of seeing him. I didn't want you worrying about it. You've got enough on your plate.'

They'd always looked after each other and her sister's advice was well meant. 'Oh, Sandy, you don't have to worry about me. I've no intention of letting any guy get to me again.'

'After all you went through with Philippe, you know I can't help but worry about you. When I think of how you were in Sydney all by yourself having the baby while he—'

Lizzie put up her hand to stop her sister's flow of words. She didn't want to even think about that time, let alone talk about it. 'I'm older and wiser now. And much, much tougher.'

'Maybe I was wrong not to warn you about Jesse being home in Dolphin Bay.'

'No. You were right. It did give me a shock to see him here. Then to find out I'll be working with him every day…' *Maybe if she'd known, she'd have found a way to put off the opening of the café until Jesse had gone.*

'Don't knock back any offers of help—even if you don't particularly want to spend time with Jesse,' said Sandy. 'It's a big ask to get this café open for business in seven days. Besides, he's only here for a few weeks.'

'Four, to be precise,' Lizzie said. 'But don't worry, Sandy. I've got very good at resisting temptation. Jesse Morgan is no danger to my heart, I can assure you. I promise I'll make an effort to get along with him for your sake.'

CHAPTER FIVE

JESSE HADN'T LIVED in Dolphin Bay for any length of time for years. If he took the new job he'd been offered in Houston, Texas, he'd rarely be back to his home town. Yet he took pride in showing Lizzie more of the area where he, his father and his grandfather had grown up.

He had seen so many parts of the world devastated by floods, tornadoes, earthquakes and other disasters he never took its beauty for granted. No matter the growth of the town itself, the heritage-listed harbour, the beaches and the national park bushland stayed reassuringly the same. Whatever the ups and downs of his life, he took comfort from that.

'All I've seen of this part of the world is the town, the beach and the road in and out,' Lizzie said when she settled into the SUV he'd borrowed from his father. She was wearing white jeans and a simple knit top that gave her a look of cool elegance, of discreet sexiness he found very appealing. 'I'm looking forward to seeing more.'

'Then we'll drive the long way around to the places we're going to visit,' he said.

Spring was his favourite time here, the quiet months before the place became overrun with summer tourists. The bush was lush with new growth, a haze of fresh green splashed with the yellow of spring-flowering wattle. The ocean dazzled in its hues of turquoise reflecting cloudless skies; the sand almost white under the sun.

After they'd left the town centre behind, he drove along the road that ran parallel to the sea and stopped at the rocky rise that gave the best view right down the length of Silver Gull, the beach south of Big Ray. He was gratified when Lizzie caught her breath at her first sight of the rollers crashing on the stretch of pristine sand, the stands of young eucalypt that grew down to the edge of it. He owned a block of land on the headland that looked right out to the ocean. One day he'd build a house there.

'I don't know if you've been away long enough to be impressed that in the evening kangaroos sometimes come down to splash in the shallows,' he said.

Her smile was completely without reticence. 'I would never not be impressed by that. If I saw kangaroos there now, I'd go crazy with my phone camera. My French friends would go crazy too when I sent them the photos.'

'You might want to bring your daughter down one evening,' he said, smiling at her enthusiasm, as he put the car into gear and pulled away.

'Amy would love that, and so would I,' she said. 'Our Aussie beaches were one of the things I really missed when I was living in France.'

'France must have had its advantages,' he said, tongue-in-cheek.

'Of course it did. Not just the food but also the fashion, the architecture—I loved it. Thought I would always live there.' He didn't miss the edge of sadness to her voice.

'I'm sorry it didn't work out,' he said.

'Thank you,' she murmured and turned her head to

look out of the window, but not before he saw the bleakness in her eyes.

He'd like to know what had gone wrong with her marriage. What kind of a jerk would let go a woman like Lizzie and her cute little daughter? But it wasn't his business. And he didn't want to talk on an intimate level with her. Not when he was determined to deny any attraction he still felt for her.

'If I remember right you used to surf when you were a teenager,' she said after a pause that was starting to feel uncomfortable.

'Correct,' he said. 'I was a crazy kid, always looking for bigger waves, greater challenges. My first year of university, a group of us went down to Tasmania to surf Australia's wildest waves. It was a wonder none of us was killed.'

'Would you do that now?'

'Go surfing?' he said, deliberately misunderstanding her question. 'Not without a wetsuit. The water's still too cold.'

'I meant surf those extreme waves. I couldn't imagine anything more terrifying.'

Should he share his worst ever surfing story with her? The experience that had completely changed his life? He wanted to keep the time he spent with her on an impersonal level. But now that she'd dropped her chilly persona, he found her dangerously easy to talk to. 'I lost my taste for extreme surfing when I had to outrun a tsunami.'

She laughed in disbelief. 'You were surfing a tsunami? C'mon, pull the other leg.'

'Not surfing. Running. Literally running away from the beach as a monster wave thundered in.'

'You're serious!'

'You bet I am.' Even now his gut clenched with terror and he gripped hard on the steering wheel at the memory of it. 'I took a gap year when I finished my engineering degree. Thought I'd surf my way around all the great breaks of the world. This particular beach was on the south coast of Sri Lanka. That morning I came out very early to surf. The boy who manned the amenities hut screamed at me to get off the beach and to run to the high ground with him.'

She gasped. 'That must have been terrifying.'

'His village was wiped out. But he saved my life. I stuck around to help in any way I could. The organisation I work for now came to rebuild and there was lots of work for a volunteer engineer. When we were done, they offered me a paying job.'

'That's quite a story,' she said. 'I wondered how you'd got into your line of work.' He felt her eyes on him but he kept his straight ahead on the road. 'The thing is, you don't look like a do-gooder type.'

Her comment so surprised him, he took his hands off the wheel for a second and had to quickly correct the swerve of the car. 'And what does a do-gooder look like?'

'Not like he could be an actor or a model. Not like… like you.'

He laughed. 'It doesn't matter what you look like when people need help.'

He knew he hadn't been hit with the ugly stick so didn't demur with false modesty when people commented on the fortunate combination of genes he'd been blessed with. Your looks you were born with. He'd learned it was the personality you developed that counted. Lizzie, for example, was turn-heads lovely but it was her energy and warmth that had drawn him to her. Camilla had been older than him, eye-catching rather than beautiful, but her smarts and confidence had drawn him to her.

'Is that why you do it? To help people? When a guy like you could do anything he wanted?'

'What else?' He went to shrug but winced at the resulting pain in his shoulder. 'That first project—the camaraderie, seeing people rehoused so quickly, it was a high. I wanted more.'

The tsunami had cured him of his adrenalin-junkie taste for extreme sports. The surfing on five-metre waves, the heli-skiing on avalanches, the mountain biking off the sides of mountains. After seeing real disaster he no longer wanted to court it in the name of sport.

But recently he'd been wondering if he had replaced one sort of thrill for another. The thrill of being called to dangerous sites of recent catastrophes, the still present danger, the high of being needed. It was a rewarding life. But he gave up a lot to do it. Regular hours, a permanent home. Of course that made for a convenient excuse to stay single. But Lizzie was the last person he wanted to discuss that with.

'It must be dangerous and uncomfortable at times,' she said. 'I admire you. I don't think I could do it. The world is lucky to have people like you.'

He liked that she got it. Seemed that Lizzie took people for what they were.

'When it all boils down to it, it's a job the same as any other,' he said. 'Not, perhaps, one I'd want to do for the rest of my life. But one I've been glad to do while I can.'

'I don't believe that for a moment. It's like a calling.'

'Maybe,' he said, not wanting to be drawn further

into a conversation that might have him facing awkward truths about his motivations.

He distracted Lizzie by pointing to a flock of multi-coloured rainbow lorikeets hanging upside down off the branches of an indigenous grevillea bush. They were intoxicated by a surfeit of spring nectar from its spiky orange blossoms. When he and Ben had been kids, they'd found the sight of drunken parrots hilarious. He was gratified when Lizzie found it funny too. And tried not to be entranced at the sight and sound of her laughter.

Lizzie carefully stacked her finds into the back of Jesse's SUV, feeling more excited about the café than she had since she'd arrived in Dolphin Bay. Jesse had driven her through unsealed roads that twisted through acres of bushland to a property where the parents of one of Jesse's old school friends had a beekeeping business.

On the spot she'd bought honey harvested from bees that had feasted on blossoms of the eucalypts growing in the adjoining national park and named for the trees: Spotted Gum, Iron Bark, River Gum.

Jesse seemed bemused she'd bought so many jars. 'This is liquid gold,' she explained as he slammed shut the door of the boot. 'Each honey has a particular flavour and they're not always available. I'm thrilled to bits. It's also considerably cheaper buying it direct from the farmer.'

'Your head is buzzing with ideas on what to cook with all this?' he asked.

She smiled at his joke and he met her smile with one of his own. When she'd first climbed into his car this morning she'd felt tense and on edge in his company but had gradually relaxed to the point she felt she could have a normal conversation without being choked by self-consciousness. 'You could say that. I love to cook with honey but I also like to drizzle it over, say, baked ricotta for breakfast.'

'Ricotta cheese for breakfast! A hungry man coming into the café won't think much of that.'

'How about served with a stack of buttermilk pancakes?'

'With a side of bacon?'

'With a side order of bacon,' she said.

'Much better,' he said. 'I like a big breakfast to start the day. I might become a regular customer while I'm in town.'

There was something very appealing about a big man with a hearty appetite. She remembered—

No! She would not even *think* about Jesse in relation to other appetites. Not for the first time she thanked heaven that her time with him at the wedding had been interrupted. She might have been very, very tempted to go much further than kisses and that would have been a big mistake of the irredeemable kind. Mere kisses were easy to put behind her. *Though not without a degree of regret that they could never take up where they'd left off.*

'Why not?' she said lightly. 'I guarantee we'll have the best breakfasts and lunches in town. If you're still hungry after one of my breakfasts I'll give you your money back.'

'Is that a challenge?'

'An all-you-can-eat challenge? You'll just have to wait and see the food, won't you?'

'What about the coffee? A café will live or die on its coffee.'

'The beans they're ordering for me through the Harbourside are single origin beans from El Salvador and Guatemala. Fair trade, of course. I have no quibble with them.' Her voice trailed away at the end. She'd decided not to complain too much about anything to Jesse in case it found its way back to Ben and Sandy.

He turned to her. 'You don't sound as confident about the coffee as you do about the food.'

'How did you know that?'

'Just an edge to the tone of your voice.'

It was scary how quickly he'd learned to read her. Was that the Jesse way with women? Or a genuine friendship building between them? Still, she decided to confide in him—this was just business. 'You're right. We've got a state-of-the-art Italian coffee machine. But I'm not sure how good the girl is we've employed to use it.'

'If she's no good, employ someone else,' he said, again displaying the ruthless business streak that surprised her.

'Easier said than done in a place like Dolphin Bay. There's not a lot of need for highly skilled baristas; as a result there aren't many to call upon.'

'I'm sure you'll sort it out,' he said. 'You're likely to have a few teething problems to overcome.'

'But I don't want teething problems,' she said stubbornly. 'I want the café to run perfectly from the get-go.'

'You really are a perfectionist, aren't you?'

'Yes,' she admitted. 'Which isn't always a good thing. It means I'm often disappointed.'

She knew there was a bitter edge to her words but she couldn't help it. *'No man is perfect,'* Philippe had shouted at her when she'd refused to take him back that final time. Was it so unreasonable to want a man who wouldn't cheat and lie? Who could manage to stay faithful?

Another reason to keep Jesse strictly hands-off. He

was a player like Philippe. With all the potential for heartbreak that came with that kind of guy.

She forced herself away from old hurts and back to the café.

'Tell me if you think this is a good idea—I want to ask your mother if she could share some of her favourite recipes from the old guest house. It would be nice to have that link to the Morgans in the café menu.'

Morgan's Guest House had been such a wonderful place, especially for a girl interested in cooking. Maura was an exceptional home-style cook.

Jesse paused for a long moment before he replied. She wondered if it had been a bad idea. She let out her breath when he answered, not realising she had been holding it. 'It's a great idea,' he said slowly. 'I'm sure Mum would be flattered. I'd certainly like it.'

'I'm so glad you think so,' she said with a rush of relief. 'I have such happy memories of helping Maura cook in the kitchen. She taught me to make perfect scrambled eggs. I've never found a better technique than hers.'

'When my mother heard you'd become a chef she was tickled pink that she might have had an influence on you.'

'I'm glad to hear that, because she was a big influence. My own mother encouraged me too.'

'And your father?'

She looked away from the car so she didn't have to face him. 'You've probably heard something from Sandy about what my father was like,' she said stiffly.

'Ben said Dr Randall Adam was an officious, domineering snob who—'

Lizzie put up her hand to halt him. 'Don't say it. After all he's done, he's still my father.'

'Sure,' he said, and she felt embarrassed at the sympathy in his voice. She didn't want him to feel sorry for her.

She scuffed at the ground near the back tyres of the car with the toe of her sneaker. 'Shall we say, he was less than encouraging when I didn't want to follow the academic path he'd mapped out for me. I wasn't the honours student Sandy was but he didn't get that. He wanted me to go to university. When I landed an apprenticeship at one of the most highly regarded restaurants in Sydney he didn't appreciate what a coup that was. He…well, he pretty much disowned me.'

Under threat of being kicked out of home without a cent to support her if she didn't complete her schooling, she'd finished high school. But the kitchen jobs she'd worked during her vacations had only reinforced her desire to become a chef. When she'd got the apprenticeship at the age of seventeen her father had carried out his threat and booted her out of home. It had backfired on him, though. Her mother had finally had enough of his bullying and infidelities. He went. Lizzie stayed. It was a triumph for her but one she hadn't relished—she'd adored her father and had been heartbroken.

Jesse shook his head in obvious disbelief. 'Isn't he proud of what you've achieved now?'

It was an effort to keep her voice steady. 'He sees being a chef as a trade rather than a profession. I…I think he's ashamed of me.' She shrugged. 'That's his problem, isn't it?'

'And not one you want to talk about, right?' Jesse said, his blue eyes shrewd in their assessment of her mood.

She had to fight an urge to throw herself into his arms and feel them around her in a big comforting hug.

At Sandy's wedding ceremony she'd sobbed, not just with joy for her sister but for the loss of her own marriage and her own dreams of happiness. Jesse had silently held her and let her tears wet his linen shirt. She could never forget how it had felt to rest against his broad, powerful chest and feel his warmth and strength for just the few moments she had allowed herself the luxury. *It had meant nothing.*

'That's right,' she said. Then gave a big sigh. 'I won't say it doesn't still hurt. But I'm a big girl now with a child of my own to raise.'

'And you're sure as heck not going to raise her like you were raised,' he said.

'You're sure right on that,' she said with a shaky laugh.

'I was so lucky with my parents,' said Jesse. 'They're really good people who love Ben and me unconditionally. I didn't know what a gift that was until I grew up.'

'Looking back, I realise how kind Maura was,' Lizzie said. 'She must have found me a terrible nuisance, always underfoot. But there was so much tension between my parents, I wanted to avoid them. And Sandy was always off with Ben.'

'Of course she wouldn't have found you a nuisance,' said Jesse. 'Out of all the guests she had over the years, Mum always remembered you and Sandy. I think she'd love to share her recipes with you. Maybe…maybe it's time to revive some happy memories of the guest house.'

They both fell silent. Ben's first wife and baby son had died when the old guest house had burned down. That meant Jesse had lost his sister-in-law and nephew. She wondered how the tragedy had affected him. But it wasn't the kind of thing she felt she could ask. Not now. Maybe never.

'Can you ask about the recipes for me?' she said.

'Sure. Though I'm sure Mum would love it if you called her and asked her yourself.'

'I just might do that.'

Jesse glanced at his watch.

'I know, the two hours,' she said, resisting the urge to ask him just what catastrophe would befall him if he spent longer than that in her company. 'We'd better hurry up and get back in the car.' She walked around to the passenger side, settled into her seat and clicked in her seat belt. 'We're heading for a dairy next, right?'

'Correct,' said Jesse from the driver's seat. 'The farmer and his wife are old schoolfriends of mine. I hear they've won swags of awards for their cheeses and yogurts. I thought that might interest you.'

She turned to look at him, teasing. 'How do you know exactly what I need, Jesse Morgan?'

He held her gaze with a quizzical look of his own. 'Do I?' he said in that deep voice that sent a shiver of awareness down her spine.

Shocked at her reaction, she rapidly back-pedalled. 'In terms of supplies for the café, I meant.'

His dark brows drew together. 'Of course you did,' he said. 'What else would you have meant?'

She kept her gaze straight ahead and didn't answer.

CHAPTER SIX

THE SATURDAY TASTE-TESTING brunch at the café was in full swing. Bay Bites was packed with people, most of whom Lizzie didn't recognise, all of whom she wanted to impress. She'd spent all of Friday prepping food and working with the staff Sandy had hand-picked for her. They'd bonded well as a team, united by enthusiasm for the new venture. Now it was actually happening and it was exhilarating and scary at the same time.

She took a moment out from supervising her new kitchen staff to stand back behind the dolphin-carved countertop and watch what had turned into a party of sorts.

So far, so good. Her menu choices were getting rave reviews. She'd decided to serve small portions from the basic menu, handed around from trays, so people could try as many options as possible. She'd gone as far as printing feedback sheets to be filled in but the Dolphin Bay taste-testers were proving more informal than that. They simply told her or the wait staff what they thought. She took their suggestions on board with a smile.

'I'd go easy on the chilli in that warm chicken salad, love,' Jesse's seventy-five-year-old great-aunt Ida said. 'Some of us oldies aren't keen on too much of the hot stuff.'

'The only problem with those little burgers was there weren't enough of them,' said the bank manager, a friend of Ben. 'Your other greedy guests emptied the tray.'

'The triple chocolate brownies? Bliss,' said one well-dressed thirty-plus woman. 'I'll be coming here for my book club meetings—it's ideal with the bookshop next door.'

Lizzie soon sensed an immense goodwill towards the new venture. Not, she realised, because of any reputation of hers. Because of Ben and Sandy, she was accepted as a member of the well-loved Morgan clan.

And then there was the Jesse effect. A number of these people were the wedding guests who had discovered her and Jesse kissing on the balcony. She was, and always would be in their eyes, one of 'Jesse's girls' and included in their general affection towards him. Who would have thought it?

From her corner behind the counter, she watched Jesse as he worked the room, towering head and shoulders above most of the guests. Was he aware of how many female eyes followed him? Her eyes were among them. No matter where he was in the café she was conscious of him. It was as if he had some built-in magnet that drew female attention. She was no more immune than the rest of them. She just had to continue to fight it if she was going to be able to work with him.

He'd insisted on wearing the same blue jeans, white T-shirt and butcher-striped full apron in sea tones of blue and aqua as the wait staff. How could a guy look so hot in such pedestrian work-wear? But then a guy as handsome and well-built as Jesse would look good in anything. *Or nothing.* She shook her head to rid both her brain and her libido of such subversive thoughts. Jesse was off-limits—even to her imagination.

He'd arrived this morning before anyone else. 'I'm here to help,' he'd said. 'If I wear the uniform, people will know it.'

'I thought you were here to taste the food,' she'd protested as he'd tied on the apron, succeeding in looking utterly masculine as he did so. The colours of the stripes made his impossibly blue eyes look even bluer.

'I can do both,' he'd said in a tone that brooked no argument.

She'd let it go at that, in truth grateful for the extra help. And he had excelled himself. It appeared he knew most of the guests—and if he didn't he very soon did. Through the hum of conversation, the clatter of cutlery, the noise of chairs scraping on the tiled floor, she could hear the deep tones of his voice as he made people welcome to Bay Bites and talked up the food while he was at it.

If she had hired an expensive public relations consultant they wouldn't have done better than Jesse in promoting the new business.

She froze as she saw him bend his dark head to chat with Evie, the pretty blonde wife of the dairy farmer Jesse had introduced her to on Thursday. Straight away Lizzie had sensed that the girl was more than a mere acquaintance. Sure enough, it turned out she had dated Jesse in high school.

How many other women in this room had Jesse been involved with? *Was involved with right now?*

Was he really a player in the worst sense of the word, moving on once he'd made a conquest? Or was he just a natural-born charmer? She suspected the latter. The nurses in the hospital where he'd been born had probably gone gaga over him as he'd lain kicking and gurgling in his crib. And she'd bet he'd been a teacher's pet all the way through school—with the female teachers, anyway.

Evie had come to the taste-testing without her husband; rather she was accompanied by a curvy auburn-haired girl who was a friend visiting from Sydney. Lizzie gripped tight onto the edge of the counter as Evie's companion laughed up at Jesse. She schooled her face to show no reaction. He could talk and laugh with whatever woman he pleased. *It was nothing to her.*

That uncomfortable twinge of jealousy she felt as she watched them was further reason to keep Jesse at a distance.

Jealousy. She had battled hard with herself to overcome what she saw as a serious character flaw. As a child she'd been jealous of Sandy, not just for her toys or pretty dresses, but also because she'd been convinced her father loved Sandy more than he'd loved her. Thankfully, her mother had identified what was going on and made sure no rift ever developed between the sisters. She'd helped the young Lizzie learn to handle jealousy of other kids at school and later jealousy when she'd thought people at work had been favoured over her. As an adult, Lizzie had thought the demon had been well and truly vanquished. Until she'd met Philippe.

She'd been just twenty-one and working at an upmarket resort in Port Douglas in tropical far northern Queensland. She had worked hard and played hard with talented young chefs from around the world on working holidays. Good-looking, charming Philippe had been way out of her league. But he'd made a play for her and she'd fallen hard for his French accent and his live-for-the-moment ways. It hadn't mattered that other girls never stopped flirting with him because he had assured her he loved only her. She'd followed him to France without a moment's hesitation.

But the jealousy demon had reared back into full flaming life after she'd given birth to Amy. For the first six months she'd been stuck at home living with his parents while he'd continued the work-hard-play-hard lifestyle they'd formerly enjoyed together. And Philippe had not been the type of man to do without feminine attention.

Just like Jesse, she thought now as he smiled at the auburn-haired girl who was hanging onto his every word. Who could blame the girl for being dazzled by his movie-star looks and genuine charm? *She couldn't let it get to her.* Women of all ages gravitated to Jesse and he gravitated to them. That was the way he was and it wasn't likely to change. It was the reason above all others that she could never be more than passing friendly with him.

If Jesse had been more than a friend, she would by now be racked with jealousy. It wasn't a feeling she enjoyed. She had hated the jealous, suspicious person she had become towards the end of her marriage; she never wanted to go there again.

Jesse must have felt her gaze on him because he said something to the two women, turned and headed towards her. He indicated his near-empty tray where a lone piece of chicken sat in a pile of baby spinach leaves. 'Want some?'

She shook her head. 'Can't eat. Too concerned with feeding all of this lot.'

'You're sure? You need to keep your energy up. It's delicious. Made with free-range chicken breast stuffed with organic caramelised tomato and locally produced goat's cheese and wrapped in Italian prosciutto.'

She smiled. 'You're doing a good job of selling it to me, but no thanks all the same.'

'Can't let it go to waste,' he said, popping it into his mouth.

'Glad you approve,' she said as he ate the chicken with evident relish. A similar dish had been one of the most popular items in the Sydney restaurant she'd worked in when she'd first come back from France. Served with a salad for lunch, she hoped it would be popular here too.

'The slow-cooked lamb was a huge success,' he said. 'Although some people said they'd prefer an onion relish to the beetroot relish.'

'*Some* people,' she said, arching her brow. 'How many people? One person in particular, perhaps?'

'One in particular has never much liked beetroot. He'd like the onion.'

'So maybe the chef was correct in her guess that that particular person would like the slow-cooked lamb?'

'Maybe.'

'You refuse to admit I was right about what you'd like best?'

'I haven't finished tasting everything yet. I'll let you know at the end. By the way, the asparagus and feta frittata was a big hit with the ladies. I told them it was low calorie, though I don't know whether that's actually true.'

Was he born with an innate knowledge of what appealed to women? Or was it some masculine dark art he practised to enchant and ensnare them? *She could not let herself fall under his spell—it would be only too easy.*

'Make sure you don't miss out on the apple pie, I'm

sure you'll love it,' she said. 'But don't even think of telling anyone it's low calorie. I might get sued when my customers start stacking on the weight.'

He put down the tray, leaned across the counter towards her and spoke in a low voice, his eyes warm with what seemed like genuine concern. 'Seriously, are you pleased how it's going?'

She nodded. 'Really pleased. I don't want to jinx myself but people are booking already for our opening day on Thursday.'

'The buzz is good. I was on door duty a while ago and had to turn passers-by away. Lucky we put the "Closed for Private Function" sign on the door or I reckon we'd have been invaded.'

'I've handed out a lot of leaflets letting people know about the opening hours and menu.'

'So everything is going as planned?'

'I'm happy but—'

'You're not happy with the staff.'

Again, she was surprised at how easily he read her. Especially when he scarcely knew her. 'No. Yes. I mean I'm really happy with the sous chef. He's excellent. In fact he's too good for a café and I doubt we'll keep him.' She glanced back at the kitchen. But with the noise level of the café there was no way the chef could hear her.

'You'll keep him. He's already got one kid and another on the way. He can't afford to leave Dolphin Bay.'

'I don't know whether to be glad for us or sad for him.'

'Try glad for him. He's happy to have a job in his home town. What about the others?'

'The kitchen hand is great with both prep and clearing up and the waitresses are enthusiastic and friendly, which is just what I want.'

'I can hear a "but" coming.'

'The waitress who is also the barista—Nikki. She's a nice girl but not nearly as experienced with making coffee as she said and I'm worried how she'll work under pressure.'

'You know what I said. With a small staff and a reputation to establish you can't afford any weak links.'

'I know. And…thanks for the advice.'

He picked up the tray again, swivelling it on one hand. 'The kitchen is calling.'

She'd noticed how adeptly he'd carried the tray, served the food. 'You know, if you weren't an engineer and helping the world, you'd have a great future in hospitality,' she teased.

'Been there. Done that. I worked as a waiter for an agency while I was at university. I'm only doing it again to help make Bay Bites a success.'

She bet she knew which agency. It employed only the handsomest of handsome men. It figured they'd want Jesse on their books even if only in university vacations.

Jesse took off again, stopping for a quick word with his mother on his way to the kitchen.

Lizzie waved to Maura, and Maura smiled and blew her a kiss. Jesse's mother was a tall, imposing woman with Jesse's blue eyes and black hair, though hers was now threaded with grey. Lizzie had taken up with her again as if it had been yesterday that she'd been a teenager helping her in the kitchen and soaking up the older woman's cooking lore.

Thankfully, Maura had been delighted at the idea of sharing some of the guest house favourites based on the cooking of her Irish youth. They'd made a date for Monday to go through the recipes. *Just to go through the recipes, not to talk about Jesse*, Lizzie reminded

herself. Or to do anything as ridiculous as to ask Maura
to show her his baby photos. Her thoughts of him being
doted over as a baby had sparked a totally unwarranted
curiosity to see what he'd looked like as a little boy.

As Jesse picked up a tray of mini muffins, he wondered
what the heck he was doing playing at being a waiter
in a café. He hadn't enjoyed the time he'd spent in the
service industry during university, had only done it to
fund his surfing and skiing trips. Being polite to ill-
mannered clients of catering companies hadn't been at
all to his liking. In fact he'd lost his job when he'd tipped
a pitcher of cold water over an obnoxious drunken guest
who wouldn't stop harassing one of the young waitresses. The agency had never hired him again and he
hadn't given a damn.

He'd promised to help Sandy with the café but the
building work he'd already done was more than his
sister-in-law would ever have expected. No. He had to
be honest with himself. This café gig was all about
Lizzie. Seeing her every day. Being part of her life.
And that was a bad, bad idea. Even for two hours a day.

Because he couldn't stop thinking about her. How
beautiful she was. Her grace and elegance. Her warmth
and humour. Remembering how she'd felt in his arms
and how he'd like to have her there again. Her passionate response to his kisses and how he'd like—

In short, he was failing dismally in thinking of Lizzie
Dumont as a family acquaintance trying to be friends.
Could it ever really be platonic between them? There
would always be an undercurrent of sexual attraction, of
possibilities. Even in that white chef's jacket and baggy
black pants she looked beautiful. He even found it al-
luring the way she tasted food in the kitchen—how she

closed her eyes, the way she used her tongue, her murmurs of pleasure when the food tasted the way it should.

Lizzie wasn't sexy in a hip-swinging, cleavage-baring way. But there was something about the way she carried herself, the way she smiled that hinted at the passionate woman he knew existed under her contained exterior.

However, his reasons for not wanting to date her were still there and stopped him from flirting with her, from suggesting they see each other while he was in town. There could be no 'fun while it lasts' scenarios with Lizzie. And the alternative—something more serious—was not on for him. The last time he'd tried serious it had taken him years to recover from the emotional battering.

He had fallen so hard and fast for Camilla he hadn't seen sense. Hadn't realised when he'd talked to her about his feelings she had answered him with weasel words that had had him completely stymied, fooled into thinking she cared for him. He cringed when he thought about how naïve and idealistic he'd been. When he'd proposed to her she had virtually laughed in his face.

No way would he risk going there again with Lizzie. He had to stop looking at her, noticing her, admiring her.

There was also the sobering truth that Lizzie didn't seem to want anything to do with him other than as a family friend. In fact he suspected she disapproved of him.

He'd noticed the way she'd watched him as he'd worked the room, offering samples of food, talking up the café, Lizzie's skills as a chef, the bookshop next door, how it would all work when Bay Bites opened. He'd talked to guys too, but it was the women who'd wanted to linger and chat. As it always had been. And Lizzie was clocking that female attention.

Ever since he'd turned fourteen women had made it obvious they found him attractive. *'You don't even have to try, you lucky dog,'* Ben had often said when they were younger.

When his mates had been trying to talk girls into their beds he'd been trying to get them out of his. Literally. More than once he'd come home and found a girl he scarcely knew had climbed through his bedroom window and was waiting for him, naked in his bed.

He'd found that a turn-off rather than a turn-on. He'd had to ask them to leave in the nicest possible way without hurting their feelings. When Jesse made love to a woman it was always going to be memorable—and his choice.

His brother Ben stopped him to snag first one muffin then another from his tray. 'Sure I can't convince you to stay in Dolphin Bay and work here? With your way with the ladies, I reckon we'll double the numbers of female customers. Look at them, flocking to your side like they've always done.'

'Ha ha,' he said, ignoring the bait, conscious that Lizzie might overhear the conversation with his brother.

As he'd said to Lizzie, his prowess with the opposite sex was greatly exaggerated. And he hadn't taken advantage of his gift with women. He had always been honest about his feelings. Dated one girl at a time. Made it clear when he wasn't looking for anything serious. Bailed before anyone got hurt. Let her tell everyone *she* had dumped *him*. Had stayed friends with his ex-girlfriends—as far as their boyfriends or husbands would allow.

But today, seeing himself through Lizzie's eyes, he

wasn't so sure he was comfortable with all that any more. Most of his Dolphin Bay friends were married now. Though the guys moaned and complained about being tied down, he didn't actually believe them when they said they envied him his life. They seemed too content.

Now he sometimes wondered what they really thought about him being single as he faced turning thirty. He knew the townsfolk had laid bets on him always staying a bachelor. It was beginning to bug him. But he had never treated their interest in his ladies' man reputation as anything other than a laugh; never talked about the reasons he'd stayed on his own.

He hadn't told anyone in Dolphin Bay—even his family—about what had happened with Camilla. Had never confided how the deaths of his sister-in-law Jodi and little nephew Liam had affected him. How terrified he'd been at seeing Ben suffer the life-destroying pain caused by the loss of love. On the cusp of manhood, Jesse had resolved he would never endure what Ben had endured. He'd put the brakes on any relationship that threatened to get serious.

Gradually, however, he'd realised Ben's pain should not be his pain. That he had to love his own way, take his own risks. He'd let down his guard by the time he'd met Camilla and hurtled into a relationship with her. Only for her callous rejection of his love to send him right back behind his barricades.

Was that enough now?

He looked over to Lizzie but she had disappeared into the kitchen again. He'd seen yet another side of her today. Calm. Competent. Ruthlessly efficient under pressure. He liked it.

He admired her for her commitment. Surely a café

serving toasted ham and cheese sandwiches—even if she called them *croque monsieur*—was a huge come-down for someone with Lizzie's career credentials. Dolphin Bay must be just a pit stop for Lizzie. She had a half-French daughter. How long before she got fed up with flipping fried eggs and turned her sights back to Europe?

Or did he have that wrong? It was logical for him to base future plans purely on his career. Maybe it wasn't so for Lizzie. She was a mother—perhaps that was why she could settle for Bay Bites? Maybe because it was in the best interests of her daughter.

He couldn't imagine how it would be to put someone else first. Wife. Child. Suiting himself had seemed just fine up to now. *A charming Peter Pan.* That was what Camilla had called him at their most recent encounter. She'd said it with a laugh. Hadn't meant it to sound like an insult. But it had stung just the same. And made him think.

He headed back into the fray. 'Be quick before these muffins are all snatched off the tray,' he said to the nice redhead friend of Evie's. 'They're made with organically grown rhubarb, locally produced sour cream—in fact from Evie's farm—and—'

The girl picked one up from the tray, sniffed it, broke off a piece, tasted it. 'And pure maple syrup from the forests of Quebec, if I'm not wrong—together with Queensland pecans,' she pronounced.

He stared at her, taken aback. 'Sounds good to me. I'll check with the chef.' He must ask Lizzie. He really wasn't cut out to be a waiter.

Lizzie slumped in one of the bentwood chairs, exhausted. The guests had gone. The clearing up was done. The staff dismissed. Only Sandy, Ben and Jesse remained.

Sandy was incandescent with joy. 'Ever since I first set foot in the bookshop, I dreamed of there being a café next door. If today was an indication of how it's going to turn out, I think my dream is on its way to coming true. Thanks to my sister.'

She grabbed both Lizzie's hands and pulled her to her feet. 'Hug,' she commanded. Lizzie smiled and did as she was told. If she could repay Sandy's kindness with a successful café she'd be happy.

'C'mon, Ben too,' said Sandy. 'And you, too, Jesse. Group hug. Family hug.'

Alarmed, Lizzie stiffened. 'I don't think—'

But, before she knew it, both she and Sandy were enveloped in a bear hug from tall, blond Ben whom she already loved as a brother. Then Jesse joined in and it was a different feeling altogether. Every nerve went on alert as she felt Jesse's strong arms around her, was pulled against the solid wall of his chest, breathed in his maleness and warmth. Could he feel her heart pounding at his nearness?

She could never, ever think of Jesse as a brother.

And right at this moment it was darn near impossible to think of him only as a friend.

CHAPTER SEVEN

THE NEXT DAY, mid-morning, Jesse drove from the boat-house where he was staying towards Silver Gull beach. He knew the surf would be flat with just the occasional swell; he'd checked it while he was on his early morning run just after dawn. But that didn't bother him. Surfing wasn't possible right now, with his shoulder injury. He couldn't paddle out to where the waves would usually be breaking and he couldn't use his shoulders to get him into a wave. That right shoulder was aching today. Carrying all those food-laden trays yesterday probably hadn't been the wisest thing he could have done in terms of shoulder rehabilitation.

But he could swim. Cautiously. No freestyle. But some breaststroke. Maybe some back-kick that left his shoulders right out of it. Heck, just to float around would be better than nothing.

The beach should be near-deserted at this time of morning. It wasn't as popular as Big Ray, which was one of the reasons he liked it. All the early morning run-ners and dog walkers would have gone home by now and October wasn't yet peak swimming season. Al-though it was gloriously sunny, with very little breeze, the water was still too cold for all but the intrepid to swim without a wetsuit.

The first thing he saw as he approached the beach access was Lizzie's small blue hatchback parked carefully off the road. He didn't know whether to be glad or annoyed she was here. The more he saw of her, the more he was perturbed by his attraction to her. That group hug the night before had tested his endurance. Having Lizzie back in his arms—well, half of Lizzie considering the nature of a group hug—had brought desire for her rushing back in a major way. He hadn't stopped thinking about her since.

For a long moment he left the engine idling. Go or stay?

No contest, he thought as he killed the engine. It wasn't a good idea for Lizzie to be swimming by herself. Not at Silver Gull with its dangerous rip undertow that could pull an unwary swimmer out to sea. He needed to keep an eye on her, keep her safe. He zipped himself into his wetsuit, grabbed a towel and headed towards the sand dunes that bordered the southern end of the beach.

As he'd thought, there wasn't another soul there. Almost straight away he saw Lizzie on the sand halfway between where the gum trees grew down to the edge of the beach and where the small breaking waves swirled up onto the sand in lacy white foam. She was lying on her back on a bright pink towel, her lovely body covered only by a turquoise and white checked bikini. Her long slender limbs were stretched out in total relaxation, her pale hair loose and glinting like silver in the sunlight, an expression of bliss on her face.

Jesse clenched his fists by his sides and a cold sweat broke out on his forehead. It would have been better if he'd kept on driving and gone to a different beach.

He could not deny there had been times since he'd

met Lizzie that he had wondered how she looked under her clothes. But the reality of her in the skimpy bikini far surpassed any fantasy—her breasts high and round, her hips flaring gently, her body slender not skinny. She was perfect in every way. He couldn't help but observe that she had certainly filled out since her teenage years.

He coughed to alert her to his presence, not wanting to be seen to stare at her for so long it could be perceived as untoward. Startled, she sat up quickly, looked up at him. She took off her sunglasses and then used her hand to shade her eyes, blinking to focus on him. 'Jesse. You...you surprised me.'

He wasn't sure whether it was shock or pleasure he saw in her eyes. 'Catching some rays?' he asked, trying to sound casual when all he could think about was how sexy she looked in that bikini. Of how, in fact, the design of a bikini didn't so much cover up but draw attention.

'I desperately need to get some colour,' she said, stretching out her arms with unconscious grace. 'Feeling the sun on my skin is heaven. There won't be much beach time once the café opens.'

Already the smooth skin of her shoulders was tinged with gold. 'Are you planning to swim?' he asked.

She turned to look towards the water, calm, translucent, sparkling in the sunlight as far as the eye could see. 'Just thinking about it now. The water looks so inviting.'

'It will be very cold in.'

She indicated the beach bag to the left side of the towel. 'I borrowed Sandy's wetsuit.'

He gritted his teeth. 'Might be an idea to put it on.'

'I will soon. I'm enjoying—'

'Put it on now, will you.' His voice came out harsher than he had intended.

She frowned. 'But—'

'I can't talk to you while you're wearing that bikini.' He spoke somewhere over her head, not trusting himself to look at her.

'But it's a modest bikini—'

'It does nothing to hide what a beautiful body you have. That's more than a guy who's trying to be just friends can take.'

'Oh,' she said and blushed so the colour on her cheeks rivalled that of her towel.

He tossed her his navy striped towel. 'Here. Cover up, will you.'

She caught the towel. 'Sure. I didn't think…' She pulled his towel around her, twisting to tuck it into her bikini top between her breasts. *Lucky towel.* Then she went to get up from the sand.

Automatically, he offered her his hand to help her. For a long moment she just stared at it with an expression he couldn't read. Then she put her narrow hand in his much larger one. He pulled her to her feet, unable to keep his eyes from how lovely she was.

She faced him, standing very still. She was tall, but he was taller and she had to look up to him, exposing her slender neck, her delicate throat where he could see a pulse throbbing. Their gazes locked. Her grey eyes seemed brighter, perhaps reflecting the blue of the sky and the sea. 'Thank you,' she murmured.

Jesse still held her hand and when she made no effort to free it he tightened his grip—now he had her so close he couldn't bear to let her go. He noticed a few grains of sand sprinkled on her cheek, maybe from where she'd pushed her hair away from her face. Reluctant to let go of her hand, he used his other hand to gently wipe off the tiny grains from where they adhered to her smooth skin.

She closed her eyes with a flutter of long fair lashes and he could feel her tremble beneath his touch as his fingers then traced down her cheek towards her mouth. He traced the outline of her soft, lovely mouth with his fingers and now it was he who trembled with awareness and a stunned disbelief she wasn't pushing him away.

Her lips parted just enough for her to breathe out a slow sigh and open her eyes. Jesse saw in them both wariness and desire. 'Jesse, I...' Whatever she might have been about to say faltered to nothing. She swayed towards him.

He dropped his hand and used it to take her other hand and pull her closer to him, so close he could feel the heat from her sun-warmed body. He pressed his mouth to hers in a soft questioning kiss—she gave him the answer he wanted with the pressure of her lips back on his. As he deepened the kiss he felt the same fierce surge of possessive hunger he'd felt the first time he'd kissed her. Had kissed her, then been parted from her through a stupid misunderstanding before he'd had the chance to think about what that flare of attraction between them could mean.

Six months between kisses and she tasted the same. Felt the same. And he wanted her just as much—more. She kissed him back with a fierce intensity that sent a surge of excitement pulsing through him. He dropped his hands so he could lock his arms around her. With a little murmur she wound her arms around his neck and pulled him close. The towel slid to the sand between them. 'Leave it,' he growled against her mouth then slanted and deepened the angle of his kiss.

The longing for her he'd been holding back overwhelmed him. All this platonic friendship stuff was bulldust as far as he was concerned. He'd wanted her from the time she'd first swept him up with her warmth and laughter, set him the challenge of that cool exterior and the promise of passion beneath. He slid his hands up her slender waist, skimmed her small, firm breasts as her heart thudded under his hand and she gasped under his mouth.

There were master chefs, master sommeliers, master chocolatiers—but Jesse was truly a master kisser, Lizzie mused, her thoughts barely coherent through a fizz of excitement. Delicious shivers of pleasure tingled across her skin as Jesse worked seductive magic with his lips and tongue. The scrape of the stubble on his chin was an exciting contrast to the softness of his mouth; the hard strength of his body to the tenderness of his hands on her bare skin. The last man to kiss her had been Jesse six months ago. The way he kissed her now was everything she'd remembered, everything that had excited her that night on the balcony and awoken needs she'd tried to deny.

She'd been daydreaming about him when she'd been lying on the beach—and then suddenly he'd been there, as if conjured up from her fantasies. She was so dazed that before she knew it she was in his arms, with no time to worry about whether it was right, wrong or ill-advised. Another public kiss with Jesse? Her craving to be close to him was so strong the possibility of being caught again, being teased again, had scarcely registered.

Jesse looked so hot in that wetsuit, the tight black

fabric moulding his broad chest, flat belly, muscular limbs. Unshaven, his black hair carelessly tousled as if he'd just run his hand through it in his hurry to get to the beach, he'd never looked more should-be-on-billboards handsome. When he'd taken her hand to help her up from the sand, she'd known where it would lead. Known and felt dizzy with anticipation.

Now she kissed him back, lost in the overwhelming pleasure of being with Jesse again. She'd found it impossible to clamp down on her attraction to him—no matter how many times she'd told herself Jesse wasn't right for her. She might be able to deny herself that Belgian chocolate—but not this.

Desire bloomed in the tightening of her nipples, the ache to be closer, and she tightened her arms around his neck, breathing in the intoxicating scent of his skin. Wanting him. Craving more than kisses. She had never been kissed the way Jesse kissed. Jesse the master kisser would be Jesse the master lover and she shivered in sensual anticipation of the discovery.

What was she thinking? She stilled in his embrace.

She could not let herself want Jesse this much. Too many other women wanted Jesse. It would only lead to heartbreak, to agony. *He couldn't give her what she needed.*

She broke the kiss and drew away, pushing against his chest, her breath ragged. He murmured a protest and gathered her back into his arms but he let her go when she continued to maintain her resistance. His expression, passion fading to bewilderment and—yes—hurt wrenched at her heart. She hated that she was the cause of that.

What had just happened was purely physical, she reminded herself. Oh, she wanted Jesse all right. And the more she'd got to like him, the more she'd wanted him. But she needed to be cherished, loved for herself, not be the latest in a line of conquests. She wanted to love and be loved—but she also wanted to trust.

How hard would it be to trust a player again?

'Jesse, I can't do this. I won't do this.' Her voice came out wobblier than she would have liked. But Jesse got the message.

He choked out just the one word. 'Why?'

Jesse gulped in deep breaths of salt-tangy air to try and get back his equilibrium. He was convinced that Lizzie had enjoyed being with him as much as he'd enjoyed being with her. He could see her aroused nipples through the fabric of her bikini top. She was flushed, her eyes dilated, her mouth swollen from his kisses. She had never looked lovelier.

But she turned away from him. Bent down and picked up his towel where it lay rumpled on the sand at her feet. With hands that weren't steady she draped it around her shoulders but it covered less than it revealed. *He wanted her so much it hurt.*

She twisted the corner of the towel until it was scrunched into a knot, untwisted it and twisted it again before she looked back up at him. 'Because all those reasons that make it a bad idea for us to get together are still there,' she said.

Somewhere in the realm of good sense he knew that. Hell, he had his reasons too. Desire this strong could lead to pain as wrenching as Camilla had inflicted on him. But his body didn't want to listen to his brain. He wanted Lizzie and he wanted her now. If not now this afternoon, this evening, tonight—and hang the consequences.

'It was…a mistake. We have to forget it happened. This…this shouldn't ch-change anything between us,' she stammered.

He cleared his throat. 'How can it *not* change things between us?'

She looked up at him, her eyes huge in the oval of her face. 'Jesse, I want you so much I'm aching for you.' Her voice caught and she took in a deep breath but it did nothing to steady it. 'If…if things were different there's nothing more I'd want than to make love with you right now.'

He made a disbelieving grunt in response.

'Oh, not on the beach. But back in my apartment. In a hotel room. At your place. Somewhere private where we could explore each other, please each other, satisfy our curiosity about each other. Even…even if that was all we ever had.'

He groaned and when he spoke his voice was edged with anger. 'Do you realise what you're doing talking to me like that? Don't be a—'

'A tease? Believe me, I'm not teasing.' She swallowed hard. 'In the six months since I last saw you, even though I thought you'd gone off with another woman, I dreamed of you. I kept waking up from dreams of you. Wanting you. Aching for you. Reaching for you, to find only an empty bed.'

'Then why—?'

'Because desire isn't enough.' She took in another of those deep breaths that made her breasts swell over her bikini top in such a tantalising way. 'I'm sometimes accused of being blunt but I have to be honest with you,' she said.

He swallowed a curse word. Whenever anyone used that 'honest' phrase he knew he was about to hear something he didn't want to hear. Lizzie's expression didn't give him cause to think otherwise.

'Fire away,' he said through gritted teeth.

'I've told you, right now there's no room in my life for a man.' She was having trouble meeting his eyes. Not a good sign. 'But if I do start to date again, I want it to be someone…someone serious, dependable, reliable. Not—'

'Not someone like me,' he finished for her, his voice brusque.

She bit her lip. 'That didn't come out well, did it?' she said with a quiver to her voice. 'It's not that you're not gorgeous. You are. In fact you're too gorgeous.'

'I don't know how being told I'm gorgeous sounds like an insult, but I get the gist of it.'

Her eyes widened. 'I didn't want that to sound like an insult. I wouldn't want to hurt you for the world.'

I wouldn't want to hurt you for the world. Jesse felt uncomfortably aware that he had used something like that phrase more than once when kindly breaking up with a woman. But those words directed at him did not feel good. They made him feel scorned like he'd felt when Camilla had rejected him—though she hadn't been as kind about it as Lizzie was being.

'No offence taken,' he said gruffly.

'I…I'm not very good at this,' she said, looking down at the ground, scuffing the sand with her bare foot.

Amazing that while she was thrusting the knife deep into his gut and then twisting it, he felt sorry for her having to deliver the message. In the interests of being *honest.*

'No one is good at it,' he said.

'I do want to try to explain. Because…because I've come to really like you.'

Like. It was a runner-up word. A consolation prize word. A loser word. How could he have exposed himself again to this?

'Continue,' he said gruffly.

'My ex was a good-looking guy with the charisma to go with it. I was always having to look over my shoulder to see what woman was pursuing him, what woman he was encouraging.'

'He was a *player*, right?' He practically spat out that word he was getting sick of hearing applied to him.

She nodded. 'I never want to endure a relationship with someone like that again. I can't live with that feeling that I'm not the only woman in my man's life. To be always suspicious of girls he works with, girls he encounters anywhere. I want to come first, last and in between with a man. Not…not always feeling humiliated and rejected.'

Jesse clenched his fists by his sides. He wasn't that guy. How could she be so wrong about him? A nagging inner voice gave him the answer. *Because that's the way you appear.* He'd done such a good job of acting the player to cover up his fears and pain that he'd given Lizzie the wrong impression of him.

It was true, over the years he'd been flattered by all that female attention. *But he didn't want it now.* He didn't want people taking bets on his marital status. Most of all he didn't want Lizzie so unfairly lumping him in a category of cheats and heartbreakers.

'What makes you think I'm like your ex-husband? You're implying that he cheated on you—I've never cheated or been unfaithful to a girlfriend. *Never.*'

'I…I believe you,' she said but her eyes told a different story. She'd stuck him in the same category as her ex and nothing he'd done—or the reputation he had acquired—had changed her mind.

He was not the guy she thought he was. He had to prove that to her.

'What happened at the wedding to cause you to think I'd gone off with another woman was a misunderstanding,' he said. 'So what makes you think I live up to my reputation?'

Her smile was shaky. 'Women adore you. Not just young attractive women who want to date you. Older women dote on you. Ex-girlfriends like Evie want you still in their life. Even children are fans. Amy was beside herself with excitement when I told her on the phone last night that Uncle Jesse would be here when she got back from France. You were such a hit with her at the wedding when you danced her right around the room.'

He frowned. 'And that's a bad thing? Would you prefer I was the kind of guy women loathed? Feared even?'

'Of course not.' She shook her head as if to clear her thoughts. 'I'm not getting this across at all well, am I? Fact is, it's not all about you; it's—'

He put up his hand. 'Whoa. If you're going to say "it's not you; it's me" forget it, I don't want to hear that old cliché.'

'What I'm trying to tell you is that I…I'm a jealous person.' She looked down at her feet for a moment as if she was ashamed of her words before she faced him again. 'A jealous woman and a chick-magnet guy are not a good combination, as I found out in my marriage. It wasn't just his infidelity that ended it; my jealousy and suspicion made it impossible for us to live with each other.'

'In my book, infidelity is unforgivable.' He clenched his jaw.

She looked across him and out to sea as if gathering her words before she faced him again. 'There…there can be shades of grey…'

He shook his head. 'Fidelity is non-negotiable. No cheating, end of story. If either party cheats—the relationship is over. For good.'

Did she believe him? Or had she heard too many lies from that ex-husband to believe an honest guy?

Her brow furrowed. 'That stance is not…not what I would have expected of you.'

'You've been listening to gossips.' He snorted in disgust. 'What would they know about my private life? You think I don't know about betrayal? You think I haven't been hurt?'

'I…I only know what I've heard.' She bit down on her lower lip, her face a picture of misery.

'I thought I'd found the woman I wanted to be with for the rest of my life. Turned out she was a cheat and a liar. But I don't lie or cheat. Never have. Never will.'

'I'm sorry, Jesse, if I got it wrong. But I can't take risks when it comes to men. For my sake and for my daughter's.' Only then came that familiar tilt to her chin. 'No matter how much I might want that man.'

He glanced down at the small scars on her hands and forearms. Scars she'd got in the kitchen, she'd told him, from burning oil and scalding steam and knives that had slipped. Now he realised she had scars on the inside too. Her ex-husband—and maybe before that her father—had chipped away at her trust, at her belief that she could inspire lasting love and fidelity. *That she deserved to be cherished and honoured.*

Whoa. He wasn't thinking the L word here. Just the

crazy attraction. Then the friendship. And the other L word. He realised how much in these last few days he had grown to like and admire Lizzie. In this context, 'like' was not a loser word. It was a feeling that built on that instant physical attraction to something that packed a powerful punch.

Lizzie was right—the reasons they both had for keeping the other at friend status were still there. He didn't want to put his heart on the line again and he didn't want to risk wounding her with further scars.

He ached to take her in his arms again but had no intention of doing so. It wasn't what she wanted. She didn't need a man like him in her life.

'I'd like to give you a big hug but…but I don't think it's a good idea,' he said, trying to sound offhand but failing dismally, betrayed by the hitch in his voice.

Warm colour flushed her cheeks. 'I agree. And… and no more kissing. I can't deal with how it makes me feel.'

He realised how vulnerable she was under that blunt-speaking front.

'No more kissing,' he agreed though he hated the idea of never being able to kiss her again.

She looked up at him, eyes huge, hair a silver cloud around her face. 'Jesse, I…I wasn't lying when I said how much I liked you. I do count you as a friend now.'

He nodded. 'Yeah. I like you too. We're friends.' But he didn't offer his hand to shake on it. No touching. No kissing. No physical contact of any kind. That was how it would have to be. No matter how difficult that stance would be to maintain when he had to see her every day.

He looked towards the water. It was still a low swell. Still good for swimming. And he needed to get in there.

Physical activity was always his way of dealing with stress and difficult situations. 'Are you going to swim?' he asked her.

She shook her head. 'I should be getting back to the café.'

Good. He didn't want her to join him in that water. Splashing around with her in a wetsuit moulded close to her curves would be more than he could endure.

'I'm going in,' he said. 'This is my favourite beach and I want to spend as much time as I can here while I'm home.'

She walked back to where her towel and bag were on the sand. She picked up her pink towel and turned her back to him as she swapped his towel for hers. Her back view was beautiful, with her hair tumbling around her shoulders, her narrow waist and shapely behind. *He wanted her but he couldn't have her.* He turned his head away. 'Just leave my towel there,' he said gruffly.

'Will you…will you be coming to the café today?' she asked, facing him again.

He hadn't given her two hours of help today but he needed distance from her. 'No. I'm driving to Sydney tonight.'

'Oh,' she said.

'I've got an appointment tomorrow with the orthopaedic specialist for my shoulder,' he said. And he had a video interview with the executives of the company in Houston. 'I'll see you when I get back.'

He was going to find it difficult working those two hours a day with her for the rest of his time back home in Dolphin Bay. But he had a commitment to Sandy that he would honour. He also wanted to be a friend to Lizzie now that they'd got this far.

But if she was to respect him as something other than a good-looking player—even in the context of a family connection friendship—he had to prove that the Jesse of his reputation and the real Jesse were not one and the same.

CHAPTER EIGHT

IT WAS SEVEN o'clock on the morning of the official opening of Bay Bites and the café doors were due to open in half an hour for their very first breakfast service. Lizzie had been working in the kitchen since five. She was confident she and her team had done all they could to prepare but still she was so nervous she had to keep wiping her hands down the side of her apron.

She'd worked at a start-up before. But not as the person in charge. It was a very different matter taking orders in the kitchen from someone else compared to being the one responsible for the success or failure of the venture. She twirled that piece of her hair that always escaped when she tied back her hair so hard it tugged at her scalp and made her wince. *What if no one showed up?*

That line of thought was crazy; she knew that—they had confirmed bookings for breakfast, brunch and lunch. Okay, so some of them were Morgan family and friends who had promised to be there to show support. But they would only be there the first few days; after that it would be up to word-of-mouth and reputation for the business to work.

Sandy, whose background was in advertising and marketing, had told her not to worry about all that—it was up to her to promote the new business. It was up to Lizzie to make the food—and the coffee—good enough for people to return again and again. It was all about the food, Sandy had said several times.

Lizzie took a deep steadying breath. She was confident the food was good, that she could hold up her end of the deal. Service had to be good too. Fingers crossed that Nikki, the young barista, could deal with the pressure.

She kept looking up to see if any early customers had arrived yet. The best marketing for a café was a line of people waiting to get in—though the line couldn't be so long that it put people off.

She was packing one of the big glass jars with freshly baked salted caramel and pecan cookies. She looked up again. And then again. But in the end she had to admit to herself she wasn't looking for early customers peering through the plate-glass windows. She was looking for Jesse.

Jesse, who had taken off to Sydney on Sunday, telling her he wouldn't be back until Wednesday evening.

One part of her was upset he would go to Sydney just days before the café was due to open. Another part of her knew she had no right to expect him to be there to help her with all those last-minute things. Especially when she had told him in no uncertain terms she would never want to date him. Both Sandy and Ben had been there after hours to help instead.

Of course the kisses on the beach had changed things between them. How could they not? The kisses at the wedding had been with a hot guy she scarcely knew. But the beach kisses had been with her friend Jesse, a man she'd got to like and in whose company she felt at ease. His kisses had been sensuous, exciting, arousing—but, more than that, it had felt somehow *right* to be sharing such pleasure with Jesse. In spite of all the strikes against him.

She missed him. She missed him more than she could have imagined. She missed his laugh, she missed his manly way of getting things done, most of all she missed that wonderful feeling of being in his arms. Had she been mistaken about him?

She thought about what she'd said to him on the beach, when she'd tried to be honest, but had succeeded only in wounding him—she'd seen the hurt in his eyes. Was she wrong in filing him under P for Player, with a sub-category of H for Heartbreaker? Had she misjudged him? After all, she still didn't know him that well. But what she'd got to know she liked. Liked a lot.

Her caution stemmed from his reputation. But surely her own sister wouldn't have warned her against him if there hadn't been something to be cautious about?

She'd met Philippe when she was twenty-one and had only had one serious boyfriend before him and none after him. Truth was, she didn't have a lot of man mileage on the clock and not a lot of experience on which to make judgements.

Delicious smells wafted into the café, reminding her she needed to be back in that kitchen. Tension was mounting. There had been raised voices, tears, the odd thrown utensil but now all was calm efficiency again.

By seven-twenty a.m. there was a line-up outside the door. By seven forty-five she was so run off her feet she didn't have time to worry about missing Jesse. By eight-thirty young Nikki was in such a fluster managing the constant orders for coffee, Lizzie could see customers tapping impatiently on table tops waiting for their cappuccino, skinny lattes, flat whites and so on. Nightmare!

As she plated an order for French toast with caramelised bananas and blueberries she tried to think what to do. Ask Sandy if she could borrow another waitress from the Hotel Harbourside? Make coffees herself? She'd run through the machine a few times to familiarise herself with it and could probably churn out a halfway acceptable beverage.

Whatever she did, she had to keep calm—if she didn't the whole place would fall apart. She'd have to expect teething problems, Jesse had said. But paying customers were harsh critics. A café would live or die on the reputation of its coffee—if she didn't fix the coffee problem Bay Bites would be going backwards on its first day.

Then, at eight thirty-five, Jesse was there. In the kitchen beside her, tying on his blue-striped apron, joking to the staff that he'd be in trouble with the boss for being tardy.

Her breath caught in her throat and her heart started to hammer so fast she felt giddy. *Jesse.* She ached to throw her arms around him and tell him how glad she was to see him. How she'd felt as though part of her was missing when he wasn't here. But that couldn't happen. They were friends. And he was talking to her as if she were the boss and he was the volunteer helper who was late for work. As it should be, of course. She swallowed down hard on a wave of irrational disappointment.

'I got caught up so couldn't get here until now,' he explained with nothing more than courtesy.

She didn't care where he'd been, just so long as he was with her now. She forced her voice to sound professional and boss-like. 'I'm so glad you're here. Nikki isn't coping with the coffee. If I can ask—'

'I'll take over the coffee machine.'

'What do you mean? How can you do that?'

'I worked a coffee machine when I was a student. Got quite good at it.'

'You didn't tell me.'

'Thought I'd be too rusty to be of any use to you. While I was in Sydney I did a barista course to get me up to speed.'

'You *what?*'

He pulled out a folded up sheet of paper from one pocket then a glasses case from the other. He put on black-framed glasses and unfolded the paper. 'It's a certificate proving I'm officially accredited as a barista. Turns out since I last did this, I first had to do a course in kitchen hygiene so I've got that qualification there too.' He added the last sentence in his mock modest, self-deprecating way she liked so much.

Lizzie didn't know what shocked her most—the fact Jesse had gone to Sydney to train as a barista or how hot he looked in glasses. It added a whole extra layer of hotness to his appeal—not that he actually needed any extra layers.

She lowered her voice so the chef and the kitchen hand who were working nearby couldn't overhear her. 'Why did you do it?'

'I knew you were worried about Nikki. I wanted to help. But I wanted to make sure I wouldn't be more hindrance than help if I'd forgotten how to froth the milk. Turns out I hadn't. And I got a good score for my coffee art, too.'

She stared at him. 'You can do coffee art?'

'Rosettes, hearts. I need some more practice to do a dolphin but I'll get there,' he said, deadpan.

'I'm seriously impressed,' she said. *He'd done it for her and her heart skipped a beat at the thought.*

'It's just steamed milk on espresso, not difficult really.'

As a chef, she knew presentation was a big part of customer appreciation. These days, people had very high expectations of their coffee; they wanted it to look good as well as taste good.

'There's more than that to it; I didn't know you were an artist.' Then she remembered he'd studied art in high school. She was beginning to realise she still had a lot to learn about Jesse. What other surprises were waiting to be discovered?

He shrugged and then winced. 'Your shoulder? What did the doctor say?' she asked.

'It's healing much better than expected,' he said. 'I can probably go back to work soon.'

Her heart plummeted to the level of her clogs.

'That's good,' she said, forcing her voice to be level.

At the back of her mind she'd thought she'd at least have a few more weeks with him around. But there was no time to ask what he intended to do. It would have to wait. Even in the few minutes she'd been speaking to him the orders were piling up.

Jesse got down to business. 'Give Nikki a break from the coffee machine. I'll take over. Let her wait tables. Later I'll spend some time training her and we'll see if she's good enough to stay.'

Lizzie was too darn grateful that Jesse was back to ask him if he was only going to be there for the two hours he'd defined as his time with her.

The last thing Jesse had thought he'd ever be doing again was making coffee for customers. He was a highly regarded engineer, considered an expert in the quick construction of mass pre-fabricated housing, who had a major corporation jockeying for his skills. He'd had a teleconference with the CEO of the company while he was in Sydney and again they had expressed their keenness in having him on board. They were, in fact, pressuring him to make a decision.

But he also wanted to prove to Lizzie he was not the shallow womaniser she seemed to believe he was. The player label she'd been only too ready to tag him with was really beginning to irk him.

The gratitude and relief on Lizzie's face when he'd told her about the barista course was enough to justify his decision. He'd sensed there'd be trouble with Nikki and had taken the steps that would enable him to help Lizzie achieve her aim of a wrinkle-free launch.

But he'd missed her while he'd been in Sydney. Missed her so much his future—be it in Texas or Asia or wherever he might end up—had seemed somehow bleak without her in it in some way. Never had a hotel room seemed so lonely. The way he'd felt raised questions he wasn't sure of the answers to. He forced himself not to think about it and focused his attention on making coffee.

Flat white, cappuccino, espresso, soy latte, decaf— the orders kept on coming and he kept on filling them. He knew half the customers and had to put up with a lot of good-natured banter.

His answer to the inevitable, 'Hey, Jesse, why the new career path?' was always, 'To help out Sandy and Ben while I'm on leave.'

No way would he admit to anyone that he was doing it with the aim of proving to Lizzie that he was not the guy she thought he was.

But there were customers he didn't know too, total strangers who'd found their way to Bay Bites. People with no connection to the family would be the lifeblood of the new business. Those and the tourists who would eat here a few times, recommend it to their friends, come back next time. He'd noticed lots of empty plates and contented faces. He'd also seen customers photographing their meals with their phones. Free Wi-Fi in the café would pretty much guarantee there would be online reviews up by evening.

He looked up to see Evie's redhead friend he'd met at the taste-test had settled herself at a table and was perusing a menu. She caught his eye and waved. What was her name? Dell, that was right, Dell.

She came up to the counter to say hello. 'Nothing like a handsome barista to bring in business,' she said with her easy, friendly manner.

He smiled. 'I'm also on the front line if they don't like the coffee. But I haven't had any thrown back at me yet.'

Dell smiled back. 'So far, so good, huh? The menu is impressive.'

'All Lizzie's work; I'm just the help.'

'Evie told me Lizzie is a chef who worked in some top restaurants in France and then in Sydney too.'

'That's true,' he said. 'She's highly regarded and has won all sorts of awards.' He felt a swell of unexpected pride in recounting Lizzie's achievements.

'So what brings her to Dolphin Bay?'

'Family,' he said firmly. He was protective of Lizzie's personal life when it came to discussing it with strangers. No one needed to know about her broken marriage, her ongoing custody issues. *The Morgans looked after their own.*

Dell nodded. 'I hope it all goes well for her.'

Just then Lizzie came out of the kitchen. Immediately Jesse felt her gaze go from him to Dell and back to him. Was that jealousy he saw glinting in her narrowed grey eyes? If so, there wasn't much he could do about it but reassure her she had nothing to worry about. Women liked him. He liked women. But he was not flirting with this girl. And Dell was certainly not sending off any flirty vibes. How could he let Lizzie know that?

He beckoned Lizzie over and introduced her to Dell. 'Dell's been saying some very nice things about the menu.'

'Yes,' said Dell with a friendly smile 'I was at your taste-test party on Saturday. Everything I tried was superb. Kudos to you.'

'Thank you,' said Lizzie.

'And I was saying to your boyfriend that every café needs a handsome barista.'

Lizzie flushed. 'Jesse's not my—'

'We're friends,' Jesse was quick to say. 'Just friends.'

'My mistake,' said Dell. 'I thought… Anyway, I'd better get back to my table and stop holding you guys up. It looks busy.'

'Nothing the kitchen can't handle,' said Lizzie a little stiffly.

Dell rewarded her with a big smile. 'I'm looking forward to my lunch. Congratulations, the café is awesome. I'll bring my guy with me next time; I know he'll love it too.'

Now, at last, Lizzie smiled back. Jesse was puzzled by her sudden change of attitude. Was this some kind of girl talk he wasn't privy too? Had Dell given her a secret semaphore message to make her thaw?

Whatever, he didn't have time to worry about it as the lunchtime coffee orders stepped up. He had worked way more than his allocated two hours but who was counting?

CHAPTER NINE

LIZZIE DIDN'T KNOW how she could thank Jesse enough for what he'd done. To train as a barista just to help her out wasn't something she'd ever imagined Jesse would do. It had caused a radical shift in her opinion of him.

'You saved the day,' she said as they shut up shop at four p.m. Everyone else had gone home and they were the last two remaining in the café, empty now but somehow still echoing with the energy of all the meals cooked, eaten and enjoyed. Bay Bites had been well and truly launched. They'd even sold two paintings. She looked up at Jesse. 'Did I tell you how much I appreciate what you did?'

'Only about a gazillion times, but you can say it again if you like,' he said with the laid-back smile that had appealed to her from the get-go.

'So here's my "thank you number gazillion and one",' she said. 'No matter how good a job we did with the food, our opening day would have been a fail if we hadn't had good coffee.'

'It was far from a fail, Lizzie,' Jesse said. 'I think you can chalk up your first day as a success.'

'Don't say that,' she said quickly. 'We don't want to jinx ourselves.'

He quirked a dark eyebrow. 'I didn't put you down as superstitious.'

'You know how theatre people are full of superstitions? So are restaurant people. No one would be surprised if I had the building blessed, maybe brought in a feng-shui expert. Or burned sage to get rid of any bad karma from the previous business on this site. Maybe even hung crystals in strategic places. And don't even think about whistling in the kitchen. Especially a French kitchen.'

'You're kidding me?'

She shook her head. 'A lot happens in restaurants. First dates. Break-ups. Celebrations. Illicit liaisons. They leave energy. We want good energy. Opening day of a new restaurant is rather like the opening night of a new play. The cast. The audience. The need to have butts on seats. So let's just say I'm cautiously optimistic about how today went and leave it at that.'

He laughed. 'Okay, I'll grant you that. But I still say—'

Lizzie swiped her thumb and first finger across her lips to zip it. 'Don't say it or I'll blame you if anything goes wrong.'

Jesse pretended to cower. Lizzie laughed and ushered him through the back door to the car park. She punched in the alarm code, followed him out and locked the door behind them.

For the first time an awkward silence fell between them. The door that led upstairs to her apartment was only a few metres to the left. Did she invite him upstairs? Be alone with him again? She hadn't been able to stop thinking about how exciting his kisses had been. How much she'd missed him. How maybe she had misjudged him. Would it be wise?

She gestured to the door. 'I can offer you a coffee

but I suspect that might be the last thing you want to face right now.'

'I wouldn't say no to a beer,' he said.

'I've got some in the fridge upstairs. I could do with one too.' She gave a sigh that was halfway to a moan of exhaustion. 'There's nothing I want to do more than take off these clogs and kick back.'

The apartment over the café was compact but Sandy had done a wonderful job of refurbishing it for her and Amy. With polished wooden floors throughout, it had been painted in muted neutral tones with white shutters at the windows. Furniture comprised simple, comfortable pieces in whitewashed timber and a plump sofa and easy chairs upholstered in natural linen. The living room window framed a magnificent view of the harbour. The effect was contemporary but cosy and Lizzie's heart lifted every time she came through the door.

'You've settled in,' Jesse said as he followed her through to the small but well-equipped kitchen.

'I just need to get a few more personal touches in place before Amy gets here. Is it "thank you number gazillion and two" if I say how much I appreciate the work you did here?' she said. 'Sandy told me how much of this place is due to your efforts.'

'Enough with the grovelling,' he said with a grin. 'Just get me that beer.'

Lizzie grabbed two beers from the fridge and cut lime quarters to press into the bottle necks. She handed one to Jesse and carried her own through into the living room. 'No food to offer you, I'm afraid,' she said. 'It's all downstairs.'

'I've been snacking on stuff all day,' Jesse said. 'I don't need any more. How do you stay so slim working with all that delicious food?' He cast an appreciative eye over her figure.

'I learned early on to only have very small servings—just tastes really. Then there's the fact that cooking is hard physical work. I'm standing all day every day.'

She flopped down onto the sofa and kicked off her clogs. 'My feet are killing me. They're always killing me. My feet, my knees, my back. It's so good to sit down.'

She wiggled her toes, rotated her ankles, but it didn't do much to ease the deep, throbbing ache in her feet. Damaged feet were an occupational hazard of being a chef.

Jesse sat down on the sofa next to her. 'Let me rub your feet for you.'

Lizzie's gaze met his and there was a question in his eyes that asked so much more than she knew how to answer.

She knew saying yes to his suggestion would be going beyond the bounds of their tentative friendship. But she longed to have his strong, capable hands on her feet, stroking and massaging to ease the pain. Stop kidding herself: she longed to have his hands on her body, full stop. She had gone beyond denying her attraction to him. But was this foot massage a good idea?

'There's some peppermint lotion in the fridge,' she said. 'It's more soothing when it's chilled.'

Jesse returned from the kitchen with the peppermint lotion. He sat down on the sofa again, put the container on the coffee table. 'Swivel around on the sofa and put your feet across my legs.'

It seemed an intimate way to start a foot massage but she didn't protest. The alternative was to have him kneeling at her feet and that wouldn't do.

Her feet were so sore that Jesse's first firm, sure strokes were painful and she yelped. 'Just getting the knots out,' he explained. He then settled into an easier rhythm, probing, stroking, squeezing with his strong fingers and thumbs, smoothing in the cool, sharply scented lotion.

She moaned her pleasure and relief. 'This is heaven, absolute heaven. Where did you learn to massage like this?'

'Nowhere,' he said. 'I'm just giving you what you seem to need.'

'Oh,' she said, not meeting his gaze.

She didn't know what to say to that. What she did know was she had to keep thoughts of other needs, and the way Jesse might meet them, on a very tight rein.

Her whole body thrummed with the pleasure of what his hands were doing to her heels, toes, soles. She'd never thought of feet as sensual zones but what Jesse was doing was nothing short of bliss.

'I'm just going to lie back and enjoy every minute,' she said, settling further back into the cushions, shifting her feet to fit more comfortably on his thighs.

'You do that,' he said in that deep, resonant voice that had become so familiar. Everything was beautiful about Jesse. His face. His voice. His hands—especially his hands. She moaned again as he massaged the pain away so that now his touch brought only pleasure.

She closed her eyes, zoned out into another world that focused on the rhythmical stroking of Jesse's hands on her feet; the scent of peppermint mingled with the faint aroma of coffee that clung to him; the sound of their breathing, his strong and steady, hers becoming slower, calmer. She could hear the tick, tick, tick of the kitchen clock in the silence of the apartment. *Please don't stop—don't ever stop.*

Eventually, when her feet felt utterly boneless, he finished by stretching out her toes one by one, squeezing her feet one final time, then stroking right up to her shins. 'Done,' he said.

'Mmm…' she murmured as she drowsily sat up, swinging her feet away so she sat near him on the sofa. He might have been massaging her feet but her entire body felt relaxed. 'You're a man of many talents, Jesse Morgan. I guess that's "thank you number gazillion and three". I…'

Her voice got lost in her throat at the intensity of Jesse's expression. She gazed into his face for a long moment, those incredible blue eyes fringed with black lashes, the dark eyebrows, his chiselled mouth. She knew she shouldn't use the word 'beautiful' to describe a man but there wasn't another word that worked as well. Handsome. Good-looking. Striking. He was more than all of those combined. A wave of intense longing for him surged through her.

Now was her chance to move away. To get off the sofa and make an excuse to go into another room. Even to yawn in an exaggerated manner and tell him she needed her beauty sleep and it was time for him to go home.

But she didn't. Instead she reached out her hand and explored his face with her fingers, stroking the tousled hair from his forehead, tracing the line of his thick brows, the ridge of his sculptured cheekbones, the roughness of the dark shadow of his beard, until she reached his mouth. His lips were smooth and warm, the top one slightly narrower than the bottom. His eyes stayed locked on hers. He caught her fingers with his strong white teeth, nipped them gently and she gasped at the unexpected pleasure-pain.

She leaned forward and caressed his mouth with hers. His lips parted under hers and she gave herself over to the sensation of lips, tongue, taste in a slow, easy tender kiss. When he pulled her to him she sank into the embrace of his strong arms around her.

But what had started as gentle rapidly deepened into something more passionate, more demanding that had her winding her fingers through his hair to bring him closer, pressing her body to his hard strength, her heart hammering.

She had been so long without the touch of a man, of skin on skin, the heady delight of breathing in a man's scent. And this was Jesse, who she liked so much, who she was growing to trust, who had appealed to her from the get-go. She wanted so badly to be close to him.

They were alone in the apartment. Anything could happen. But it shouldn't. Not now. Not yet. Sex too soon with Jesse was not a good idea.

She harnessed all the willpower she could muster and pulled away from him. 'That…that wasn't a friend kiss,' she said when she got her breath back.

'No. No, it wasn't,' he said, his voice husky, his breath ragged. 'I like you as much more than a friend, Lizzie. I'd be lying if I said otherwise.'

She shifted a little further away from him on the sofa. With their thighs touching she found it difficult to keep her thoughts straight. 'Me too. I mean…there was a spark between us at the wedding. Now it…it's grown.'

'We got off onto a bad start with each other. You thought I was a guy who picked up and then discarded women just because I could.'

'And you thought I was a…I don't know what you

thought I was. Someone too quick to jump to the wrong conclusion?'

'Someone who's trying so hard to protect herself she might not see what could be there,' he said.

She paused to let the implication of his words sink in. 'Perhaps,' she said.

'You seem to have a distorted idea of who I am based on gossip and innuendo. I want to prove to you I'm a decent guy.'

Again she realised that some of her reactions to him might have hurt him. She hastened to reassure him. 'You've shown me that in so many ways. The fact you went off and trained to be a barista just to help me is the latest example.' She looked away and then back. 'It's just...just the other women thing.'

Jesse sighed. She didn't like the sound of it. 'I saw the way you watched me as I talked to Evie's friend.'

'Dell.'

'Were you jealous?'

'A...a little. She's very attractive.'

'Is she? I didn't notice. She's friendly, pleasant.'

'How could you not see how cute she is?'

'Contrary to that bad old reputation of mine, I don't look with lust at every female I meet because I want to bed her and run.'

She managed a weak smile. 'I never thought that for a minute.' Though she'd certainly been told that was what Jesse was capable of. She was beginning to realise the gossips had got him wrong.

Jesse shifted on the sofa, a movement that brought him closer to her. 'I haven't spent much time in Dolphin Bay in recent years. I don't like people knowing my business. It's suited me to let them think Jesse the player has waltzed through life unscathed. If I'd brought

Camilla home to marry her it would have been a triumph. But when it turned out such a disaster I was glad I'd never mentioned her. I didn't want anyone to know I'd been brought down so low.'

Lizzie was shocked at the slight edge to his voice. 'Camilla?' she asked.

'She was a photojournalist who came to do a feature story on our team. We were rebuilding tsunami-ravaged villages in Sri Lanka a few years back. I wasn't attracted to her at first but she singled me out for a lot of one-on-one photography.'

'I bet she did,' Lizzie murmured under her breath.

'What was that?' asked Jesse.

'Nothing,' she said and decided to keep her comments to herself. She couldn't be jealous of someone in Jesse's past and it sounded petty to criticise the unknown woman.

'I spent a lot of time with her being interviewed, being photographed.'

'And you fell for her.'

'Hard and fast.'

Lizzie jumped down hard on an unwarranted twinge of jealousy. Her imagination was running crazy wondering what kind of photos Camilla had taken of Jesse and whether he'd been wearing any clothes. But she couldn't ask.

'Her time with us was limited,' Jesse continued. 'It was a pressure cooker environment. I managed to get hold of a sapphire ring. I proposed. She laughed. Then turned me down.'

'She *laughed?*' Indignation for Jesse swept through Lizzie.

'Seemed what I'd thought was a serious relationship was a casual fling to her. She already had a fiancé at home in London. That was the first I'd heard of him. She had never told me she was anything other than single.' The delivery of his words was matter-of-fact, emotionless, as if he didn't care. But the rigid line of his mouth told Lizzie otherwise.

'You must have been devastated.'

He shrugged. 'You could say that.'

'So what happened?'

'She went home to London to marry the poor sucker.'

'And you never saw her again?'

He paused. 'Not from choice.'

'What…what do you mean?'

'She showed up in India at the start of this year to do a follow-up feature.'

'On you?'

'On the organisation I worked for. I wanted nothing to do with her.'

Something about the tone of his voice made her ask, 'But she wanted you?'

'To take up where we left off. Another fling. She was married by then and prepared to betray her husband.'

Under her breath, Lizzie uttered some choice swear words in French.

'I don't dare ask what that meant,' Jesse said with a shadow of his grin.

'Don't,' said Lizzie.

'Probably nothing I wouldn't have said myself,' he said. 'I told her what I thought of her and got transferred to another site.'

Lizzie put her hand on his arm. 'I hate her on your behalf,' she said vehemently. 'How dare she do that to you? And what an idiot to…to have let you go. I would have…' Her voice tapered off as she realised what she had said. What she had revealed. 'I…I mean—'

Jesse cradled her face in his hands, dropped a kiss on her mouth. 'That's sweet of you,' he said.

She managed a weak smile. 'I...I think you're kinda wonderful. I can't imagine every other woman wouldn't think so too.'

'I'm glad you think I'm wonderful.' He rolled his eyes in self-mockery.

'You...you must know I do. I don't mean that as a joke.'

Her breath hitched with awareness of how attractive she found him but it was so much more than the way he looked. 'I missed you terribly while you were away in Sydney. It...it scared me. The thought of what it would be like when you leave for your job.'

'I missed you too. I thought about you every minute of that four-hour trip to Sydney and all the way back.'

He took her hand in his, twined his fingers through hers. 'So what are we going to do about it?'

Jesse tightened his grip on Lizzie's hand. 'What's to stop us being more than friends? From seeing what else we could be to each other if we gave it a chance. What are the real issues—issues that can't easily be resolved? Can we discuss that?' They could beat about the bush for weeks over this—and he didn't have weeks.

She answered the pressure of his hand with hers. 'There's the fact we don't live in the same country for a start. You seem to be in a different place every few months.'

'That's the nature of my current job.'

'Current? There's something else in the offing?'

'A job that would still involve travel. But I'd be based in Houston, Texas. That is *if* I choose to take the job.'

She released her hand from his, smoothed her hair

away from her forehead in a nervous gesture that was becoming familiar. 'Texas is a long way from here. Even further than the Asian countries you seem to work in now. That's a real issue.'

'In the short-term. Long-term, Houston is a good city to live in. With plenty of good restaurants.'

She found her favourite errant lock of hair and twisted it around her finger. 'But there's not just me to consider. There's Amy. She needs stability in her life. She's already been uprooted from France, then from Sydney. And her father still wants her with him every long school vacation. I don't want to disrupt her again.'

'Does it make a huge difference where she lives when she's only five years old?'

Lizzie threw up her hands in an exaggerated shrug. 'I don't know. Maybe. Maybe not. I'm still learning to be Amy's mum. Trying to do my best for her when at times it's been quite difficult. I can't tell you how much I miss her when she's away, like now. But, for her sake, I do everything I can to keep up the relationship with her papa. She loves him and she loves her French grandparents.'

'I can understand that,' he said. That didn't mean he had to like the guy.

Lizzie shifted on the sofa; the movement took her further from him. 'I guess we've already segued into the next issue that might stop us being together—my daughter. Bringing a man into our lives would have ramifications I haven't really thought through. All I know is Amy has to come first.'

'It's not an issue for me,' Jesse said. 'You and Amy come as a package deal and I'm okay with that. We'd have to play it by ear what my role would be with Amy.'

'You know I'm not looking for a father for Amy?'

'I get that.'

'She has a father. Philippe has his faults but he loves his daughter.'

'You said he wants custody?'

'He and his parents want her brought up French. His parents love her too. And she loves her *grand-maman* and *grand-père*. They're wealthy. They think they can give her a good life.'

'Not as good as with her mother.' He felt a fierce surge of protectiveness towards both Lizzie and Amy.

'That's another point I have to consider. Amy is the reason I'm in Dolphin Bay. Thanks to Sandy I've got a job and a home and family nearby. Your mother has said she'll help me with Amy. The local school seems good. I wouldn't give all that up easily.'

'You'd have to weigh up the pros and the cons of another possible change.'

'Yes. That's exactly what I'd have to do.'

He spoke slowly. 'And I have to think about what a possible commitment would mean for me.'

Her quick intake of air told him he'd hit the mark with that one. He knew about the wagers laid on his ongoing bachelor ways. He knew even Sandy called him a 'commitment-phobe'. He wouldn't be surprised if she'd warned her sister off him.

'Did what happened with Camilla make you…make you back away from relationships?' Lizzie asked.

'Yeah. It did. Just when I'd…I'd got over the fire.' Lizzie was the first person he had confided in about Camilla and now this. If he wanted to take their attraction further he owed it to her to be honest.

'The fire that burned down the guest house? When… when you lost Ben's first wife and little boy.'

'It affected us all. We probably should have had

trauma counselling. But Morgans don't go in for that. You know what happened to Ben. He was so deep in despair no one could reach him. Until Sandy came back.'

'Thank heaven,' she said.

'Mum doted on her little grandson. Dad as well. She went extra dotty over dogs after we lost Liam and Jodi.'

'And you?' Lizzie's eyes were warm with compassion.

'I was gutted.'

'But everyone was probably so concerned for Ben they didn't think about the effect on you.'

'And rightly so. But seeing what happened to him made me decide it was never going to happen to me.'

'If you didn't love, you couldn't lose.'

'Something like that. By the time I met Camilla my defences were cracking. I'd realised I had to take my own risks. Make my own way.'

'And then you got hit with Camilla's betrayal.'

'And went backwards.'

Lizzie's smile was shaky at the edges. 'We're quite a pair, aren't we? Both scared of what happened to us in the past happening to us again. Me with Philippe. You with Camilla.'

'I don't know that I'd use the word "scared",' he said.

Jesse thought of the defences he'd thrown up around the idea of a committed relationship with a woman. The job. The travel. His ongoing career.

Mentally, he pulled himself up. *Stop kidding yourself, mate.*

Work was the wimp excuse. *The wussy versus the brave.* From somewhere deep inside him he had to drag out the truth. At the wedding, he'd felt a real connection to Lizzie that he had never felt before—a connection that had been severed with a painful cut by the way she'd behaved. Now he realised that link could easily fuse together again. *Go further with her and he could get hurt.*

And there was nothing wimpy about avoiding the kind of hurt that could destroy a man. Like the pain he'd felt when Camilla had ended it with him so brutally. Like when Ben had lost his family.

But Ben had found new happiness with Sandy. All around him were people in settled, fulfilling relationships. And he was headed for thirty, older and wiser, he hoped. He realised just telling Lizzie about Camilla's behaviour and hearing Lizzie's outrage on his behalf had done him good.

It had also made him realise how very different the two women were. He doubted that blunt, straightforward Lizzie had it in her to be as devious as Camilla. What good reason—what real, valid reason—was there left for him not to be brave when it came to Lizzie?

'What are we waiting for to happen?' he asked her. 'If we don't take this chance while we're actually both in the same country, will we live to regret it?'

She got up from the sofa, walked across the room, stood with her back to him for a terrifyingly long moment. Then she turned to face him again, took the steps to bring her closer to him again. He got up from the sofa to meet her.

'I've had a horrible thought,' she said, still keeping a distance between them.

'Tell me,' he said, bracing himself for her words.

She tilted her head to one side. 'What if we walked away from this and kept up the pretence we were just friends, then the next time we met was at one of our weddings to someone else?'

A shudder racked him at the thought. 'That is a horrible thought.'

'Too horrible to contemplate,' she said. 'I don't know that I could bear it.'

'Me neither. I say we forget the pretence of friendship. If there's something real between us then we can address my job, your jealousy and any other barriers we've put between us.'

She covered the distance between them in a few steps, opened her arms and put them around him. 'Yes,' she said. 'I say yes. We give it a go.'

He drew her tightly to him. This. This was what he wanted.

Lizzie stood close to Jesse in the circle of his arms. She couldn't remember when she'd last felt this mix of happiness and anticipation. Facing the future—even if they were only talking the immediate future—felt so much less scary when she was facing it with Jesse. She could almost feel those barricades she'd put up against him falling down one by one with a noisy clatter.

Her voice was muffled against his shoulder. 'One more thing. There might be a puppy to throw into the mix of things we have to consider.'

He groaned. 'You've been talking to my mother.'

Lizzie pulled away from him so she could look up at his face but stayed in the protective circle of his arms. 'How did you guess?'

'Her house is full of foster dogs and she's always on the lookout for homes for them.'

'Amy would love a puppy. So would I. My father would never allow us to have pets. I always wanted one.'

'Needless to say, we always had dogs when I was

growing up. How could I not love them? I admire Mum for her commitment to rescues.'

'I hear a "however" there,' she said. These days, she picked up on the slightest nuances in his voice.

'Some of the parts of the world I've worked in, children live worse lives than our pampered pooches. It's charities for kids I support.'

Was Jesse saying the things he knew she wanted to hear? She shook her head to rid herself of the thought. She had decided to trust him.

'Are you too good to be true, Jesse Morgan?' she asked.

He shook his head. 'I'm just me, Lizzie—take me as you find me. I didn't tell you that looking for praise,' he said. 'But it's a good way to segue into the fund-raising dinner the dog shelter my mother supports is having on Saturday night.'

'Maura did mention it, so did Sandy. But I said no. I can't afford a late night when I'll have such an early start next day. I'm expecting Sunday to be one of our busiest days at the café.'

'What if you made it an early night?' he coaxed. 'Just come for the dinner and then I take you straight home?'

Her smile was teasing, mischievous. 'Are you asking me on a date, Jesse?'

'I guess I am. Surely it can't be all work and no play for you.'

'No, but—'

'Where's the "but", Lizzie? You can't use the "just friends" argument any more.'

'I…I don't want everyone in Dolphin Bay knowing our business.' She would never forget that dreadful moment at the wedding when that raucous crowd had discovered her and Jesse kissing on the balcony.

'I understand. And feel the same way. So we keep it private,' he said.

'Even from my sister and your brother?' Sandy was the last person she'd want to know about the change in status of her relationship with Jesse. She didn't want any more warnings or disapproval. Not when she'd decided to switch off her own inner warning system when it came to Jesse.

'If that's what you want,' he said. 'I've never confided in Ben about my relationships.'

'And Amy too, when she gets here on Wednesday. Until…until we know for sure where we're going.' If Jesse were to be a part of her life, they would have to introduce the idea to her daughter with great care.

'Fine by me,' he said.

He cradled her face in his hands. Kissed her briefly, tenderly. Even on that level of kiss, he was a master.

'I'll come to the fund-raiser with you,' she said. 'To everyone there we'll just be friends, but to us—'

'We'll be finding out if we can be so much more.'

'Yes,' she said.

CHAPTER TEN

SATURDAY MORNING WAS so busy at Bay Bites that Lizzie had to call in a casual waitress for extra help. It wasn't just for help with table service; the phone was also ringing off the hook with advance bookings. She was elated and also somewhat surprised that the word had spread so quickly. Don't jinx it, she reminded herself.

She was in the kitchen checking a new batch of the rhubarb and strawberry muffins that had just come out of the oven when Sandy burst in the back door, fizzing with excitement. She grabbed Lizzie by the arm. 'Forget those—they look perfect, smell divine and will probably be gone in ten minutes. Come outside, will you.'

Bemused, Lizzie let herself be dragged outside by her sister. Sandy waved the Saturday edition of Sydney's major newspaper in her face. 'Check this out in the Lifestyle section. Bay Bites has been included in an article about the foodie scene on the south coast.'

Lizzie felt her stomach plummet to below the level of her clogs. There had already been positive reviews from customers on the internet review sites. But to be reviewed by this newspaper was something different altogether. The review would go on its website too and find its way into prominent positions on search engines.

A bad review could seriously damage them at this baby steps stage of the business.

She took hold of the newspaper with shaking hands and focused on the page with some difficulty. The headline was bold and black: *Take the South Coast Gourmet Food Trail*.

She scanned the first paragraphs. They talked about 'the ever-growing food and wine scene', mentioning the lush soil, mild climate, and singling out for praise some of her newly sourced suppliers.

Then there was a list of 'Six Foodie Hotspots' on the south coast. The television chef's restaurant was included. But high on the list was also, to her heart-pounding excitement, Bay Bites.

'Read it out—I've read it ten times already but I want to hear it again,' urged Sandy.

'I…I don't think my voice will work,' Lizzie said.

'Sure it will; come on—read.'

Lizzie cleared her throat and started to read in a voice that started off shaky but gained in strength and confidence as she read:

'"France's loss is the south coast's gain. Talented Aussie chef Lizzie Dumont has returned home to Oz from stints in top restaurants in Lyon and Paris to bring her particular flair to must-visit café Bay Bites in the charming coastal town of Dolphin Bay. The menu is a clever blend of perfectly executed café favourites and more innovative specials that showcase locally sourced ingredients. Don't miss: sublime scrambled eggs; rhubarb and strawberry muffins; slow-cooked lamb with beetroot relish. Then there's the excellent coffee served by the most swoon-worthy barista you'll see this side of Hollywood."'

The review was accompanied by a photograph of

the café interior looking bright and fashionable and another close-up of a muffin broken open with crumbs scattered artfully alongside. Jesse was there beside the coffee machine but his image was blurred, as if in motion, so you couldn't readily identify him.

Lizzie sagged with relief. She looked at the by-line of the journalist who had written such a gratifying review. Adele Hudson. She peered closer at the small photo that accompanied it. She blinked then looked again to make sure she hadn't got it wrong. 'I don't believe it. It's Dell. Adele Hudson is Dell.'

'Who is Dell and how do you know her?' said Sandy.

'She's a friend of Evie from the dairy farm. She was here for the taste-test and then again on our opening day.'

'The redhead flirting with Jesse?'

'Turns out she was interviewing him, in a subtle way,' Lizzie said slowly. She'd thought Dell had been flirting with Jesse too. She felt sick at the memory of the jealousy that had speared her. The review could have gone completely the other way if she'd acted on it.

'Wait. There's more,' she said. 'Adele Hudson is also a well-known food blogger with tens of thousands of followers.'

'Not so well known to us,' said Sandy. She pulled out her e-tablet from her handbag, scrolled through. 'Her blog is called "Dell Dishes". Look, she's written about Bay Bites here, too.'

Lizzie read it out.

'"Good food and good books—two of my greatest loves. I got a taste of both with the newly opened Bay Bites café that's an extension of my favourite south coast bookshop Bay Books."'

She looked up, her excitement rising. 'And there's so

much more about how good the food is. She's picked up on the link between the café and the Hotel Harbourside too and called the hotel restaurant "pub grub at its best".'

'We're on the map now,' said Sandy with a great sigh of satisfaction. 'Along with those five-star ratings on the user review websites, I think we're on our way.' Lizzie laughed as her sister danced her around in a little jig of joy.

'I wondered how word of mouth spread so quickly; we've got a truckload of advance bookings,' said Lizzie. The glowing review certainly took some of the sting out of her demotion in status from fine dining to café cook.

Just then the door from the café opened and the man who had been taking up so much of her thoughts emerged. 'I'm on the hunt for our missing boss,' said Jesse with great exaggeration. He looked from Lizzie to Sandy and back again. His expression grew serious. 'Is something wrong?'

'It's very, very right,' said Lizzie exultantly. She wanted to throw herself into his arms and share with him her excitement and relief.

Sandy rolled her eyes heavenward. 'Better show the review to the "most swoon-worthy barista you'll see this side of Hollywood".'

'What are you talking about?' said Jesse as he grabbed the newspaper. He scanned the pages then groaned loudly and theatrically. 'This will do wonders for my reputation. Please let's hope my mates don't see it.'

'Your handsome face is doing wonders for butts on seats in our café,' said Sandy. 'Would you consider a full-time career change?'

Jesse laughed. 'It's nothing to do with the barista

and everything to do with this one.' He swept Lizzie up in his arms and twirled her around. 'Congratulations, boss. You deserve this.'

Now Lizzie felt really elated but as Jesse swung her to a halt she noticed her sister's narrowed, appraising eyes. Sandy's words came back: 'Jesse is so not for you.'

She caught Jesse's eye and, in one of those silent moments of communication they were having more often, he got the message. *Keep Sandy in the dark about us.*

Jesse immediately swung Sandy up and twirled her around too. 'The incredible Adam sisters triumph.'

'I'm a Morgan,' corrected Sandy.

'Dumont for me,' added Lizzie.

Both she and Sandy had been glad to kiss goodbye to their father's name when they'd married. She'd thought of reverting to her maiden name when she'd divorced Philippe but had decided against it for Amy's sake. It had been disruptive enough for her without Mummy having a different name. *Morgan was a nice name.*

She refused to let the thought go further. Anyway, that would be weird. Two sisters marrying a pair of brothers? *Never going to happen.*

CHAPTER ELEVEN

THE STAR OF the fund-raiser for Dolphin Bay Dogs, the shelter Jesse's mother Maura was involved with, was the cast of dogs, ranging from cute puppies to venerable senior citizens with grey around their muzzles.

They sat in a row along the raised platform that acted as a stage for the ballroom of the Hotel Harbourside. The volunteer carers who kept the dogs in check were busy either soothing the nervous ones or calming the excitable ones who just wanted to be part of the action.

It was clever marketing on his mother's part, Jesse thought. He was sure people would be more inclined to open their wallets when they saw those pleading canine eyes.

But, appealing as the puppies were, Jesse's eyes were only for Lizzie. They'd agreed she'd arrive with Sandy and Ben so as not to draw attention to the way their 'friendship' had escalated into something so much more.

And now she was here. As she made her way across the room to him he was literally lost for words. His heart thudded into overdrive and his mouth went dry.

Last time he'd seen her she'd been wearing her chef's jacket and black pants, her hair pulled tightly back from her face and her cheeks all flushed from the heat of the kitchen. He'd thought she'd looked lovely then. But the transformation from chef to seductress was nothing short of sensational.

Her dress clung to her slender shape and left her shoulders bare, with a tantalising suggestion of cleavage, and its colour was a tint of aqua that glistened like the underside of a wave on Silver Gull beach. Her hair puzzled him for a moment until he realised it looked so different because her wild curls had been tamed into a style that was straight and sleek and falling around her face. She looked sophisticated. Elegant. And sexy as all get-out.

'Lizzie,' he said in the most casual just-friends voice he could muster, 'you're looking very lovely.'

'Thank you,' she said in the tone she used to accept a compliment about the food from a customer, but lit by a mischievous sparkle in her eyes. 'So glad you approve.'

'I approve, all right,' he said, his voice more the hoarse whisper of a lover than the light tone of a pal, no matter how he tried to keep it casual.

The silver high heeled shoes that strapped around her ankles brought her to easy kissing height. She kissed him lightly, first on one cheek and then the other. 'Just friends, remember,' she murmured into his ear.

It was an effort not to clamp her possessively to his side. To beat away anyone who came near her. She aroused caveman instincts he hadn't known he possessed.

'You look so beautiful,' he murmured back. 'No man would want to stop at just being friends.'

She laughed as she pulled away from him to normal conversation level. He had better try and mask the hunger in his eyes.

'I bought this dress in Paris years ago. It's so long

since I dressed up I could hardly remember how. I thought it was going to be a big fail.'

'Count it as a first class honours pass,' he said.

She wore make-up too, dark stuff around her eyes that brought out a purple ring around her iris. And deep pink lipstick on her sweet, seductive mouth. It only made him want to kiss it off.

'This is the same room where Sandy and Ben's wedding reception was held, isn't it?' Lizzie asked in a low murmur. 'Do you get a feeling of déjà vu?'

'In a way,' he said. 'You're the loveliest woman in the room again.'

'I bet you say that to all the girls,' she said in mock flirtation, but he saw a touch of wariness in her eyes.

'No, I don't, and that's the truth,' he said. He bent to whisper in her ear. 'You have to learn to trust me, Lizzie.' *As he had to trust her.*

She nodded. 'I know.'

He wanted to kiss her to reassure her, but of course he couldn't. Not with the eyes of a sizable number of his family and friends upon them.

'One thing is for sure,' she said, as if she'd read his mind. 'Nothing could take me out onto that balcony again.'

He didn't want to share her. Wanted her all to himself somewhere very private. But she was right—that place wasn't the balcony. No matter how beautiful the view of the full moon over the bay.

He was about to tell her that when Ben came up beside them. He slapped his brother on the shoulder in greeting. 'It's not you I've come to talk to,' Ben said. 'It's Lizzie.'

'Okay,' said Lizzie. Did she feel as annoyed as he did at being interrupted?

'Mum wants to show you something special,' Ben said to Lizzie. 'She's over there near the stage. Please don't be surprised if it's a dog.'

Lizzie laughed. 'I don't mind at all if it's a dog. Isn't that what we're here for?'

She casually brushed her hand against Jesse's arm as she left—he got the message she would rather stay with him and it pleased him.

'I actually do want to talk to you,' said Ben. He went from smiling to serious, as he did when money and investment was concerned.

Jesse's interest was sparked. When he was younger, he'd trusted Ben with financial advice that had paid off very handsomely. A generous inheritance plus business savvy and wise investment meant that at his age he was very well off. Well off enough to be able to take the weight right off Lizzie's feet if that was what she wanted; maybe into a job that wasn't so physically demanding. It concerned him to see her so exhausted and in pain at the end of a long day in the kitchen.

'I want to talk to you about a business proposition,' Ben said.

'If you want to hire me as a full-time barista, forget it,' Jesse said with a grin.

'Sandy would sign you up in a moment,' Ben said. 'But that's not the money-making proposal I have for you.'

As Lizzie walked away from Jesse, she was surprised to realise how much she was enjoying herself. She couldn't help but contrast the last time she'd been in this room for Sandy's wedding.

Then she'd been the bride's sister who didn't know anyone. Now, even after only a few weeks in Dolphin

Bay, she recognised lots of faces and they were all very complimentary about Bay Bites. Several people told her they'd put in bids for the prize of lunch for two she'd donated to the silent auction.

Maura came bustling up and swept her up into a hug. 'Gorgeous, gorgeous dress,' she said. 'So glad to see you having a night out.'

'We had another busy day in the café today,' Lizzie told her. 'The fish pie I made from your recipe was a sell-out. And we've already got customers asking us to put your strawberry sponge cake on the regular menu.'

'Only serve that cake when strawberries are at their finest,' Maura advised. 'It's at its best with the freshest, sweetest strawberries. Anything else is a compromise and the flavour will suffer.'

Lizzie smiled. Maura truly was a woman after her own heart when it came to food. 'I'll keep that advice in mind,' she said.

'I'm pleased about that, dear. But we're not here to talk about cooking. There's someone I want you to meet.'

Lizzie followed Maura up onto the platform where the dogs were waiting to play their roles for the evening with varying degrees of good behaviour.

'If we can appeal to people's hearts for adoptions tonight that will be grand,' said Maura. 'If we can get them to open their wallets, too, that's all the better.'

Lizzie suppressed a smile. It appeared the Morgan family were born businesspeople. That augured well for the future of Bay Bites—and her own security in Dolphin Bay.

Maura led Lizzie to where a puppy snuggled with a teenage girl. 'He's sad, Mrs Morgan,' she said. 'He misses his brother and sister who got adopted.'

'Sad? Maybe a little lonely,' said Maura. 'But he's quiet because he's exhausted from being run around the yard all afternoon.' She turned to Lizzie. 'Meet Alfie.'

At the sound of his name, the puppy sat up. He was black with a few irregular white patches, soulful dark eyes and long floppy ears that made Lizzie think he had some spaniel in him. He gave a sweet little whine and lifted up a furry paw to be shaken.

Lizzie was smitten. 'Oh, he's adorable.' She shook the puppy's warm little paw.

'Mother, are you up to your "get the puppy to shake paws" tricks again?' Jesse spoke from behind her and Lizzie turned. Her heart missed a beat at the sight of how devastating he looked in a tuxedo. She hadn't thought he could look more handsome than he did in his jeans and T-shirt but he did. Oh, yes, he did.

'And if a few tricks help a homeless animal find his way into someone's heart, who am I to miss the opportunity?' said Maura with the charming smile that was so like her son's.

'He's won my heart already—can I pick him up?' Lizzie asked.

As soon as he was in her arms the puppy tried to enthusiastically lick her face. Lizzie laughed. 'Jesse, isn't he cute?'

'He is that,' said Jesse with a smile she could only describe as indulgent.

'Amy would adore him.'

'Yes, she would,' said Maura. 'A dog can be a great friend to a little girl.'

'Her *grand-maman* in France has a little dog that Amy loves. She's heartbroken every time she says goodbye to her. It might help her to settle here if she had a dog of her own.'

'But is it practical for you to have a puppy?' Jesse asked.

'Not right now,' Lizzie said reluctantly, kissing the puppy's little forehead. 'Who knows what the future might bring for us? But he's utterly enchanting.'

She turned to Maura. 'Amy will be here on Wednesday. If Alfie hasn't found a home by then I'll bring her to see him.' She gave the puppy one more pat, to which he responded with enthusiastic wagging of his tiny tail, and reluctantly handed him back to his carer.

Maura put her hand on Lizzie's arm. 'You have to do what's best for you and your daughter. But a dog brings such rewards.'

If Lizzie stayed in Dolphin Bay a dog would be possible. For one thing, she'd be happier if Amy had the comfort of a puppy while she settled into her new home and made new friends. But it was still early days yet.

It wasn't just the possibility of something serious with Jesse that made her hesitate. She only had a job here if the café was a success. Otherwise she'd be back in Sydney flat-hunting in a difficult rental market with the added hindrance of a dog in tow.

And then there was Jesse's career. If they had a future together, where might it be?

'Don't you have to give your speech soon, Mum?' Jesse said.

'Yes, of course I do,' said Maura. 'You just keep little Alfie in mind, Lizzie.'

Jesse put his arm casually around Lizzie's shoulder as he led her down from the platform. 'Don't let her talk you into something you're not ready for. A dog's a big commitment.'

'Don't I know it,' she said.

She was silent for a long moment. Holding the squirming little bundle in her arms had brought back memories of Amy as a baby. Amy often asked if she could have a little brother or sister, but another baby had never been on the agenda. Why was she thinking about it now?

As the evening progressed Lizzie couldn't help being overwhelmed by that déjà vu. They were in the same room as the wedding reception. She was enjoying the opportunity to wear a beautiful dress, do something special with her hair—she loved the effect of having it straight—and wearing more make-up than usual.

With the Parisian dress she felt she had donned some of her old Lizzie party-girl spirit. That Lizzie had been pretty much smothered by maternal responsibilities and anxieties. She loved Amy more than she could ever have imagined loving another person. But there were times she wanted to be Lizzie, not just Mummy or Chef. This was one of them. She was determined to enjoy every second of the evening.

She even enjoyed the speeches. She wasn't the only one near tears when Maura spoke about the homeless dogs and cats in the area and the maltreatment some of them received before they got to the shelter. Someone else spoke convincingly about spaying and neutering to help bring down the number of unwanted kittens and puppies.

When Maura returned to the table after the speeches, she saw the pride in Jesse's father's eyes as he helped his wife of heaven knew how many years back into her chair. She realised Jesse had been brought up in a family where love and kindness ruled.

How very different from her family, where her father, a specialist anaesthetist, believed in excessive discipline, rigorous academic achievement and ruthless competition. No wonder both she and Sandy had rebelled. No wonder her mother had eventually divorced him and moved to another state.

Her father hadn't been a part of her life for a long time but he had asked to see her when she'd brought Amy back to Australia. She'd hoped he'd regretted the way he'd treated her, maybe wanted to make up for it by developing a relationship with his granddaughter. But no. He wanted to pay to send Amy to an exclusive girls' boarding school where she could develop her academic potential, away from her mother's influence. Needless to say, Lizzie had declined the offer.

The food at Maura's function was good, but not as good as she'd expected from the Hotel Harbourside catering. 'Should I mention it to Sandy?' she whispered to Jesse. They were seated together at the Morgan family table, surreptitiously holding hands under cover of the tablecloth.

'When the moment is right,' Jesse said, keeping his voice very low, pretending not to be too interested in what she was saying. 'You'll need to be diplomatic.'

'Aren't I always diplomatic?' she started to say in a huff.

He smiled. 'You can't pride yourself on being both blunt and diplomatic at the same time.' He squeezed her hand to emphasise he didn't mean it as an insult.

'Point taken,' she said.

Again she marvelled at how quickly Jesse had got to know her. She didn't feel she knew him as well but was enjoying each revelation of what lay beneath the heartbreakingly handsome exterior. So far she'd discovered he was a thoughtful, highly intelligent man with a good heart, a good head for business and a whole lot of common sense. That was on top of being a master kisser.

'Do you know what I'm missing?' she said. 'The music. I wish I could get up and dance with you. Do you remember how we danced together at the wedding?'

'How could I forget?'

'I think dancing with you was when I—' She swallowed the words that bubbled to the surface. *When I thought I might have found someone special.*

'When you...?' Jesse prompted.

'When I...when I realised you were so much more than the best man who I, as the chief bridesmaid, was obligated to spend time with.'

And now? *Now she was falling in love with him.* She'd fought it so hard she hadn't let herself recognise it. *Could you fall in love this quickly?*

'You okay?' asked Jesse. 'You seem flustered.'

'Yes. Yes. Of course I'm okay.' *How did she deal with this?*

'I want to dance with you too,' said Jesse in a husky undertone. 'The evening is winding up. In half an hour we leave separately, then—'

'Yes?' she asked, her heart thudding.

'Then we have our own private dance on the beach.'

CHAPTER TWELVE

JESSE WAITED UNTIL a moment when his mother had got back up onstage and was introducing the audience to the dogs. She held up a particularly cute puppy with one ear that flopped all the way over. All attention was on the puppy as the other guests oohed and aahed at its cuteness. He didn't think anyone would notice him slip away and make his way out of the hotel.

Ten minutes later he saw Lizzie creep out of the Hotel Harbourside exit and cross the road to where he waited. For a moment she didn't see him and her wary look made his heart leap.

He couldn't have anticipated how fast things were moving with her. But he was a man used to making quick life-or-death decisions. He had decided he wanted to take a chance on Lizzie Dumont—and no obstacle was going to be allowed to stand in the way of them becoming a couple. That included his own doubts.

She caught sight of him and smiled—a joyous smile tinged with mischief, just like the smile he had fallen for when he had first met her at the pre-wedding outing. She ran over the road to meet him under the palm tree that edged the beach. 'I feel like a naughty schoolgirl sneaking out like this,' she said with a delightful giggle.

Funny, he hadn't been attracted to her when she was a schoolgirl. It was the woman she'd become who'd caught his attention.

'So where's the dance floor?' she asked.

'Down there.' He indicated the beach with an expansive wave of his hand. 'If we dance down there and to the left we'll be out of sight of the hotel.'

Her gasp of pleasure was the biggest reward he could have asked for. 'So we twirl and whirl on the sand,' she said.

She balanced on his shoulder as she leaned down to unbuckle the straps on her silver shoes and slip them off. She tucked them alongside his own shoes, socks and bow tie where he'd discarded them at the base of the palm tree.

'The wet sand near the edge of the water will be firmer,' he said with his engineer's brain.

The full moon was high in the sky and its reflection lit a shimmering path of palest gold from the horizon, over the water to where the tiny waves of the bay sighed onto the sand.

'Magic by moonlight,' she breathed.

It was so light he could clearly see Lizzie's eyes, her face pale, uplifted to the moon, her hair glinting like silver. She looked ethereal, like some kind of fairy princess in her shimmering dress.

Jesse could hardly believe he was thinking such thoughts. He was an engineer. Practical. Mathematical. *Madness* by moonlight, more like it.

She wound her arms around his neck. 'I feel like I'm in some kind of enchanted world,' she whispered. 'And you're the handsome prince spiriting me away to dance on moonbeams. Have I found my way onto the pages of one of Amy's fairy tale books?'

He kissed her, lightly, possessively. 'If that's the case, you're the fairy princess.' *Had he actually said that?*

'I had no idea you were so romantic, Jesse,' she murmured.

'I'm not usually,' he said. 'It…it's you.'

This was the Lizzie who had captivated him at the wedding. During the last ten days he'd got to see the other sides of Lizzie. And the more he got to know her, the more he wanted her in his life.

She laughed and the slightly bawdy edge to her laughter reminded him how utterly real and womanly she was. 'Where's the music, Prince Charming? Can you conjure it up from the moonlight?'

'The prosaic engineer in me would tell you I can play music through my smartphone.'

'Whereas Prince Charming might say we can dance to the music of the stars,' she suggested.

'And the rhythm of the waves,' he said.

'With those chirping crickets adding some bass.'

He laughed. 'If you say so.'

'It's perfect,' she whispered.

She went into his arms and together they danced barefoot on the cool, wet sand with the occasional tiny cold wave swishing over their feet and making her squeal. They danced not with the expertise of ballroom dancers—he'd never mastered that art—but in their own rhythm, making up their steps as they went along, her glittering skirt twirling around them.

'I don't know that the music of the moon and stars is enough; it hasn't quite got a beat,' she murmured. 'Shall I hum? I can't sing, so humming will have to do.'

'Go ahead and hum,' he said, falling more under her spell each minute, totally enchanted by her.

He stood quite still as she started to hum the tune of

the old song about Jesse's girl that had tormented him for so many years. But in her slightly tuneless hum, it was the most melodious music he'd ever heard. And her particular version of the words echoed in his heart as she murmured them.

He smoothed her hair back from her face, cupped her face in his hands. 'Do you really want to be Jesse's girl?'

Her eyes were luminous in the moonlight. 'Oh, yes,' she said.

Lizzie pulled Jesse back for another kiss. She couldn't bear to spend a minute out of his arms on this magical evening where her own Prince Charming was dancing her along an enchanted beach. Only too soon her prince might have to go across those waters to the badlands to fight his own battles and maybe never come back to her.

She'd not been one for fairy tales. As a mother, she'd tried to steer Amy in the direction of feminist tales of hard-working women who met men on an equal footing, who had no room for Prince Charmings riding to their rescue on white chargers when they could rescue themselves perfectly well, thank you very much.

But tonight with Jesse she felt differently. Whether it was indeed the magic of the full moon or because she was falling in love with him, she wanted Jesse to be her prince, sweep her up into his arms and carry her away to make her his.

Even if it was only for tonight she wanted this, wanted him. She lost herself in his kisses, yielding to his lips, to his tongue as his mouth claimed hers, trembled with pleasure at the sensation of his hands on her bare shoulders.

'It's about at this stage Prince Charming sweeps

the princess off to his fairy tale castle,' she murmured against his mouth.

Jesse lifted his head to meet her gaze. 'To make her his?'

He had never looked more handsome than at this moment. His hair raven's wing black in the moonlight, his eyes reflecting the indigo of the deep night sea.

'Yes,' she breathed. 'To make her his in every sense of the word.'

'Are you sure?' His voice was deep, husky with a slight hitch that betrayed his fear she might say no.

There was no risk of that. She nodded. 'My Cinderella garret above the café is all mine right now. On Wednesday the junior princess will be in residence. You might find I turn back into a pumpkin then.'

Jesse laughed, his perfect white teeth gleaming in the moonlight. 'I think you're getting your analogies mixed. Even I know it was the carriage that got turned back into a pumpkin. You've left your shoes on the beach. It will be the prince doing the rounds of every house in the magical town of Dolphin Bay trying to find whose foot fits the silver stiletto.'

She smiled. 'So, not a pumpkin. But it's true that at five a.m. I'll turn back into a servant wearing rags and clogs as I stoke the fires of the café kitchen. Well, maybe not rags but—'

He dropped a kiss on her nose. 'The clock is ticking.'

'My castle or yours?' she said.

'As I'm staying in the boathouse, your garret might be more private.'

'My garret it is,' she said.

Laughing, kissing, Jesse danced her over the sand and back up to where they had stashed their shoes. He knelt in the sand and helped her wipe off the sand from her feet. Then he kissed the arch of each foot before he slipped on her silver stilettos.

'I had to stop myself from doing that the night I massaged your feet,' he said.

Delicious ripples of pleasure shimmered through her. 'No need to stop now,' she whispered.

Totally engrossed in the magic of being with Jesse, Lizzie didn't care who might see them make their way hand in hand towards her apartment. There, in true fairy tale prince fashion, he gathered her into his arms and carried her up the stairs and into the magical kingdom of her bedroom.

CHAPTER THIRTEEN

JESSE HAD AGREED with Lizzie to keep secret the new turn their relationship had taken. In the three days since their dance on the beach they'd managed not to arouse suspicion. Neither of them wanted to be subject to the inevitable teasing the revelation they were dating would bring. To him, Lizzie was not just one in a stream of 'Jesse's girls'. As far as he was concerned, she was the one and only Jesse's girl.

This wasn't something short-term. He was convinced of that. Lizzie wasn't underhand and dishonest like Camilla had been. He trusted her.

He intended to talk to her today about the proposition he had discussed in depth with Ben. His brother had suggested they pool some of the land they each owned around Dolphin Bay and form a property development company.

Jesse had been involved in the building of the Hotel Harbourside and was a part-owner of the new spa resort Ben was building. At the back of his mind he'd always wanted to go into business for himself; he came from a long line of entrepreneurs. It was a logical—and exciting—next step.

Relocating back to Dolphin Bay would also knock down the major barrier that remained between him and

Lizzie—that they lived in different countries. It was a move that checked all the boxes. Importantly, it would give them time to really get to know each other.

He'd arranged to meet Lizzie after the café closed for the day. The young waitress Nikki had responded so well to his training and confidence-boosting, he'd done himself out of his job as a barista. His role at Bay Bites now comprised helping out for a few hours over lunchtime—and that was only an excuse to be with Lizzie. His two-hour time limit? Twenty hours of Lizzie's company a day wouldn't be enough.

She was already there when he got to the lookout, a block away from the café, with the best view in Dolphin Bay of the harbour. It was a perfect afternoon, the water sparkling aquamarine under a cloudless sky. Fishing boats and pleasure craft of all shapes and sizes bobbed on the water and the melodic chime of rigging against masts carried across to where he stood.

Lizzie wore a pink sundress that bared her shoulders and arms. Fine tendrils of her pale blonde hair had escaped from the band that held it back from her face and wafted in the slight breeze. There was no reason for her to be anything but happy and relaxed. But he could see straight away that something was bothering her—he'd learned to read the way anxiety tightened her face and dimmed the light in her eyes.

They greeted each other with a discreet kiss on the cheek—as friends, colleagues and family connections would. After a night of lovemaking, he'd left her warm and satisfied in her bed when he'd exited before dawn. It had been difficult to leave her but they both wanted to keep their new intimacy a secret.

'What's up?' he asked.

'How do you always know?' she asked with the shadow of a smile.

'Just observant,' he said.

But it was more than that. The connection between them grew stronger with each minute they spent together. It was a bond he'd never had before. But it also brought fear of the inevitable pain if that connection was ever severed. *Wussy versus brave,* he reminded himself. He'd chosen to take the brave path, to let feeling grow rather than stifle it with fear. So, it seemed, had she.

Lizzie took his hand and gave it a surreptitious squeeze. He knew without further words being spoken that she valued the depth of their connection too.

She looked up at him 'You know Amy is due back tomorrow?'

'I know how much you're looking forward to seeing her. Why the glum face?'

'Philippe is escorting her on her flight from Lyon. I was going to drive up to Sydney to meet her plane. Now he'll hire a car to bring her here.'

'Your ex? Here in Dolphin Bay?' He was hit by a blow of dismay. Lizzie's ex-husband played an active role in Amy's life. But having him here on home turf was not a move he welcomed.

'It's as much a surprise to me as it is to you,' she said.

For her sake, he suppressed the stab of jealousy that knifed him. 'That's good for Amy.'

'Yes. The airline does a wonderful job of escorting her. In fact she enjoys the fuss the attendants make of her so much she's probably protesting having her papa with her. But I worry every second she's on the plane by herself so in that way I'm glad he'll be there.'

'Of course you are.'

He admired Lizzie's dedication to her daughter. Amy

was a fantastic little kid, smart, funny, outgoing. If—
and it was still a big if—he got to be a permanent part of
Lizzie's life he would welcome a role in Amy's life too.

'I'm worried about why Philippe wants to see me
so much he's flying all the way to Australia.' That favourite stray piece of hair was getting another workout
between her fingers.

'Maybe because he's missing you.' Jesse spoke
lightly but his gut roiled.

'Nothing like that,' she said, shaking her head with
a vehemence Jesse should have found reassuring but
didn't. If he'd had Lizzie for his own, he would never
have let her get away. Her ex-husband must have regretted it a million times. Maybe that was what he wanted
to tell her. Perhaps he had a good story to spin about
how he'd changed.

'He says there's something important that has to be
said face to face,' Lizzie continued.

The ex wanted her back. Jesse just knew it. 'So what
do you think your ex wants?'

'I'm terrified he's going for full custody of Amy. He's
used it as a threat before to try and keep me in France.
I can't think what else he would need to see me about.'

Jesse thought he knew only too well what her ex
would want: Lizzie and Amy back with him. But he
didn't share his thoughts. Instead he reassured her.
'You're a wonderful mother. You can provide a secure
home for Amy. No way would he have grounds to say
you're unfit for custody. Don't the courts usually rule
in favour of the mother?'

Lizzie snatched her hand to her mouth. 'The courts?
Please don't let it get that far.'

'You'll know tomorrow what he wants. There's nothing you can do in the meantime. Try to stop worrying.'

He didn't want her to be preoccupied with her ex on the last night they had together alone before Amy came home. The dynamic between them would be changed when they had to fit their private time around the needs of a five-year-old.

'If their flight is on time and all goes well, he and Amy should be here by midmorning.'

She banged the railing of the seafront wall with such force it surely must have hurt her hand. 'Why is he doing this to me? After all he put me through before? I've done everything I can to be civilised about the divorce, to make it easier for Amy. Letting her go to France half of every school holidays. Video calls every week. Why?' She muttered under her breath in what Jesse could only assume was a string of fluent French swear words.

It was the closest to anger he had seen her, though he'd heard a few explosions coming from the kitchen at Bay Bites. 'You really don't want to see him, do you?'

'Of course I don't. Why would I?'

Jesse's spirits lifted at the thought. Sounded as if any possible reunion could be wishful thinking on the ex-husband's part.

'Do you want me to be there when you meet with him?'

'No.'

Her answer came with such swiftness that Jesse felt as if he'd been hit with an unexpected punch between the eyes. 'Whatever,' he said.

Her face filled with contrition. She reached out and touched him fleetingly on the cheek with slender, cool fingers. 'I didn't mean to sound hurtful. Of course I would like you by my side when I confront Philippe. But if he's after sole custody, I wouldn't want him to know I was in a relationship with a man.'

'I don't want to jeopardise anything,' Jesse said. 'But I'll be at hand. Just in case.'

'No need for that,' she said. 'Philippe hasn't got a violent bone in his body. I wouldn't let Amy spend so much time with him if he had any tendencies that way. No. I can handle this by myself—like I did with the issues that ended the marriage.'

Jesse muttered assent. But no way would he let Lizzie go into this by herself. When she met with her ex he would be nearby.

But, to help her, he needed to know what had happened to end the marriage in such a drastic way she'd come back to Australia to raise her child on her own.

'Lizzie, we've skirted around this. But what actually happened to end your marriage? To make you so wary of men like your ex.'

Lizzie hated reliving the past. She and her sister had handled what had happened with their father by having a 'water under the bridge' policy that had so far served her well.

But Jesse deserved to know.

'I don't really like to talk about this, so I won't linger on the details,' she said.

'Fine by me,' he said. He leaned back against the lookout wall with his back to the view. Lizzie couldn't help thinking she'd rather look at Jesse than any number of rustic stone breakwaters and charming boats in the harbour, no matter how picturesque.

'I met Philippe when we were both working at a hotel up in Port Douglas. When he left to go back home to France I went with him. It was an adventure—and good for my career. Living in Paris was a ball, working all hours then partying hard.'

'I hear a "but" coming on.'

She nodded. 'I fell pregnant. It was unplanned. But we got married, made the best of it. When there were some complications in the pregnancy, I wanted to go home to have the baby. My French had improved out of sight by then but I didn't feel I really understood the doctors and the hospitals. Philippe didn't much like it—and his family were horrified—but I came home to stay with Sandy.'

'Why didn't your husband go with you?'

'He had a really good job; I didn't want him to give it up. Not when we were about to have a child to support. Neither of us wanted to accept money from his parents with the strings that went with it.'

'I wouldn't have let you go by yourself. Under any circumstances.'

'You're you. Philippe was Philippe.' She looked up at Jesse. 'I really, really hate talking about this.'

'I wish I could hug you but, in case you hadn't noticed, a couple of my mother's friends are walking on the other side of the road. If I touch you, the whole town will soon know.'

Lizzie turned around. Sure enough, two older ladies who had become regulars at the café and drank more cups of tea in the space of an hour than she had imagined anyone could possibly drink, had drawn level to them. She forced a smile and waved to them.

She turned back to Jesse. 'I see what you mean. I want to hug you too. More than you could know. But I'll get on with the story so I can be done with it.' She gritted her teeth. 'I got back to France and knew immediately something was different.'

'To cut a long story even shorter, he'd met someone else,' said Jesse with a scowl.

'How did you know that?'

'Lucky guess,' he said.

He must dislike hearing this as much as she disliked saying it. She appreciated how difficult it must have been for him to tell her about that dreadful Camilla.

'She was a *commis,* a junior chef, in the restaurant where Philippe worked. He said it meant nothing.'

'He was lonely; she threw herself at him,' Jesse drawled, contempt edging his voice.

'All that. He confessed and begged my forgiveness.'

Jesse's mouth tightened to a thin line. 'You know my opinion. No cheating under any circumstances.'

Was Jesse judging her? She wished she hadn't started this conversation.

'What choice did I have? I was twenty-three, had a brand new baby. We moved to Lyon to make a fresh start. I went back to work when Amy was six months old. But things were very different. No more party girl Lizzie.'

'I think I can predict the rest.' Jesse's hands were curled into fists.

'He swore he was faithful but I couldn't believe him. I was so jealous and suspicious I became a horrible person no one would want to live with. I stuck it until Amy was four. You know the rest.'

'Did you love him?' Jesse's question came from left field.

'I thought I did.'

'What do you feel about him now?' Jesse's voice was tight, his eyes guarded.

She frowned. 'That's a strange question to ask after what I've been telling you. Philippe is done and dusted as far as I'm concerned. Not only do I not love him, I don't actually like him.'

Jesse's face darkened. 'Best I don't meet the guy to-morrow. You might not be able to hold me back.'

'I've probably said too much. But now you know why I resisted getting involved with someone I thought might hurt me in the same way.'

CHAPTER FOURTEEN

THE NEXT DAY Lizzie was so nervous about the upcoming confrontation with Philippe she felt nauseous. She had organised extra help in the kitchen so she could spend the day with Amy. That also allowed her time for a private meeting with her ex-husband. Dread that he might try to take Amy away from her put her so on edge she wasn't fit to work anyway.

In the fairy tale her life in Dolphin Bay with Jesse had become, she cast Philippe in the role of the ogre who could take her happiness away. She was ready with sword and shield to fight him. She had given up her career and moved to Dolphin Bay for Amy's sake. She could give her daughter a good life here. She would never, ever let her go.

The reunion with Amy had been ecstatic, as it always was when they'd been apart for any length of time. She'd held her darling girl tightly to her, breathed in the apple shampoo freshness of her, laughed and pretended to squirm at Amy's exuberant hugs and kisses.

As usual after Amy had been with her father and his family it had taken her a few minutes to adjust to speaking English, to being a little Australian girl again. But after Lizzie had shown her the café—where the staff had made a huge fuss of her—and her new home upstairs, Amy had happily gone off with Maura. No doubt she would be introduced to little Alfie and then the begging and pleading to keep him would start. Lizzie decided to keep an open mind on that one.

Maura had so much grandmotherly love to give—and Amy was the only child in their family she had to lavish it on. Lizzie was aware of the thread of sadness underlying Maura's warmth, stemming from the tragic loss of Ben's little son.

With Amy settled with Maura, now it would be just her and Philippe, squaring up against each other as adversaries with their child the spoils of battle. She hadn't seen her ex-husband for more than a year. Sometimes she liked to imagine he didn't exist. But he was here in Dolphin Bay. She took a deep steadying breath to centre herself and headed to the Hotel Harbourside. *Let the battle begin.*

She'd chosen neutral territory, a quiet corner of the guest lounge. At this time of day, during the week, there should be no one to disturb them. She regretted the hurt that had flashed across Jesse's face when she had declined his offer to accompany her. But this was something she had to do by herself.

She cast a quick eye around the room. Jesse had said he would be nearby in case he needed to rush in to her defence—like a true Prince Charming would. She couldn't see him anywhere, but she trusted he was there. Jesse was true to his word. Although she knew the confrontation with Philippe wouldn't get physical—unless he'd changed out of sight—it was reassuring to know that Jesse was close.

Then Philippe was there, greeting her with his accented English that had charmed her years ago. She braced herself and looked up at her ex, his handsome face with his prominent nose and Amy's eyes, his dark blond hair. He had once been so dear to her; they had started off with such high hopes, now he meant nothing. There was an element of sadness—of failure—to her thoughts but no regret. If it wasn't for Amy, she would be happy never to have to see him again.

Jesse knew the layout of the Hotel Harbourside very well. It had not been difficult to find a spot where, with the help of a large wall mirror, he could sit in a large, high-backed lounge chair and keep an eye on Lizzie without her—or her ex-husband—seeing him. He held an open newspaper in front of him and flicked through its pages without seeing a word. It was like a stake-out. Cloak and dagger stuff. Only this was a game where the stakes were very high.

Lizzie had come into the guest lounge by herself. She was dressed more formally than he had seen her, wearing narrow black trousers and a tight cropped jacket with the sleeves pushed up. Her hair was pulled back in a thick plait that hung in pale contrast down the back of the black jacket. She looked elegant, stylish and so unfamiliar it disconcerted him.

He could tell by the way Lizzie squared her shoulders and measured her stride that she was nervous. Was that why she had dressed like that? As armour? The ugly thought intruded. Or to look good for her ex?

She only had seconds to pace the floor by herself before she was joined by a tall guy wearing grey trousers and a lightweight sweater. Lizzie had always said her cheater of an ex was a good-looking guy. Yeah. He could see that. The Frenchman was big with broad shoulders and a powerful body.

The first thing they did was kiss each other. Twice.

Once on each cheek. Jesse knew that was the European way, but still he gripped tight onto the arms of the chair at the sight of Lizzie in an embrace with another guy. Not just another guy. The man she'd married, had intended to spend her life with, the father of her child. *Someone she'd loved.*

Ex-husband and ex-wife started to talk. Jesse hadn't hidden close enough to hear their actual words, just the sound of their voices. The conversation seemed to be more intense than angry with Philippe doing a lot of the talking. They were switching between English and French.

It was a shock to see Lizzie speaking French. She looked different—her mouth, her face—and she gesticulated with her hands in a Gallic way. This was a Lizzie who seemed to slip right back into a different persona altogether. It made him wonder how well he actually knew her.

He wished he'd sat closer so he could hear but he would have risked exposure. Was Philippe laying down terms for custody of Amy? Or was he putting his argument for his family to return to him in France? If the dude got angry with Lizzie, Jesse would be up there like a shot to protect her.

But, far from being an angry confrontation with her ex, Lizzie's meeting seemed amicable. Very amicable. *Too* amicable.

Lizzie smiled. She laughed. She *hugged* the guy who she'd told Jesse had made her life hell. The ex smiled too. He seemed too damn happy for a man who was being told his ex-wife would not give him custody of their daughter. Any sense of fun Jesse had felt in staking out Lizzie and her ex was quickly replaced by bitter disbelief.

There was too much laughter and goodwill going on. Lizzie had said she dreaded the meeting but it looked to Jesse as if she was enjoying every minute of it.

Lizzie had problems with jealousy? Jesse had never before been bothered by it, had never understood the emotion. He sure as hell understood it now. Violent jealousy flamed through him at the sight of Lizzie with her ex-husband.

He felt excluded and it wasn't a feeling he liked. All the foundations he'd been building around Lizzie felt threatened.

They hugged *again*. Then they walked out to the lobby and towards the exit, chatting as they went.

Jesse got up from his lounge chair, slammed the newspaper on the table and headed towards the side door that led to the terrace. From there he would actually be able to hear their farewells unless Lizzie walked her ex to his rental car.

But no. They stayed put and did the one-kiss, two-kiss thing again. Then Lizzie looked up into her handsome ex-husband's face and said very clearly in English. 'I will see you in Lyon. For the start of a new life.'

Then she watched him get into the car and waved as he pulled out of the hotel driveway and headed north to Sydney.

Those final words reverberated through Jesse's mind. *I will see you in Lyon. For the start of a new life.*

What the hell had that meant? It was difficult not to draw the obvious conclusion.

He'd been played for a fool again.

He wouldn't make the same mistake he'd made with Camilla. He was in deep with Lizzie, but he had an out. The job in Houston.

But first he'd give her a chance to explain herself.

If she didn't come clean then he'd know he had been lied to again. That Lizzie intended to have her fun with him until it was time to go back to her other man. Like Camilla had.

His hands fisted by his sides, he stepped out from the terrace so Lizzie could see him as she approached.

Her face lit up when she saw him and she hastened her steps to get to him quicker. It made his gut churn at how much he had come to care for her.

'So there you are,' she said. 'I've been looking for you. I've got good news.'

'Fire away,' he said gruffly.

'Philippe has dropped his plans to sue for sole custody. He flew all the way here to apologise about the way he behaved during our time together and to tell me—and to tell me...' She spluttered to a halt.

'To tell you what?' He felt choked by a grim foreboding.

'To...uh...to tell me how much he cared for Amy and how she would always be his first priority.'

She was lying. He couldn't fail to notice how she'd pulled herself up. No way would her ex come to the other side of the world just to tell her he was sorry for his behaviour of years ago. He believed the guy had apologised. But what had come next? Reconciliation? There'd been a lot of smiling and hugging. What the hell had that been about?

'That's good,' he muttered.

'You were a big hit with Amy, by the way, Uncle Jesse.' Lizzie chattered on, seemingly oblivious to his dark change of mood.

'Yeah, she's a great kid.' He'd been working at the café, educating Nikki in the finer aspects of pulling espresso shots, when Lizzie had brought Amy in to show her the café. Her little face had lit up when she'd seen him and she'd come tearing up to him to hurtle herself at him with a squeal of delight. 'Uncle Jesse!'

Laughing, he'd swept her up into his arms. It had taken him a long time after the fire to be comfortable around kids. He'd loved Ben's little boy Liam. It had seemed disloyal to pay attention to other children when his nephew had gone. He had taken his role as uncle very seriously. What role in his life might Amy play?

'Be flattered,' Lizzie had said. 'She doesn't take to everyone.'

'I wanted to introduce you to Philippe,' Lizzie said now.

He frowned. 'Why would you do that?'

So he'd be friendly to him when they got back together?

He thought back to one of the reasons he'd resisted pursuing Lizzie—if things went wrong he'd still have to see her at every family gathering. Her and her current man—perhaps her reconciled husband.

Not if he was in Houston, he wouldn't.

'Because, well, because he was here and because he's Amy's father I—'

'You told me how this guy cheated on you and made your life hell. Why would I want to shake his hand?' He paused. 'Unless things have changed between you.'

She looked confused. 'Well, yes, they have changed.'

Here it came—the confession.

'What I meant is, *he's* changed. Grown up at last. Admitted his mistakes.'

'And?'

She frowned. 'What do you mean "and"? I don't know what you're talking about.'

'Haven't you got something to tell me?'

She flushed. 'Well, yes. I do.' She looked around her. 'But this isn't the time or the place to talk to you about it. What it means for us.'

He cursed inwardly. *So he hadn't misunderstood those overheard words.*

'There's something *I* need to tell *you*,' he said, unable to meet her eyes. 'The company in Houston contacted me this morning. They want a decision by close of business today and a start date of Monday if I accept. I'd have to leave Dolphin Bay tomorrow.'

The blood drained from her face. 'Oh,' she said. 'Wh-what will you do?'

'I'm going to take it.'

'Wh-what about your shoulder?'

'It's healed enough for desk duties.'

He hadn't meant to be so harsh about it. Hadn't wanted to wound her. But hell, she had dealt him a body blow. Just like Camilla had.

'You'll be gone tomorrow?' Her voice was so faint he had to strain to hear it.

He nodded, unable to find the words that would take that stricken look off her face. Yet she still wouldn't admit she was going back to her husband. Or give him an explanation of why she'd lied. Why she had no explanation for those words he'd overheard.

He wanted to tell her he loved her. That he wanted to make decisions based on *their* future, not just his.

But she wasn't giving anything away. Not a word about her plans for going back to France to take up a new life with her old husband. Or why she was going to Lyon if it wasn't for that.

'So,' she said, with that familiar tilting of her chin. 'You'll be leaving Dolphin Bay?'

'Looks like it,' he said.

'Wh-what does that mean for us?' She turned her face away.

'You still don't have anything you want to tell me?' Anger and frustration and disbelief that he'd been caught again raged through him.

'It's not anything you'd want to hear,' she said in a very small voice.

That sealed it.

Then she met his gaze straight on. 'You'd better go make that phone call.'

She turned and he let her go.

CHAPTER FIFTEEN

LIZZIE WALKED AWAY from Jesse, expecting him to come after her. To tell her it was all a mistake. Reeling in shocked disbelief, she got halfway back to her apartment before she realised it wasn't going to happen. *Jesse had dumped her.* After all the emotional ups and downs she'd been through today, she was finding it impossible to stay steady on her feet. She had to stop and lean against one of the famous dolphin rubbish bins. Its smiling mouth seemed to mock her.

In a daze, she dragged her feet one step after another until she reached the door to her apartment and then hauled herself up the stairs.

The empty rooms derided her. Jesse was everywhere. His handprint all over the place—the tiles he'd laid, the walls he'd painted, the room he'd prepared for Amy. He was on the sofa where the aroma of peppermint still lingered. Most of all, he was in her bedroom. How could he have made love to her with such tenderness and passion, only to dump her when her daughter came home?

Her heart contracted with the agony of the realisation of what it felt to be one of Jesse's disposable girls.

She'd cleared the bedroom of every trace of him so Amy wouldn't be aware Uncle Jesse had been sleeping over in Mummy's bed. She and Jesse had agreed it was too soon for her to know. She laid her head on the pillow where only this morning his beautiful dark head had rested. Where they had slept entwined in each other's arms. She lay where he had lain, breathed in deeply, hoping for a lingering trace of his scent but she'd stripped the bed and washed all the linen. There wasn't a trace of him left.

What had gone wrong?

He'd given her no clue. His change of heart had come completely out of the blue. Was it something to do with her meeting with Philippe? The meeting that had released her from the chains of resentment that had held her back from fully trusting Jesse.

The first thing Philippe had done was to apologise for the way he'd behaved during their marriage. Then he'd told her he was getting married again. To a French-Canadian girl named Thérèse who was also a chef.

Lizzie's first thought had been for Amy. But Philippe had reiterated his love for his daughter and said Thérèse wanted to be a good stepmother. In fact she wanted to meet Lizzie so she could discuss Amy's shared care when her little girl spent time in France. There was no longer any question that Philippe would seek sole custody.

For Amy's sake she had accepted the hand of reconciliation that Philippe had extended. 'We learn from our mistakes, yes?' Philippe had said.

She had agreed and, in doing so, had realised how unfair it had been of her to judge Jesse on the mistakes she had made with her ex-husband. *The men were nothing alike.*

Her relationship with Philippe had been founded on youthful passion fired by rebellion. She and her ex-husband had never been friends like Jesse and she had become. Jesse was both friend and lover—it was a formidable combination. She doubted her ex had understood her after several years together the way Jesse already understood her.

As she'd spoken with Philippe, something in her heart that had been frozen with bitterness and resentment had thawed. She'd felt freed from heavy chains she hadn't realised had been tethering her so tightly.

The revelation had had nothing to do with Philippe and everything to do with Jesse. Her feelings for him had changed everything. Had made her ready to forgive and move on with no lingering fears from the past to poison the present with jealousy and suspicion.

Jesse was the real deal. The happily ever after. The till death us do part.

Then she'd sought out Jesse, anxious to tell him what had happened—and to explain how the burden of Philippe's past behaviour had lifted so she was free to love again without the hindrance of bad old energy from the marriage gone wrong.

But Jesse had blocked her every way. Grim Jesse with the charming good looks gone dark and glowering. *Black Irish.* Jesse with the harsh voice, the eyes with the shutters suddenly down against her.

Jesse who, to all intents, had done exactly what she'd feared he'd do. *Made a conquest of her and then dumped her.* And boy had she been an easy conquest. She'd barely put up a struggle before she'd fallen so joyously into bed.

Just another of Jesse's girls after all. She'd believed she'd been so much more. How could she have been so naïve, so stubborn, not to listen to her own sister's advice? She'd listened to her heart instead and it had led her wrong.

And yet.

She'd grown to believe in Jesse so strongly it was hard to let that trust go. She had truly thought he wouldn't do this to her. But there was no escaping that he had.

If she looked at it brutally, dispassionately, the timing was right for him to get rid of her. Amy had come home. With a five-year-old in residence, they would have to snatch time together, might go days without intimacy. He needed to free himself for new conquests. Those Texan girls didn't know what they were in for. Jesse the Player. Jesse the Heartbreaker.

She thought back, puzzling, seeking clues. *Philippe.* It all came back to his visit. Maybe Jesse was concerned about the ongoing contact with her ex-husband. There wasn't anything she could do about that. Amy deserved to have a loving relationship with her father and she was determined to facilitate that in any way she could.

What had Jesse meant? He'd asked her if she had something to tell him three times.

Did he want to know he had a place in her and Amy's life when there was a father still so actively involved with his daughter—even though said father lived on the other side of the world?

Maybe Jesse wanted assurance.

Maybe Jesse wanted her to tell him how she felt.

Maybe she needed to tell Jesse she loved him, wanted him, would go to Houston with him. Would go anywhere with him—the Philippines, India, any old where. Because she realised with a huge whoosh of pain that made her double over with the agony of it that life without Jesse would be intolerable.

She got up from the bed. She had to find him. Tell him she loved him. And if it all blew up in her face, if she was after all the latest in a long line of discarded Jesse's girls, at least she would have tried.

She clattered down the stairs of her apartment, waved to one of the waitresses who stood outside the door of the café talking on her phone. She kept her demeanour calm, her face controlled. As far as anyone else in Dolphin Bay knew, she and Jesse were just friends. It wouldn't look right for her to be stressed and tearful and hunting around town for him.

But where could she find him?

She didn't want to call him on his mobile phone to alert him she was coming after him. She went to the boathouse. No Jesse. His car was gone too.

If Jesse was indeed taking off for Texas tomorrow, surely he'd want a farewell swim at his favourite beach. She'd take a punt he'd gone to Silver Gull. If he hadn't gone there she'd keep on looking until she found him. Even if she had to drive to Sydney and confront him at the airport.

No way was she going to let Jesse go until she'd made absolutely sure there was no hope left for them.

Jesse swam up and down the length of the beach, churning through the freezing water until his shoulder ached too much to go on. He'd had to fight a strong swell to get out beyond the breaking waves. That was nothing to the fight he'd had against himself. But the salt water and the vigorous exercise had cleared his head.

He'd been an idiot. The worst of the wussies. He'd let all the pain and fear from his early decision to avoid love make him act like an irrational, bad-tempered fool. He'd let the pain of Camilla's old betrayal blind him to the fact that Lizzie was not Camilla. Lizzie had not set out to hurt him. *He had hurt her.*

While he'd raged against the idea that Lizzie was going back to her ex-husband, she had never actually said she was. Remembering the bewildered look on her lovely face made him realise his anger had stopped him thinking straight.

Now he understood what Lizzie had struggled with—jealousy could turn a person crazy.

He should have asked Lizzie outright about what he'd overheard. Instead he'd set her a test of honesty she hadn't even known she had to pass. He'd been totally out of order. Cruel. Cowardly. Worse, he had betrayed the trust she'd worked so hard to build up from a baseline of emotional abuse.

He strode out of the water. Slung a towel around him and headed towards his car. He had to find her. Grovel. Apologise. Grovel some more. *Tell her how much he cared for her.*

Only to see Lizzie walking across the sand towards him. Her face was a mass of contradictions. Fear. Determination. And something else shining from her eyes that made his heart leap inside his chest.

He ran to meet her. But as he got closer she put up her hand to stop him. 'Before you come any further, Jesse Morgan, I want to answer that question you kept asking me before—have I got anything to tell you?'

He groaned. 'That was a mistake. I—' But she spoke right over him in that blunt, determined Lizzie way.

'I *have* got something to tell you. I don't know if it's what you wanted to hear but you're going to hear it anyway. I love you, Jesse. I fancied you the moment I met you. Then I fell in love with you when you danced me around a deserted beach in the moonlight to the sound of the stars. Or maybe when you massaged my feet. It could even have been when you pulled coffees all day just to help me out. Whatever. I nearly lost you the first time through a silly misunderstanding and I don't want to lose you again through another one. Is that what you wanted me to tell you?'

Her eyes were huge and her mouth quivered as she waited for his answer.

She loved him.

How could he have been such an idiot as to risk losing her?

He wanted to pull her into his arms and tell her he loved her too and that she was the most amazing woman he'd ever met. That she had become his favourite person in the whole world. That it would be like wrenching out his soul if he couldn't have her in his life. But that was beyond his limited skills as an orator. And he feared she wouldn't welcome his touch. Especially as he was dripping salt water.

'No, it wasn't,' he said. 'You gave me a better answer.'

'What do you mean?' she said, hope struggling to life amid the woeful expression on her face. 'You're talking in riddles, Jesse, and I'm in no mood to try to solve them.'

He took a deep breath. 'I overheard you talking to your ex. You hugged him, kissed him and said: "I will see you in Lyon. For the start of a new life."'

Why the hell hadn't he asked her that directly?

She frowned. 'You were there? Listening?'

'I heard every word of your farewell. Then, when we met up afterwards, I wanted you to tell me what you had meant by that promise to see him in Lyon. Did it mean you were going back to him? That's the conclusion I jumped to. But if you say you love me, I guess you won't be boarding a plane to France any time soon.'

She crossed her arms in front of her. 'I certainly

won't be going back to Philippe. That was never, ever on the cards. Why didn't you just ask me?'

'Because I was a stupid, insecure idiot, too blinded by fear of losing you to think straight. So I'll ask you now. Why *are* you going to France to see your ex-husband?'

'You might be going too,' she said.

'Now you're the one talking in riddles.'

'Let me explain,' she said, uncrossing her arms.

'Please do,' he said. *Man, had he made a mess of this.*

'Philippe asked me to keep this secret for Amy's sake. But you're more important than keeping his confidence. He's getting married and his fiancée wants me and Amy to be there at the wedding next April in Lyon. You're invited too. Actually, I invited you. But Philippe didn't want Amy to know until closer to the time and he asked me not to tell anyone in case she overheard.'

'Your ex is getting married?' That was the last thing he had expected to hear.

'Is it so surprising? People do get remarried, you know. And I'm happy for him.'

'I thought he wanted you back.'

Now her eyes were accusing. 'How could you possibly think I'd go back to him after what you and I have shared together? The…the fairy tale magic. What kind of a woman do you think I am?'

'Obviously one I'm not worthy of,' he said slowly. He tasted regret, bitter and stinging.

All her indignation and anger fled from her face and her eyes softened. She reached up and laid her fingers across his mouth. 'Oh, Jesse, don't say that. After all we've been through to get here.'

He took her fingers in his hand. 'Can you forgive me?'

'If you'll forgive me for keeping secrets from you. I

should have told you straight away about the wedding in Lyon. I love you, Jesse. I couldn't bear to lose you.'

Relief swelled through him. 'That's twice you've told me you love me. Can you give a man a chance to catch up?'

He couldn't wait another second to gather her close to him. She squealed. 'You're wet and cold but I don't care.'

He claimed her mouth in a kiss. 'I love you, Lizzie,' he said, revelling in the sound of the words and how it made him feel to say them. 'I love you, Lizzie,' he repeated. 'That's twice I've said it. We're even.'

She locked her arms around his neck. 'I'm going to tell you how much I love you a lot more times than that. I'm coming to Texas with you. Amy too.'

'You'd leave the café?'

'Funnily enough, though it didn't seem the best job in the world when I came down to Dolphin Bay, I've got attached to it. But not as attached as I am to you. So yes, I'll leave it after training someone else to take over so I don't let Sandy down.'

'You don't have to leave. I'm staying right here in Dolphin Bay.'

'What do you mean?'

'I'm going into business with Ben.'

She frowned. 'Is it what you really want? You're not compromising for my sake? Because if—'

'It's what I really want. I want you too. No more pretending to be "just friends" either. No more being jealous because we're not certain of each other.'

'Jealous? You?'

'You turned me into a jealous guy when I saw you hugging and kissing Philippe.'

She shrugged in that Gallic way. 'It's just a French thing. The kissing. Nothing to be concerned about.'

'I didn't like it.'

'So we're both jealous. Do two people being jealous cancel out the jealousy?'

She was making light of it. But he knew how concerned she was about her jealousy causing problems.

'I have a better idea,' he said. 'Love. Security. Commitment. Knowing the other person is always in your court. That could go a long way to cancelling out the jealousy.'

She went very still. He was aware of the sound of the waves. The thudding of his own heart. 'I…I'm not sure what you're getting at,' she said.

He'd thought about this when he'd been swimming up and down in the surf. How he couldn't bear to be without Lizzie in his life. How he could think of nothing better than making her and Amy his family. How what she needed had become what he needed. 'A wedding ring firmly circling your finger is my idea of a jealousy buster,' he said.

'And a matching one circling yours is mine,' she said. Her wonderful warm laugh rang out across the beach. 'Did you just propose to me, Jesse Morgan?'

'Did you just accept my proposal, Lizzie Morgan to-be?'

'I did,' she said, planting a kiss on his mouth. 'And… and I couldn't be happier.'

'Me too,' he said and kissed her back. His heart actually ached with joy.

She broke away from the kiss. 'You realise there will be a lot of upset people in town when this news leaks out?'

'Who? My family will be delighted.'

'The punters who laid bets you'd never marry.'

'Serves them right for giving you the wrong impression of me and making it so tough for me to win you.'

She smiled. 'I'm glad you changed my mind about that. I love you, Jesse.'

'I love you too,' he said. 'That makes three times we've said it.'

'Shall we try for thirty times before the day is over?'

'Why not?' he said. 'I'll never tire of hearing those words from you.'

EPILOGUE

Two months later

AS A CHILD, Christmas had not been Lizzie's favourite time of year—her family Christmas Days had always seen the sad cliché of every bitterness and conflict getting a good airing over the roast turkey and plum pudding.

As an adult, she had embraced Christmas as a joyous celebration, growing to love festive traditions whether celebrated in the winter of Europe or the Australian summer.

But this year's Christmas was going to be the most magical and memorable of all—because this year Lizzie was celebrating Christmas as a bride.

On Christmas Eve—a perfect sunny south coast morning—Lizzie let Sandy fuss around fixing her hair, which had been braided into a thick plait interwoven with white ribbons and creamy frangipani flowers. In her ears were the exquisite diamond studs Jesse had given her as an early Christmas present.

The sisters were getting ready in a location van parked on the approach to Silver Gull beach. As the most significant moments of their courtship had taken place on beaches, she and Jesse had decided Silver

Gull would be the perfect venue for their exchange of vows.

The location van had been Sandy's idea; she was familiar with such luxuries from her days working on advertising shoots. Lizzie marvelled at the set-up—the interior was like a dressing room complete with mirrors and even a small bathroom. It was the ideal place to prepare for a wedding at a beach.

'Now, let me check the dress,' said Sandy, who was taking her duties as Lizzie's bridesmaid very seriously.

Lizzie was so happy to be getting married to Jesse she hadn't imagined she'd be plagued by any wedding day nerves. Not so. She wasn't worried about the details of the ceremony; they had all been organised by Kate Lancaster, who had done such a marvellous job as wedding planner for Sandy and Ben's wedding. Or about the reception—a small informal affair which was to be held back at Bay Bites. Lizzie's team had all that under control.

No. Lizzie's concern was that she wanted to look beautiful for Jesse.

She did a twirl as best she could in the confines of the van. 'Do you think Jesse will like it?' she asked Sandy, unable to suppress the tremor in her voice. She loved the ankle-length dress for its elegant simplicity: a V-neck tunic in soft off-white tulle lace layered over a silk under-dress and caught in with a flat bow in the small of her back.

'Jesse won't be able to keep his eyes off you,' said Sandy. 'I've never seen a lovelier bride, and I'm not saying that because you're my baby sister. That dress is divine—simple, elegant, discreetly sexy. Just like you.'

Lizzie hugged her. 'You're okay about me marrying Jesse, aren't you?' she asked. 'You warned me off him so many times. But he isn't what people said, you know. He makes me happier than I ever could have imagined.'

She was taken aback by Sandy's burst of laughter. 'Ben and I couldn't be more delighted you two are getting married. You and Jesse are perfect for each other. But you're so stubborn you would have run the other way if I'd told you that. You had to find each other in your own way.'

Lizzie's first reaction was to huff indignantly. But instead she smiled. 'You did me a favour and I'm grateful.' She paused. 'Sisters married to brothers. It's worked out so well for us, hasn't it? Our guys from Dolphin Bay.'

'Yes,' said Sandy. Her hand went protectively to the slight swell of her belly. She and Ben were expecting a baby in six months' time—an event anticipated with much joy by the Morgan clan. 'We're both getting our happily-ever-after endings.'

Then Sandy bustled Lizzie towards the door of the van. 'Come on, bride, your gorgeous groom is waiting for you.'

Lizzie waited at the start of the 'aisle' formed by double rows of seashells that led to a white wooden wedding arch adorned with filmy white fabric and sprays of the small red flowers of the New South Wales Christmas bush. The aquamarine waters of the ocean with the white waves rolling in formed the most glorious backdrop for her wedding ceremony. When she drew in some deep calming breaths, the salt smell of the sea mingled with the sweet scent of the frangipani in her hair.

Both Sandy and Amy, her only attendants, had preceded her down the aisle. They both wore pretty knee-length dresses in a shade of palest coffee. Barista coffee, Lizzie had joked. They were all barefoot, with their toenails painted Christmas red in honour of the festive season.

There was one more thing to do before Lizzie took her journey down the aisle. She laid aside her bouquet of Christmas bush. Then slipped off her diamond engagement ring from the third finger of her left hand and transferred it to her right hand. Jesse had surprised her with the superb solitaire in a starkly simple platinum setting just days after he had proposed to her on this very beach.

She watched as Sandy reached the wedding arch and took her place beside Ben, Jesse's best man. On her other side, Amy held her aunt's hand. Then it was Lizzie's turn to walk down the aisle to get married to Jesse.

The sand either side of the aisle was lined with well-wishers but they were just a blur to Lizzie. She recognised Maura standing by with Amy's adored Alfie and Ben's golden retriever Hobo firmly secured by leashes. But the only face she wanted to see was Jesse's.

And then she was beside him; he was clean-shaven, his black hair tamed, heart-achingly handsome in a stone-coloured linen suit and an open-neck white silk shirt. Any doubts she might have had about him finding her beautiful on her wedding day were dispersed by the look of adoration in his deep blue eyes as he took her hand in his and drew her to his side.

'I love you,' he murmured.

'I love you too,' she whispered.

'That's three thousand and sixty-three times we've said it,' he said.

'And we have a lifetime ahead of us to keep on saying it,' she said, tightening her clasp on his hand.

The celebrant called the guests to order. Before she knew it, they'd exchanged vows and Jesse was slipping the platinum wedding ring on her finger and then her diamond ring on top. 'I declare you man and wife,' said the celebrant.

'Now I can kiss my bride,' said Jesse, gathering her into his arms. 'Mrs Lizzie Morgan.'

Their kiss should have been the cue for classical wedding music to play through the speakers placed strategically near the wedding arch.

But, as Jesse claimed his first kiss as her husband, Lizzie was stunned to hear instead the distinctive notes of Jesse's signature tune rearranged for violin and piano.

'Where did that music come from?' she asked Jesse.

Jesse laughed. 'No idea. But I like it. Now you truly are Jesse's girl.' He kissed her again to the accompaniment of clapping and cheering from their friends and family. 'My wife—the best Christmas present ever.'

* * * * *

She realized that in that instant if there was one thing she wanted as much as to know who she really was, it was Braden.

She ached to feel his hands on her, to feel him inside her, to know what it was like.

"Braden," she said, her voice so thick his name almost didn't come out.

"I feel you," he murmured.

His choice of words at once seemed odd and yet right. He wanted to know her first, but he knew essentially all there was to know about her, the pathetic story of her search for self and place. Maybe part of that search could be answered right now with him. Maybe she was afraid of knowing any more about her past, but she wasn't afraid of this.

To just be a woman at her most basic seemed like the greatest gift on the planet. To stop being guarded, to stop censoring herself, to stop fearing. To just *be*.

* * *

Montana Mavericks:
20 Years in the Saddle!

A VERY MAVERICK CHRISTMAS

BY
RACHEL LEE

MILLS &
BOON®

Published in Great Britain 2014
by Mills & Boon, an imprint of Harlequin (UK) Limited,
Eton House, 18-24 Paradise Road, Richmond, Surrey, TW9 1SR

© 2014 Harlequin Books S.A.

Special thanks and acknowledgement to Rachel Lee for her contribution to the Montana Mavericks: 20 Years in the Saddle! continuity.

ISBN: 978-0-263-91339-2

23-1214

Harlequin (UK) Limited's policy is to use papers that are natural, renewable and recyclable products and made from wood grown in sustainable forests. The logging and manufacturing processes conform to the legal environmental regulations of the country of origin.

Printed and bound in Spain
by CPI, Barcelona

Rachel Lee was hooked on writing by the age of twelve and practiced her craft as she moved from place to place all over the United States. This *New York Times* best-selling author now resides in Florida and has the joy of writing full-time.

**To my family,
who have blessed me in so many ways.**

Chapter One

"I'll meet you there in fifteen minutes," Vanessa said over the phone. "Okay?"

"I'm almost ready," Julie answered, looking around for her boots. "See you." Spying one under the bed, she clicked off the call and made a grab for it.

Going to a Christmas pageant? She wondered if she was losing her mind. All those people… The only thing that was going to be worse was Thanksgiving, right around the corner, a day she was going to spend determinedly by herself.

Trying to feel at home constantly troubled Julie Smith. She had come to Rust Creek Falls nearly six months ago in June, had made a few friends at the Newcomers Club, but she still didn't feel as if she belonged.

But how could she? she wondered as she finished dressing to join her new friends for the Christmas pageant. She had no memory older than four years, and no idea who she was. Julie Smith was a name conveniently tacked to her by the people who had cared for her after the incident that had erased her memory.

But coming out here to Montana to live in this tiny ramshackle cabin sometimes struck her as the ultimate grasping at straws. She looked into the mirror that hung—oddly, she thought—beside her front door and touched the necklace she wore, her only touchstone to her past, gazing at the tarnished coins that hung from it. A specialist in antique coins had told her she was wearing a small fortune around her neck, and that the most recent information he had been able to find about the collection was that it had last been owned by a man in Montana. No name, as collectors preferred to protect their identities, and insurance companies wouldn't give out private information.

So here she was. All because of a necklace and an online blog by someone named Lissa Rourke that had somehow roused a sense of familiarity in her.

Stupid? Maybe. Desperately hunting for a place in this world? Definitely.

For sure, what she found most familiar was the deepening winter. Little enough to cling to.

She smoothed her blue wool sheath over her body and looked at her shoulder-length blond hair. She preferred jeans and Western shirts, and the dress felt awkward. Four years, and she still somehow didn't look right to herself, either. Something was wrong. The hair, she decided, and quickly pulled it back into the ponytail she favored. Better, but the bright blue eyes that stared back at her held no answers to the mystery of who she was. Sometimes she thought she ought to just cut off all her hair, but stopped herself. She'd been able to sell one of her coins, which had given her enough to live on for a while, but that didn't mean she could afford to splurge. Nor did she want to part with another piece of what might be the only clue to her identity.

Sighing, she went to get her coat, wishing she had a longer memory, wishing things in life really seemed to fit somewhere in her experience. But she was woefully inexperienced now. A grown woman with a four-year-old memory. Pathetic. Frustrating.

It struck her, though, as she pulled on her coat, that while Montana was a big state and some conviction that this wasn't the right town kept gnawing at her, things did strike her as familiar. Cowboys. Horses. Even the occasional family name. Those small familiarities kept her here, kept her hoping.

She felt more at home here, if she could feel that at all, than she had at any time since her memory loss.

But what was home? She didn't even know. And if she ever found out who she really was, could she be sure she would feel that other woman was really her? Or would she meet a stranger inside her own head?

Stop it, she told herself. Time to look forward to whatever tonight would bring, and stop peering backward into a black hole.

It had been hard enough to join the Newcomers Club. She suspected she hadn't always been so uncomfortable with people, but how would she know? Going to the pageant tonight had taken some persuasion from her small group of friends. Big groups still overwhelmed her, mainly because she felt out of context. Always out of context and unsure how to react. She didn't have a list of anecdotes to tell about herself in casual conversation, and much of her experience since the amnesia was off-limits. She couldn't bring herself to expose that flaw to anyone.

So she kept quiet, tentatively reacting, speaking only rarely about the most recent events around here, and that left her little enough confidence or conversation. Somehow she had to build enough of a future to have a past.

Because she suspected she might never regain her full memory. As time passed, it became less likely. But maybe she could find at least some snatches of who she had once been.

Maybe someday she'd feel less like she'd been born spontaneously into adulthood.

Headlights flared through the window of the tiny, two-room cabin she rented on the outskirts of town, casting the battered furnishings briefly in harsh light. Her new friends were here.

All she had to do was take one step at a time. Minute by minute, she just had to forge ahead.

It sounded easier than it was. She touched her necklace again before buttoning her coat. It was the only good luck in her new life and her only proof of her past.

Sitting near the front in the auditorium, near Mallory Franklin and her fiancé, Caleb Dalton, Vanessa Brent and Cecelia Clifton, Julie felt mostly uninterested in the show. It was a typical Christmas pageant, although she had no idea how she knew that. But then Mallory's niece, Lily, entered garbed as a darling angel, and the world seemed to stop for Julie.

All of a sudden she had a flash of wearing a similar costume, mouthing similar lines. Then, in an instant, the vision was gone.

She felt herself tremble as she came back to the crowded room, and wondered if she'd had a flash of real memory. Could she have ever played an angel in a Christmas pageant? Soon she realized that the people around her were applauding, and she halfheartedly joined in, trying to paste a smile to her face.

As the applause died away, and everyone waited for the show's little actors to emerge from backstage, Vanessa started talking. She was a tall, lovely woman with curly brown hair and sparkling eyes that for some reason Julie couldn't help but envy.

"I always love Christmastime," Vanessa said. "Don't you, Julie?"

"It's beautiful," Julie answered cautiously. She couldn't understand her reaction to little Lily's angel outfit, or why she still felt shaken.

"We used to have this family tradition," Vanessa continued. "I think I'm going to start it with my family." Over Halloween, Vanessa had gotten engaged to architect Jonah Dalton, and she clearly couldn't wait to begin their new life together.

"What's that?" Julie asked.

"Everyone—siblings, parents, cousins—got holiday pajamas exactly alike. Then on Christmas Eve we'd all gather on the staircase and take a group photo."

"Ooh, I like that," Cecelia said. She tossed her dark hair back over her shoulders. "Mind if I steal it?"

"Help yourself, if you can find the pajamas." Vanessa giggled. "It wasn't always easy."

Mallory spoke. Beside Vanessa she appeared especially petite. She looked ready to jump up from her chair the instant her niece, Lily, appeared. "I think my tradition for a while is going to be making costumes for Lily. She loved this whole pageant idea. But as for family traditions, oh, we had loads. From who did which job decorating the tree to the foods we had for dinner." She smiled at Julie. "What about you?"

"I…" There it was again. Just the big blank that held her back from being a part of all this. "I just loved the season no matter how we celebrated."

"No traditions?"

Julie had to fight an urge to flee. She hadn't told anyone in this town about her amnesia, and this wasn't the place to start. "None that stuck." At least not stuck to her memory.

"Maybe you can start your own," Mallory said, then jumped up and grabbed Julie's arm. "There's Lily. Let's go tell her how wonderful she was." Caleb had already moved toward his soon-to-be daughter. Julie was touched by his eagerness to reach the girl. She wondered what it must have been like to be loved like that…but she couldn't remember.

Lily was a perfect little doll with a mouth that often embarrassed her aunt. She'd been adopted from China by Mallory's sister, who had died. With long, inky hair and almond eyes, she promised to become a stunning beauty.

Except for that costume. Something about it made Julie hesitant to approach. Mallory just kept tugging her closer, and she forced herself to don a smile and get ready to congratulate the little girl.

The Traubs and Daltons were already gathered, telling Lily how beautifully she had done. Julie had already met some of the Daltons through Mallory, but the Traubs were still utter strangers to her. As they approached, Vanessa suddenly poked her gently in the ribs. "Look at who showed up."

"Who?" Julie asked blankly.

"Braden Traub. The last single Traub brother. He's gorgeous enough that I might have given him a second look except I met Jonah. I hear the whole family gives him a hard time about still being a bachelor. Anyway, I guess he managed to come in from the ranch for once."

"But you got Jonah Dalton," Julie said with passable cheer. "Complaints?"

"Absolutely none. I just wish he could be here. Nick, too. You should hear Cecelia complain about her loneliness. The guys are working too hard right now."

"Needs must." Julie attempted to sound light, but she

knew all about loneliness, she figured. She had no one at all. How nice it must be to have someone to miss.

Julie, who, unlike many of the women she had met at the club, hadn't come to Rust Creek looking for the cowboy of her dreams, finally picked out Braden from his family. They all shared similar good looks, but Vanessa was right. He was drop-dead gorgeous.

Apparently, amnesia hadn't deprived her of the ability to feel a quiver of response to a handsome, muscular man with brown hair and eyes that seemed to hold a sparkle. She'd been putting her sexuality on the back burner since her amnesia, for good reason. Her sudden reaction to Braden was almost disheartening. If she didn't know herself, she shouldn't even consider such things. No guy would want her in this condition anyway.

They reached Lily at last, and Julie squatted before the child to tell her how wonderful she'd been. Then before she could stop the words, she said, "When I was five I got to be the angel, too. I was so scared." Where had that come from?

"I wasn't," Lily answered confidently. "It was lots of fun." She beamed at the gathered adults, who all smiled and laughed. As soon as Julie straightened, Lily, clearly feeling like a queen bee at the moment, introduced her to everyone, Traubs and Daltons both, including little Noelle. They plunged into a discussion of past Christmas events, clearly trying to include her in a neighborly way.

Wondering how she could talk about something she didn't really remember, Julie started looking for a graceful escape. She could wait outside until Vanessa was ready to go.

Before she could take a step, Lily spoke again, freezing her. "Julie? I think you should talk to Braden. He hasn't got anybody yet, either."

Mallory gasped. "Lily! I've told you to stop saying embarrassing things to people."

Julie looked down in time to see the girl's face fall into a frown.

"Making friends is good. What's embarrassing?" Lily asked.

Plenty, Julie thought, wanting to sink through the floor.

But Braden pretended nothing had happened. His brother Dallas spoke. "About time you met the recluse, Julie. The last of the living Traub bachelors."

Braden offered his hand with a smile, and Julie reluctantly took it. His palm felt warm and callused, but it had more of an impact than a simple handshake should. Her urge to flee grew. She couldn't risk wanting a man, or becoming involved with one. But nothing about him suggested he was feeling anything more than friendly. Oddly enough, given her state of mind, that almost disappointed her.

"Nice to meet you, Julie. Don't listen to Dallas. I'm not a recluse at all."

"No, you just bury yourself in work."

"Only because you guys are so busy romancing the ladies. Or were." Braden released Julie's hand but continued to smile at her. "Why don't you join us at the Triple-T for our after party, and maybe we can get past the Lily-inspired awkwardness."

"What's awk...awkness?" Lily's question dissolved everyone into laughter, breaking any tension that remained.

"Seriously," Braden said. "You don't want to miss the after-show fun. Mallory? How about you and Caleb come, too?"

"I've got to get this little hellion home to bed," Mallory answered. "Sorry to miss out." She turned to Julie. "You really should go. A lot of people will be there, and it's always a great time. Vanessa can take you, or I can drop you to get your own car."

"I'll think about it," Julie said, while firmly convinced that she was going to bolt. Then she met Braden's friendly gaze again. Or maybe not.

She had apparently recovered a memory tonight. Maybe getting out more into larger groups would jar something loose.

With her heart in her throat, she agreed to go. But only for a short visit, she promised herself.

Braden knew his brothers were going to rib him about inviting Julie to the Triple-T, but he was so used to being ribbed about his dating life—or lack thereof—that he really didn't care. He'd dated before, he'd date again when the time was right. Just now it didn't feel right.

But something about Julie Smith had managed to reach out to him. For some weird reason, she made him feel like she needed a protector. Yeah, she was beautiful all right, but with an aura of innocence that cried out for shelter. And something else, something uneasy. Julie Smith was not a truly happy young woman, and that affected him.

She touched him, striking some kind of responsive chord, and it wasn't just those huge blue eyes, her soft face, her great figure. Those things were just a package, and at thirty-four, Braden wasn't often deceived by the packaging. He'd managed to learn a few lessons over the years.

But he'd always been a sucker for someone or something that needed protecting, whether a friend or a new foal. He could be all wrong about her, but he supposed he'd figure that out quickly.

At first he left her pretty much alone among the family and friends at the Triple-T. A party was underway, and he was one of the hosts. But he kept seeking her out with his eyes, and every time he noticed how uncomfortable she looked. The folks in his home were all friendly, but apparently, as a newcomer, she felt awkward. In fact, she looked as if she wished she could melt into the walls. He was sure people weren't trying to ignore her or make her feel out of place. Instead, she seemed to be creating her own bubble, emerging only when she had to so she could return a greeting or shake a hand. Welcomed but not feeling it.

His curiosity about her began to grow. She was definitely *not* just another one of the women who had showed up here hoping to find a husband as they rebuilt the town after the flood. Not to say all those women were bad or anything. But this one seemed to be looking for escape more than company.

Curiosity might be his worst failing, he thought with some amusement as he realized he was steadily circling through the room toward her. He just loved a mystery.

He amused himself even more because he'd seen this woman around town a few times but had never felt the least urge to meet her, until tonight. Ah yes, mystery. Well, he'd try to find out what it was, kill his curiosity and move on. Things were too hectic on the ranch with all his brothers distracted by their families and girlfriends for him to spare the time for much more anyway.

He saw his parents get to her first. It was mostly a family party, and apparently they didn't want her to feel like a loose end. As he drew nearer, he heard them greeting her as if she were some kind of celebrity guest, glad she had taken the time to join them, hoping she would visit often. They even threw in a little matchmaking of their own, extolling Braden's virtues.

And Julie, whether they knew it or not, was beginning to look almost frightened. What the hell?

His parents moved on finally, and he prepared to step in. Whatever was going on, he didn't want her scared.

She started to walk around the room, looking at family pictures on the dark wood wall. His opening, if he could catch up to her. He didn't miss the fact that she was drawing ever closer to Vanessa, who was her escape route.

He quickened his step and caught her finally as she stopped to look up at the portrait of his grandfather.

"My grandfather," he said to her.

She started, then looked at him with those huge blue eyes. "You have a big family."

"Yeah. When I was a kid, I sometimes wished I was an only child. Now everyone's moved out with their new families and when I stay here, I sometimes feel like I'm rattling around in this place."

She gave a tentative laugh.

"What about you?" he asked. "Large family?"

"Only child."

The brevity of her response invited no more questions, but he was determined. "Parents?"

"Gone."

God, he thought, that was sad. She was truly alone. Friends couldn't make up for the absence of family, something he'd learned as his brothers moved out to be with their brides and girlfriends. "I'm sorry."

Just then Dallas appeared at his side, having left his wife Nina to talk to their mother, and bumped his shoulder. "Coon dog smelling possum?" he asked.

"Damn it, Dallas." Some women wouldn't appreciate that kind of rough humor. "Go back to your wife and lay off."

Dallas simply grinned.

Braden glared at him then turned to apologize to Julie. Too late. In just those few moments, she'd managed to reach Vanessa. The two women were talking, and Vanessa nodded. They were leaving.

"Strike out?" Dallas asked.

"I'll never know, you big idiot. You scared her off."

"Looked to me like you were doing a pretty good job of that yourself."

Braden paused. Had he been?

His instinct told him to go to the door to say goodnight, but Dallas's words held him back. That woman didn't need any more scaring. Instead, he watched as his parents bade the women good-night and made them promise to come back again soon.

"Damn it," he said again.

"You can always invite her to help at Presents for Patriots. Innocent enough."

"I don't need your advice."

"Wanna bet?" Dallas asked.

Braden realized the room had nearly emptied. It looked even emptier with most of the furniture moved back against the walls to make room. The gals had apparently gone to the kitchen to help with cleanup. That left the merciless crew of Sutter, Dallas, and Collin to stand around with him, converging like vultures who spied a meal. They'd tussled and teased with each other since their earliest days, and Braden didn't need a map to know what he was in for now. He'd actually talked to a single woman.

"Brother Braden," Sutter said, "has the hots for a cute little blonde."

It was hopeless, but Braden argued anyway. Silence might only make it worse. "I was just trying to make her feel welcome here. I said maybe a half dozen words to her."

"Yeah, but it was all about what was in your eyes," Collin retorted.

"Since when did you read eyes?"

Dallas snorted a laugh. "Since you started broadcasting. About time you looked at a woman that way. Stuck here all by yourself as a bachelor. Mom and Dad are worried."

"Mom and Dad are less worried than you four. What is it about people who get married? They want everyone to join them? Doesn't matter if you're happy or not?"

"You don't know if you'd be happy," Clay remarked. "You never stuck with anyone long enough."

"Because I wasn't happy."

"I think you should go for that woman," Dallas opined. "Get on your horse and ride over to her place and make her swoon at the sight of a real cowboy."

Braden reached for a throw pillow from one of the couches and threw it at him. "I don't think she's in the market for a cowboy. Besides, I'm not in the market, either. Now will you just lay off? I was trying to be courteous."

Of course it didn't end there. It never did. His brothers continued to razz him until the his mom and the growing crowd of his sisters-in-law and soon-to-be sisters-in-law reappeared. He took a few more verbal jabs, but the presence of the ladies toned them down.

And that, thought Braden, was a good reason not to get involved with a woman. Next thing you knew, you'd be leaving your boots outside the door and turning all proper-like.

That was just an excuse and he knew it. His brothers changed a bit around their ladies because with them they could show a different side, a gentler side, than they did with each other.

A good thing, he supposed. But sometimes he really did feel like the odd man out, now that they'd all found their mates. Hell, he was the last man standing. The thought brought a wry smile to his lips.

But he was sure his interest in Julie Smith had entirely to do with the aura of mystery around her and nothing to do with how pretty she was. He almost asked if anyone knew anything about her, but stopped himself just in time.

He could take the razzing, but right now he didn't feel like taking it about Julie. She'd reached some place inside him that he didn't want anyone else to touch.

Some dangerously protective place, which meant keeping his brothers out of this as much as possible. More remarks like the one Dallas had made tonight, and Julie Smith might vanish from town as suddenly as she had arrived.

Later, though, in a quiet moment as he was getting ready to sleep in his old bedroom rather than head over to his own place, his mother spoke to him.

"Braden?"

"Yeah?" He had one foot in the doorway of his bedroom.

"That Julie Smith."

He tensed. "Mom…"

"Just listen to me. She's very pretty and seems very nice. I know Vanessa, Mallory and Cecelia all like her. But no one knows anything about her, really. So, while I'd like to see you settled and happy…"

He looked into the face that had loved him since birth and turned to give her a big hug. "I'll be careful, Mom. I always have been, much to your disappointment."

Ellie Traub laughed. "Maybe. I'm surprised she hasn't dated while she's been here. And it's not for want of guys asking, I believe."

"She's a wounded bird, Mom. That's all. I just want to know what's going on."

Ellie's smile faded. "That's dangerous, Braden."

"I know."

"Just be careful. If I'd known how you were going to turn out, I'd probably have named you Parsival."

"Thank God you didn't." He laughed. "I'm no knight errant on a quest, just a frustrated detective."

"I hope you're right." She put a hand on his shoulder and drew him close for a kiss on his cheek. "Good night, my boy."

He watched her disappear toward her room then entered his own and closed the door. The woman who'd earlier been acting as if the answer to her prayers had arrived that night was now cautioning him.

He didn't miss her point. Not at all.

Chapter Two

For the next few days, Julie felt as if the inside of her head had become a huge jumble. Her memory, if that's what it was, of being an angel in a Christmas pageant when she was young, was really niggling her.

She pulled up that flash over and over, trying to wring every possible detail out of it that she could. Standing on stage, wings on her back, scanning a sea of faces trying to find her parents and not seeing them.

"Damn," she cussed out loud. If that was a real memory, why couldn't she see her parents?

But even if she had, could she rely on what she thought she remembered? She'd had some counseling since the amnesia, but it had mostly been pithy claims about how she just had to trust her memory, such as it was, and perhaps her past would return to her.

Trust it? She couldn't even be sure it was a true memory. It might have been some kind of daydream, resulting from a desperate need to fill in the huge hole her past had become.

But maybe, just maybe, there was some link in her head with the holidays. She should make more of an effort to enjoy the season as it ramped up. Maybe it would jar some more memories loose for her. Maybe little shards would grow into big pieces.

But somehow, one little girl in an angel costume had

managed to throw her entire being into some kind of blender. Conviction and doubt warred within her, alongside hope and despair.

Then there was Braden Traub. She told herself he'd just been being nice to her, but he might as well have warning flags all over him. For the first time since she lost her memory, she felt attracted to a man. Seriously attracted. Forgotten urges had wakened in an instant. Dangerous, because she had no memory. She was sure that the instant a guy found out she was amnesiac, he'd head for the hills. But apart from that, she was a babe in the woods. No memory to guide her about dealing with men. About dating.

Hell, she couldn't even carry on much of a conversation unless it was about the last few months. So why take a risk?

She sighed and rubbed her aching head. Again and again she had been warned about trying to force her memory, but she kept trying anyway. Desperation gnawed at her.

Like looking at those family portraits at the Triple-T. She'd hoped one of them would jog her in some way, but none of them had. Instead, all they had done was make her feel even lonelier. She didn't even have one photo tied to her past.

But then, she didn't even know what had happened to her. The doctors theorized she might have been mugged or had an accident, but she'd been found wandering with nothing to show for her experience except a cracked skull and no memory. And her necklace. Her talisman.

And a desire for cold and snow that had led her to New England, where she'd met the man who had researched her necklace and told her the last owner had lived in Montana. Then she'd come across that blog and felt drawn here like a homing pigeon.

But what did any of that mean? Again, she was without context. In some ways that was the most frustrating thing of all: urges and impulses that drove her without having any idea why.

If she couldn't explain herself to herself, how could she explain herself to anyone?

When she realized she was thoroughly cleaning the cabin again for the third time in as many days, she stopped and tried to give herself a wake-up call.

One of the two rooms she was working so hard on was a bathroom. Otherwise the cabin contained a larger room that held a small kitchen at one corner, an alcove beside the bathroom where she had a bed, and a beastly woodstove that terrified her because she'd never had to use one before, at least not that she could remember. As winter deepened, she prayed the power would stay on, because if it didn't the heater wouldn't work and she was going to get very cold. Maybe she should buy a kerosene space heater, although those were dangerous, too.

Sighing, she rubbed her temples. For three days she hadn't gone out her front door, not since the party at the Triple-T. What was with her? The town was familiar enough now that she felt all right when she walked the streets and shopped. The woods around the cabin were like a personal cathedral for her, offering peace and serenity. So what was she doing being a hermit?

She stuffed her feet into her warm winter boots and pulled her parka off the peg. A bracing walk would do her good, clearing out cobwebs and probably settling her frantic ramblings. The winter snow was not yet deep, although she had been warned that it would get there soon enough. For now, though, she could walk in the woods or into town.

She locked up the cabin behind her, then hesitated on the stoop. The woods or town? She needed a few things from the grocery, and increasingly she had a desire to find some splash of color to add to the cabin. The inside of it was almost dismal; age had faded everything so much. A throw pillow or two, or maybe just a small throw she could wrap herself in when it became drafty. The bedding was her only addition, and sadly she'd chosen a wintry look that right now didn't help at all.

Why did winter call to her anyway? What she needed as the days grew shorter, colder and darker, were some really bright colors.

God, she couldn't even bring herself to put a mark on the place where she lived. She seemed to spend all her time feeling as if she might have to bolt at any moment, a purely ridiculous idea. Certainly no one had made her feel that way.

She figured she'd winter in this town then perhaps move on again if she unlocked nothing about herself. That, she thought, was her real problem: trying on places and people, then hitting the road to search for the key to her memory.

But how could she put down roots? She had two huge fears: that she might plant herself in the wrong place and thus lose any chance of finding out who she was, and that she'd find out and not like what she learned. Given that those were polar opposites, she sometimes wondered what the heck she was doing.

She turned toward the woods then changed her mind. If nothing else, she could bring at least one piece of cheer into that cabin. Maybe something Christmasy, given her reaction to Lily's costume. Maybe Christmas held some kind of key for her.

She'd bought a battered, secondhand car with some of the money she'd received for the sale of her coin, and she climbed into the blue monster now in case the day turned colder, or in case she actually splurged on something besides a few groceries. A Christmas tree? But then she'd have to decorate it.

Shaking her head at her own indecision, she turned over the ignition. This heap might not look like much, but it had turned out to be amazingly reliable so far. Probably the good thing about buying locally. The garage owner had a reputation to maintain in a relatively small town.

She was driving up Cedar toward the Crawford General Store when she spied that psychic Winona Cobbs, her white hair flying in the breeze. That woman made Julie uneasy, although she wasn't sure exactly why. When Winona had given a talk back in August about listening to inner voices, she'd seemed slightly dotty but not crazy. Afterward, as Julie had been drawn forward to meet the woman, she had felt an almost electric zap. In that instant Winona had snapped her head around, looked at her then shrugged and returned to her conversation.

Whatever it was that had happened, Julie had no desire to repeat the experience. It had been weird, even creepy.

On a weekday morning, finding parking near the General Store was easy. Julie slid into a spot then pondered exactly what she intended to do there. Most folks here drove to Kalispell for major shopping, but the General Store had a bit of everything. She could not only get a few chicken breasts and veggies for dinner the next few nights, but she could also wander through a miserly selection of Western clothing and even some decorator items. She was almost positive she could find a pillow and a throw in here, although she'd have a bigger selection in Kalispell.

That didn't entice her to pull out. Small things that mattered very little weren't enough to drag her to a bigger town. Her needs, both psychological and physical, could be met here.

At least until she decided she needed to move on again.

Shaking her head at herself, she climbed out and headed into the store. Although it hadn't been destroyed in the flood last year, some repairs had obviously been necessary regardless, because the store had clearly been freshly painted not that long ago. It was certainly jammed with merchandise. The Crawford family was doing their best to give people a reason to shop locally.

She didn't get two steps inside the door before she was greeted by Nina Crawford Traub.

"Nice to see you, Julie. Can I help you find something?"

"Groceries, eventually, but I'm looking for a little color to add to my place."

"I can help with that," Nina said cheerfully. "Got a whole bunch of new Christmas stuff in."

Which would be useless in little more than a month, Julie thought as she followed Nina. On the other hand, she *was* wondering if Christmas might hold some kind of key for her.

Nina finally waved her hand expansively at an area clearly marked out for the holiday season. Thanksgiving items were marked down as the big day was nearly upon them. Christmas colors shrieked from a heaped table and some nearby racks.

"Christmas tree decorations are in the back." Nina pointed to her right, then her left. "If you want nonseasonal, look over there. Call if you need me."

A pretty impressive display for such a relatively small space, Julie thought as she began to wander around the table. Stockings, pillows, tree skirts, even some holiday-themed costume jewelry. Someone had tried to hit every possibility, including a basket of inexpensive stocking stuffers.

But nothing struck her. Nothing touched her. Nothing seemed to jar anything within her. Well, if she was going to spend any money at all on brightening the place, she guessed the nonseasonal area would be the place to look.

She was just fingering a bright blue throw, almost electric in its brilliance, when a familiar voice caused her to freeze.

"Hi," said Braden Traub. Then when she didn't immediately answer, "I'm sorry. I didn't mean to intrude."

Suddenly galvanized, embarrassed by what might appear to be rudeness, she turned and saw him half smiling at her. "You're not," she blurted, once again struck by how attractive he was. He wore a shearling jacket with gloves hanging out of the pockets, jeans and boots. An iconic man most women would drool over. She hoped she avoided that embarrassment.

"I tore up a couple of shirts over the last week," he said casually as if he didn't mind starting a conversation in the middle. "Damn barbed wire. So I'm replacing them. That's a pretty color you're looking at there."

She glanced at the soft wool fabric between her fingers. "Yes, it is." Then she made an effort. "I need to brighten my place up a little."

"You're at the old cabin outside town, right?"

"Yes."

"It needs brightening," he agreed. "I haven't been in there for a few years, but it needed some back then, too."

"Um…"

"Yes?" he said encouragingly.

"How could you tear shirts on barbed wire? Did it cut through your jacket?"

His smile widened. "No jacket. I was dealing with some rolls in the barn and got careless. I'm lucky I didn't need stitches."

"Shirts might cost almost as much." It pleased her immensely when he laughed.

"There is that," he agreed. "And the fact that I was careless more than once. I ought to know better."

"I hope they were old shirts."

"On their last legs. Are you thinking about decorating for Christmas? I could help you get a tree to your place."

She blinked. A man whose own brothers claimed he was a recluse was offering to help her get a tree and bring it to her cabin? Then it struck her they might have been joking. "You and your brothers joke a lot."

Surprise widened his dark eyes a bit, then he laughed again as he apparently caught her reference. "Oh, you mean what Dallas said about me being a recluse. Yeah, we joke a lot. The teasing is merciless. That's the only thing I don't mind about them all being at their own places now. It's so dang peaceful."

She felt a smile begin to dawn on her own face. "Things can be too peaceful."

"Well, sometimes, but they come back often enough to keep me on my toes. I think they'll all calm down when they have their own little Noelles."

"That's your niece? She's so cute."

"I think so, but I'm biased. Well, let me know if you need help with anything. I'm going to be in town for a few hours." He started to turn away then paused. "Are you coming to the church to help with gift wrapping for the troops?"

"I've already promised Vanessa I will."

"Great. See you there." Then he paused again. "Unless you'd like to get some coffee when you're done here?"

The invitation completely startled her. She'd been asked out a few times since she arrived here and had turned down all the offers. But it felt different to be casually asked for coffee. Part of her wanted to flee, because it was so tiring to conceal all the gaps in her memory, but another part of her wanted to keep looking at him, listening to him.

Becoming a hermit, she told herself sternly, wasn't going to do the least thing to solve her problem. In fact, it might hinder her.

"I'd love coffee," she answered, hoping her hesitation hadn't been too noticeable.

"Great!" His smile widened again. "How long do you need?"

"Well, I have to pick out…" She stopped herself. Delaying tactics weren't going to help anything. "I need to grab some groceries. Nothing that won't keep in the car for a while. Twenty minutes?"

"Twenty minutes. Just enough time for me to pick and pay for my shirts. See you at checkout."

She envied him his easiness, his ability to seem comfortable in his own skin. She often hoped she didn't look as skittish and frightened as she sometimes felt.

On impulse, she grabbed the electric-blue throw and a couple of red, glittery Christmas pillows, both with angels on them. Cost be hanged, she thought as she headed over to the groceries. Color seemed imperative now, and it was apt to get more so as the winter deepened and darkened.

Coffee with the mystery lady, Braden thought, feeling as if he'd just made a huge leap. Of course, if anyone saw him having coffee with Julie Smith, the teasing was going to go through the roof.

Oh, well. He was used to it. Being the last Traub bachelor in town had not only increased the teasing, but had taught him that he seemed to be under some kind of local microscope, too. All the women who had come into town in a veritable wave looking for husbands had added to the local curiosity about a guy who seemed impervious to all those wiles.

He could just imagine what some folk suspected, although he didn't really care. When the right woman came along, well… It was as his mother had once said, "Dating is a series of no, no, no until you finally get to yes." Well, he'd had a few nos, enough to realize that dating could be a huge investment. Better to be picky before you really got started.

He pulled four plain Western shirts off the rack, glad that he hadn't given in to a whim to go to Kalispell for a few hours. All he'd wanted were work shirts, and now he was going to have coffee with Julie Smith. His curiosity quickened again. At the very least he wanted to know why such a beautiful young woman seemed to hang back in some very noticeable ways.

Sort of like him, he thought humorously. Maybe she had some bad romances in her past.

"Stocking up again," said Nina as she checked him out. "You're hard on shirts, Braden Traub. Dallas takes better care than you do."

"Blame it on the barbed wire."

Nina rolled her eyes. Once his shirts were in a paper bag, he saw Julie approaching with a cart that contained two red throw pillows, the electric-blue blanket she'd been admiring, and some packaged chicken breasts, frozen vegetables and a couple of potatoes.

Bachelor fare, he thought as he stood back and waited. And given how cold it was outside, sunshine notwithstanding, if she put everything in her trunk, it would probably freeze before she got home.

Assuming he could keep her from bolting before she'd spent ten minutes with him.

God, she was pretty. Each time he looked at her, he felt it anew. And it wasn't just those big blue eyes, blond hair or figure. It was an aura of, well, innocence. She reminded him of a lamb exploring the world for the first time, trying bravely and then showing huge timidity at something startlingly new. But she had to be somewhere in her early twenties, and that didn't seem to fit with the whole innocence thing. More innocent than he was, certainly, but not a child.

He hoped he'd find out something about her. If he could quiet his curiosity, maybe he wouldn't feel so drawn to her, and he could safely escape another entanglement doomed for failure.

He offered to help with her bags, although he was sure she could have carried them herself. Manners had been ingrained at an early age. A kind of old-fashioned chivalry, judging by much of what he saw of the world today. He had no doubt, however, that Nina would report back to Dallas, and he'd take another round of ribbing. Sometimes this town could be too small.

She blushed, but let him take a couple of the bags and carry them to her car. Then she lowered the boom he'd half expected.

"I should get this food home and into a refrigerator."

Braden didn't often give anyone a hard time, but some stubbornness reared in him. "It's freezing out here. You put the chicken and frozen vegetables in your trunk, and it'll stay colder than it would in your fridge while we have coffee. Not the potatoes, though. Don't want them to freeze."

In the bright morning sunlight, with the air as clear as fresh-washed glass, she looked even prettier. He saw emotions chase across her face, and she bit her lip.

"It's just coffee," he said gently.

"Just coffee," she repeated. Then, at long last, "Okay."

"Let's go to Daisy's donut shop on North Broomtail," he prodded gently. "You can bring your own car and run as soon as you need to."

Her face darkened in a way that told him he'd said exactly the wrong thing, but then, making an effort, she smoothed it over. "Sure. I'll see you there."

Wondering if she'd even show up, he went over to his mud-splashed truck, climbed in and left it to her to follow. He wasn't going to force himself on any woman, even for a chance to talk.

After Braden drove off, Julie dithered in her car for a few minutes, letting it warm up. Well, that was her excuse anyway. Braden appealed to her, undeniably. She felt a jolt of sexual awareness every time she saw him. But was that enough to take this kind of risk?

What did she have to talk to him about? Her few months here in Rust Creek? His family, whom she did not really know? Maybe she could ask enough questions to keep him talking. But what if he asked questions?

She sat like a terrified rabbit for maybe five minutes until she realized the heat was blasting in her face, and if Braden was waiting for her, she was being rude. He'd helped her load her car. He must be wondering why she hadn't followed right away. That's what any normal woman would have done, wasn't it?

She put the car in gear and headed for the donut shop.

There'd be other people there, limiting their topics of conversation, she assured herself. Besides, as she'd been arguing to herself this morning, being a hermit was unlikely to get her any closer to the answers she wanted.

Stupid, she thought, to so desperately want to know about her past yet be equally frightened of finding out. Normal reaction, the psychologist had said, but how could anyone really know what was normal for someone who'd lost all memory of her past until she woke in a hospital unable to even remember her name? Her kind of retrograde amnesia was extremely rare, so rare that at first the doctors hadn't seemed to believe her.

Some memory loss happened. Total memory loss was in a class of its own, evidently.

It didn't take long to reach the donut shop. Braden's truck was there, and she glimpsed him through the window. He waved when he saw her pulling in. The gesture warmed her a bit, and took the edge off her nerves. At least her knees didn't feel like rubber as she climbed out and walked toward the door. She'd get through this, the way she had gotten through everything so far.

She had certainly gotten through a lot. Her memory of the last four years, short though it was, reminded her that she was made of sterner stuff than she sometimes thought. Maybe she should congratulate herself on getting this far, instead of fearing the next twenty minutes.

But his remark about her being able to run as soon as she wanted returned to her, and she wondered if she was giving everyone the impression that she wanted to bolt. Well, sometimes she did. Sometimes she seriously wanted to bolt from this whole situation. But where could she go? This was one of those things she would take with her wherever she went. No escape.

To her surprise, Braden opened the door for her. She

hadn't expected that, just walking into a coffee shop. His smile was welcoming, his voice kind as he teased, "I thought I'd lost you."

His eyes were warm, just like his smile, and she felt some inner tension let go. "I just warmed up the car a bit. The guy I bought it from said I shouldn't make a habit of running with a cold engine."

"Good advice, usually. You can see how well I pay attention to it."

He motioned her to the booth, and she loosened her coat.

Braden remained on his feet until she slid into the bench facing where he'd been sitting. Only then did he sit facing her. "I'm going to have a latte," he said. "Don't let anybody know. I'll be hearing from my brothers how I need to drink *real* coffee. The manly stuff."

More of her tension seeped away, and she laughed. "Grow-hair-on-your-chest coffee, huh?"

"Something like that, although that day is long past. Did you ever wonder why they tell you coffee will stunt your growth when you're young, and then when you get older it'll make you manly?"

She laughed again. "No, sorry. Wrong gender."

His head tipped a little, a laugh escaped him, then he leaned toward her a bit, his eyes dancing. "The things your gender has spared you. What will you have? My treat, and the sky's the limit."

She looked up at the menu hanging over the counter. "I'll have the mocha cinnamon latte," she decided, then nearly patted her own back for finding it so easy to order. So natural. Some things didn't feel at all natural to her anymore. So maybe her previous self had liked that kind of coffee?

Pointless question.

Braden called the waitress over. "Candy? When you have a sec?"

She returned her attention to Braden as he ordered for them, adding a couple of blueberry muffins. "I hope you like them," he said to her as the waitress walked away.

"I do," she admitted. Then a thought occurred to her. He'd called the waitress by name. "Do you know everyone in town?"

"Certainly not you," he said lightly. Then more seriously, "No, I don't know everyone. We've had a lot of new people come to help with the floods and other things."

"And you're very busy at the ranch?" Keep asking questions, don't give him a chance to pry.

"These days, yes. My brothers are busy with their personal lives. They have their own businesses and families to take care of these days. Can't say I blame them."

Her smile came easily. "Me neither. Which is how you came to be wrestling with barbed wire?"

He grinned. "Exactly. And wrestling is a good term for it. Are you ready for our winter?"

The change of subject seemed abrupt, but at least she could answer truthfully. "I love winter."

"Maybe not winters here so much. We get dang cold. Where'd you come from?"

"New England." Which was truthful insofar as it went. "Part of what drew me out here was the idea of snow-capped mountains. Real mountains. And Lissa Roarke's blog, of course. Though I gather she's now Lissa Christensen." Julie had learned from local gossip that Lissa had married her own Rust Creek cowboy, Sheriff Gage Christensen, a few months after her arrival in town last year.

"I never had much time to read her blog," he said, leaning back as the waitress, Candy, served them. He thanked her. "I hope she didn't make us seem overly romantic."

"Depends on what you mean by romance. I just knew I wanted mountains and snow, and this place sounded friendly."

"Do you ski?"

She blinked. A blank wall answered that question. "Not really," she hedged.

"Most people who like snow do. Just asking. I don't have a lot of time for it, myself, but if I can arrange it, I like cross-country. I don't need a slope and don't have to risk permanent disability."

He was cute, she thought, and he made it so easy to laugh. She wanted to keep her guard up, but she was beginning to feel safe with him. For now, at least. Growing warm, she slipped the coat off her shoulders and reached for her coffee.

"Want me to cut the muffins up?" he asked.

"It might make it easier."

Again that twinkle in his eyes. "Depends on who's eating and where." But he unwrapped the flatware that was rolled in the napkin and cut the two muffins into bite-size pieces. Crumbs tumbled all over the plate, but he didn't seem concerned.

"That's an interesting necklace you're wearing," he said, pushing the plate toward her in invitation. "It looks old."

"It is," she admitted. She at least knew something about it for certain. "It's an heirloom." She reached for a piece of muffin and pulled a napkin out of the dispenser to place it on, while she tensed for the next question.

"It's nice to have something like that," he said, picking a piece of muffin for himself. "I like things that pass down through the generations. They create a great sense of connection."

A cowboy philosopher, she thought, and wondered

what he'd think if he knew that necklace was her *only* connection. Probably find an excuse to head back to his ranch and pretend they'd never met.

She picked up her coffee, nearly hiding behind it, wondering why she was so ashamed of her amnesia. It wasn't some kind of personal failing. She'd been severely injured, probably in some awful accident, and should just be grateful to be alive. Why did she feel so embarrassed by it?

Because she wasn't normal. She wasn't anything approaching normal. Missing a limb was more normal than missing your entire past, and most people would probably think she was making it up, or crazy in some way. *That* was the problem. Her dirty little secret.

"I've never experienced winter in New England," he said when he'd swallowed more muffin and coffee. "I wonder how it compares."

"I can't answer. This is my first time here."

Again that devastating grin came to his face. "Maybe we should track the weather this winter and compare the two places. Betcha we get colder."

Remembering the last winter, she felt a smile play around her mouth. "I wouldn't be so sure. We got pretty darn cold last winter. Colder than normal, though." She knew that because she'd heard it countless times.

"Then maybe we beat you in the snow department." When she didn't answer immediately, he winked. "Say, aren't you willing to get into an argument about whose home has the worst winter?"

"You might have better luck with your brothers."

He laughed with pure pleasure. "Good one. Points for you."

She felt her cheeks warm at his approval. Maybe this would become easier.

"You seem thick as thieves with Vanessa."

"She's great. She and Mallory and Cecelia and Callie. They've all been wonderful to me. And I just adore little Lily."

"She's easy to adore, although I suppose I should defend the Traub honor and claim that for Noelle."

"She's adorable, too."

"I just hope she doesn't grow up quite as mouthy as Lily. That girl! Whatever pops into her head comes out of her mouth. I actually like it. Caleb does too except for when it seems to bother Mallory."

"She'll grow out of it. I kind of like knowing where I stand with her."

"Until she tries some matchmaking."

Julie's cheeks flamed. "That *was* a little awkward."

"Actually, it might have been a good idea."

Julie froze. The urge to flee warred with the urge to stand her ground and not look like a fool by running.

"People *do* need friends," he said as if he didn't notice her reaction. Maybe he hadn't. "So, that kind of ended the awkwardness. Then she was so cute when she couldn't say that word."

"She was," Julie said around a thick tongue.

"I guess I shouldn't have brought it up." He looked out the window. "Winona Cobbs keeps saying we're going to get a heckuva blizzard soon. One to remember. I wonder if she's right."

At last, a topic that made Julie feel safe. "Do you believe her predictions? I don't know why, but she makes me a little uneasy."

He returned his attention to her. "We're at the time of year for blizzards. I won't put much stock in a prediction like that unless it flies in the face of meteorology. As for being uneasy around her…well, some folks are. She's essentially a harmless, nice person, but when those eyes settle on you, it's possible to feel like she sees your soul."

Remembering the strange electric tingle she had felt when Winona fixed her gaze on her, Julie could only nod. "There's something about her…"

"Which is why some people listen more than maybe they should. But she means well, I'll give her that. If she's psychic, I don't really know, but she's not cheating widows out of the life insurance, if you get me."

Julie didn't know. She had no memory of psychics. "What do you mean?" she dared to ask.

"Oh, there are some scam artists around who'll charge an arm and a leg to give you some ridiculous reading. Never knew one, just read about them. At least we don't have one of them around here. Winona gets paid for speaking, but never charges for any information she volunteers. To my way of thinking, that makes her honest, even if it doesn't necessarily make her right."

Julie nodded, stuffing some more of the blueberry muffin in her mouth, savoring it then washing it down with her latte. "Great flavor combination," she said after dabbing her lips with a napkin. She didn't want to gossip about local people, even if gossip sometimes seemed to be a favorite pastime. She was willing to listen, but talking was a dangerous thing. There was no way to know, if she said something wrong, whether it would come back to haunt her. And sometimes she feared she simply didn't know what the wrong things to say might be. She seemed to have retained most of her skills from her past, but she couldn't be sure, without memory, how many of them were working right.

"So where in New England are you from?" Braden asked.

At once she tensed, and her mouth started to dry out.

Now would come the questions she couldn't answer because there were no answers. At least she knew the last place she had lived. "Outside Boston, in a town called Worcester."

"I always liked the way that word doesn't sound like it's spelled. I had a terrible time when I was a kid learning to say *Worcestershire*, that sauce. Love it on my steaks. Anyway, mastering that one took long enough that my brothers were merciless. I think I finally got it."

"I'd say so."

"You must be missing your friends."

She felt her face start to freeze. Time to go, before he grew too personal. "I moved a lot," she said finally, glancing at her watch. "And I really need to go."

"So soon?" He studied her. "I said something wrong."

"No, really. I just have some other things I need to do." Like examine her own head, explain to herself why she'd been stupid enough to accept this invitation, even if the guy awoke her entire sexual being. What the hell was she thinking? Yes, she needed to be out more and talk to more people if she was ever going to jog her memory, but her few friends here had stopped asking most questions a while back. A new person meant more questions, and each question caused her to evade and face the blank wall all over again.

"I wasn't trying to pry," he said, lifting his hand for the waitress. When she came over, he asked her to put both coffees in takeout cups, and the blueberry muffin remains in a bag.

Afterward, he passed the bag to Julie. "Sorry I cut it into mostly crumbs. I thought we had a little longer. It's been great getting to know you. Thanks for the company, Julie."

"Thank you for the coffee and muffin." She stood and

pulled her coat on quickly, not so quickly that she appeared to be in headlong flight, she hoped.

He stood, too, offering to shake her hand. She took it reluctantly, and once again met those brown eyes. They seemed to hold some kind of understanding, although what he was understanding she couldn't imagine. She was acting like a nut.

"See you soon," he said, and let her make her way out on her own. He watched her get into her car and drive off, and it wasn't until she was out of town and nearing her cabin that she realized just how tense she had become; that reaction was making her shake.

One man, one coffee, a few casual questions and she became a basket case? God, she had to get over this. He appeared interested in her. She knew for a fact that she was interested in him. Then she turned into a nut and ran from what she wanted?

Oh, she definitely had to get over this, at least enough to reach for the future.

But the only way over it seemed to be recovering something that remained stubbornly elusive: her past.

Chapter Three

Braden wasted a lot of time over the next couple of weeks wondering about Julie and what her problem was. Since he spent the time doing manual labor around the family spread, the mindless kinds of tasks he needed to do for the most part opened up his mind to wander—and no matter what he did to distract himself, it kept wandering right over to the mysterious blonde.

Pitching hay and stacking bales didn't exactly require many brain cells. Making sure it would be easy to feed the cattle when the snow got deep, making sure the bales provided windbreaks against the worst weather, took a lot of time but not a lot of thought.

So he was thinking about Julie and telling himself he was a fool. At least Dallas was over on a different section of their pastures, because he would have noticed his woolgathering and given him a hard time about it. Someplace deep inside, he did *not* want to be teased about his fascination with Julie Smith.

That alone should probably have warned him, he thought almost grimly.

What was it about the woman anyway? She seemed frightened of almost everything, poised on the edge of taking flight…and then she'd relax briefly, and he was sure he saw the real woman peek through. Maybe.

Will the real Julie Smith stand up? he thought with

sour amusement. She looked so innocent, so angelic with those big blue eyes, that he couldn't believe there was anything bad about her. She'd been in town since June, and there sure hadn't been any unkind whispers about her. If she were a bad sort, he'd have heard something by now.

But even on the rumor mill it was almost as if she were invisible, which was kind of hard to do. People who knew her mentioned her briefly; she did things with the Newcomers Club; she'd made some good friends. Upstanding friends. If they thought there was anything wrong with her, they wouldn't keep her in their circle.

So whatever was going on had to be something other than that she was a fleeing felon.

He almost laughed at that thought. Yeah, right.

But the urge to protect her remained; the desire to know more about her goaded him. The coffee experience…well, he didn't know for sure how to characterize that. Maybe she *had* just had something to do. After all, the meetup had been impromptu, and she could well have had some chores awaiting her.

He slung another bale onto the wall he was building to give the cattle a windbreak, and hoped like hell that Winona Cobbs was wrong about a record-breaking blizzard on its way. The weather reports certainly showed no indication of any big front coming, even as far away as the Pacific Coast. So far it looked as if they were in for a relatively normal December.

He didn't want to ponder Winona, however. She could be intriguing at times, but mostly he thought of her as a character, part of the charm of the place. For some reason, that brought his thoughts around to another character, Homer Gilmore. The old coot was a little crazy, wandering around and telling everyone he was "The Ghost of Christmas Past."

Weird, but the weather was going to take a severe turn for the worse eventually, and he couldn't imagine that Homer could get by relying on charity handouts. Lord only knew where the guy was sleeping. Grunting as he hefted another bale, Braden decided that something needed to be done for the man. Surely there was a warm hidey-hole somewhere in this town where they could shelter him for the winter. If it came to it, Braden would pay for it himself.

It would be heartless to leave the man's fate to the elements.

His mother's remark floated back to him, and he suddenly grinned. Parsival, huh? If she had any idea where his thoughts wandered on the subject of Julie Smith, she wouldn't liken him to a "pure and perfect knight." Hah!

A laugh escaped him even as Julie rose in his mind's eye. That wool sheath she had worn to the pageant had draped her gentle curves in a way that drew a man's thoughts far from the angelic. Her face might bring to mind an angel, but the rest of her called to a man's demons.

He paused for some coffee from his thermos and wiped his brow. Cold or not, a man could work up a sweat doing this. And apart from sweat, there was the damn prickly hay. It had managed to get inside his jacket, and probably his shirt.

He scratched a bit, letting his mind wander over Julie's gentle curves. Closing his eyes as he sipped warming coffee, he imagined running his hands over them. Even through that wool sheath they'd be able to set him on fire. Hell, picturing them was enough to put his motor in high gear.

Leaning back against the wall of hay, he gave himself up to the daydream for a few minutes. Julie in his arms. Her lips welcoming his kiss, her soft curves pressed against his hardness. He imagined pulling down the zipper on that dress, reaching inside to feel warm, silky skin.

Damn it! His eyes popped open, and he stopped himself in midfantasy. Just that little bit, and he was ready to bust out of his jeans. Over a woman he hardly knew, one who seemed a damn sight too skittish to be interested in any kind of intimacy. In fact, she seemed to be avoiding it.

Mentally, he stomped down on his male urges as if he was trying to put out a small grass fire. *Cool it*, he ordered himself.

It might have been easier to call a halt if he hadn't remembered that tomorrow was the Presents for Patriots event at the Community Church. Holy hell. He was going to see her again, and it suddenly struck him that she might spend the whole time avoiding him.

He drained his coffee, wondering if he should skip the whole evening, then realizing he'd never hear the end of it if he let down the Traub family by failing to appear.

Stuck, he thought. Shaking out his cup, he then screwed it back onto the thermos and hit those bales again with every bit of energy in him.

Work could drive out demons, even if it couldn't make him forget an angelic face.

Living a lie didn't make Julie happy. And while she was mostly engaged in just surviving while she hunted for some evidence of her past, it didn't make her happy to realize that she was surrounded by a web of deceit of her own making.

Vanessa and Mallory called a couple of times, asking

what she was up to, and the lie came too easily to her lips. "Writing," she said.

Because that was her cover story. She had to explain why she was hanging out here, why she didn't have a job—mainly because she wasn't at all sure she could hold much of a job successfully. She'd managed working in retail shops and one antiques store, but the strain had overwhelmed her. All the strangers, her uncertainty about so many basic things, the other employees who asked way too many questions about her…well, she had a little money now, thanks to selling that coin, and that meant she didn't have to try to pull off the role of a shop-girl while she was here, a huge relief for her. In a town this size, her seeming standoffishness would eventually be noted and commented on.

So she claimed to be working on a novel on the cheap laptop that sat on a wooden table. It explained how she survived, why she didn't have an ordinary job and why she disappeared sometimes when she felt too troubled.

But it was a lie. She hated the lies so much that she'd even taken a stab at writing something. The problem was, fiction seemed like a way to escape the really important things she needed to deal with, and nonfiction all came down to "My journey as a woman without a memory." As if.

It didn't help that her life seemed like a plot ripped out of the pages of a novel, or that her writing was mostly a meandering diary.

So she wasn't being honest with her new friends, which didn't make her feel one whit more comfortable. Maybe she should just blurt the truth, tell everyone that she'd been born and given a name only a short time ago. Yeah, they'd probably call her crazy and drop her like a hot potato. Who was going to believe that?

So much had happened in the weeks after she returned to awareness of where she was, things that had made her feel that even professionals suspected she might be lying, and finally just made her feel like a bug under a microscope.

Go forth and build a life sounded easy, but it was hard.

Like coffee with Braden. It should have been so simple, but the evasions began to get to her. You couldn't have a relationship based on lies, and the truth was too painful.

Pulling on her outdoor gear, she decided to take a walk in the woods. She left her phone behind, even though she knew she should take it in case she had an accident, but she didn't want another call reminding her about tomorrow, asking how her writing was going, and did she ever intend to come out of her cave.

For the first time she wondered how anyone wrote a book when people were so disrespectful of a writer's time. But maybe writers learned not to answer the phone, not to go to the door, not to feel guilty for ignoring a friend's call.

Somehow she doubted it. Her acquaintance with guilt was growing by leaps and bounds. She seemed to be building it constantly and adding to it with every evasion.

Telling herself it was necessary didn't much help.

They'd tried to convince her that she would be building a new past for herself each day that went by. It sure wasn't enough of a past to satisfy her. Yes, she could talk lightly about the few jobs she'd held in her wanderings, some of the people she'd met, but there was always that wall she couldn't surmount.

Dang, she thought, scuffing her toe in the light layer of snow and bringing up some loam from beneath.

Braden. He was another problem. Though she didn't

have a lot of experience she remembered so she could call on it, she was almost certain that he'd looked at her several times with male interest.

Well, she'd looked at him the same way. He drew her, attracted her, made her want to be a normal girl who could just date and get to know a guy. But since there wasn't much he could get to know about her, she was a fool to even cherish such dreams, and even more of a fool when he hadn't tried to reach her in over a week.

But she couldn't help wishing, and Braden made her wish. The warm, roughness of his palm when he shook her hand seemed to have imprinted itself vividly on her memory. She liked just looking at him, which she supposed was utterly silly, and she reacted like a woman to his scent, to his broad shoulders, to the sight of his butt in those snug jeans he wore.

Oh, man, the bug had bit, but it couldn't go anywhere. Not unless she told him the truth, and she could just imagine the horror that would come to his face. "You don't know who you *are*?" The question that most terrified her.

For heaven's sake, she didn't even know how old she was. When her birthday was. Who her parents had been. Where she had gone to school. All those simple but important things. Not even whether she was a virgin.

Man. Self-disgust filled her again, even though she knew it wasn't fair. She'd been seriously injured. She was lucky to be alive.

Except that she had only part of a life.

Tomorrow was going to be another rough day unless she found a way to excuse herself from the big community gift wrapping. But no, she wasn't going to excuse herself. She had no idea what had drawn her to this town, what had made her feel so compelled to come here, and hiding out wasn't going to answer the question.

But that compulsion... As she stepped out of the trees and looked up, she saw the snowy peaks of the Rocky Mountains, like the Alps, although how she knew that, she had no idea. They called to her, those mountains in all their majestic height and cragginess. They seemed to be a part of her.

They felt more like home than anything else since her accident. They kept her here.

The church hall was full of people by the time Julie arrived. So many people, all very busy at sorting through gifts and wrapping them, then labeling them for "A soldier" or "A soldier's family." Ages were placed only on toys.

Vanessa grabbed her at once and dragged her to the table where she, Mallory and Lily were busy wrapping things.

"The others will be here later," Vanessa told her. "Except Jonah, who has a bad cold. Caleb's finishing some work, and Cecelia and Nick got delayed. I don't want to know how they got delayed." Vanessa rolled her eyes suggestively, drawing a laugh from Julie, who then greeted everyone and asked, "If we were going to do toys, why not send them to Toys for Tots?"

"We work with what people give us," Mallory explained. "Sometimes I think we send enough cologne and aftershave to perfume the entire military."

Julie laughed and allowed herself to relax. This wasn't going to be so hard. "So it really gets to the troops? I thought the military was difficult about that, and these are wrapped." Where that came from, she had no idea.

"It's all going to nearby bases. No problem there. They know who we are."

"Ah."

Lily spoke. "I can't get the triangle right."

At once Julie leaned over to her and showed her how to fold the paper at the end of the package. Sometimes it amazed her that she could remember to do things like this without remembering she had ever done them before.

"I like the triangles," Lily said. "They're prettier than just sticking lots of tape on."

"You're right about that," Julie agreed.

Lily triumphantly placed the last piece of tape and looked up with sparkling eyes. Then she looked past Julie. "Hi, Braden. Are you and Julie friends now?"

"We're working on it," came the answer.

Julie was almost afraid to turn around, but after taking a breath she did, and found him smiling at her.

"Room at this table?" he asked.

"Of course," said Vanessa, scooting over before Julie could respond, making room for him right beside Julie.

It seemed more than Lily were involved in a little matchmaking, Julie thought. Her cheeks heated.

"Hi," he said, still smiling.

"Hi," she managed to answer, then quickly dragged her gaze back to the half-wrapped package in front of her. He looked good enough to eat, and her heart speeded up nervously. He smelled good, too, fresh from a shower, not wearing any aftershave or cologne that she could detect. For some reason she had never found that attractive in a man. At least not in her present incarnation.

He chatted pleasantly with the others who joined the table, appearing comfortable with everyone. She envied him that comfort. Sometimes she wondered if she had ever been someone who had a circle of family and friends that she had known for a long time, a group of people where any reasonable conversation was easy. Small talk certainly didn't come easily to her now, not at all.

And less so, being crowded against him at the table. Inevitably their arms and shoulders brushed, and sometimes they reached out simultaneously for the tape. Each contact, however minor, seemed to zap her with electricity.

A different kind of electricity than she had felt from Winona Cobbs. This kind made her start wondering what it would be like to have this man's arms around her, his lips on hers.

She tried to imagine it and wondered if her imaginings had any basis in experience, or if she was just making it up. How would she know? The not knowing was apt to drive her crazy. She ought to be getting used to this discombobulation, but it didn't seem to be getting any easier, not with a handsome, sexy man standing so close.

"Julie? Julie?" Vanessa's voice punctured her preoccupation. She snapped her head up.

"I'm sorry. Woolgathering."

"Nothing new in that," Vanessa teased. "The tape, please?"

Julie leaned over and passed her the dispenser. Somehow that twist and lean brought her hard up against Braden's side.

In an instant, everything else vanished. A web of desire cast its spell, making all her worries and wondering seem like a waste of time. All that mattered was that man and what his closeness was doing to her. What she'd like him to do with her.

Mallory excused herself to take Lily to the bathroom. Vanessa went off in search of a cup of coffee. All of a sudden she was alone with Braden, who was busy cutting paper for the next package.

Desperate not to appear like a dummy, and certainly not disinterested when he was filling her thoughts so much, she hunted for something to say. "Does everyone in town help with this?"

"Of course not." He flashed her a grin. "Some folks are working, some don't have time, some don't care, and could you imagine trying to fit all of Rust Creek into this place? Nah, we'll stay a short while, and you'll see new faces start to arrive."

"That makes sense. How did *you* find time?"

"I worked extra hard the last few days."

She dared to eye him. "Not with barbed wire, I presume."

He laughed. "Nope. Hay. And you know what? That's almost as bad when it finds its way inside your clothes. Prickly and itchy."

"But no danger of stitches."

He looked up from the package he was wrapping, and their gazes engaged. Julie felt as if the air had vanished from the room.

"No stitches," he agreed. Then, "Julie?"

"Jennifer."

He looked startled, but probably no more than she. Where had that come from? She stared at him without seeing him as her mind once again jumped on the hamster wheel. Jennifer? Somehow that sounded right, better than Julie. My God, was that her real name? But for once, something felt as if it fit.

"Julie?" he repeated. "What's wrong?"

She shook herself out of the moment, promising herself she could ponder this revelation later. "Sorry," she said. "It's just that I used to go by Jennifer. I don't know how it came about, it just did. I haven't used it here." Because she didn't know it. "I shouldn't have blurted that."

"Well, if it's the name you prefer, I don't mind using it." His smile was friendly as he returned to wrapping. "Jennifer it is. I like it. Or can I call you Jenn? I like that, too."

Only then did it strike her how many people were going to wonder about this name change. How many questions she might have to answer. Oh, God, she needed to stop blurting things like that. Not that there were too many of them so far.

"Oh, just stick with Julie," she dared to say. "If I go changing my name now, everyone's going to get confused."

"I doubt it. It's your nickname. I think most of your friends would like knowing that."

"I don't know. It seems stupid after all this time to come out with that."

"Let me handle it."

She was glad to, but wondered why he should even bother. Or why she should let him. God, she'd like to find some backbone and take control of this roller-coaster ride she lived on.

Then she reminded herself that she'd had the gumption to move clear across the country on her search to make a new place for herself in an entirely strange town. That wasn't cowardly. She only grew skittish when dealing with people who came close, close enough to figure out that something was wrong with her.

Maybe she should stop making such a big deal out of that. Maybe it was high time she let go of all her anxieties, stiffened her shoulders and let the chips fall wherever.

It sounded good. Not so easy to do.

The room was becoming truly crowded with people now, everyone talking and wrapping presents. Exactly the kind of situation that made Julie nervous. She returned greetings pleasantly enough and began to wonder how soon she could gracefully bow out. Wrapping gifts for the troops and their families seemed important, so she forced herself to attend only to the work. Still no Caleb or Nick.

Vanessa returned with coffee in a covered cup, and Mallory and Lily returned only long enough to bid everyone farewell. "Bedtime for the pip-squeak," Mallory said.

"I am not a pip-squeak," Lily insisted. "I don't squeak much."

Mallory squatted. "No, you don't. And it was meant to be affectionate, not a bad name."

Lily frowned. "I don't like the way it sounds." Then she looked at Julie-Jennifer and Braden. "You keep making friends," she said. And an instant later she was skipping toward the coatroom with her aunt in tow.

Vanessa's cell phone rang, and a frown lowered on her face. "Well, I'm outta here, too," she said after she disconnected. "There's a problem at the hotel. See you later."

"Watching that woman work on the hotel design is purely an experience," Braden remarked. "She sees things I'd miss."

"Artistic eye." Or maybe Jonah needed her. Now she was alone at the table with him, and her discomfort grew. Surely someone else would join them? But they were almost done with the rack of gifts that had been given to them. Nobody, it seemed, had to do that much. Many hands and all that.

"Say," he said as he reached for the last gift, this one a set of scented soaps. "Why don't we try the coffee thing again, Jenn? I hate to head home without my latte."

Considering how she'd fled the last time, she might

have said no. But temptation was standing there in a fantastically gorgeous package, and he had just called her Jenn. Hearing that name on his lips warmed some place inside her that hadn't felt warm in a long time. She couldn't resist, though some wiser part of her cried that she might be making a big mistake. Blowing her cover. Revealing her inadequacies.

"Sure," she heard herself say. "I'd like that." Who was running her mouth now? Julie or Jennifer?

"Good." He wrapped paper around the last package and asked her to hold it with her finger while he reached for the tape. "I was afraid I'd offended you last time."

"Me? No!" The thought horrified her. "No, Braden. I just had...something I needed to do."

He turned his head, and his eyes smiled at her. "I'm glad to know that. I don't usually send people into headlong flight to get away from me."

She felt her cheeks burn. "I'm sorry. I didn't mean to make you feel like that."

"Which you just proved by agreeing to go out with me again. Hey, lady, it's my evening out, my day off. I'd enjoy it a lot more with your company."

A very kind and flattering thing to say, and pleasant heat shot through her. Maybe she was walking on a tightrope, but in this instance, the fall might even be fun.

Twenty minutes later they once again sat in the donut shop. It being Saturday night, it was packed, but they managed to grab one of the few small tables. Once again they both ordered the same things.

"I've been talking to Homer Gilmore," Braden said. "Do you know who he is?"

"I've seen him around, but no one seems to know his story."

"No one does, at least, no one I've talked to," Braden

agreed. "I'm working on getting him a place to stay, maybe at the church, before he freezes to death out there."

Jenn—she really *did* feel better thinking of herself that way, perhaps another piece of the mystery solved?—shook her head. "He seems sad. I hear he doesn't even say anything intelligible."

"That's part of the problem. He wanders around mumbling unintelligible stuff, and nobody knows what to make of him. He seems harmless. I mean, he's been hanging around and hasn't really bothered anybody, unless mumbling crazy things to people is bothersome."

Jenn felt herself warm to him even more. "It's kind of you to try to find a place for him to stay."

"Not really. He deserves at least as much care as any stray, don't you think?"

Considering she was a stray of sorts herself, she nodded. "Don't diminish what you're doing. I don't see anyone else running around trying to find the guy a home."

He leaned back as they were served and gave her a crooked smile. "If Winona's right, I need to get cracking."

"She's still predicting that blizzard?"

"Not only that, but every time she gives a prediction, it seems to have grown bigger and worse. Which brings me to a question. Are you going to be okay in that cabin if the power goes out?"

"I was thinking of getting a kerosene heater."

He shook his head. "Better to use the woodstove. If you want, I'll check it out for you when we leave here, make sure the chimney is clean."

"That thing looks like a monster to me."

He laughed quietly. "It's not. I'll make sure it's safe then show you how to light a fire. Have you got any wood out there?"

"Some, alongside the cabin."

"I guess you couldn't tell me how much."

Surprisingly, she felt herself smile then laugh. "What I know about wood you can put on the head of a pin. There's a stack. I have no idea how much or how long it would last."

"A very good reason to take advantage of a willing neighbor. Me."

Take advantage of him? She hoped he had absolutely no idea the visions that wording brought to her head. "Well," she said, "if you're going to do that for me, I ought to stop by the grocery before it closes and pick up what I need to feed you a late meal. Unless you've already eaten."

"I haven't but it's not necessary," he said. "Which is not to say I wouldn't enjoy it. I just don't want you to feel obligated."

She was almost relieved by his refusal, but then relief gave way to disappointment. She really *did* want to spend time with this man, even though it would mean tiptoeing through the minefield of evasions and nonanswers.

Torn again. She was getting tired of *herself*, she realized. "It'll be something simple, and I'd really like to do it, if you have time."

"I have time. Okay, that would be great. But when we're done here, I need to stop by the church again. I've been working on the rev to turn over some storage space to Homer. It's empty now." His eyes sparkled. "All those gifts will be shipped on Monday, and there's this nice warm room."

She laughed again. "I think you're going to win."

"It's not winning. He's a charitable man. It's just that no one is really comfortable with Homer. I think the good reverend is afraid he might burn the place down or something."

Jennifer nodded. "That's not an unreasonable fear."

"The thing is, while I think Homer may be crazy, I don't think he's stupid. There's a huge difference. He's made it this far under worse circumstances. I'd find him space at our ranch, but he wanders too much, and he'd be even more alone. No, he needs to be in town where someone can make sure he's okay and that he's eating."

"Do you often collect strays?" The question wasn't as light as she tried to make it sound. She hoped she wasn't another stray like Homer to him.

"Me? Nah. Now when I was young, yes, but now?" He shook his head. "If I find them, I put them at the shelter for adoption. Sometimes I don't find them in time." His face darkened.

"What do you mean?" That look on his face made her nervous. She liked it better when he looked happy. Plus, she wondered if he had deliberately diverted the subject from stray people to stray animals. She desperately hoped he didn't see her that way.

"Just that people dump pets they don't want on the ranches and farms. I guess they think the animals can take care of themselves. Well, they can't. They don't know how. So unless we find them..." He shook his head. "Sorry, that's a downer. How about a more cheerful topic?"

"Got one?" she asked, again trying to sound light.

"Of course. I'm a generally cheerful guy."

But before either of them could say another word, a familiar voice interrupted.

"Well, well," said Dallas Traub. "Look who's having coffee with the new lady."

Jenn wanted to sink into the floor. Braden looked annoyed, and his evident annoyance appeared to grow as

Dallas grabbed a chair and turned it around so he could sit at the end of their booth.

"Dallas, cut it out. Jenn's not used to us."

"Jenn?" Both of Dallas's brows elevated. Julie-Jenn—which was it?—wished him to the devil as her crazy name change came out in the worst way possible.

Braden didn't give her a chance to speak. "We just came from wrapping presents. Did you do yours?"

"On my way there as soon as I get coffee for me and Nina, and hot chocolates for the kids. So what's with the name?" Clearly he wasn't going to let it drop. Just then, one of his young sons, dressed in a puffy down coat, came bursting through the door and ran up to him. He tugged the bottom of Dallas's jacket, and the man reached out and arm to hold him close. Braden gave the boy's shoulder a squeeze, though he was busy staring at Dallas.

"Simple," said Braden in a voice that seemed edged with warning steel. "It's her nickname. She shared it with me while we were wrapping presents. Seems only courteous to call a lady by the name she prefers, without making a big deal about it."

Dallas lifted both hands, palms out. "Easy, brother, easy. I was just curious." He smiled at Julie. "Hi, Jenn. That is, unless only my bachelor brother is allowed to use the name."

"God, Dallas." Braden nearly groaned.

"I don't mind anyone using it," Jenn answered bravely. "After all these months, though, I'll probably need to get used to it again. Who's your adorable shadow here?"

Dallas chuckled. "This is my youngest, Robbie." The boy gave Jenn a shy smile but stayed close to his father. "As I was saying, there's names and there's names.

You know, like Mule here. That's what we used to call Braden."

"Until I got big enough to shut some mouths," Braden said.

"He's still stubborn," Dallas went on as if his brother hadn't spoken. "Makes up his mind, and that's it. Or in the case of women, never makes up his mind." He looked at Braden. "So tell me, man, are you waiting for some kind of perfect female saint? It'll take one to put up with you."

At that moment, the waitress put a cardboard tray full of cups in front of Dallas.

"Daddy, hurry," said the boy.

"That's your cue," Braden said firmly.

Dallas laughed. "I can take a lead-footed hint." He looked at Julie. "Jenn. I like it. Good nickname. But look out for this guy. Love 'em and leave 'em, that's him."

"Damn it, Dallas!"

Still laughing, Dallas stood up and put the chair back. Grabbing his coffee, he headed for the door. Alongside him trotted his son, who was asking in a piping voice, "You really called Uncle Braden a mule?"

Jenn sat waiting quietly, not quite sure what to say.

"Numbskull," Braden said. "That should be *his* nickname. And he's wrong. But you try getting to know a woman with those guys always butting in like that. Are you ready to shake me off? I wouldn't blame you because I come with all of that attached."

Jenn hesitated. She was beginning to feel scattered inside, between her new name and the things Dallas had said and Braden talking as if they already had some kind of relationship. A bit uncertain how to proceed. God, she wished she knew who she was. "We're just having coffee," she said finally. "No biggie. Right?"

The warmth in his brown eyes seemed to deepen. "No biggie," he agreed. "Just friends having coffee."

"Then I'm not shaking you off. Even because of Dallas."

He smiled then. "You're braver than most, Ju-Jenn."

Somehow that struck her as funny. She giggled. "You poor man."

"Most of the time I don't mind it," he admitted. "Except when they get ham-fisted at the wrong time."

"Which apparently happens sometimes."

He nodded. "As just proved."

She relaxed then, somehow feeling comfortable with him. He'd been the one most disturbed by Dallas; he hadn't done one thing to make her feel uneasy, and he'd handled the name business beautifully. She was content to sit and listen as he talked casually about the kind of winter preparations they were making at the Triple-T, and the things they'd be dealing with in the months ahead. He was clearly a very busy man.

Before long, they were done with their coffee. As they rose, he said, "I'll meet you at your place. Maybe half an hour or a little longer, depending on how much time I spend at the church. We'll master that monster stove."

Damn, he was charming, she thought as he walked her to her car and opened the door for her. She waved to him as she backed out.

Then the dam broke. Who was Jennifer? Was she really Jennifer? She turned the name around and around in her head, feeling it, tasting it, finding it seemed to fit comfortably on her, like a warm shawl on a chilly day. Okay, so she was Jennifer. Whoever Jennifer was. She wondered how her friends would react to this news, because she suspected it would get around even if she didn't say anything herself.

But why *shouldn't* she say anything? If she felt more comfortable with that name, she could explain it the same way she had explained it to Braden. He'd accepted it easily enough.

Somehow, she promised herself for the millionth time, this was all going to be okay. She'd make it.

Chapter Four

She stopped at the market just in time and got the necessities to make Chicken Cordon Bleu, actually a very easy recipe despite the fancy name. It would be nice if she could remember how she had learned to make it. Or all the times she must have made it in the past.

On the way back to her cabin, tension began to creep into her again. Dallas had acted as if it were a big deal that Braden was having coffee with her. What did that mean? Just brotherly teasing? Or something more?

She'd already heard more than once that Braden was the last single Traub, but she couldn't understand why that seemed like something worthy of mention. He wasn't all that old. Were people supposed to get married out of the cradle here?

But even with her lack of memory, she sensed that Braden's interest in her was more than casual. That could become a problem. She knew it but didn't want to call a halt. Not yet. Twice now she'd been with him when she'd had a flash of her past. Maybe he had nothing to do with it, but what if he did?

Then she forced herself to shrug the thought aside. An attractive man was showing interest. That was a good thing, even if it didn't last long. She needed that kind of reassurance, although again she didn't know why. Maybe because she'd been feeling so unsure of herself and everything else?

Regardless, she was attracted to him, and despite her nerves was looking forward to having him over, to his help with the stove, and to sharing dinner with him. It shouldn't cause much talk because she was definitely off the beaten track out here. Nobody would probably even find out, which might keep his brothers off his back, and her friends from teasing her, as well.

She ought to be able to take the teasing, but the truth was, she was so aware of what she lacked that she sometimes felt fragile and unsure about how to respond. Which made her a weakling, she supposed, and she had no reason to feel weak.

Stiffening herself, she carried the groceries inside and began to get ready for dinner. She was a woman who had chased her own identity all over the country. She was tough. She could handle just about anything.

Finally smiling, she began to hum. Enough of herself. Time to think about having a man over for a little while. Because anyway she looked at it, it struck her that they were having a date. Of sorts.

By the time Braden drove up, she had the rolled chicken cutlets in the fridge, awaiting cooking. A pan of flour and paprika stood ready for coating them, the ingredients for the wine sauce waited at hand, and she debated which vegetables to serve with it. Well, she supposed she could ask him what he preferred.

Overall, it was an easy meal to make, but she'd gone a little overboard on her budget by buying ham and Swiss cheese to stuff the breasts, and white wine for the sauce. A little splurge, but surely she deserved one for a special occasion?

And surely Braden deserved a special meal for doing all of this for her. She was still regarding the woodstove dubiously, and wondered if he'd be able to banish her fear of it.

The phone rang. It was Vanessa, proving that in a town this size, gossip flew faster than the speed of light. "I hear," she said knowingly, "that you had coffee with Braden Traub."

"I wouldn't have thought that interesting enough to be worthy of mentioning." A lie. She herself had certainly found it interesting.

"Dallas mentioned it. Apparently, he's gloating that his brother has been snared."

"Because of a cup of coffee?" Jenn blinked in astonishment.

"Oh, he's just being an annoying brother. It's not like Braden hasn't dated before. They just like to give him a hard time, those brothers of his. From what I've seen, he gives as good as he gets. But that's not really why I called. Coffee doesn't add up to wedding bells."

"No, really it doesn't. What's up?"

"Your nickname."

Something inside Jenn or Julie or whoever froze and tried to curl into a tight knot. "Why?"

"Listen," Vanessa said, "I'm not trying to give you a hard time. I just wondered if Dallas was making up stuff or if that really is your nickname."

"It was," Jenn answered as truthfully as she could.

"I wish you'd told us all. I hate to think we've been calling you by a name you don't like. So it's Jenn or Jennifer? Middle name?"

Jenn didn't know how to answer that. Honestly, she was getting confused by this herself.

After a moment, Vanessa spoke cheerfully. "Well, I

like it. So okay, I'll tell the others. Jenn or Jennifer. It'll probably feel more like home around here if we use your nickname."

"Thank you." Jenn felt a wave of warmth toward Vanessa. "How'd the problem at the lodge go?"

"No biggie. Someone dinged my mural and I needed to touch it up. Time is getting so tight, Nate is afraid to let anything wait."

"And Jonah? How's he feeling?"

Vanessa laughed again. "Men, like mighty oaks, fall hard when they get sick. I need to take him some more chicken broth. Talk to you soon?"

Jenn disconnected and leaned back against the counter, waiting for Braden with more impatience than she would have believed possible. And wondering at the same time about this Jennifer thing. It fit, it felt right. It felt like it belonged to her more than the name Julie. But still, how could she be sure? Sure or not, she definitely liked having Braden call her Jenn, so Jenn it would be.

Did it matter? Finally, she shook her head once again, and her fingers wandered up to feel the long scar in her scalp, a scar successfully covered by her hair.

She would never know what had happened to her, and she would never, ever be really sure if any memories she regained were real. Not unless she ran into someone who had known her before.

Oddly, that scared her. Wouldn't confirmation be a positive thing? But it could also turn into a kind of misery, she supposed, a person or people who knew a past that she'd forgotten. It might answer some general questions, but it would give her very little. A name, a few recollections that would seem like they belonged to someone else. Maybe it would be best if it never happened. Yeah, she wanted to know who she had once been, like it or not, but she also feared the discovery. The thought that she might not like her old self plagued her.

Sometimes she thought it would be best to just let it go. To never know, the way she would never know what had happened to leave her with a cracked skull and no memory. She was *sure* she didn't want to remember that.

But she needed a place, physically and in time. She was trying to build that here, because somehow this town felt comfortable to her. Like something she had once known in the distant mists of time. But there were lots of towns like this, so no way could she know if this was the right one.

But she'd made some small strides toward building a life here, and since she found some strange kind of comfort in this mountain town, she might as well stay and see what happened.

Before she could get too locked in the endless spiral of her thoughts, she heard Braden's truck pull up. A minute later came his knock on her door.

He was smiling as she opened it, and she saw that snowflakes were falling lightly from a sky the color of steel. "Are you ready for me?"

"Absolutely." She stepped back to let him in. "Did things go well at the church?"

"Homer should have a place to stay come Monday. Then the problem becomes finding Homer."

She giggled a little at that. "He seems elusive."

A cold draft had blown in with him and lingered after he closed the door. "Hey, Jenn?"

"Yes?"

"You really need to master this stove. Then you wouldn't be so worried about electric and propane that you keep it this cold."

"I like the cold." She knew that with a certainty she felt for little else in her life these days.

"Not all the time." He astonished her by taking her hand. "Cold fingers. Not good. You need some warming up."

Before she could react, except with a thrill that raced to her very center and made her insides clench with delight and longing, he dropped her hand.

"First things first," he said, becoming all business. "Have you got an old piece of cloth I can drape around the stove?"

"Why would you want to do that?" she asked, surprised. Wouldn't it burn?

"Because if I knock ash and soot out of that chimney, it's going to come out any and every nook or cranny on that thing. Believe me, you don't want soot settling all over this place."

She remembered the old curtains she had taken down when she first moved in. Frayed and aging, they had long since passed any useful life. "I have just the thing."

"Good. Sorry I took so long getting here," he said as she went to the cabin's one closet. "I had to borrow a chimney brush from one of my brothers."

"That must have been fun."

"I didn't have to say much," he laughed. "Apparently, everyone has heard that we had coffee together."

"Vanessa called and mentioned it." She turned with the curtains over her arms and he took them. There wasn't a whole lot of room in this place.

"Well, dang," he said with a wink. "I'd better buy the ring this week."

He made her laugh. It was so easy to laugh with him, despite the winding spring of tension inside her, a tension that eased and strengthened almost constantly as she tiptoed her way into her new life.

A thought struck her. She not only felt maimed in some essential way, but she also felt like an imposter in her own life. Quickly she brushed that idea away for future consideration. How could she be an imposter anyway? She was what she was, just like anyone else.

She watched as he swaddled the stove, covering the door opening completely, and around the base of the chimney.

"The nice thing about the soot," he said, "is that anywhere it turns up on this cloth I'll know if I need to do a little sealing. The air should be getting into the firebox only through the vents. I'll show you how to use them." He paused, looking at her. "You resemble a nervous rabbit."

"I'm just not used to this whole idea. Fire is a scary thing."

"By the time I'm done, you won't be scared, and you'll be ready for winter. Believe me, Jenn, even if we don't get Winona's big blizzard, there'll be other times when power is out, or a propane delivery can't get to you. You can even cook on this stove."

Considering she'd sought this place out, sure that these mountains and winter held some answers for her, she felt like an utter neophyte. She was also feeling wimpy.

"Okay," she said. "I'll put on my pioneer hat."

"Good." His eyes crinkled at the corners as he went back to work.

A short time later he was satisfied. "Okay. I'm going to go get my ladder and the chimney brush. This won't take long."

"I really appreciate this," she hastened to say. She meant it, even though it meant she'd now have no excuse to avoid that stove. Why it loomed like such a large threat in her mind, she couldn't imagine. Maybe she was transferring other anxieties to it. That wouldn't surprise her. "But Braden, it's dark out there."

"There's enough light to do this job. Don't worry."

She listened to his footsteps on the roof. Shortly they were followed by the sound of metal scraping on metal. She could imagine him running the chimney brush up and down the inside of the stovepipe. It must be a messy job.

From inside, however, she couldn't tell how messy it might be. The curtains draped all over the stove successfully prevented any soot from escaping. Ten minutes later, the sounds of his footsteps disappeared from the roof, and she could faintly hear the clatter of his booted feet on the ladder he must have brought with him.

Peeking out the window, she watched him collapse the ladder and carry it back to his truck along with the chimney brush. He was right about the light. The snow seemed to magnify the light spilling from her windows.

Once he had them stowed, he tossed work gloves into a metal box on the bed and headed toward the door. She opened it before he even knocked.

"It was pretty clean," he said. "Either the last resident knew how to build a fire, or he cleaned it before he left. I think I knocked down a bird's nest, though." He must have caught something on her face because he smiled. "Not to worry. It's been empty for a long time."

"Wrong time of year for hatchlings," she agreed, wondering why it had even concerned her. For heaven's sake, it was winter out there, and snow was still falling very gently, just a light dusting.

He began to pull the drapes away from the stove, checking for soot. "A few cracks at the base of the pipe," he said when he was done. "I'll patch them. I have some compound in the truck."

"You carry everything, like a handyman," she said with surprise.

"When you work on a ranch as big as I do, you learn to carry everything you might need." Then he flashed her a smile. "I cheated. I knew I'd be working on the stove, so I stopped at the hardware store." He rolled up the drapes. "Do you want these? The stove is pretty sound, but there's a little soot from the stovepipe. You don't have a washer here, do you?"

"I use the laundry in town. And no, I don't need to save those."

"Then I'll cart them to the dump." He dashed out with them then returned with his work gloves and a can full of something.

It occurred to her then that she wasn't even being a good hostess. "Would you like some coffee? I can make it."

"Sounds great."

She left him to his work while she went to the kitchen area and started the coffee. One big room. Two people could trip over each other in here if they weren't careful.

"That needs a couple of hours to set up," he said. "Then we'll get to fire-making."

Startled to realize that he was right behind her, she almost jumped. God, that was ridiculous, considering that six of his paces would carry him across the entire space.

"Do you want to eat soon?" she asked, hoping her start hadn't been visible.

"Whenever you'd like. But you're stuck with me for a while. Let's have coffee before anything else."

"Sorry it's not a latte."

"Hey, I love coffee any way it comes…except weak."

Soon she was able to fill mugs for both of them, and they settled in the two battered armchairs, one of which she'd tossed the blue blanket over. The angel pillows sat on a scarred wooden chest that looked at least as old as the cabin. As the only seasonal color in the room, they almost looked forlorn.

"You really should have a tree," he remarked.

"Is that your next rescue mission?" She tried to sound light. "The thing is, you're talking about me building a fire in that stove. Where the heck would I put a tree that would be safe?"

He glanced around. "Point taken. But maybe a small artificial one that you could put on the table."

She laughed, suddenly amused. "Knight-errant," she said.

"Oh no, you don't. I swear, I hear enough of that from my mother. Have you been talking with her? I just want you to feel at home here, and it looks like you haven't been able to do a lot so far."

How could she possibly tell him that her commitment to staying here kept wavering like rippling water? She wasn't at all sure she was at journey's end, and doing too much to this cabin seemed like a waste of money, and possibly effort. "I'll think about it."

"Fair enough, and I'll shut my trap." He glanced toward the window. "More snow. I'd better bring in some wood for the fire before it gets buried. Is that your woodpile I saw near the back corner?"

"You tell me. Like I said, I'm a total tyro on wood and woodstoves."

"We're about to take care of that." He drained his mug and rose, reaching for his jacket. "Be right back."

Through the window she watched him dig out his gloves once more, and disappear around the end of the cabin. This place had few enough windows—only two large ones at the front—but it was enough for her.

Before very long, he returned with a hefty armload of wood. He placed it beside the stove in a heavy canvas hammock-type thing she had always wondered about. "There's a box of kindling, too. I'll bring some in. And it might be a good time to think about reading the newspaper occasionally."

He bounced out once again and returned with some more wood. "I'll have to get you more wood. You don't have enough out there to get you through much more than a few days. A really bad blizzard could cut you off for up to a week."

"I guess I should lay in supplies then, too."

"Nonperishables. Seriously, you can cook a lot of things on the top of that stove. Just remember, it's apt to be hot, and you can't control the temperature very well."

He was a good teacher as he led her through the intricacies of how to build a fire and control its output with the vents. "You don't want it to blaze, once you get it started, so you pretty much close the vents. Just let a tiny bit of air in. It'll burn hotter and longer and make less soot."

And so on. She wondered how much of this she would even be able to remember, and if she should be taking notes.

Soon he had a pleasant fire going, and she could feel warmth beginning to seep through the cabin. It was certainly more comfortable than the sixty-six degrees she had the thermostat set to.

"We'll run through this again once I get you some more wood."

She hesitated. He was being awfully generous. "I can order a delivery, can't I?"

"Why should you? We have enough split wood out at the ranch to get us through four years without any other heat. We can spare the little you'll need, no problem."

The fire did make the cabin seem cheerier, especially since she could see the flames through the glass door on the stove.

"I wonder who put that stove in?" Braden mused. "It's a good one, and that door even makes it pretty."

"You're not familiar with who lived here before?"

He cocked a brow at her. "People who live out here tend to keep to themselves. It was kind of a surprising place for you to choose."

She hesitated, then used her cover story. "I was mainly thinking about peace and quiet for writing."

"You're a writer?"

"Hope to be."

He half smiled. "There are all kinds of difficult jobs in the world. I'd put that near the top of the list. I'm doing good if I can write a list of chores."

She was pretty sure he was exaggerating, but there was one thing she could say with perfect truth. "I haven't made a whole lot of progress yet."

"Be patient. It'll come. Most things do."

"I guess I'm going to see."

He offered to help her make dinner, but she declined. Cooking was one of the few tasks where she felt reasonable confidence. Once again she thought how odd it was that she seemed to remember how to do so many things without actually *remembering* them. One thing she knew for certain, however: she felt absolutely no familiarity with a woodstove.

He turned out to be a good dinner guest, keeping her company while she cooked, commenting on how delicious everything smelled. When she brought out the plates and flatware, he insisted on setting her little table for two.

When at last they dined, he took one mouthful of the chicken, closed his eyes as he savored it and announced it was the best thing he'd eaten in a very long time.

"We tend to go simple at the ranch, most of the time. So many mouths, so many varied taste preferences. Mom decided a long time ago that we were beans, potatoes and meat men."

She smiled. "Doesn't look like it at the moment."

"It's just easy, like I said. Must have been really interesting for her when we were youngsters. Six brothers, everyone wanting something different. About the only time we all reached agreement was over hamburgers and hot dogs."

She laughed. "Fun times."

"For us. Not so much for her, probably. I guess we survived our pathetic food tastes because we all liked vegetables of any kind. We have a garden every summer and freeze or can any overabundance."

It sounded so… Well, she couldn't think of the proper word for it, but she liked the picture he was painting of his life. A family. Working together. Growing a garden together. Putting up food for the winter.

She was probably romanticizing a whole lot of work, she warned herself. She'd already heard about the way Braden worked nearly every day, so much so that getting away for a brief stint in town was a rarity, at least for now.

"Does your work slow down in the winter?" she asked.

"If we're properly prepared. We have more free time, some of which goes to taking care of things we've had to let slide during the busy times. Do you ride?"

"Horses?" She blinked, once again facing her internal blank wall. Hadn't he asked this before? Why was he asking again. No, that was whether she skied. And she still had no idea how to answer.

But before her silence became obvious, he spoke again. "If we get some decent weather, I should take you out for a gentle ride. I think you'd love it."

"I think so." She thought she might enjoy it but had no way to know. Maybe once she was on the horse's back, her feelings would change.

Their conversation remained light enough and general enough that she was mostly able to relax and just enjoy his company. He seemed to have a knack for bringing up simple matters, and for entertaining with stories about his childhood. He put few demands on her, and she felt her liking for him growing. An easy companion. Easier than even her girlfriends.

He insisted on washing the dishes while she had after-dinner coffee; he raved about her cooking, and all in all made her feel pretty good.

She smiled more than she had in a long time, and laughed more freely. But she was also very aware that the more time she spent with someone, like her girlfriends, the more danger lurked. Covering up had become almost second nature, but it never ceased to fill her with anxiety.

"Have you visited any of the other towns around here?" he asked her as he hung the dish towel over the stove handle to dry.

"Not really. I've been thinking about it. I picked the wrong time of year to feel a yen to get up into the mountains, I guess."

"Not really. We can still take a drive if you like, maybe over to Thunder Canyon to see my brothers Forrest and Clay and their families. If you feel like it. Say Tuesday? I should be all caught up on chores."

At once she felt herself pulled in differing directions. More time with Braden? Possibly tiptoeing around the rabbit hole in which she seemed to live? But the mountains called to her, and if she were to be honest, so did Braden. Before she could catch herself, she said, "I'd love that." Except for the Thunder Canyon part. She didn't want to go visiting, and wondered how she could divert him from that without being rude.

"Great, I'll give you a call." Then he pointed at the woodstove. "I need to get going before tongues start wagging, but let me show you how to keep that fire banked overnight so that in the morning all you have to do is throw on a couple more logs."

So she squatted beside him in front of the stove. The blast of heat that emerged when he opened the door astonished her, and gave her some indication of how gently the stove was radiating the heat. Yes, she could tell the stove was hot this close, but nothing like the blast-furnace effect of opening the door.

The banking part was something she was sure she could manage. He mounded coals together and scooped ash on top of them. "In the morning all you should have to do is stir this a bit and throw a log or two on top."

"Very cool," she said as he latched the stove door closed.

They were still squatting, and she felt him look at her, so she turned. What happened then seemed as inevitable as the flow of the seasons.

"You're beautiful," he murmured, then leaned toward her until their mouths met.

One of those glowing coals from the stove might have touched her lips. A very different kind of fire instantly ignited in her. God, this felt so good!

She dropped to her knees to keep her balance, and he

never broke the kiss. Without thinking, she raised one hand to grip his shoulder and keep him close.

She couldn't remember ever having wanted anything as much as she wanted this man's kiss. It hit her out of nowhere, like a racing train, fresh, unexpected and utterly powerful. She had never seen it coming, despite the attraction she felt, never guessed that a mere kiss could inflame her so fast and so furiously.

Warm. Gentle. Nothing forceful, nothing demanding. Just a gentle caress.

Then it was gone.

"Oh, very nice," he whispered, then jumped to his feet. "I really have to run. See you Tuesday."

Very *nice*. Nice? That's what he thought? As the door closed behind him, she remained kneeling in front of the stove, and all she wanted to do was cry.

Nice. Her whole world felt as if it had just been turned upside down again and he said *Nice*?

Braden was grateful for the chilly night air. The cold bathed him, and he didn't even turn on the heater in his truck. He'd kissed more than a few women in his life, but his response to Julie—Jenn—had left him feeling like he needed to run fast and hard to save himself.

Because, damn it, one kiss and he'd been on fire for her. Perilously close to sweeping her beneath him on that rug and exploring every nook and cranny of her body until she begged for more.

He knew better than that. What he had just experienced was dangerous in so many ways. She was still the mystery woman about whom he knew very little. He still caught her hesitations when she needed to answer a question, still saw a mixture of doubt and uncertainty in those incredible blue eyes.

Sex would only complicate the entire thing for both of them. It might take them places both of them would regret. Hell, he wasn't a kid anymore. He knew that a relationship had to come first; there had to be some understanding, some friendship, some liking. He liked her so far, but he felt they were a long way from friendship and understanding.

Crap. He was driving too fast and eased up on the gas. The flurries earlier had made this lousy road slippery, and the last thing he wanted to do tonight was call to get towed out of a ditch. If his cell would even get a signal out here. There were still dead zones where a phone wouldn't work, although since last year's flood they'd been trying to improve that, too. And if he got on the satellite phone they used for the ranch, he'd be talking to one of the very people he most didn't want to have to explain himself to. Gradually, he began to cool down, and to wonder what it was about that woman that brought out the devil in him. Why he wanted her so badly. Why he was deliberately inserting himself into her life.

Loneliness? He simply shook his head. He didn't have time to be lonely, and had too many friends and family to need someone else. It was one thing to help her deal with her woodstove, and another to start craving her like a starving man.

But one little kiss, just a teeny little kiss, and everything inside him had responded instantly. Kinda scary.

First he had to solve the mystery of Jenn. Learn more about her, about why she sometimes looked lonely in a crowd, why she seemed to back away from the simplest of questions. What was her secret? What was she hiding from?

Those questions *had* to be answered first.

Well, maybe he'd get some answers during their drive

on Tuesday. Mentally he crossed out any thought of going to see his brothers in Thunder Canyon. He wanted to share his biggest infatuation with Jenn, and Jenn alone. He loved running up some of the roads into the mountains, and the winter still hadn't deepened enough to make it risky. Beautiful vistas, majestic peaks, the deep shadows of the evergreen forests. The place seemed magical to him.

It would be interesting to see Jenn's response. If she didn't feel the magic, too, then he'd know for sure she wasn't for him, at least not beyond casual friendship.

So yeah. He felt a little better. Tuesday he'd find out more about her. Like whether he should ever see her again.

Chapter Five

Jenn joined her friends at church on Sunday morning and heard all about Winona Cobbs's increasingly bad predictions. When she glimpsed Winona Cobbs emerging after the service, she panicked. She didn't know what it was about that woman, but she didn't want to be around her.

"Gotta run," she told Vanessa, Callie, Mallory and Cecelia.

"Hey, what about coffee and donuts?" Callie protested. "We said we would head over to Daisy's this morning."

"I can't, really," Jenn said hastily, watching as Winona grew closer. "I'm in the middle of something in my…writing."

"Okay, then," Vanessa said lightly. "I get it, being an artist and all. Go. Be flaky. Your calling gives you permission."

Jenn would have been a whole lot more amused if she hadn't felt the overwhelming need to flee. Briefly, her gaze met Winona's. She felt again that electric shock, but Winona didn't seem to be interested in her at all. The woman turned away to speak to someone else and Jenn fled.

Writing gave her permission to be flaky? Only as she left town behind did Jenn begin to relax, her anxiety about Winona easing, and Vanessa's remark penetrating. She felt a little bubble of laughter in her stomach but it didn't escape.

So now she had an excuse for being weird? Who would have thought? Instant cover. Just say you're some kind of artist. Maybe they were accepting her name change as the same kind of flakiness.

Anxiety drained away as she pondered the words. An excuse, built in. *Thank you, Vanessa.*

But she also wondered what it was about Winona Cobbs that bothered her so much. She was sure she didn't know the woman, and the woman didn't seem to even want to meet her. So why this reaction, followed by such an urgent need to escape?

Maybe she was a little crazy herself, no artistry to excuse it.

But the hard part of having no memory was lacking touchstones for her own reactions. Maybe Winona reminded her of someone she couldn't remember. Maybe it had been a bad experience.

And she might never know.

What did she have to go on anyway? A name that felt like it belonged to her, a fleeting memory of a Christmas pageant, her reaction to Winona, and her love of the mountains around this town.

Not a whole heck of a lot.

Back at home, she followed Braden's directions and put a few more logs on the fire after stirring the coals. They caught quickly, and soon the cabin was warm, and she nearly closed the air intakes.

Treating herself, she turned her small wobbly desk so she could see the red glow from the fire and decided she could get used to this. Maybe even become proficient at it. Stepping outside, she went to her woodpile to bring in a few more logs.

When she looked at it, she quickly guessed Braden was right about her needing some more wood. She might have enough for a few more days at this rate. Each day that she burned the stove, the pile shrank. Of course, she'd noticed that her heat wasn't turning on, and given the cost of propane for the heater and electric to run the blower, it was probably saving her loads of money. As for the rest…well, there was no way to reduce her electric, and the stove still operated on propane. Maybe she should try cooking on the top of the woodstove. Little things, like an egg, or using the metal percolator she'd found at the back of the cupboard instead of the drip coffeemaker.

A sense of adventure overcame her, and she decided coffee was the safest starting point. She could hear if it started to boil over, and smell when the coffee was ready.

She stacked the pot as best as she could remember, if memory it was, and set it on the stove. Then she sat down to her laptop. Browsing the web tempted her, even on her slow dial-up service, but instead she forced herself to write.

After all, that's what she had said she was going to do.

Her random scribblings weren't very impressive, though. Mostly she'd been keeping a kind of diary, as if somewhere within it she might find answers. It gave her thoughts more order than the mental hamster wheel she too often got stuck in. She had no idea if the order was any more useful, but sometimes she felt reassured that she could look back over her meanderings. A written record couldn't be erased by accident, unlike most of her life.

Because a terrifying possibility kept haunting her. What if she woke up one morning and discovered she had lost the last four years as well as everything that came before? What if she once again woke up a blank slate? It had happened once, and there was no reason to think it couldn't happen again.

Such an event was unlikely to be sure, but recording things on her computer made her feel safer somehow, and she always kept everything backed up on a flash drive, tucked safely away, in case the computer crashed.

So she sat at her computer, watching the fire, and little by little recorded her impressions of her day with Braden, how he'd made her feel, how he'd been so helpful. *A tendril of belonging*, she thought as she typed the words. The girls, and now Braden. Little Lily. People who had come to mean a whole lot to her.

Finally, afraid of getting way too sappy over Braden, who had done nothing but kiss her and call the experience nice, she scrolled back through the other things she had written down.

Lifting her hand, she fingered the tarnished coins that hung around her neck. She wore them all the time, but not because she had learned they were worth a lot of money. They were all she had left of her former life, for one thing, but even more important, they might be recognized by someone. Hope on that score had nearly died, but she wasn't ready to abandon it yet.

Finally, she shook herself from reverie, pulled the coffee off the woodstove and found it had turned out perfectly. Pouring herself a mug, she sat sipping her coffee, feeling a rare spell of contentment. She had Tuesday and a drive into the mountains to look forward to. She could hardly wait. She hadn't so far dared to go up there all alone, for fear something might happen.

Something bad had happened in her past, and she no longer thought awful things only happened to other people. In a very real way, she had been stripped of her sense of security.

She still had a long way to go. A very long way.

* * *

Monday night, Braden called Jenn to confirm their drive, saying he'd pick her up at ten the next morning. He liked hearing the pleasure in her voice, and didn't mind the ribbing he got from Dallas when he asked his brother to finish up a few things for him.

"Getting a little serious here, brother?"

Braden rolled his eyes. "A drive in the mountains? You gotta be kidding. Way too early for serious."

"I don't know about that. Sometimes it strikes you fast and hard, like a falling rock. Speaking of which, take it easy on those hairpin turns. I hear there have been some rock slides."

"I seem to remember having driven those roads before."

Dallas laughed. "Yeah. Like the time we got a little too liquored up for our own good in our wild youth. Lucky to be alive."

"Sutter's reflexes had something to do with that luck."

"And you screaming 'rock' like a girl."

Braden couldn't help laughing, but then he noticed Dallas's demeanor change. "What?"

Dallas eyed him gravely. "Be careful, Braden. Nobody seems to know a whole lot about her, and she's a bit... quirky. Nina said she thought she was evasive at times."

"I've noticed. Thanks for your concern, but at the moment I'm more interested in solving the mystery than anything."

Dallas let it go, but Braden knew the warning was a fair one. The things he had begun to feel for Jenn were already surpassing mere curiosity. Danger signs loomed on the road ahead.

He could handle it, he decided. He wasn't by any means in too deep yet, and a casual drive in the mountains wasn't likely to get him in much deeper. He could do that with anyone.

As for the flame of desire she lit in him—well, it wasn't the first time that had happened, and he'd made it out in one piece.

Humming, he went back to work, thinking about which route would be best to follow. Dallas was right about rock slides. It might turn out to be a very short drive, indeed.

Tuesday morning, on his way to pick up Jenn, Braden stopped at the donut shop to have them fill a thermos for him, and added a couple of their sandwiches. No telling when hunger might hit or how long this drive might become. That, he knew, would depend on Jenn and the roads.

He was stepping out of the shop when he ran into Winona Cobbs. He smiled at once, asking lightly, "Storm still coming?"

She frowned at him. "Nobody's listening."

"Maybe because the weather forecast is promising clear blue skies for the next week."

She shook her head. "There are things they don't know. Clouds are growing over this town."

"Winona…"

But she cut him off and smiled suddenly. "Don't believe me, Braden Traub. It doesn't matter. Soon enough you'll know." Then she paused. "I want to talk to that girl you're seeing."

Braden hesitated, unsure of what Winona knew or didn't know. Other than his brothers, he figured no one in town knew he'd seen Jenn for more than coffee. Of course, there was no guaranteeing his brothers hadn't gabbed somewhere. They had an unfortunate tendency to make jokes that sometimes revealed too much.

"That girl," Winona said, her gaze growing vague. "Something about her. I want to see her."

"I'll tell her," he said, although he had no intention of doing so. Jenn had been quite up front about how uneasy Winona made her.

Winona's eyes snapped back into focus, fixing on him. "Ignore me, young Traub, and that girl will not find something she desperately needs."

With that, Winona continued on her way. Braden stared after her, wondering what it was with that woman. While he was inclined to believe most of what she said was mumbo jumbo, every so often he had the weirdest feeling that she could see something invisible to others.

Well, if her damn blizzard materialized, he guessed he'd change his opinion.

There hadn't been any snow since Saturday, not even the light flurries they'd had then. The sky overhead was that incredibly clear, almost painful winter blue; the mountains appeared to gleam as if they wore sparkling white coats, and the breeze seemed to be holding its breath.

Jenn hardly waited for him to park the truck in front of her cabin. Her eagerness pleased him as she appeared in her door, waved, then stepped out and locked up. She was dressed for the weather in a decent parka and snow boots, ready for just about anything except getting stranded in the woods. Which wasn't even a remote possibility. He knew the terrain like the back of his hand, and could keep them safe. He even had a few survival skills tucked up his sleeve. Besides, Dallas—and probably the whole family by now—knew where he was going. If he didn't return or call by nightfall, the search parties would be out.

He did manage to climb out and open the passenger door for her before she reached it.

"This is exciting," she said as she slid in. "I've been wanting to get up into those mountains since I got here, but I haven't wanted to do it alone."

"Not in that old beater of yours, reliable as it may be," he agreed. She was making him smile, and he liked it. Imagine a woman being this pleased about a drive in the mountains. In his experience, most wanted more expensive entertainment, or something more exciting. A drive sounded tame, but apparently, not to Jenn.

"Any particular way you want to head?" he asked as he drove away from her place.

"Just mountains. You know the area. I've just been admiring from afar."

"Not very far in this valley. I'll go southwest then. There are some beautiful vistas that open up so you'll get to see more than a tunnel of forest."

"Great!"

"And by the way, I've decided not to go visit my brothers and their families today. Bad timing for them." He patted the insulated bottle on the bench seat between them. "Coffee, if you want. I also got us a sack lunch, so don't be afraid to tell me if you get hungry."

"Maybe later. I just had breakfast."

They didn't talk much as he took a road outside town that linked up with the drive he had chosen. "We won't be able to go over the passes now," he remarked. "Closed for the winter up here."

"Do we get really closed off here?"

"Well, not completely. We can usually head down to Kalispell and from there get most everywhere else we need to go. But we don't have any major roads passing over the mountains here. It gets a little sticky sometimes."

"Around your butt to get to your elbow?"

He laughed. "That's about it. Occasionally, we might

even be cut off from Kalispell for a couple of days until the plows finish, but that's rare. We have pretty good snow removal for the most part."

At last they began the climb, gentle at times, steeper at others, but always winding. He cracked his window just a bit to let in the fresh smell of the evergreens and the slightly sharp one of the fresh snow.

"Have you thought about that Christmas tree?" he asked.

"It seems silly just for me."

"Not if it makes you smile. If you got a very small, real one, think of the way it would scent the cabin."

He felt, rather than saw, her nod as he negotiated a tight turn. The pavement was still black, although a of bit wet from snowmelt could be seen on either side of the road.

"I'm going to have to turn back by one or so," he remarked. "Sorry it can't be longer."

"How come?"

"See how wet the pavement is? That's snow melting. If the temperature starts to drop, it could turn into black ice. Not good."

"Oh. I guess there's a lot I don't know."

"Surely you ran into this in Massachusetts. You did say that's where you're from?"

Again he noted the slight hesitation. "I didn't get out of town much."

"Ah." He let that lie, though he wondered. Didn't get out of town much? What had her life been like before she arrived here? He didn't know how to ask without seeming intrusive. "No car?"

"Public transportation usually. It's great."

Well, he could believe that. She *was* young, and if

there was a convenient alternative, why get a car? "So did you have a job?"

"Yes." That came quickly enough. "My last one was at an antiques store. I spent an awful lot of time dusting and oiling old pieces. They were fascinating, though, and the owner could tell me about most of them. Maybe not specific history, but how they were used. She had this one pharmacy cabinet that she wouldn't part with. It was huge, full of cubbies and drawers with a big counter and cabinets beneath. It might've been the biggest piece of furniture I'd ever seen, and it looked so useful."

"But if it was that big, where would you put it?"

She laughed. "It wouldn't have fit in most rooms, that's for sure. We also sold a lot of old iceboxes, the kind that look like chests, with doors on the front. People liked to use them for kitchen islands, so we were always on the hunt for more of them."

"Did you help with the hunt?"

"Mostly from catalogs and computers. She spent a lot of time traveling to shows to find special things."

"I find the antiques business, um, strange."

He felt her turn in her seat to look at him. "Why?"

He shrugged one shoulder. "One person's junk, another one's treasure, that's all. I'm sure there are pieces in my parents' house that would qualify, and maybe some in my own."

"You have your own house?"

"Of course, right on the ranch. Built most of it myself. I won't mention the help from my brothers. Just a snug little place. But back to antiques. I have a whole thing about that. I mean, we keep a lot of serviceable pieces at our place. Some of them go back to when the family first came west. I bet some of them would fetch a nice price in an antiques store, and I can't imagine why."

She laughed quietly. "I did wonder about some things."

"How could you not? They can need a lot of work, but because they're old, they're worth more?"

"I can see I'll never sell you an antique."

"Probably not," he admitted, and flashed her a grin. "I'm more interested in usefulness."

The switchbacks were coming closer together now, and he fell silent as he paid close attention to the road. As they climbed in altitude, the possibility of ice in shady places grew. No complaints. He liked the quiet; he loved the beauty of the winter woods; he loved being away from everything, and his companion seemed comfortable for a change.

Before long he had slowed to little more than a crawl. Trees and sharp curves occluded sightlines, and he didn't want to come around a tight bend and hit rocks that could take out the bottom of his truck. Cliffs dotted the landscape to either side, not everywhere of course, but enough of them to make him cautious when they weren't rolling between tall trees.

Just as he was thinking it might be best to find a place to turn around and head back, they came around a tight curve and Jenn gasped.

"I dreamed about that mountain!"

He wondered what she meant, but he didn't take time to ask. The rising alpine peak wasn't very visible from town, but up here it seemed to dominate the whole world, and he knew it could be seen from other mountain towns, as well. He looked around until he found a safe place to pull over on gravel and snow, then parked the truck.

The mountain was now concealed by trees again, but he had an idea.

"You like it?"

"It's gorgeous!"

"That's Fall Mountain, quite a landmark. Let's hike back to where you can see it. It'll only take a few minutes, and that's sure a sight to be admired."

She was climbing out before he could help her. He grabbed the thermos, certain that coffee was going to be necessary before long. It was far colder up here than below, and the wind could whip around those curves like a lash.

By the time he climbed out to follow, she was marching steadily back down the road like a woman with a mission. Quirky much? he wondered with amusement. She was certainly different from most of the women he knew. They didn't generally leap out of a car in a hurry to take a look at a mountain.

Something about her determination gave him pause, however, and he followed slowly, feeling that she might need some space, although he couldn't imagine why.

Finally, he reached her side, and she stood looking up at that dang mountain with wonder. Almost awe. Then she said something that stilled everything inside him.

"I belong here."

Her tone warned him that this was important to her, though he couldn't begin to understand what she was driving at. Damn, he needed to figure this woman out, to understand the mystery that made her do things like this.

She belonged here? He suspected she didn't mean on this road. For some reason, that mountain seemed to mean something to her. Well, it was a helluva landmark.

Or maybe she was just responding to the beauty of the place. A lot of people took one look at these mountains and wanted to find a way to stay.

But something in her face seemed to glow. As if she had discovered a treasure.

Then, slowly, it faded. She became aware of him again,

of her surroundings, as if waking from a dream. "How could I know that mountain?" she asked.

He didn't believe she was asking him, so he didn't even attempt an answer. Finally, when she darted an embarrassed look at him, he decided it was time to act as if nothing at all had happened.

"Beautiful view," he said. "Takes the breath away. Want some coffee?"

Jenn refused his offer. She was too entranced by the mountain, and stared up at it for a while longer, feeling something deep within her mind vibrate a response, like a harmonic frequency. She *knew* that mountain. She was sure of it in the way she had been sure the name Jenn fit her.

So she was in the right place. At least, in the right vicinity. If she could have hugged that peak, she might have. It seemed to reach out to her like a call home. Like a mother.

But while she could have stood there forever, even she couldn't ignore the cold indefinitely. It had begun to penetrate her jeans, her parka, and make her ears burn.

A gentle touch on her elbow forced her back.

"We need to go," Braden said. "Sorry. I'll bring you back another time, but right now you're starting to turn blue. Pull up that hood before your ears get frostbite."

Reluctantly, she obeyed, surprisingly glad that the snorkel hood not only warmed her ears but also hid her face a bit. Man, he must think she was nuts.

If he did, though, he gave no sign of it. Once they were back in the truck, he turned them around and headed back down. When he suggested she pour them some coffee, she did so without argument, realizing for the first time how deeply the cold had penetrated.

"Next time we do this," she tried to say lightly, "maybe I should wear some snow pants."

Almost as soon as she spoke, she realized she had inadvertently suggested a second date. She darted a nervous look his way, wondering if his offer to bring her up here another time had been merely polite.

Though he was still driving, he reached sideways and stroked her cheek lightly with the back of his fingers. A hunger for more mushroomed in her instantly. "We're certainly going to make sure you're warmer," he agreed. "Either that or the weather. We might still get a few warm days this month, though. It's only December. Next one we'll come back."

Relaxing finally, she leaned back and sipped the hot coffee. Then he lowered his hand and let it come to rest lightly on her thigh. The heat of his touch penetrated to her very core. Life could feel so good sometimes.

Chapter Six

Three days later, utterly without warning, Winona's predicted blizzard blew in. Nothing on the weather reports had prepared the town, but here it was, blowing like the very devil, the snow falling so heavily it nearly blinded. Icy, too, stinging exposed skin like needles.

Aw hell, Braden thought. The ranch had been prepared; there wasn't a whole hell of lot more he could do in this, but he'd screwed up.

He'd failed to get more wood to Jenn. Thinking he'd had time, remembering her reluctance to use the stove, it hadn't exactly seemed urgent.

After a quick breakfast he hit the woodshed and filled the back of his truck with enough wood for a week or so. Then he went inside the main house for a quick coffee and found his mother and father in the kitchen.

"Everyone's safely in their homes," Bob Traub announced. "Predictions are we'll lose all power, and all of a sudden the weather reports are talking about forty or fifty inches of snow."

"The meteorologists who didn't know anything about this storm?"

"The same. Some kind of anomaly. You can listen to them blather on about how the mountains make their own weather if you want."

"I'll skip it. I promised Jenn I'd bring her a truckload

of wood, and the way it's building out there, I'm not sure I'll be able to see where I'm going before long."

Ellie rose. "Grab food out of the pantry while you're at it. I'm sure that child isn't at all prepared for this."

She probably wasn't, Braden thought. Probably not at all. Twenty minutes later, his father had helped him load a whole bunch of canned goods into the cab along with a three-pound can of coffee. "Must have the essentials," the senior Traub said, winking.

"I don't know if I'll be able to get back."

His father grew serious. "Son, just take care of her. She's a babe in the woods, and this is building from bad to dangerous. And dang me if I ever fail to listen to Winona again."

"She forgot to predict the exact day and hour," Braden retorted. His dad's laugh followed him as he climbed into his truck to go to Jenn.

It was bad, really bad. Whiteout conditions hit from time to time, and it was a damn good thing he could have driven these roads blindfolded. He might as well have been.

Another hour or so, and no one would be going anywhere.

Jenn had heard the wind during the night. It had made the cabin creak a bit, but it was a pleasant sound and didn't frighten her. Besides, she had other thoughts to occupy her, like her reaction to that mountain.

She belonged here? Had she really said that? Really felt it? But when she closed her eyes and cast herself back into that moment, she experienced it all over again. Finally, at long last, she had felt familiarity for something besides a Christmas pageant and a name. Familiarity for a place.

God, she'd been looking for that so long!

She made coffee with the drip coffeemaker. She'd let the fire in the woodstove go out because she was down to her last few logs, and the man she'd called for delivery said he couldn't get to her for a week. She might need those logs, she thought, especially since this previously cozy cabin seemed to have developed a whole bunch of chinks overnight. No matter where she stood, she could feel a strong draft when the wind howled.

Finally, afraid of what she would see, she pulled the curtain back and gasped. She knew a blizzard when she saw one, and this one looked positively evil. How long would it last?

She had no TV because reception here stank. Her computer was hooked into a phone line, so slow on dial-up that she rarely used it for going on the web. Talk about going back to pioneer days. The thought made her almost giggle until she realized that she might be in trouble.

She had taken Braden's advice to stock up on some canned goods, but if the power went out, keeping warm was going to be a problem. The only heat she could make, now that her wood was almost gone, was with her gas stove.

She stood at the window, gnawing at her lip, wondering if she should try to make it to town. What she saw didn't hearten her. The trees surrounding her house almost vanished in the blowing snow. She doubted she'd be able to see more than a foot beyond the front bumper of her car, and she knew she couldn't drive that miserable road blind.

What had possessed her to take this place anyway? In June it had seemed perfect. Right now it felt like madness. She could freeze to death out here.

Just as she was considering the possibility that there

might be more wrong with her than amnesia, she saw Braden's blue truck emerge from the snow like a ghost.

Her heart leaped. He was riding to the rescue. Maybe he'd take her out of here. Although with the conditions so bad…

He pulled up right in front of her stoop and jumped out, bending against the wind as he approached her door, holding his hat on his head. He almost looked like a ghost, too, and in those few steps he actually vanished in the snow twice.

As soon as she heard him pound his feet on the stoop, she opened the door. He darted inside and closed it quickly behind him.

"Do you like living in an icebox?" he asked without even greeting her.

"This place seems to have become leaky overnight. The heater is blasting and it can't seem to keep up."

"I'm not surprised." He pushed his cowboy hat back a little on his head. "I brought wood. I brought food. And you may be stuck with me until this passes. I could hardly see where I was going."

"I was thinking about that just before you appeared," she admitted. "I was wondering if I could get to town, but everything out there is almost invisible." Stuck with him? Part of her wanted to leap exuberantly at the thought. Still…no, she wouldn't even think about her fears over intimacy. If she had to get "stuck" with someone, she was elated that it was Braden.

"We'd have found your frozen body inside your car at the first thaw." He shook his head. "Wise decision to stay here. Let me bring in some wood, and we'll deal with the heat first. Do I smell coffee?"

She had to smile. "Want some?"

"First let me get a few armloads of wood in here.

Dang, you have a lousy heater. Cold as it is outside, I didn't feel a whole lot warmer when I came in."

She couldn't disagree. Dressed in her warmest fleece pants, a heavy shirt and sweater, she still hovered near the point of shivering. "Thanks for coming, Braden," she said sincerely. Just the sight of him made her feel better and less alone. And the thought of having him here through the storm was as pleasurable as it was reassuring. All kinds of sensual possibilities began dancing through her head, an anticipatory excitement she didn't want to shut down. At least not yet.

"Can't leave a pretty lady to become a winter statistic," he said cheerfully, then headed back outside to start unloading the back of his truck.

"Can I help?" she called after him.

"Stay in here where it's warmer. Slightly. A little bit. I'm used to hauling stuff around. Pack mule, that's me."

"I thought it was just Mule."

He laughed as he disappeared into the swirling snow.

A pretty lady? Those words brought a secret smile to her heart and thrilled her deeply. He thought she was pretty. She sure hoped he meant it.

He'd covered the wood on his truck bed with a tarp, so as he brought in four armloads, there wasn't much snow on it to melt.

"I'll get the food in a bit," he said, "and wood as we need it. Let me get this going, then we'll turn off your heat. I think you'll find this blaze will more than make up for it."

She brought him coffee. He drained half the mug in one draft before he started working on the fire. He was amazing to watch, she thought. Every movement sure and practiced. Almost like magic, he soon had flames leaping inside the box. When he at last closed the door, he left the air intakes wide open.

"First we warm up." He smiled and rose from his squat. "I sure as hell am glad I came out here."

"I am, too."

He surprised her by reaching out to touch her cheek lightly. A shiver of a different kind ran through her, but he dropped his hand swiftly. "Let's see if we can find where all these drafts are coming from."

The swift change left her off balance. After a moment she collected her scattered thoughts. It would have been so easy to just sink into the pleasure his lightest touch could cause her. "I looked and couldn't figure it out."

"As hard as it's blowing, it wouldn't take large chinks to create a problem. You might also have been losing some heat up the chimney pipe since you didn't have a fire, and then there's those windows. Single-paned. Not good." He paused. "I guess Winona was right."

"Was she? I haven't been following the weather."

"Out here you should. But yeah, this storm wasn't predicted by the meteorologists. My dad said they're busy trying to explain that mountains create their own weather."

"Do they?"

"Oh, yeah. But a storm like this?" He shook his head. "I need to be careful or I'm going to start believing in Winona."

She laughed. "Would that be so bad?"

"Terrible." He winked. "Okay, now for some more of that coffee and a hunt for chinks."

She was happy to refill his mug. It was such a little thing to do for the man who had come riding to her rescue. Worry about him being here for a few days settled onto the back burner for now. As long as they had impersonal subjects for discussion, she was safe. And her delight seemed to be overcoming her instinctive worries anyway. It was a happy change, as far as she was concerned. "What could we do about them anyway?" she asked. "I mean, to fill them?"

"Depends on how big they are. I could use all your socks. Or some of that caulking in my truck might be enough."

She glanced out the window again. "Won't it freeze out there?"

For once *he* was the one who appeared startled. "You're right. And the food. Okay, let me get that stuff safely stowed in here. I'm running ahead of myself."

More boxes appeared inside, some near the kitchen and stocked with canned and dried goods. He put a couple of tubes of caulking on the small table, then began to hunt around the cabin for where the cold air was getting in.

Meanwhile, the stove began to elevate the temperature, doing far better than the heater had.

He had no more luck than she. He finally pulled out a chair at the table, shucked his jacket and remarked, "Maybe it's just temperature differential. You do have those windows. They need thermal drapes."

"I didn't think of anything like that when I moved in."

His smile was crooked. "Of course not. It was June. But I'm through reorganizing your life. I'm surprised you haven't snapped at me yet. I'm sure you're perfectly capable of making your own decisions."

She sat across from him, wishing she was sure of that. "I don't know," she said finally. "There are a whole lot of things I never thought about when I came here. I just wanted to be here."

"God's country," he said quietly. Pivoting on his chair,

he reached for the coffeepot and topped off both their mugs. "As long as we have coffee…"

She laughed at that. "Who needs anything else, especially now that it's getting warm in here."

"Too warm?" he asked immediately.

"Maybe warm enough to ditch the sweater. That would be nice. But no, I'm not uncomfortable."

Then came one of those long silences that she dreaded. She realized in theory that people could be comfortable with silence, but for her those quiet spells had become fraught with threat. She didn't have the small talk; she couldn't summon some past memory to share with humor. She quite simply had little she dared to mention except the immediate. If the silence went on long enough, he might start asking questions she couldn't answer, just to chat.

But he leaned back, looking out the window at the blizzard that had cut off the world, seeming content to sip his coffee.

After a while he remarked, "Can I say I'm having a good time? I don't often get to relax like this."

"Working a ranch must be hard."

"It's certainly busy. You get used to the work at an early age, though. We're not gentlemen ranchers, but honest-to-goodness working cowboys. We do almost all of it."

She bit her lip, hesitating. It was hard when you weren't even sure what questions to ask. "The cattle? How do they get through something like this?"

He looked at her then. "They huddle together, we built windbreaks out of hay for them, and if we're lucky, most of them will make it, as long as it doesn't get too cold."

She pondered that, trying to imagine the loss in real terms. "So this storm could really cost you?"

"Yep." He paused. "We're luckier than most. Ranching is getting harder every year, but we have resources to fall back on. We'll be okay. But I admit, we don't like losing cattle. Every single one counts."

She eyed the storm outside the window, seeing it in a different way. Braden must be sitting there worried about his livelihood, yet he'd come here to bail her out. She couldn't imagine the cattle standing out in this, trying to stay out of the wind and keep as warm as possible. Yet, he seemed almost philosophical about it.

"You've faced this before?" she asked.

"We face winter every year. Other times it might be drought. We get by, though. Actually, we do better than just get by. We're lucky to be such a large operation."

She'd heard mentions around town that the Traub family did quite well with their ranching, although she had no idea exactly what that meant. Apparently, they were nowhere near dirt poor. That was, after all, a fairly new truck he drove.

She let her mind wander away from the threat the blizzard posed, deciding he had judged it from experience, and he didn't seem too awfully worried. Her stomach growled unexpectedly, and her cheeks heated. "Sorry, I haven't eaten yet. I'm a bad hostess. Would you like breakfast?"

"Just more coffee for now. I had breakfast right before I headed out here. You go ahead and eat."

While she prepared her egg and toast, he carried his mug over to the window and stared out into the blizzard. It gave her a nice view of his broad shoulders and narrow hips, and the opportunity to just gaze.

It struck her that he might be feeling caged at the moment. He must be a man used to spending the majority of his time outdoors, and right now he was trapped inside. He was also accustomed to working a lot, and he had not a thing to do here, really. He had done what he had come to do, and now he was a prisoner of the storm and these four walls.

And maybe he was worrying more than he let on. That storm out there was dangerous for man and beast alike.

She could think of no distraction to offer. She had no games lying around, no way to wile the time. There was just the two of them, and conversation, or silence. Given how she felt about conversation, silence seemed preferable.

But she wanted him to like her. A vain hope considering that if he found out the truth about her, he'd probably head the other direction as fast as he could. Still, it would be nice to make him smile, to be able to entertain him, to make him enjoy time with her.

To feel once again that she was truly worth something to someone. If she had ever felt that way. How would she know?

That damn wall in her memory reared up again, and she stared at its blank granite face. Blank, except for a name, a mountain and a pageant. It was a huge wall, and that was little enough to put on it.

"Winona wants to talk to you," he said, turning from the window.

Her heart skipped several beats, and for a second she felt lightheaded. "Why? I don't want to talk to her."

He half smiled. "I already figured that out. But I ran into her the other day, and she said she needed to talk to you. Nothing about why. Nothing about what. Winona can be the definition of cryptic. Regardless, if you don't want to talk to her, you'd better keep your distance."

"I don't like the way she makes me feel," Jenn admitted reluctantly. "It's kind of weird. Nobody's made me feel like that before." At least not in the short period of her life that she could remember.

"Maybe she just pulled lottery numbers out of the thin air for you."

She gave a halfhearted laugh, but there was no way on earth she could explain to herself why she reacted to Winona the way she did. That sense of an electric shock. An unreasoning fear, she supposed. But if she planned on staying here, she doubted she could avoid the woman forever.

Braden came her way and began to make a fresh pot of coffee. Then he went to his jacket, which he'd hung on one of the cabin's most useful items: a peg beside the door.

"I have a deck of cards. Care to play?" He pulled out a battered pack. "I can't guarantee you can't see through them."

"Why not?" She wished her heartbeat would slow down.

"You will never know how many poker games get played around a campfire at night. Or on a long evening. This is my lucky deck, though, so I won't replace it."

"Lucky deck?" she repeated, blinking, her anxiety easing a bit. At least he wasn't going to keep talking about Winona.

"Sure. I've cleaned out my brothers a few times with it."

"Cleaned them out? For real money?"

He laughed. "No way. I have to see them often enough. So I have a box of plastic chips in the truck. But we don't have to play poker. Any game will do. We can keep track of points if you have a pad and pencil."

The wind never stopped howling. The density of the cabin walls toned it down some, but the keening was still audible, and the way the windows rattled sometimes couldn't be ignored.

Braden was glad he was here. From what he'd seen, if the power went out, Jenn would have been in a world of hurt. He'd barely made it here as it was, a certain recklessness and determination drawing him over here in weather he would never have otherwise tried to drive through.

He even patted himself on the back for bringing out the deck of cards. He had the pleasure of seeing her seriously relax, forgetting whatever those things were that sometimes disturbed or frightened her. She focused entirely on the games they played, and he was careful to direct his conversation mostly the same way.

They played hearts and spades, and finally he taught her seven-card stud. Poker wasn't the best game in the world with only two players, but she seemed to enjoy learning how it worked. If he'd had another deck of cards, he'd have suggested pinochle.

They lunched on the bread and cold cuts he'd brought with him, made even more coffee, and soon they were chatting and laughing, if not like old friends, certainly like comfortable card game buddies.

None of that answered his questions about her, but he figured now wouldn't be a good time to pry. If he upset her, she couldn't even throw him out.

He went outside to bring in some more wood, noting that the storm seemed to be worsening. Two-foot drifts had appeared against the cabin, and the sky hadn't lightened one bit. If anything, the sky had darkened; the gray clouds seemed like a portent of worse to come.

When he'd finished bringing in the wood and checked the fire, he straightened to find her standing with her hands clasped, looking at him.

"When is this going to stop?" she asked. "I get that it could go on all day, but it seems to be getting worse. Is it?"

"Yeah, it is. We had more light a couple of hours ago. I think the clouds have thickened. As for when it'll be over, I don't know. Want me to call Winona?"

He'd meant it as a joke, but saw again that fear flicker across her face. He couldn't imagine why anyone should be afraid of the psychic. She was harmless; you could listen to her or not as you chose. Why should Jenn even care?

But clearly she did, and that heightened his curiosity even more. The woman was like a box of secrets, and every little thing whetted his appetite for more answers.

He'd noticed, for example, that when he occasionally had recalled childhood memories today, like jumping in the cattle pond only to come up so covered with muck, he'd needed to be hosed down in the barnyard, she hadn't volunteered a single story from her own childhood. Not one amusing memory. Not any kind of memory at all.

"I won't call Winona," he said after a moment. "I will note for the record that while she said this storm was coming, she didn't tell us a date. Now how could I ask her to know when it ends?"

A little laugh escaped her, and her tension fled. "Good point. But I kind of meant, you've lived here all your life. How long do these things usually last?"

"It varies. Are you tired of me already?" He was joking, but her response made it clear she hadn't taken it that way.

She stepped toward him, hand out. "No! Oh, no, Braden, this has been fun so far. And you came to my rescue."

He waved a hand. "Forget the rescue part. Just as long as I'm not overstaying my welcome."

"I don't think that could happen."

The words appeared to startle her as much as they did him. What was she saying? Should he move in closer? Did she want something more from him?

Before he could do a thing, the power went out. At once the cabin was concealed in dark shadows that danced in the red glow of the stove.

"Oh, man," she breathed.

"Well, now comes the fun," he said with deliberate cheer. "Might as well nest out here near the stove. I was getting tired of the table anyway."

She sighed. "So was I. I think I have some candles. And a flashlight."

"Well, we don't exactly need them right now. The stove is giving off enough light."

"Not if you want to play cards."

He tilted his head. "Do you?" Because he was getting the distinct impression that playing cards had taken some kind of pressure off her. That pressure interested him. Was she afraid of just having an ordinary conversation? Why in the world could that be?

"Not really. Not just yet," she said slowly.

Right then and there he made up his mind not to say anything much unless she initiated a conversation. One of these days he wanted to get to the root of whatever her problem was, but there was no reason to push.

"Well," she said after a moment, "I guess we could treat this like a camping trip."

She turned and went to pull the comforter off her bed, along with the pillows. She spread them on the floor in front of the stove, but not too close. Then she returned to a small closet and pulled out another comforter. "The floor is hard," she said by way of explanation.

Only if you wanted to sit on it, he thought. He took

one of the ancient armchairs, careful to leave her some
unthreatening space. She even took the bright blue blanket she'd bought and spread it with the rest. Then she
plopped down in the middle of the nest, her back to him.

He might as well have not even been there. It was as
if she was shutting him out in some way. With anyone
else he might have felt stung, but not with this woman.
He was beginning to believe that her problems were huge
and went deep.

All he knew was that he wished there was some damn
way he could help her. It bothered him to see her troubled, to sense that she felt alone even among friends, to
feel that she was frightened of something. But how could
he ask? If he did, he wouldn't blame her for driving him
out into the blizzard.

They were hardly acquainted, after all, and right now
were sharing an intimacy that had been manufactured
by the storm, not something they had built themselves.

An intimacy they would apparently never share as
long as she kept her secrets. He rubbed his chin, staring at the back of her head, resisting an urge to sit down
beside her and wrap her in his arms in the hope that an
embrace might make her feel safer from whatever demon
she harbored.

Another reason for her to kick him out, he thought
ruefully.

Then she astonished him, leaving him to hold his
breath and wait.

"Can you keep a secret?" she asked.

"From everyone?"

"Yes. From your family and everyone else. I don't
want anybody to know."

"I can do that, unless you're about to tell me you're
a bank robber."

Her laugh sounded almost bitter. "I can't stand it anymore," she said quietly. "I just can't. I'm all alone inside my head, damaged, afraid. You may as well know, since you're being so nice. I'm not normal. And after this you'll probably want nothing to do with me ever again."

"I can't imagine that."

She finally twisted on the blankets, looking at him. "You're attracted to me?"

He supposed it had been written all over him, and he wasn't ashamed that she knew. That's how men and women got together. Nature and all that. "Hell, yeah."

"Well, I'm attracted to you, too." She faced the stove again. "And nothing can ever come from it."

For some reason, his heart almost stopped. He'd expected a whole lot of things, but not her to turn him away before he'd even made a real approach. The idea pained him, although it seemed extreme considering the short time he'd known her. "Why? Are you married?"

"That's just it," she said finally, her voice sharpening and rising a bit. *"I don't know!"*

Chapter Seven

Braden didn't know how to react. He wanted to slide down beside her and hold her, but he feared that something important was happening inside her, something that shouldn't be interrupted. Her emotional earthquake was almost palpable to him, as dramatic as the storm that battered Rust Creek Falls.

He was in over his head; he knew that before she even began speaking. But he bit back any sound, any gesture, that might interrupt her. Whatever this was, she desperately needed it to happen.

"I haven't told my girlfriends," she said, her voice thin. "I haven't told anyone. I'm so ashamed."

"Of what?" he dared to ask quietly. Never would he tell her all the imaginings that popped into his head at that confession. The matters that might shame her created a long list, but certainly not what came out of her next.

"I have amnesia," she said, her voice breaking. "I don't know who I am. I don't remember a single thing before I woke up from a coma in the hospital four years ago. I don't even know what happened to me."

He saw her hand reach up to touch the back of her head, stroking something he couldn't see.

"I was found wandering without any identification. All I had were the clothes on my back and this necklace. God, Braden, even the doctors didn't really believe at first that I couldn't remember anything of my past at all. Do you know how rare that is?"

"No," he admitted. Inside he felt rocked to the core by what she was telling him. It was as if everything he had felt and noticed about her imploded until one great big monolith in his mind covered it all. Her skittishness, her lack of conversation, her occasional evasions... It was enough to leave him stunned.

"I'm someone, obviously, but I don't know who. I've been searching, and my search brought me here, but I still don't know anything about who I was, what kind of person I was. Or, like I said, whether I'm married. Although I'm probably not because the cops hunted the missing persons reports and I never came up. Whoever I was apparently didn't make friends or have family."

He hesitated, sorrow replacing shock. "You can't be sure."

"Of course I can't be sure. All I can be sure of is that nobody gave enough of a damn to report me missing."

"Maybe you'd moved on for some reason, and they didn't expect you to come back."

She swiveled her head, looking at him from the corner of her eye. "That's a kind explanation. The truth is probably not as pretty. Part of me is desperate to recover my past, and part of me is terrified of it. What if I don't like the woman I used to be?"

"But you're the woman you are now," he argued quietly.

"Who is she? I don't know!"

"She's Jenn or Jennifer. You got that much, right?"

"Maybe." She pulled up her knees, resting her chin on them, wrapping her arms around her legs. "How can I be sure?"

"I don't know," he admitted. "But you seemed awfully certain when you told me. And then there was the mountain. I don't think you could come from this town. By now someone would have recognized you, but there are other towns that mountain is visible from. Maybe we need to check them out."

"Or it could just resemble a mountain I used to know."

He fell silent for a while, but when she offered nothing more, he left his chair to sit beside her on the blankets. Hesitantly, he reached for her hand and was relieved when she didn't snatch it back. He squeezed it, holding it and caressing it gently with his fingers, clamping down on the desires she always evoked in him.

"This must be enough to make you crazy sometimes," he remarked.

"Sometimes I think I *am* crazy. I just know… Well, I don't know a whole lot. I feel like I'm running in circles in a hamster wheel, looking for a way off. I've had a few flashes that seemed to come from my past, but I don't know whether to trust them."

"Why not?"

"Because that big empty hole has been there so long now that I may be filling it with wishful thinking."

God, he hadn't even thought of that. Not that he'd had a whole lot of time to think of anything yet. He still felt rocked back on his heels by her revelation; he ached for the pain she must endure. But there was one thing he could be utterly frank about. "I can't imagine it, Jenn. I just simply can't imagine what it must be like for you."

"Nobody can," she admitted. Her chin still rested on her knees. "I don't even know if I can explain it. It's like there's this huge, blank wall in my mind, and I can't reach anything that's behind it. Sometimes, for brief periods, I forget it. I'm just in the moment. Then something will happen to remind me. A question I can't answer."

He turned it round in his mind. "So that's why you sometimes seem evasive."

"Yeah. Because I just don't know. And I get so tired of having to slip away from questions I should be able to answer, or come up with something noncommittal enough that I don't get asked more questions."

He gave her hand another gentle squeeze. "Has it occurred to you that maybe folks would understand better than you think? I'm not running. Maybe you noticed."

"Where can you run to in the middle of this storm?"

That ignited a spark of anger in him. "I wouldn't run if it was a clear day out there. Let's get that straight from the start. I'm not sitting here thinking about me. I'm thinking about you."

She turned her head, until her cheek rested on her knee, and looked at him. "You're a very nice man, Braden Traub. Look at me. I'm not normal."

"What's normal?" His voice held a slight edge of anger. "Why do you even ask yourself that? Why torment yourself? You have a big enough problem already without walking around feeling abnormal."

She lifted her head. "You can't possibly think total amnesia is normal!"

He was relieved to see that flare in her. "Think about all the soldiers coming back from war with traumatic brain injuries. They've changed, but just because they've changed, that doesn't mean they're not normal. They're normal *for what they have been through*."

"That's a false argument," she said and averted her face.

"No, it's not. It's the truth. Normal is a relative thing. Do yourself a favor and recognize that much, at least. Then you can get on with life without feeling like you can't possibly find a place to belong."

Her head pivoted sharply around toward him. "How do you know that?"

"It's a feeling I get from you. You don't feel you belong, and you're afraid you never will. Tell me that isn't true."

He watched her open her mouth, as if she wanted to respond, then she slumped again, burying her face against her knees, curling into a tight ball. He wanted to pry her out of that ball, to help her relax, to let her know that she really *wasn't* alone unless she chose to be.

But he was well and truly in over his head and he knew it. He thought about what little he'd seen of her, and realized that even though she was surrounded by girlfriends sometimes, she didn't really let them close to her. It was as if she walked in an invisible bubble, unable to reach out, unable to be reached.

He wished he had some magic wand to wave, some perfect words to speak. Something to reach her, to let her know it was safe to let someone inside her shell.

Her obvious retreat frightened him, though. He felt as if she were slipping away, and that if he didn't stop her withdrawal, she might just disappear like a mist.

Shoving himself to his feet so he couldn't do something stupid like grab her and force a hug on her, he paced the small cabin. The storm that raged outside didn't hold a candle to the one she faced inside, he guessed. He couldn't imagine all that she endured and would continue to endure.

But he had to get through to her, to make her understand that her loss of memory wasn't some kind of scarlet letter. Whoever she had been before, she needed to understand that people liked the person she was now. He'd seen it in a group of women he admired, women who called her friend and had invited her into their circle.

In himself. He hadn't come barreling out here to help

someone he didn't like. He'd known he was going to be stuck here until this storm cleared and the roads opened up again. He'd *wanted* to go through this blizzard here, with her.

But he was afraid he would scare her if he told her that, even though it might reassure her that someone truly wanted to be with her. Damn, he wished he understood better, but there was only one way that would happen. She had to talk, and right now she resembled a clam that had pulled back into its shell.

"Jenn?"

"Hmm?" The sound was muffled.

"Want some more coffee?"

She lifted her head a little. "I think I'm wired enough."

"Or maybe not. Milk? Something to eat? A lesson in how to cook on the woodstove?" He didn't care what pulled her back to him. Hell, he'd go out into the blizzard and build a snowman for her amusement right outside the window.

"I'm sorry," she said after a moment. "I don't know why I dumped on you."

"Don't be sorry. I'm glad I'm here. I'm ready to listen to anything you want to say. But I'm trying really hard not to push you."

At last she sighed and let go of her crouch. Moving a bit gingerly, as if she had stiffened, she straightened out her legs, then stood up. "I'm not being much of a hostess."

"I don't remember being an invited guest. I'm not looking for a hostess anyway."

She turned slowly in place and tried to give him a smile. The expression was wan, and her eyes were pinched, even a little frightened.

"Relax," he said after a moment. "I still like you, I'm

still attracted to you, and frankly I don't care who you might have been before. I like who you are now."

Exactly the wrong thing to say. He saw it instantly, but it was too late to swallow the words. He wanted to kick his own butt.

"What if I remember? What if I'm really some awful person?"

At least he could answer that one. "You're not an awful person right now. If you *used* to be one, that doesn't mean you have to be one again."

Well, at least that appeared to be the right answer. She relaxed visibly and took a step toward him. "I am a little hungry," she admitted. "For a light snack."

"I'm sure I brought some of those. The Traub household can't function without easily portable snacks."

He checked the boxes he'd brought in and came up with a package of pretzels. "These look good?"

"Yummy. I'll get a bowl."

"Good heavens, you don't eat out of the bag?" He was teasing, and it pleased him when her smile became more natural.

"Not when I can reach a bowl."

"My mother would love you. She's death on bag eaters."

Jenn laughed, and the tension eased out of the cabin. No telling for how long, but he was willing to bide his time and see what came down the pike. Given the weather out there, he was fairly certain they would be here for a few days. Long enough for her to confide in him again as long as he was careful.

Because he really *did* want to know more about her, about the time since her injury, since she couldn't recall anything before that. It occurred to him that she must be a really amazing person, to have faced all that and somehow come through it until she found a place and friends here in the middle of virtual nowhere. Hell of a risk, he thought, given that it would have been easier for her to remain anonymous in a big city. Around here, everyone knew who had sneezed and when.

They once again sat at the table, the glow of the stove barely reaching them. She seemed to have little interest in light at the moment, and he supposed she felt safer right now in the shadows. He wished she'd just say so, but what she had confided already was huge. He hoped she didn't wonder if she'd made a mistake.

He peered into her darkened fridge and pulled out two soft drinks. "They're getting warm," he said as he placed the cans on the table."

That made her laugh quietly. "You can always stick them outside the front door."

"I'm already using Mother Nature's freezer. There are steaks in my truck, and some burgers."

Her eyes widened. "Did you overlook anything?"

"Hey, I like my food. I hope you do, too."

"Food and I get along pretty well."

Safe ground. He was relieved to see her cheering up, but hoped that didn't mean the end of her confidences. He glanced at the deck of cards that had gotten them through the early part of the day, then dismissed them. No more diversions. Just him, her and whatever she wanted to talk about.

But she didn't say anything for a while, so he decided to open the can of worms again. "You know, this is like a mystery."

"What?" She looked uncertain.

"Yeah, as in 'Who is that gorgeous woman and how did she get here?'"

She could have reacted in a lot of ways, but this time

she didn't choose to dance around. "You really want to know?"

"Everything you're willing to tell me. I'm interested. I like you. I kind of feel like now we're in this together."

"I wouldn't ask that of anyone," she said, her face shadowing a bit.

"You didn't ask. I'm volunteering."

She studied his face as if trying to read him. He waited patiently, figuring this was something that had to come in her own way in her own time.

"It's been hard," she admitted finally. "The worst was at first. I was so terrified, I can't even tell you. I had no past and no memory older than a few days. They gave me some therapy to help me deal, and then told me my memory might return spontaneously, all at once or just some bits and pieces from time to time."

"Or never at all."

"They didn't like to mention that. Anyway, I'm grateful that I didn't forget a lot of things, apparently. I can still do most of the things I need to do."

"Like walk and talk."

At that she actually laughed, a small one. "And dress myself, and cook."

"I'm glad you remembered how to make that chicken we had the other night. Fabulous."

Her smile widened a hair. "Folks were good to me, Braden. They had to get me a whole identity so I could work, then the psychologist encouraged me to find a job that didn't make me feel threatened. It wasn't easy without references, but I found one working in a small dress shop. Little by little I gained at least some confidence. I could use a cash register, I could count change, I could pass a few easy pleasantries. But I also felt overwhelmed. I still hate to be in large groups. I still feel uncomfortable with most conversation unless it's about some immediate matter. I have no answers to common questions, so I'd like it if people didn't ask them. But of course they do. It's natural. Like at the pageant, the girls were talking about family holiday traditions, and they wondered about mine. All I could say was we didn't have any."

She fell silent, clasping her hands on the table in front of her.

"I'm still trying to imagine it," he said presently. "I just can't wrap my head around what it would be like not to be able to remember my family, or our holidays or the dumb things my brothers and I did."

"And I can't imagine what it's like to remember all of that."

"You must feel awfully adrift."

"I do. Even now, with some experience and memories under my belt, I'm still not sure who I am, where I've been or anything else. And I'm scared of something else," she admitted.

"What's that?" He leaned toward her, intent on every word.

"That I could wake up again without any memory." Her voice stretched thin. "It happened once. I can't quite believe it won't happen again."

That was too much for him. Way too much. That this woman was actually sitting here, having found the courage to come all the way to Montana in search of something she couldn't even identify, awed him. "You've got more courage than anyone I've ever known."

Then he was up out of his chair and around the table, drawing her up until he held her tightly against him, burying his face in her hair, feeling every delicious curve of hers against him, but aware beyond anything of her amazing courage and determination.

He'd found the qualities in her that he'd seldom seen in anyone else.

She didn't push him away. After a momentary stiffening of surprise, she melted into him as if his embrace filled some aching, empty place inside her.

Maybe it did, he thought as he held her. Jenn was the most alone person he had ever met.

Braden's arms felt so strong, warm and reassuring. Jenn allowed herself to relax into them, to lean against him and close her eyes. He hadn't run, hadn't rejected her. Instead, he had reached out to offer the most basic comfort in the world, a hug.

She didn't even know when last she had been hugged. If she let herself think about it, she'd get on that stupid hamster wheel again, and she didn't want to do that right now.

She wanted to pretend she was an ordinary woman with an unshadowed life, resting in the arms of a lover. She wanted to give in to all the attraction she felt for this man, to find out—maybe for the first time in her life, but certainly for the first time in *this* life—what it was like to make love with a man. And not just any man, but this one. From the start she'd felt the longing for him, no matter how hard she tried to hide it from herself. Braden called to her in the most elemental way possible.

She wanted to throw caution and worry to the winds and lie in this man's arms. Tentatively, she turned her face up to look at him. Her heart nearly stopped when she saw an answering fire blazing in his warm brown gaze.

"I could," he said quietly, "make love to you right this instant. I want to. But would that be right? Are you really ready for that? Because I don't want to be just an escape."

The justice of his concern felt like lead in her heart.

Escape right now would be easy, and it was certainly tempting. But it would only be a temporary escape, and in fairness to him, she couldn't use him that way.

"So where do we go from here?" she murmured.

"You could tell me more about what you do remember since you woke up. What you've been up to. How you got here. We could just talk, Jenn. I'm old enough to understand that hormones are no substitute for getting to know someone."

"But you can't really know me."

"You think not? I already know how brave you are. Suppose you tell me how resourceful you are, as well."

With that, the escape hatch closed. She sighed, backed away then curled up on the blankets again, sitting cross-legged this time. He paused to put another log on the fire then came to sit on the floor beside her.

He finally pushed her a little when her silence lingered. "Pretend you don't have that blank wall on much of your past. Tell me how you got by after you awoke. I'm really curious how you came to be here."

She rubbed her free hand along her thigh, trying to ease the tension that had returned. She'd already told him the worst, that she didn't know who she used to be. How hard could it be to discuss the time since she left the hospital? She'd certainly been over it in her head enough times, hoping some little clue would leap out at her.

"Abbreviated version," she said finally. "I told you they helped me with some therapy, that they managed to give me an identity, and my psychologist found me my first job. With a friend of hers. Did I tell you that?"

"Not that it was her friend."

"It was. Nobody else would have taken me on, I'm sure. I had no past, no references, no prior job experience, at least to my knowledge. So her friend gave me a

part-time position. I'd probably still be there except..."
After a moment she just blurted it out. "I was restless.
Very restless. I kept feeling like I was in the wrong place.
Something wasn't right. It was too warm. There wasn't
enough snow. So I started moving around. Kind of a roll-
ing stone. I managed to find temporary and part-time
jobs until I wound up working in that antiques store in
Worcester."

"And that's where things came to a head?"

"In a way. I started dreaming about snow and mountains, and I knew I still wasn't in the right place. Hilda,
the lady who owned the antiques store, got most of my
story from me, and I guess she felt some sympathy. She
told me to go to the library and start looking around. She
said it would be easier and safer to search for places on
the web, rather than packing up and moving yet again."

She glimpsed his nod from the corner of her eye. "And
that brought you here?"

"Partly. I mean, I realized that every time pictures
of the Rocky Mountains would come up, I felt drawn to
them. But the Rockies are a big place. I needed something narrower. That's when Fred Krieg came into the
shop one day and noticed my necklace. He was fascinated
by it, told me he was a coin specialist, and he wanted to
know all about it."

She fell silent again, moving back in time, into that as-
tonishing moment of pure luck. Finally, she spoke again.
"I told him all I knew was it was an heirloom, but I didn't
know from where. Well, that really roused his curiosity.
Next thing I knew, he asked me to come to his shop so
he could investigate it."

"And you went?"

"I went. It took him a few weeks, but finally he told

me the last owner of these coins had lived in Montana. That's all he could tell me."

Braden stirred. "Really? Not a name? Nothing? I'd think that would be some kind of public record or something."

"They were insured. That's how he found out where the last owner was from, but insurance companies, according to him, don't divulge private information. Not a chance he could find the name or even the city of the owner. He said we were lucky to get what we had."

"Wow."

She clearly remembered her despair at the news. It sounded so clinical, but she had placed so much hope in his figuring out who had owned that necklace that she had felt nearly crushed by the dead end. Her whole life, she had thought at the time, was one big dead end. The news had kept her away from Fred's shop, because she couldn't stand another disappointment. Another lead that went nowhere, not that she had had many leads.

She'd haunted the library computers and found Lissa Roarke's blog about Rust Creek Falls. "I started reading Lissa's blog. I knew this wasn't exactly the right place, but it seemed like as good a place as any to start. I just didn't know how I was going to do it. Every time I had changed jobs, it just made getting the next job harder."

"I guess it would."

She shook her head. "I knew I was coming to some kind of end. I had to take one last step, and had become a little obsessed with this place. I read about your flood last year, about all the people who were coming to help with the recovery effort, and I thought I wouldn't stand out too much, and maybe I'd figure out something. With all the people coming to help, maybe someone would know me."

"I think you stood out a little more than you expected."

A short laugh escaped her. "Maybe. Lots of new people around. That's why I joined the Newcomers Club. I hoped maybe I'd meet someone who would have an answer. Instead, I just got a lot of questions. But anyway, I finally went back to Fred, asked him how much he'd give me for one of my coins. He was awfully generous, or at least it felt like it. He gave me my seed money to come out here and stay awhile. So here I am."

He stroked the back of her hand then astonished her by lifting her onto his lap, facing forward so that her back rested against his chest. He ignored the inevitable throbbing need she caused in him, because comforting her was far more important.

"I say again, you are one courageous, resourceful woman. I don't know many who would have moved all the way out here with so little to go on."

"It was *all* I had to go on. It was my last hope. I'm not brave."

"I disagree."

Then, to her amazement, she felt him press his face to the back of her head. All of a sudden, before she could truly enjoy the sensation, she felt him stiffen.

"Is that a scar?"

Her hand flew up instinctively and touched the narrow ridge on the back of her head. "Yes," she said quietly, almost choking on her hammering heart. "That's what caused it all."

He lifted his hands, loosened the band holding her ponytail, then gently parted her hair with his fingertips. Shivers of pleasure ran through her at the gentle touches. "God," he said quietly. "Whatever happened, it must have been bad. What *did* happen?"

"No one knows what caused it, crime or accident. I

was found wandering with a skull fracture. Bleeding inside my head. I'm lucky to be alive."

"You certainly are. But you don't feel that way, do you?"

"Sometimes. I mean, sometimes it overwhelms me, you know? I could be dead, and I wouldn't even know."

He startled her with a laugh. After a moment she realized how that had sounded, and a laugh escaped her, too.

"Okay, that was stupid," she admitted.

"I didn't say that. It just sounded funny. But you meant something else, didn't you? How many times did you wish you *had* died?"

"More than once, right afterward. It doesn't happen anymore. But for a while I thought it would have been easier."

"Yeah, I can see that. I really can." He dropped his hands. "Sorry I messed up your hair."

But she wasn't. This time when he leaned into her, she could feel the warmth of his lips on that scar. He was kissing it! Warmth spilled through her, followed by a sudden need so searing that her insides tightened.

She realized that in that instant if there was one thing she wanted as much as to know who she really was, it was Braden. She ached to feel his hands on her, to feel him inside her, to know what it was like.

"Braden," she said, her voice so thick, his name almost didn't come out.

"I feel you," he murmured.

His choice of words at once seemed odd and yet right. He wanted to know her first, but he knew essentially all there was to know about her, the pathetic story of her search for self and place. Maybe part of that search could be answered right now with him. Maybe she was afraid of knowing any more about her past, but she wasn't afraid of this.

She wanted him, and for once she wasn't afraid of what she didn't know. Wasn't afraid of what she might learn about herself, or discover that she didn't know. Being held like this was heaven, and if he refused to take it any further, she promised herself she wouldn't despair…but she knew she would. Driven by obsession all this time, she was now driven by something else even stronger, and she loved the feeling. The need. The release that need gave her.

To just be a woman at her most basic seemed like the greatest gift on the planet. To stop being guarded, to stop censoring herself, to stop fearing. To just *be*.

It might not be the best rationale in the world, but that didn't matter. She didn't want a rationale. She wanted Braden. All of him. However he chose to share himself with her. She had leaped past all the inhibitions she had developed because she wanted him more than anything on this planet.

Her heartbeat had grown heavy, and her body throbbed in time with it. She hadn't dreamed she could get so aroused so fast. Nor was she going to question it. Not now. In the thrall of these moments, nothing else mattered.

The wait seemed endless, though it couldn't have been but a minute. Then he lifted her from his lap. Just as she started to crash, thinking he was going to reject her, he lay down beside her on the blankets. Propped on his arm, he leaned over her, cupping her face with his hand, catching a few stray tendrils of her hair.

Outside the storm still raged. Dimly she heard the wind keen, and almost jumped when something thudded against the side of the cabin.

"Easy," he murmured. "The storm's just reaching a peak now."

She was reaching a peak, she realized, and hanging on tenterhooks now, wondering what would happen next. He might just be letting her down gently. Or... Anticipation leaped in her, deepening the demanding throb inside her.

"Have you done this before?"

The question was asked kindly, but it jarred her, and for a moment the heavy deepening pool of desire faded. "I don't know." The words came out stretched as fine as thin wire, because it was so painful to have to keep facing the fact that she didn't know *anything* about herself. Not even this.

"It's okay," he said, still cradling her cheek. He bent and kissed her ever so lightly on her lips. "I just want to know where I'm at. So I guess I shouldn't play the caveman and give in to my wildest impulses just now."

Her eyelids fluttered, then opened wide. "Really? I don't know what you're talking about, not really, but it sounds good."

He laughed quietly. "We'll get to that. But for right now this is a first time, most especially for you. But for me, too."

"How can it be for you?"

"Because I've never made love to Jennifer before."

That eased her apprehension in ways she couldn't begin to describe. She wondered if this man had even a vague idea how large was his innate kindness.

"You're sure about this?" he asked. "I know I'm sure. I've been craving you for what seems like forever. But..."

A new kind of courage seemed to fill her. She lifted a hand and pressed her fingers to his lips, silencing him. "I'm sure. I *need* this."

* * *

Maybe she did, he thought as he bent his head and kissed her, taking her more deeply this time. Some corner of his mind warned him that unlike his past girlfriends, this time he was wading into deep emotional waters, and not just because of her problem. Thing was, he wanted her, but somehow he had come to care for her. Something about her seemed like a piece made to fit him, emotionally.

That was a bigger danger to him than sex. Sexual attraction eased eventually, as he'd discovered, while emotional connections stayed forever. But he also knew that dangers might await her in this. It might stir memories, or reactions for reasons she couldn't remember, and they might not be good ones. She was walking into uncharted territory, and even as his body pounded and throbbed with hunger for her, he knew he had to keep at least a corner of his mind in gear, to be aware of her reactions.

Well, it was a good idea anyway. One that rapidly faded as her arms wound around him, as her lips opened to his tongue, as her body arched in response as if she were already almost there.

"Damn, I hate clothes," he muttered. They were both swaddled in them. He was surprised when she laughed in response, and encouraged, he struggled to his feet and pulled her up.

"Let's get rid of them, right now. All of them. Game?"

Sleepy-eyed, smiling faintly, she nodded. "Cut me loose, Braden."

Wow, what an invitation. The shreds of his self-control were steadily snapping like rubber bands pulled too tight. Pounding need dominated him, and from what he could see, her, as well.

"Hurry," she said thickly. "Now. Please, now!"

Gentlemen first. He stripped quickly, cussing once at his boots, then stood before her as naked as the day he was born. His erection, freed of confinement, only throbbed harder.

Some part of him expected her to turn tail, but he waited as her amazing blue eyes wandered over him, as her breaths quickened, as her eyelids drooped. The instant her hands reached for the bottom of her sweater to pull it up, he became galvanized. Good intentions flew out the window.

He ached for her, and to hell with taking it easy. She was going to get him however passion demanded. If that wasn't going to work for her, best to know it now.

He stepped toward her, pushing her hands aside, and ripped the sweater off her. The fleece shirt followed quickly, revealing a surprisingly simple bra that cradled full breasts. Then her jeans and boots, another cuss word there, until she stood before him in her plain white underwear.

He filled his eyes with her, admiring her gentle curves, from breast to belly to thigh. Made for a man's hands, made for *his* hands.

"You're perfect," he mumbled, but speech was rapidly escaping him. Slow? No way. It couldn't be slow now.

Nor did she seem to want it. With her own hands she released her bra, allowing her breasts to spill free. Not too full, but fuller than he expected with pebbled pink nipples that begged for his mouth. Dropping to his knees, he tugged down her panties with his hands while finding her breast with his mouth. The groan that escaped her as he drew her nipple into him goaded him even more.

Her hands clutched his head, pulling him even closer, filling him with triumphant pleasure. She was with him.

All awareness of everything except this woman and the pleasures she offered flew from his mind.

She wanted loving, and he wanted to give it. All the loving he was capable of.

He gripped her hips as she groaned again, keeping his mouth latched to her breast. He sucked hard, loving the little sounds she made, then managed to pull back enough to move to other breast. More groans. He felt her legs tremble, then almost without warning, she was on her knees facing him.

"Braden…" His name escaped her on a shuddery sigh, the most beautiful sound in the world. He caught her behind the knees and lowered her to the tangled blankets and clothing. Straddling her, he began to explore her with his mouth, struggling to hold back the urge to just enter her, claim her, make her his.

Propped on an elbow, he trailed kisses over her breasts and belly while his hand stole downward and found the cleft between her legs.

A cry escaped her, and she bucked upward, letting him know she was ready. Truly ready.

Too fast. The thought zipped across his mind, ephemeral as fog. It didn't slow him down. They were already at the top of the mountain, and ready to tumble over the edge.

He put a knee between her legs. At once she opened herself, spreading her legs, inviting him inside. Then the next knee. He looked down and saw her dewy core, open and ready for him, swollen with the passion that had built as fast as the damn storm outside.

He couldn't wait. For absolutely the first time in his adult life, Braden Traub lost his self-control. Completely and utterly.

Forgetting everything but the demands of their bodies, he found her opening and pressed into her. He barely noticed an instant of resistance inside her, then he was fully sheathed in her hot, wet depths. They were one.

Her legs lifted, winding around his as if she wanted him even closer. He obliged, burrowing as deeply as he could, his entire body throbbing in time to his strong, deep thrusts. She rose to meet him, fingers digging into his shoulders, legs locking him in place.

He flexed again and again, driving into her as if every answer in the universe awaited him there. When he felt her jerk and stiffen, felt the shudder run through her, heard the cry escape her, he let go and jetted into her until he felt he had emptied even his soul.

Dimly he knew he'd just gone somewhere he'd never gone before.

Then he collapsed on her, welcomed by her arms and legs, filled with her heady scent, filled with a need to never let go of this miracle.

Chapter Eight

Braden had no idea how long they lay like that. Eventually, reality began to pierce the beautiful bubble of hazy satisfaction. The storm still howled, and he felt grateful for its fury, because it had cut them off. Then he noticed the fire was dying, probably because the winds outside were sucking air up the chimney and causing it to burn faster. He needed to deal with that.

But mostly he noticed Jenn, curled in his arms like a trusting kitten. He reached out to pull a corner of blanket over her, and wondered if he really needed to move at all. Freezing to death in her arms didn't seem like the worst fate in the world.

But reality refused to back off. Brain cells, drugged by pleasure, began to flip back into action. He raised a heavy arm and tipped her face so that he could look at her.

"How are you?" he asked. Because he had a dim memory of something that now, and only now, shook him to his core.

"I am wonderful," she said softly but firmly then smiled. "You?"

"Fantastic. I don't want to move. But the fire…"

"Can wait another minute," she insisted, burrowing her face into his shoulder.

"Well, it could but… Jenn…I think that was really your first time. And I was so out of control."

"Hush," she said. "No apologies. It was perfect. Never apologize for something so good."

"But I must have hurt you…"

"Not enough to notice." Then she stirred, tipping her head to look at him. "I'm glad you were my first, that my first was so awesome."

A caveman-like impulse brought a smile to his face. He could have pounded his chest. "Really?"

"Really. Actually, if I ever learn any more about who I am, I'm glad it won't be that."

He turned that around. "So one less thing to worry about?"

"Yes. And one more thing to celebrate."

He could deal with that. In fact, he *liked* it. Swooping in, he stole another kiss. "So much for my self-control. I intended slow, easy, careful…"

A little laugh escaped her. "That can wait. This was perfect. Absolutely perfect." Then she surprised him by rolling away, revealing her full naked beauty, and flinging her arms up. "Damn, I am so *happy!*"

He suspected there was little enough of that in her life. Giving it to her made him feel as tall as the mountains. "You're good for my ego."

"Unlike your brothers," she said tartly.

He chuckled. "They're not so bad."

"Maybe not. I don't really know them. They don't all live here anymore, right?"

"Not all of them do anymore. Forrest and Clay live in Thunder Canyon with their wives and kids."

"So really you do most of the ranching by yourself."

"Mostly it's me. The others pitch in when they can, to help Mom and Dad out."

"No wonder you're so busy." She closed her eyes a

moment. "Thunder Canyon. I like the way that sounds. It kind of rolls on the tongue."

"Have you been there?"

"Not yet."

"We'll have to remedy that."

He linked his hand with hers, waiting, but when she said no more, he sat up. "I've got to take care of that fire. And I don't know about you, but I'm getting really hungry. Once I get the fire going, I'll cook us a meal. Okay?"

Her eyes popped open, and she smiled. "Okay. The rest of the world can go hang for now."

"You bet it can. I'm so glad Winona was right about this storm."

"So am I," she admitted, and for once he didn't see tension in her when he mentioned the psychic. "I could melt into a puddle."

"Not yet, we'll do that later."

Her laugh followed him as he forced himself to leave their little nest and hunt up his jeans and boots. As soon as his bottom half was safely covered, he helped her wrap herself in her new blue blanket and move back to a chair. "I don't want any sparks to reach you."

He moved everything else well away from the stove then opened the door to put another couple of logs in. The cabin *was* getting colder, he noticed. Either the wind was sucking all the heat up the chimney pipe, or this structure wasn't as good an insulator as he would have thought.

She surprised him with her next question. "Do you think Homer is okay?"

"He's no fool, crazed though he may seem. He knows he's welcome at the community church, and the pastor said he'd already gotten a cot for Homer. I'm certain he's there, and the pastor will make sure he has food."

He sat back on his heels as he closed the stove door

and peered at her over his shoulder. "You worry about others, don't you?"

"Of course. Who wouldn't?"

He turned his attention back to the logs, waiting for the moment when flames would seem to emerge from them, letting him know they'd caught. "Some wouldn't," he said. "You meet them every so often."

Staring into the fire, waiting for the coals to ignite the logs, he sorted through everything Jenn had shared with him that day. She had acted almost as if she thought she was protecting him by spilling the truth about her amnesia, exposing to him just how defective she was. Far from making him think of her as deeply flawed, however, he found himself full of a desire to give her back something, so that she could find joy in life again. He understood her fear of discovering that the truth about herself might be hideous, but he'd seen enough of her to guess with fair certainty that she'd never been an ugly person. Oh, anyone could be awful at times, but this woman didn't seem to have a mean bone in her body. Plenty of scared ones, but no mean ones.

For some reason, she seemed to trust him. Why? Because he hadn't flown the coop when she told him about her amnesia? That was little to go on. Maybe she had become trusting out of necessity. How else could you get on with anything when you had no memory?

As the logs started to catch, he realized he'd reached a decision. He was going to move heaven and earth to find out why Jenn had chosen this part of the planet to continue her search for her past. And if that meant bringing Winona Cobbs to her, then he'd do it.

But he wasn't going to tell her about it. She'd raise a ruckus, and he'd rather deal with that once Winona had seen her. Once he found out why Winona wanted to see her. That storm outside had helped make a kind of believer out of him. Or, maybe, Winona had learned something about Jenn's past by other means. Either way, the psychic didn't usually demand to see anyone, so she must know something.

If nothing else, it would be a good starting point.

Brushing his hands on his pants, he stood. "Dang, you can sit and watch a fire for hours without moving."

"Mesmerizing," Jenn agreed.

He turned and saw her wrapped in her blue blanket. Some of the uncertainty had returned, and it was his fault. He must have appeared to be ignoring her, and right now the least little thing would seem huge.

After all, she'd just lost her virginity, and could have no way to be sure how much she had thrilled him and pleased him. A smile began to play about his mouth as he thought about all the ways he could reassure her.

Then his stomach growled loudly. He was relieved when she laughed. "Feed yourself," she said.

"I'm gonna feed both of us, lady. Just you watch."

Curled up the soft wool of the blue blanket, Jenn felt almost decadent. Naked beneath the blanket, she was swaddled in warmth and comfort, and Braden refused any help as he sorted through her fridge and the supplies he had brought and began to manufacture a meal for them.

Her entire body still tingled with pleasure and new-found knowledge. Effortlessly, her mind summoned their lovemaking, bringing along with it the memories of sensations, sounds, scents, until the ache began to build in her again. She seemed to have developed an instant addiction to Braden, and while she knew it might lead to nothing—in fact, probably would lead to nothing, given her amnesia—for right now she didn't care. For right now the storm sealed them in a perfect cocoon.

Looking out the window at a world darkened by heavy clouds and hidden behind whirling curtains of white, she felt again her love of winter. Why winter drew her, she had no idea, of course, but draw her it did, and this storm seemed like an answer to a craving almost as deep in her as the craving she now felt for Braden.

Snowy mountains, that dangerous weather outside… she had been hunting for them as much as she had been hunting for her past. Somehow, she and the winter were linked, and she wondered if she would ever know why. But maybe there was no link at all, simply a love of the wild forces of nature.

Drawing her knees up to her chin, cuddling herself inside the blanket, she watched the snow and felt truly at home with it. At home, too, with the fire burning nearby, casting its flickering, ruddy glow over everything. She knew this the way she had known that mountain. At some level out of conscious reach, this was all part of her.

Braden carried a frying pan and the coffeepot to the woodstove, adjusted the vent and announced, "You had some eggs, so rather than let them spoil, we're going to have loaded scrambled eggs. It'll be ready fast, because this stove is hot."

"You could use the propane and have some control," she reminded him.

He arched a brow at her. "What? And give up my sturdy, reliable woodsman image? I think not. However, if I burn the eggs…"

Another laugh escaped her. He took her to a place where laughter was possible. "Then we eat something else?"

"Precisely. As in canned baked beans." He began to

use a spatula to keep the eggs moving in the pan. "What would you have done if you hadn't found out about your necklace, or run into Lissa's blog?"

She didn't want all that to intrude, but there was no escaping it. She couldn't hide in this private little moment forever. Of course he had questions, and now she felt she owed it to him to answer them. "I don't know. I was thinking about going to Canada."

"Really? Why? Do you feel like you're Canadian?"

"I don't know. I just knew the winters in Worcester weren't bad enough, and the mountains weren't high enough."

He waved briefly toward the window. "I give you a winter, madam. How does it feel?"

"Perfect, actually."

"I'm not sure everyone would agree with you." He pulled the pan off the top of the stove. "Stay where you are. I'll bring you a plate." Just then the coffee started to perk.

She took the opportunity to tuck the blanket under her arms, covering herself decently while leaving her shoulders bare. Part of her found this act of modesty amusing, but another part insisted that one didn't eat while naked.

Apparently, Braden agreed, because he returned with his shirt back on and offered her one of the two plates he held. Then out of his breast pocket he pulled a couple of forks. "I couldn't find the napkins."

"I use paper towels." And few enough of them.

"A woman after my own heart. Never could understand why I needed different paper to wipe my mouth from the paper I used to wipe up a spill."

"Cuz your mouth is special?"

In an instant the air seemed to leave the room. He stood stock-still, but all of a sudden his brown eyes appeared to blaze like the fire behind him. "Keep talking that way, and we'll both go hungry."

"Tempting," she admitted, but as if to disagree, her stomach rumbled, making her flush.

"Food first," he announced in response. The coffee was perking faster, and he went over to peer at the little glass knob on the top. "Almost ready."

He left his plate on the small table between their chairs and returned with mugs. "Dig in, Jenn. I hate cold scrambled eggs."

They were excellent scrambled eggs, still moist and full of bits of green pepper and onion she'd had, even some ham he had rustled up from somewhere. She complimented him between mouthfuls.

"Having to cook over a campfire and eat your own cooking has its rewards," he said, a twinkle in his eyes. "If you're still hungry after this, I'll make some trail toast."

"What's that?"

"Slabs of buttered bread browned on the stove. Or over a fire."

"Oh, yum." But it wasn't toast she was thinking of as she spoke. No, she was looking at him and drinking him in with her eyes as if he were nectar and she a bee. Behind him, through the window, the storm raged, and the day began to darken even more. She wanted that storm to go on forever.

He brought them both mugs of coffee then set the pot on the flange in front of the stove door. He hadn't tucked his shirt in yet, and she enjoyed watching him as he carried his mug to the window and looked out.

"How come you've never married?" she asked. "It seems impossible to believe that no one snatched you up by now."

He laughed. "A few tried. I tried a few times. It didn't work out. I finally figured out that attraction is great, but it's not enough. You have to really like a person, too. Like my parents. If they weren't best friends, I doubt they'd have been able to weather all these years together."

"So you think being best friends is important?"

"I think it's the most important part. Love is a hell of a lot more than great sex."

She liked that. A whole lot. Whoever got Braden Traub was going to get something enduring. She wanted something like that. But she also wanted him. She brushed away a moth wing of fear. Not now. Not in these precious moments with him.

"This doesn't look like it's going to end any time soon," he remarked as he sipped his beverage.

"Would you be appalled if I told you I was in no hurry?"

He glanced over his shoulder, smiling. "I wouldn't. Unfortunately, it might be better for my herd if the wind died down some. I wish Winona had indicated how long this was supposed to last."

"Believing her now?"

He turned from the window, and his expression had grown serious. "Don't you? This wasn't in the weather forecast. Not even a hint of it. How the hell did she know?"

Jenn looked down, uneasiness creeping into her. "I don't know."

"Me either." He turned back to the window. "Maybe you should talk to her."

"Why?" Jenn felt herself stiffening, all relaxation leaving the day. "To hear some useless psychic claptrap?"

He faced her. "I don't know that's why she wants to talk to you. She's been around for a while, that woman.

And not just here. Maybe she learned something about you."

"Nobody else seems to know a damn thing about me."

"Nobody else is Winona. She's been around these parts longer than most, and she hears a lot that folks don't tell anyone else. She might have heard something. Hell, for all I know, she recognized you."

"Then why didn't she just come out and say so?"

He shrugged one shoulder. "Would you want her telling anyone except you? And you're avoiding her."

She looked down, blindly staring at the blanket snugly wrapped over her breasts, at the mug she cradled in both hands. He was right, but that only made her stomach sink more.

"I get the problem," he said. "You want to know and you don't want to know. You're afraid of both. The question is which scares you more?"

"I came all the way out here looking," she said quietly, as her nerve endings began to jitter with anxiety.

"I know. Then you kind of stopped dead in the water, didn't you? How hard have you looked since you got here? Are you just waiting for the decision to be taken out of your hands?"

That was a fair question. Was that what she was doing, just waiting for answers to drop into her lap? Certainly, finding friends here had made the empty spaces in her memory somewhat easier to tolerate, uncomfortable though she often was with her own evasions and her inability to fit. Was she moving on in some way or dead in the water, as he suggested? Certainly, the compulsion that had carried her to this town seemed to have changed in the months she had been here.

Her psychologist had advised her to make the present her life, and not pursue her past, a past that might or might not return to her. If anyone was proof of the old saw that the only moment you really had was the instant in your grasp, she was it. Had she been making peace of a sort with that? Or had her compulsion waned out of fear that she had come close to her answers?

All of a sudden, Braden squatted in front of her. He took the mug from her and placed it on the table then grasped her hands. "It's your decision," he said quietly. "I'm sorry if I upset you. I'm just trying to understand."

"If I can't understand, how can you? Damn, Braden, I was driven, I couldn't give up the looking, the searching. The need for answers. Now...I don't know. It's like I got halfway and then stopped."

"Maybe because you don't know how to move forward now? You found a place that fits what you were looking for. Like you said, it's probably not the exact place, but it's a close enough fit. If you don't want to know any more than you do right now, that's okay. I'm not trying to push you. I'm certainly not the one with the need to know your past. I kinda like the woman in front of me right now."

God, she liked this man. With just a few words, he could warm her emotional soul. Freeing her hand, she reached out to cup his cheek, feeling the day's growth of beard stubble, reveling in his warmth and his very solid reality. "So it wouldn't bother you not to know anything else about me?"

Her heart nearly stopped as he said, "Oh, there's a lot more I want to know about you." But he was smiling, and as he continued, her moment of fear faded. "Lots more, but all about you now. If you never find out what came before you were hurt, that doesn't bother me. I'm only concerned about it bothering you."

Maybe, she thought, it was time to step out. To just admit to her friends the secret she had been keeping.

Maybe it wasn't so awful after all. It wasn't as if she had walked into some place and told them to erase her memory. "You're sure?"

"Life deals and then we deal. What more is there?"

Good question. She dropped her hand, and he clasped it once more. Closing her eyes, she leaned her head back. "Okay," she said, a decision made before she even knew it.

"Okay what?"

"I'll talk to Winona. But you better be with me because that woman makes me nervous."

"I'll be there if you want," he said. Then he chuckled. "I never thought of Winona Cobbs as a fearsome woman before."

At that, she opened her eyes and found him grinning. In spite of her anxiety over agreeing to meet the psychic, she couldn't help smiling back at him. "Well, she is."

He dropped down so that he was sitting cross-legged in front of her. "What exactly about her scares you? Did she say or do something?"

"She's never talked to me directly. It sounds crazy, but when our eyes meet, I feel something like an electric shock."

"Hmm." He dropped his gaze briefly. "I wonder if you used to know her."

She had barely considered the possibility. The one time it had occurred to her, she'd skipped away from it. Her fingers tightened around his as her heart skipped. She had to draw a deep breath, then exhale slowly to ease the sudden tension that filled her. "I don't know. It's possible, I guess."

He fell silent, clearly lost in thought, and she let him be. It was a nice picture anyway, the man who had just loved her, so handsome and appealing, framed against the flames in the stove behind him. She wished she could paint it, or that she had a camera to capture the moment.

He sighed quietly, the sound almost lost in the racket from the wind and the muffled crackle of the fire. "I'm trying to imagine what it would be like to forget my past. How it would feel not to remember all the things I do. It seems like memory is so much a part of me."

"It is," she admitted. "I miss it, though I don't know what I'm missing. But we talked about memory during my recovery, and I guess no memory is really reliable. We rewrite them all the time. That's why two people can recall the same incident and describe what happened so differently."

He looked at her. "So in a way, we're all amnesiacs."

That startled a laugh out of her. "Well...I guess you could look at it that way. How do you know your memories are accurate? I bet you rely a lot on external things, like old scars and other reminders. And continuity. Continuity is so important."

"And yours was interrupted."

"Totally. So I don't even know if the occasional thing I seem to remember is real in any sense of the word. Like telling you my name is really Jennifer. It feels right. But nobody else calls me that, so how can I be sure? You know your name is real because that's what everyone calls you."

He nodded, clearly thinking again. "A rose by any name..." Then he leaned back, propping himself on his hands. "I can't imagine it. What I *do* see is a woman who's more afraid than she should be. I watch those moments come over you, where you seem to pull inside yourself and hide. I hear the evasions."

Jenn flushed. "I'm sorry."

"I'm not. That's what first grabbed me, even more than

your beauty. It's what moved you from being a lovely wildflower by the roadside to one I wanted to pluck."

Her flush deepened. "That's awfully poetic."

He shrugged. "It's true. I saw a beautiful puzzle I wanted to solve. Well, it may never be solved, and surprisingly enough I'm okay with that. Now I don't give two figs for satisfying my own curiosity. What I want more than anything is to see you comfortable with yourself. Happy. You're so young, Jenn. The notion that this might continue to shadow your life, every word you speak, every thought you have, is damn near heartbreaking."

She had no idea how to respond to him. If he found her heartbreaking, surely he'd want to be done with her. How depressing it would be to be forever looking at someone who lived with a dark shadow and might always be unhappy because of it.

I'm learning," she said, sounding way too defensive. "I'm learning to live with it."

"I see that. Maybe I shouldn't have pressed you to talk with Winona. Hell, it just never crossed my mind that you might be making some kind of peace with yourself. You kept talking about why you'd come here, what you were seeking, and I should have considered that the reason you seemed to be holding back was because you were reaching a place where it doesn't matter as much as it did before."

"I didn't say that." Her tone took on an edge. "I know it's impossible to deal with this mess. *You* don't have to."

His face darkened. "I'm almost positive that's not what I was trying to say. Do you want me to try again, or do you just want to have a fight?"

Her hands had tightened into fists, and urges warred in her. She didn't really want him poking around inside her, yet she didn't want him to stop. God, she was getting sick of her own internal struggles to go one way or the other on anything. Yes, no, she had turned into one big flip-flopper.

She squeezed words out past a throat every bit as tight as her hands. "Try again."

"I'm working my way toward understanding. I'm not the most tactful of guys. Hell, I spend my life with animals and cowboys, not exactly good practice for dealing with sensitive things. I like to bull my way through, knock over barriers rather than go around them. So all I was saying was, I guess I didn't think this through all the way. Not unusual. And all I meant was, I'm sorry if I've been pushing you in ways you don't like. No promises that I won't do it again."

He sat up. "In fact, if you change your mind about seeing Winona, I won't argue. How the hell would I know for sure if it would help? I like to solve problems, yes, but this is *your* problem, and you get to decide how it's done. That's all I was trying to get at. As for me not having to deal with it, well, it's kinda late for that. I care and want to help. Don't ever think I don't. But that doesn't mean I'm not that old bull in the china shop."

Her hands had knotted tightly around a fold in the blanket, but as she listened to him, they loosened. She couldn't doubt his sincerity and let go of the flare of anger. This poor guy. He was trying to be careful and nice, the situation *was* impossible, from the inside or out, and she needed to share it with him. She couldn't do that if she pushed him away.

"I'm sorry, Braden," she offered.

"No need to be sorry. I'll put my foot in it again. All I ask is that you let me know when I do."

"Fair enough." She watched as he rose to his feet and

walked over to the window. Nightfall was coming early, even for here.

Why, she wondered, *did* she feel compelled to share this with him? She was only just getting to know him. One of her girlfriends would have been the more obvious choice. But she guessed she had been afraid of her own attraction for him, and didn't want to risk getting any closer if he might run when he learned the truth.

He hadn't run. He was trying to understand the incomprehensible, and in his own way to help her with it. Like asking her to speak to Winona. She still wasn't sure she'd do that, but his suggestion had been meant to be helpful. Like he said, he wanted to solve problems. Unfortunately, she couldn't be solved.

Struggling free of the blanket, she stood and wrapped it around her, going to stand beside him at the window.

He reached out an arm and drew her close to his side without a word. That simple welcome made her eyes prickle with tears. God, how she needed that. Welcome. Warmth. Caring without secrets. He quieted everything inside her, and she was content to just lean against him and soak it up.

It was a dangerous feeling, that she was at home in Braden's arms, but she couldn't argue with it. Instead, she savored the peace he gave her.

Braden was glad that she trusted him enough to come stand with him and let him embrace her. He felt as if they'd traveled a lot of hard ground today together. Their lovemaking had been like fireworks on the Fourth of July, an interlude of awesomeness and pleasure, but so far just an interlude.

This woman had serious problems, problems he couldn't really help her with. He hadn't been kidding when he said he liked her just as she was, and it didn't matter to him whether she ever had a past, but he knew it mattered to her.

He hated the helpless feeling. He'd never liked being helpless, always wanted to do something, a character facet that had gotten him into trouble at times. Maybe it was getting him into trouble again, this time on totally unknown territory. What the hell did he really know about what this might be like for her?

She could speak the words, try to explain, but he couldn't get inside her head and experience it. He could never really know.

That was true with everyone. He wasn't a fool. All you ever got to know was what they showed on the outside, what they told you. You could try to imagine walking in their shoes, but in a case like this, imagination fell way short. He had no comparison at all.

He just knew he liked her, wanted her, and wanted to help however he could. Wounded birds had led him down a path to trouble before. It was the main reason he didn't date much anymore.

But here he was again. A smart man would bail. Not him. He might be as stupid as all get out, but he knew Jenn elicited something in him no other woman had. Couldn't put his finger on it, but it was more than wanting her and wanting to help. Standing with her like this, holding her, he felt a quiet inside. A good quiet. Like everything was right for once.

So okay, they'd deal. *He'd* deal.

"Braden?"

A long time must have passed. It was damn near pitch-black outside, and all he could see was the snow near the window, catching the firelight from inside and blowing around like a million sparkling embers. "Hmm?"

"That bull in the china shop?"

"What about it?"

"I saw a TV show where the hosts actually put a couple of bulls in a china shop setup. They didn't bump a thing."

Was she trying to tell him something? He twisted to look at her, and he saw a small, quiet smile on her lips. "Yeah?" he asked.

"Yeah."

His spirits lifted. Everything was okay. "You asked for it now."

"What did I ask for?" She looked a bit confused.

"Me. You. Lady, I'm about to ravage you again."

"If that was ravaging earlier, I'll take a double helping."

Then she laughed, and the sound filled his heart with gladness. For a bull in a china shop, he clearly hadn't managed to break anything. Yet.

He made their nest of blankets once again in front of the fire. "Is this soft enough for you?"

"Like I'd even notice?" Wrapped in her blanket, she stood watching him with a passion-softened smile that made his heartbeat quicken. Then she dropped the blanket, revealing her full glory, and stepped into the middle of the pallet. Offering herself.

He stripped as fast as he could then paused to caress her with his gaze. "You are exquisite," he murmured. Every line, every curve of her, called to him. Her breasts, just right as far as he was concerned, nipples already puckering in their ring of pink areolas, and not from the cold. It was warm in here now, very warm. Perfect for being naked together.

Her hips flared, not a boy's but a woman's, begging

for a man's hands to grip them. The tight thatch of golden curls between her thighs covered secrets he wanted to explore in more ways than one.

Down her legs, nicely shaped, to delicate ankles and small feet with high arches. A woman built to be the stuff of a man's dreams for years to come.

The stuff of his dreams.

Then he saw that she was eyeing him in the same way. Realizing it ratcheted his hunger up even higher. But instead of acting, he forced himself to hold still. Except that he spread his arms a bit.

"Help yourself," he said. He wasn't surprised that the words sounded thick. He'd been almost unable to push them out. The air in the room began to perfume with their own musky scents, a heady brew.

She took him at his word, shyly at first then more boldly. Stepping toward him, she placed her hands on his shoulders, tracing the muscles hard work had built into him, following the lines of his arms to his hands, then sweeping back up to trace over his chest. She learned something when she brushed over his small, hardened nipples, and he saw the knowledge appear on her face.

Leaning in, she drew one into her mouth and sucked it the way he had done to her. Throwing back his head, he pulled in as much air as he could, wondering if he could hang on to his self-control much longer, telling himself he must. But passion pounded in him, reaching to the farthest corners of his being.

Then she released him. He had to fight an urge to pull her back, in order to let her continue her exploration.

She walked around behind him and ran her palms over his shoulders and back. "You have a lot of scars," she murmured. "Barbed wire?"

"Mostly. Other things, too, nothing very serious."

"What's serious?"

"Anything that can't be patched with some gauze and tape. I've only needed stitches a few times." And talking was all but impossible. How could she want to talk?

Her hands wandered down to the hard hills of his rump. He drew a ragged breath and forced himself to hold still even as his entire body tightened with an urge to pounce.

"Buns of steel," she said, her voice holding a teasing note.

How could she want to tease right now? He could barely breathe and hold still. "Saddle," he said shortly.

"Long, long hours," she surmised.

Oh man, just let him hang on a little longer.

Then she came back round to his front. "Am I torturing you?"

Considering she looked like a cat that was enjoying a bowl of cream, he supposed she wanted to think so. That kind of tickled him through the haze of desire that verged on blinding him.

"And this," she said.

She might as well have hit him with an arc welder as her hand closed around his erection.

"Mmm," she whispered as she stroked him. "I like this…"

That did it. Galvanized, he grabbed her and carried her down to the blankets. His turn now.

He made her pay. With mouth, tongue and hands, he traced her all over, tormenting her breasts with licks, sucks and nips until she cried out, and her nails dug into him. A despairing cry escaped her when he pulled back for a moment, but only a moment. Then downward he moved, across her smooth belly, causing ripples of excitement to pass through the muscles there. He could feel them, could feel the way her hips had begun small helpless movements.

With his hands he pushed her legs wide open and upward. Her eyes fluttered, widening briefly, then closing as she accepted her vulnerability.

He dove then, bringing his face down to that thatch of curls, parting her, using his tongue to lash that most sensitive nub of nerves until her restless pitching and moaning told him she was past ready. Still he kept on, plunging his tongue into her as he meant to plunge himself soon. Shudders ran through her; she bucked.

But he wasn't done. Back to that silky, swollen knot of nerves, using his tongue, he drove her onward until she was helpless to the needs, helpless in her drive for completion. Finally, she crested, with a keening so tight and thin he could feel the moment himself.

Only then did he settle himself between her legs and plunge into her. He had another secret to show her about her womanhood.

Jenn didn't think she'd ever move again. Three orgasms. *Three*! She'd heard about it, but had never believed she would know what it was like. But Braden had just shown her, carrying her to the top and over repeatedly.

She was exhausted, amazed and filled with stars of a new kind. Weakened, she lay in his arms, totally unaware of everything but her own wonder and Braden. Everything else that had preoccupied her for so long faded into the background as she emerged into the discovery of a whole new world.

Finally, she had to move, however weakly. He surprised her by lifting her until she rested on top of him, bathed in the warmth from the fire. Her head collapsed onto his shoulder, and her face tucked into his neck. He smelled so good!

"Wow," she whispered.

"Wow," he agreed, his voice rusty.

He reached up to stroke her hair, to run his palm over her back and bottom, gentle caresses. This time they brought her no fire, just the quietude he had given her earlier. Peace, such a stranger to her, found her in his arms.

For the first time, building a future without her past actually seemed possible. Her therapist had suggested she try it, and if her future could be full of memories like this, who needed a past? Whatever she might remember would pale to insignificance beside this.

Of course, there was no guarantee there would be any more of this, either. No promises had been made, nor could they make them at this point. It was entirely possible that he would walk out of here after the storm passed and there would be nothing more between them except friendship.

Could she deal with that? She supposed she could. She'd dealt with worse, like being alone and rootless in a strange world. He had showed her life could still be wonderful anyway, and that she could conceivably find happiness despite everything. Maybe the answers didn't lie in what she'd forgotten, but in the person she became now.

She stirred a little, wondering at the direction of her thoughts. It seemed like such a seismic shift after her obsession with her past. Maybe it wasn't to be trusted. Maybe when Braden walked out of here, she'd find herself back on the same hamster wheel, with an added wrinkle: longing for something she could never have. Because she doubted she would be the woman who put an end to Braden's bachelorhood. She didn't feel as if she could possibly measure up to all he must want. Given that at thirty-four he still hadn't married, or from what she gathered even had a long-term relationship, there was no reason to think she might be the one he was looking for. If he was even looking.

Crazy thoughts, she told herself. Looking so far ahead along a road that was as blank as most of the way behind her...just an exercise in wishful, foolish thinking. The only moment she could truly claim was the present one.

Drawing a deep breath, yanking her mind back from the chasm of the future as well as the chasm of the past, she returned to the now. Lying in Braden's arms. Being held and caressed by him. This was the purest magic, and she needed to focus on it. On him. On whatever time he chose to give her.

Tomorrow would take care of itself. Somehow, through all her travails, it had always managed to do so.

A thought struck her. At once she stiffened, rolled off him and sat up.

"Jenn? What's wrong?"

She drew up her knees, wrapping her arms around them, and turned to look at him. "Nothing. I just had a thought."

He sat up halfway, propping himself on his elbow. "Which was?"

"That I don't know any more about tomorrow than I know about my past. Sure, I imagine it's there. I imagine I'll see you. I imagine that if the storm's gone, I'll get back to town. Or see my friends, or talk to them on the phone."

He nodded encouragingly.

"But I don't know that. I fill my picture of tomorrow with imagination because I can't really know. I guess..." She hesitated, trying to find the words. "The future is only as real as I imagine it. I could say the same about the past. Both are only as real as I make them in my head. Maybe I'm obsessing too much about my lost memories. Yeah, I'd like to know who I was, but if I never remember…well, maybe it's an uncertainty the same as the ones I could have about the future."

Now he sat up the rest of the way. A few minutes passed and she waited, though for what, she didn't know. His approval? His disagreement?

"You know," he said finally, "that's a pretty heavy thought."

"Silly?"

He shook his head. "Not at all. It drew me up short, thinking about it that way. It's kind of like what you said about continuity. That's the only thing that really gives us a sense of our place."

She nodded. "Exactly. We assume there's this unbroken flow, but mine got interrupted, like you said. I don't know who I used to be. But I could just as easily say I don't know who I'll be tomorrow. Change is constant."

"Think that'll work for you?" He cocked a brow at her.

"I don't know," she admitted. "It's just a thought. Right now I feel so good, I don't care about any of it. I could feel differently again tomorrow."

Yes, she could, he thought as they dressed. The stove was still making heat, but something had come into the cabin with them. Maybe it was the shadow of her past, or the difficulties that still lay ahead of her as she tried to find some peace within herself. Whatever, the interlude was over for now. Reality had firmly stepped back into the room.

Although, what they had just shared was reality. He hoped she understood that. Beautiful, exquisite, mind-blowing reality. Not everything real had to be bad. He wondered if she could even understand that anymore, given her long search for self and place. Maybe for her, life could be seen only as a struggle, one full of unmet needs and a whole lot of fear.

That notion disturbed him deeply. He'd led a mostly blessed life, and he knew it. Family, friends, work that he loved. The little clouds that had visited his life had been minimized by all those he cared about.

She didn't have that support network. She'd been left alone with a private, raging storm, one every bit as bad as the blizzard outside.

They sat at the small table again, as if she wanted some distance. Their lovemaking still perfumed the air, but it was fading. Maybe she needed it to. He simply didn't know how to figure her yet.

"I'm sorry," she said a little later. "I feel like I just crashed a party and sent everyone running."

He shook his head a little. "You didn't crash anything. You didn't ruin anything. We can bring the magic back later if you want."

"So you're not mad at me? I feel utterly self-centered."

"I'm not mad. Not even a little. Just wish I could help more. And I don't think you're self-centered. You've been wrestling all alone with a big problem for a long time. It's not the kind of problem anyone could just forget for long. And I think you've got a lot of stuff inside you probably need to share, especially considering you haven't even told your friends about this. I'm willing to listen. I don't mind at all. I'm still wrapping my brain around all of this, but like I said, no amount of wrapping is going to let me know what this is like for you."

"I wish, I truly wish, I could just give all this up, just forget, just move on."

"I'm sure you do, but this is a little bigger than most things. It's right up at the top of big things, in fact. Harder to just put behind us. I actually think you're doing pretty well for someone who's had such a major trauma."

"I wouldn't know." She drummed her fingers briefly. "See, that's the other thing. I don't know what I know. I remember how to cook, obviously. I can still speak and understand. I never forgot how to drive, how to dress, any of that stuff. But I lack comparisons for a lot of things, because I don't have a memory of where I've been and what I've done. Sometimes I'll make a judgment about something and then wonder if I'm right because I don't have a storehouse of memories against which to measure it."

"Such as?" He was genuinely interested in this part. Jenn was such a fascinating, beautiful puzzle.

"Like what you just said. I know total amnesia is rare because they told me so. I also know I had a trauma because of the scar on my head. Whether I'm dealing with it well or not… How would I know?"

"Not many of us would have an answer to that, I'm afraid."

It pleased him to see her relax into a smile. "True that," she said.

But he understood what she was trying to say. "Do you spend a lot of time questioning yourself?"

"At the beginning I did a whole lot more of it. I questioned pretty much everything I did, so maybe it was good that I felt so driven to find my place, if not myself. It gave me a purpose. Otherwise, I might have dithered myself to death. But now…not so much. I can accept that at some level I knew coming to Rust Creek Falls was a good decision. That I feel it's close to whatever I needed, and I don't question the fact that I don't feel like I came from here. I'm learning to trust myself more, I guess."

"That's a good thing."

Even in the dim firelight, he thought she looked embarrassed.

"Evasion," she said, "has become almost natural. I don't think I'm lying, but how would I know? If I don't have an answer, I try to find a truthful way not to answer. But you noticed that, didn't you?"

"It was one of the things that first got my attention. I thought you were beautiful the few times I'd seen you around, but that night at my parents' house, you seemed to slip away like a stream rushing downhill."

"You have a nice way of describing things. Also a nonjudgmental one."

He couldn't resist. "How would you know?"

Her eyes widened, and for an instant he thought she would blow up at him, then she got it and laughed. "Good one, Braden. Well, that's my reaction, and I'm sticking to it."

He had no doubt she was a spirited, determined woman, but it was nice to see her drop her guard enough to let it show. "You're safe with me," he blurted, then wondered if he had just promised more than he should have. He knew nothing about her beyond what she had shared. There was always the possibility that she might turn out to have once been a very different woman. Well, he'd cross that river if they came to it.

Because as the evening deepened, and the storm continued to batter the world, he felt tendrils growing between them. Links, ties, bindings. She was melding herself with him in a way that ought to heighten his caution, especially under these circumstances.

But he liked what was happening between them. Liked getting to know her, liked seeing her face across the table, liked the way they had made love together. Despite the risks, he didn't want to damage even a single tender shoot of the intimacy they were beginning to share—the real intimacy of her problems, her fears, her efforts to deal with them. For the first time, he wished he was more than just a cowboy. Someone with the training to really help her somehow. What, a private detective?

He almost laughed at himself. If the cops hadn't been able to figure out who she was, what made him think he'd do any better? All he had to offer was Winona's insistence on talking to her, a pretty slim lead. Maybe the woman had heard something. Maybe she had recognized Jennifer somehow. But as it stood, he didn't know what the psychic had to offer, and in a way he felt bad for pressing Jenn to see her when Winona clearly made her so uncomfortable.

But, he thought, maybe there was a reason for that. Maybe Winona was connected in some way with Jenn's past. Maybe at some level, Jenn recognized her.

Which made her desire to avoid Winona even more interesting. Assuming that was the case, of course. She wanted to know but didn't want to know. She'd said as much herself. She feared not liking what she might learn, which was perfectly understandable, but she also couldn't live with not knowing.

A hell of a dilemma.

"Okay," he said, "a man's gotta eat. Eggs aren't going to carry me through. Hungry?"

She seemed glad to change the subject. This time he didn't make the decision, but invited her to look through the supplies he'd brought and whatever remained in her fridge that looked good while he put some more wood on the fire. He'd made the last pot of coffee with snow because when the power went out it had taken her well pump with it, so he hunted up the biggest pot he could find and went to get some more snow to boil on the stove.

"You need a bigger pot," he remarked as he prepared to step outside with one of her saucepans.

She laughed, and the sound followed him until it faded into the winter squall as he closed the door. The move outside was bracing, moving him from a warm, snuggly cocoon into the harsher world of nature's rage.

He gave himself a lecture on common sense, caution, not moving too fast, watching his step…and then forgot it all when he went back inside.

The cabin had transformed. She had lit a few candles, bringing light to the darker places, and her smile was brighter than all of them combined. He didn't want to be anywhere else in the world.

And he didn't care how dangerous this might be.

Chapter Nine

Morning brought a brilliant, snow-covered world. Sometime during the night, the wind had died and the storm had passed. By noon the plow managed to find its way to Jenn's cabin, and Braden departed after a few lingering kisses. He had to check on the herd, had to know how much damage they'd suffered.

Jenn understood, but ached as she watched him drive away. He'd said he would call, but there was still no cell phone reception, and the power hadn't yet been restored.

Before leaving, Braden had dug her car out of the snowdrift that had buried it. She wondered if it would even start, but a strange sort of ennui seemed to fill her. She thought of going to town to check on her friends, then assumed they were probably better off than she was.

She had reached some kind of cusp, she realized. Caught between past and present, trying to cling to the idyll she had shared with Braden, reluctant to go out into the world and shatter it.

She had decisions to make. Friends to see. It might be easier to get by in town. She had no doubt that Vanessa, Mallory, Cecelia or one of the others would offer her a sofa if she needed a warm place to stay.

But Braden had left her with the supplies and a truckload of wood right outside her door. She had no *need* to go anywhere. Not right now.

Things inside her seemed to have rearranged, and she spent the afternoon sitting in front of the fire, trying to sort through them.

Pursuing her past could end right here and now, she realized. Braden had opened up possibilities that overwhelmed her. Maybe he would be part of her future, maybe he wouldn't, but he had certainly taught her that there *could* be a future.

As for her past, what did she want from it? The sorry fact was, even if she had the details, such as where she had come from, what her real name was, who her parents had been, they would mean little to her in any real sense. Without her memory of all that, she would probably feel no real connection at all.

But even those bare facts could still anchor her. Answers to the simplest questions eluded her, such as exactly how old she was, when her birthday was, where she had been born. She supposed there were people in the world without amnesia who couldn't accurately answer those questions, too, but in this country, everybody she met had an answer.

Well, searching or not, she had to start making firm moves toward a future. She couldn't continue to live as if she were going to pack up and move at any moment. She needed work, she needed to plan, she needed to settle.

She needed to accept the way things were.

Easier said than done, of course. The desire to fill in the blanks had been driving her almost since the beginning, when it became clear she wouldn't have a spontaneous recovery. It had given her the purpose that had been riven from her by amnesia.

Maybe it was time to find a new purpose, if she could. Searching hadn't done a whole lot for her. She'd remembered her name, or at least the name that felt right, spontaneously. She'd recognized that mountain, but it was utterly without context. She'd come to a town that she knew instinctively wasn't her home, but it felt close to home.

All that effort for a few little tidbits, none of which really anchored her, especially since she didn't know if any of it was real. The name Jennifer had popped out of her; it had felt right. But for all she knew, it was the name of a character from a movie or book that she liked.

If someone walked up to her and handed her her birth certificate, she wasn't sure she would feel any more rooted. Not without the all-important memories.

She had to push her search for answers onto the back burner and get on with life. Otherwise, she'd end up as crazy as Homer Gilmore, wandering the world and muttering strange words that nobody could understand.

He was another one that made her nervous, she was sorry to admit. She cared that he was homeless, but his rambling kept her at a distance. Maybe because she somehow recognized that she wasn't so very different from him. She had a roof now. With the coins around her neck, she would probably always have a roof, but otherwise? Otherwise, she'd become a daft old lady on an endless quest.

Winona and Homer. Two people she avoided like the plague. Now she wondered why.

Damn, she was getting a headache. She'd boiled some snow earlier for drinking water, and went to take a couple of ibuprofen. Maybe she needed another pot of coffee.

But she nixed that idea as soon as she realized she was pacing her tiny cabin, rubbing her arms, and fighting a deep-rooted anxiety again.

Think about Braden, she told herself. Think about the hours they'd spent making love. She had been very much in the present then, and now she had a past to remember: those hours with Braden. A past *worth* remembering.

She wanted more memories like that.

"Slacker." That was the first word out of Dallas's mouth when Braden got back to the ranch. His brother, bundled up like the Abominable Snowman, was carrying a calf into the barn, its mooing mother right at his heels.

Braden didn't answer directly. "How bad?"

"Not that bad," Dallas admitted. "We've got most of the calves who seem to be suffering from the cold in the barn. The herd did pretty well with the rest. We're okay, bro, just need to help these few along."

"So no losses?"

"Not yet. You should ride out and check some more. I'm not sure we got them all. So how's your new lady?"

Braden wanted to ignore that question. He didn't want his brothers trampling all over his time with Jenn in their usual teasing way. He wanted to protect those hours, and her, from their raucous commentary. And that was about as likely to happen as waving his arm to make all the snow vanish. "Any place you haven't checked yet?"

"Snow's deep in places. We could have missed some out there. So it's like that?"

"What?" Braden tensed, ready for the inevitable jibe.

But Dallas surprised him as he set the calf on its weak legs next to the mother. It began to suckle almost immediately. Compared to the outside world, the barn was warm and cozy. Then his gaze settled on Braden. "Just wondered if I'd ever see you so taken."

Braden didn't even know how to reply to that. Was he taken? More than he ever had been before. He felt as if he was carrying something special inside him, something he didn't want to have sullied by anything. Without replying, he simply went to saddle his horse. Livestock first. Always first. Then everything else. He hoped Jenn could understand that, because if she couldn't, it wouldn't matter how taken he was with her. She just simply wouldn't fit into his world.

The afternoon stretched into long, cold hours until waning light forced him to head back. As far as he could tell, they'd skipped their way through this blizzard with no real loss. Amazing. Despite his confident comments to Jenn yesterday morning, he'd been worried. The older cattle could pretty much find their windbreaks and keep moving enough to share their heat. The calves had less endurance, and he'd feared some losses, if not big ones.

But somehow their luck had held. He found no more troubled calves, nor any sign of dead ones. A storm like this in the spring, right after calving, often had a different ending. Or an early-season storm in October.

Which was not to say the herd was looking happy. Some of those bovine eyes seemed to regard him with reproach, as if he were responsible for this messy weather. Overhead, the cloud cover continued to break up, showing patches of dark blue as the day waned. They sure needed a few sunny days now.

Back at the barn, he helped throw hay to the sequestered cows, and check the calves for any sign of frostbite. So far so good, but the barn was filled to the rafters now. He hoped they'd have less to do by morning.

They couldn't shovel fast enough, he thought with mild amusement.

He heard the dinner bell clanging from the main house, but instead of joining his brother on the trek to a huge, warm dinner, he tried his cell phone again. On the ranch they used satellite phones so they wouldn't have trouble keeping in touch, but Jenn was on a cell phone, and he hoped the towers were functioning again. He needed to hear the sound of her voice.

When she answered, he felt as if warmth poured into his heart through his ear. "How's it going?" he asked her. "I can tell you got your phone back, but what about your power?"

"Not yet. But I'm positively becoming a pioneer woman. I've got a good fire going, and I was about to cook over it. See what you've done to me?"

He laughed. "I wish I could get over there."

"How's the ranch? Your herd?"

He was touched that she even asked. He'd dated a few women who wouldn't have given a damn, and a few who'd only pretended to. It hadn't taken him long to decide they weren't cut out to be part of his life. Everything revolved around this ranch.

"We're fine. We have a barn full of chilled calves and their mamas, but we didn't lose a one."

"That's great news!"

"I think so. Especially since I bailed out yesterday."

She fell silent for a moment, and he could hear noise on the line. Then she said, "You didn't have to come to my rescue, Braden. I'm not saying I didn't appreciate it, but considering how important those animals are…well…"

"Stop," he said. "There wasn't a whole lot I could do anyway until the storm finished. All I lost was a few hours, and my brother took care of it. Another time I might have to make a different decision, but I'm glad I made the one I did."

"I'm glad you did, too," she said, her voice seeming to hold secret promises, and warming him even more.

"Did you get into town today?"

"No," she admitted. "I wasted the whole afternoon. And Mallory's on call-waiting right now. I suppose she wonders if I'm still alive. The phone just started working again."

"You go talk to her. If I can, I'll try to come over after dinner. If that's okay?"

"It's always okay."

He hoped she meant that. Suddenly very happy, he whistled as he walked up to the house. He was sure he was in for the teasing that Dallas had avoided, but surprisingly he didn't care anymore.

Jenn spent a while on the phone with Mallory and Lily, who wanted to add her own two cents. She, it seemed, quite liked Jenn's new nickname and wanted her to know it. Mallory didn't ask any questions about it, which was really tactful of her, but talked instead about how she, Lily and Caleb had spent the whole day shoveling snow. "Damn, it built up between the buildings. Some of our older neighbors really needed help. Is your cabin buried?"

"Along one side, but it's not in the way. No complaints here."

They chatted for a few more minutes, then got off the phone to take care of their own matters.

Her dinner was interrupted by calls from Vanessa and a couple of others from the Newcomers Club, and by the time the calls stopped coming, she realized that Rust Creek Falls was trying to make her feel at home. Only her own resistance stood in the way.

Then Cecelia called just as she started to boil water in which to take a stab at washing dishes.

"Hey," Cecelia said. "You're still alive."

"That's the rumor."

Cecelia laughed. "Got your power back? We have it, but I hear it's still a little spotty."

"I'm probably at the bottom of the list, out here."

"But you're okay? Do you need anything?"

"If I did, I'd come to town. I'm learning how to take full advantage of a woodstove."

"I thought that thing terrified you."

"It used to," Jenn admitted, without telling Cecelia how the change had come about. "We do what we must and all that. So what's happening? You all are okay, right?"

"We're fine. We were prepared, thanks to Winona."

That woman again. Jenn's hand tightened on her phone, and she feared she might disconnect by accident. Finger by finger she eased her grip and tried to answer lightly. "I guess I should have listened. But really, I'm okay. I have everything I need."

"You can get out of there, can't you?"

"All shoveled and plowed out."

That was when she heard Cecelia hesitate. "Julie? I mean Jenn. Damn, I *will* get used to this."

"I'll answer to either," Jenn assured her.

"It's not that. It's...well, I had to run to the grocery today because while we got ready in every other way, I forgot birdseed."

"Birdseed?" Jenn practically gaped into the phone.

"Hey listen, I've got a hundred sparrows dependent on the feeder Nick gave me as an early present. If you had to look at them all fluffed up out there, huddling on windowsills to stay warm, knowing that feeder was empty, you'd run to the store, too."

"Someday I need to see this. Okay, you're right. If I had a hundred birds looking all pathetic here, I'd have run to the store, too."

Cecelia laughed, but it didn't sound quite natural. Jenn had had enough. "Cecelia, what's wrong?"

Cecelia's sigh was audible. "Nothing really. It's more like weird."

"So spill."

"When I was at the store, I ran into Winona Cobbs." Tension filled Jenn all over again. "And?"

"Look, I know you don't like her. Not everyone does. There are plenty who think she's a crackpot to be avoided. But anyway…"

Jenn waited impatiently, wanting this conversation to come to a conclusion, feeling like she was on tenterhooks. "What?"

"She said she wanted to talk to you. I was to tell you that. Then she said something that was really weird. She said Homer knows. Now what in the hell would Homer know? Wandering around talking about babies lost and found, the past being present and all that stuff. I'm surprised the guy remembered to come out of the storm."

"You're disturbed because she said something about Homer?"

"No," Cecelia answered. "I'm disturbed because…well, only a couple of us know you decided you wanted to be called by your old nickname. Not a problem, but not exactly anything anyone's gossiping about. It's only been a few weeks, and it's just not that important. Julie, Jenn, who cares, right?"

Jenn closed her eyes and leaned against the short little counter. She could hear the water bubbling on the stove now, but it seemed a long way away. "So? I don't care who knows."

"I imagine not. I just want you to know that because it'll explain why I'm so…weirded out by this. When I saw Winona, she said I was to tell *Jennifer* that she wanted to talk to her. I must have looked astonished because then she said she meant the Jennifer everyone called Julie."

* * *

For a long time after the phone call ended, Jennifer ignored the boiling water and sat staring at the fire. Winona must have heard from somewhere what had happened at the gift wrapping. Someone must have overheard.

But that didn't answer the question of why the psychic had now told two people she wanted to talk to Jenn.

She must know something. Braden was right; she might have just heard something or figured out something. It didn't have to be all spooky or weird, just casual knowledge Winona had come by in a conversation. Or something she might have remembered from the past. Simple, ordinary knowledge.

Or she might know nothing, really, might have sensed Jenn's antipathy, and wanted to make a point of some kind.

But for all Winona made her feel uneasy, Jenn didn't think the psychic was that kind of person. People might be weirded out by her, but she'd never heard anyone accuse the woman of unkindness.

All of which left her staring into the gaping maw of her past again. Did she want whatever information Winona might have? Could she believe it regardless? She was certainly a perfect victim for lies. When she thought about it, she was lucky she hadn't been scammed a dozen times over. Like her necklace. Only her good fortune had brought an honest expert to her. Someone else could have taken advantage of her to get the wealth off her neck.

Or maybe not. She fingered the coins again and knew that she didn't want to part with her only link to her past. She'd had enough trouble emotionally just selling one of them, and she'd done that only so she could get out here and...

Search for her past.

Damn, she was going to be haunted forever. Every time she made up her mind to let it go, she faced once again her utter inability to do so.

The sound of a truck engine caught her attention, and she went to the steamy window. That boiling water was turning this place into a sauna. Dang, she hoped the pot wasn't ready to boil dry.

Using her sleeve, she wiped away the steam and peered out. Braden was pulling up out front, his truck a now-familiar sight. He'd managed to come!

In an instant her heart soared. She'd been moony all day over him, remembering his every word and touch, and hoping against hope that she'd see him again soon. Her very first crush, insofar as she knew, and she was suffering all the aching, yearning pangs that evidently went with it.

Braden, Braden, Braden. His name had become a constant drumbeat in her blood. Every memory of him caused her heart to jump. The need to see him was becoming as overwhelming as her search for her past.

Smiling now, she went to open the door for him. His smile seemed to stretch from ear to ear.

"Damn," he said, kicking the door closed behind him. He swept her into a hug, pressing her against his cold outer clothes. "This day was endless. I thought I'd never get back to you."

"I couldn't wait," she admitted.

"Music to my ears." Then he kissed her, long, hard and deep. Inside she melted into a puddle of yearning, but instead of taking the kiss further, he broke it off. Disappointment speared through her.

He started stripping his outerwear. "My God, are you trying to turn this place into a sauna?"

She laughed easily enough. "Not on purpose. I was

boiling water for dishes and got distracted by phone calls."

He finished hanging his gear then brushed another kiss on her lips and headed for the stove. "Um, we need water here."

"Maybe I should just give up the project." And make love with him. For hours and hours…

But he seemed in no rush, and she began to wonder if he didn't want her again. Instead, he grabbed another saucepan from her kitchen, ducked outside just long enough to fill it with snow, then dumped the snow into the boiling pot. "How desperately do you want to wash dishes?" he asked.

"Not very," she admitted. Not now that he was here.

"I'll help. Sorry, I'm frozen. Dinner didn't even warm me up. I'm not usually such a wuss, but I spent all afternoon on horseback, and I think the cold reached my bones. I blasted the heater in my truck, and I still feel like ice."

Sympathy began to replace her disappointment. "I'll make us some coffee. You sit close to that fire."

He sat on the floor while she put the pot on the stove. "Maybe I should just stop boiling water."

"Nah," he said. "I just realized that this is the first time in hours that I could actually breathe through my nose."

"Is this unusually cold or something?"

"No." His eyes were smiling as she turned, and he reached up to tug her hand until she sat in his lap, her back cradled against his chest. "I think I didn't get enough sleep last night is all. The tank is low on energy. Now I wonder who could have been responsible for that?"

Instantly, all her worries and fears fled. He couldn't have made it any plainer that he wasn't here to tell her he was through with her. "I'm sorry."

"I most definitely am not."

She let her head fall back to rest against his shoulder. "So the cows are okay?"

"Everything is okay. I took a little ribbing, but that was inevitable. My family's not used to me being gone when there's bad weather. But what good is it to have Dallas hanging around if I have to do everything?"

She laughed again, feeling gloriously happy that he was here. The shadows that had plagued her afternoon evaporated. At least for now.

"Do you get any time off?"

"Yeah, I can take a few weeks away if I want to. Dallas could hire a hand to fill in for me. Of course, there are better times of year to do it. Calving season, for example, is one time you couldn't pry me loose from the place."

"All hands on deck?"

"Believe it. As many as we can get and hire."

"I hope I get to see it."

"If you're still here come spring, I can promise you."

If she was still here? She guessed she could understand why he might wonder. With a jolt, her thoughts came back to Winona. Her heart started hammering, and her hands tightened. She had to face this. She *had* to. She couldn't keep living with anxiety every time one woman's name came up. This was a kind of craziness on her part.

"Jenn? What's wrong? You stiffened up."

"Winona," she said through tight lips.

"What about her? Did she bother you?" He sounded ready to ride to her defense.

"No, no. It's just that Cecelia says she wants to talk to me." Then she outlined the conversation, and how weird it seemed that Winona had called her Jennifer.

Braden ran his hand down her arm. "That's strange,

all right. The only person I told you were Jenn now was Dallas, and he'd have no reason to tell anyone else."

"And I just told the girls it was my old nickname, and I wanted to go back to it. They didn't seem to care one way or another."

"Probably not." The coffee smelled done, so Jenn made herself get up to pour them some. When she returned from the kitchen area with mugs, Braden had moved to one of the chairs.

"So," he said as she poured, "what do you want to do about it?"

What she wanted was to tumble onto the floor with him, or into her bed and make love until everything else in the world vanished. She wanted to forget that anything else existed except Braden.

But she knew it wasn't going to work. No way. Winona kept popping up, and forgetting about it for a few hours wouldn't make her go away. "I'm going to have to talk to her."

Braden glanced at his watch. "I could go get her right now."

"But it's late."

"It's not that late. I know where she lives. If you want, we can just deal with this and make it stop bothering you. Man, you must feel almost stalked."

"It can wait." And yes, she was starting to feel stalked, but surely sometime tomorrow would be soon enough?

"No, it can't." He stood up and began reaching for his outerwear, showing her a determined and stubborn side she should have expected, given what he did for a living, but a side she hadn't seen before. "You need not to be worrying about this. You wanted me present when you talked to her, and given the results of this storm and all the work I have waiting for me, I can't absolutely guarantee when I'll next be able to arrange that. Will I be back tomorrow night? I hope so. But sweetie, I can't promise right now. So let's just get this problem off your plate."

"But…"

"No buts." He bent to kiss her as he started buttoning his jacket. "We're crossing this one off the list now."

She could have gone with him, but dread began to fill her so much she stayed where she was, hoping he couldn't find Winona, that she could postpone whatever this was for another day.

Facing her own cowardice never pleased her, but she was feeling like a coward now. There was so much she thought showed how tough she was, surviving the amnesia, the hunt for her past, moving across the country…then one woman reminded her of how afraid she truly was.

"Chicken," she said aloud to the empty cabin as Braden drove away. Then, mad at herself, she took the boiling water off the stove. Washing dishes could go hang.

Braden drove as fast as he dared on the slick roads. He knew he was pushing Jenn, but he was beginning to believe she needed a little pushing. It was clear to him by now that she *needed* to know something. She could talk all she wanted about moving on, but somehow everything kept coming back to her need to know her real identity.

No matter how firmly she resolved to move forward, she was far from ready to let go. And maybe Winona knew something that could help her settle it. Something that at least could give Jenn an anchor to cling to even if she never remembered. A sense of her place.

Jenn was like a leaf blowing in the wind. She needed to land somehow, and maybe all it would take were some tidbits of information. Assuming Winona really knew anything, of course, but from all he'd heard about the psychic, she didn't strike him as one to shoot her mouth off in a way that might hurt someone.

She was also as old as the hills and knew more about this area and the people in it, its history, than anyone. She'd lived in many of the towns around here, or so he'd heard. She might honestly know something. Jenn owed it to herself to find out. And he was damn sure not going to let her put off something so important when it was dangling right in front of her.

Winona answered her door on that third knock. Braden was relieved to see she was still dressed. At her age, she might have already gone to bed.

"The youngest Traub," Winona remarked. "You got through the storm."

"Yes. Ms. Cobbs…"

"Winona," the woman said sharply. Her white-as-snow hair made a wild halo around her. "It's about Jennifer. That's why you're here."

In spite of himself, Braden felt a flicker of amusement. "You don't miss much."

"I don't miss anything. When is she going to see me?"

"Right now, if you're willing."

Much to his relief, Winona was willing. She invited him in, and as she struggled to get into her winter coat and boots, he helped her as much as she would let him. Touching her reminded him of just how frail and old she was. What was he thinking, dragging her out on a cold night like this?

"About time," Winona muttered when at last she was ready to go out the door. "Been looking at that girl for months. Something about her…" She tapped her head and looked at Braden just before they stepped outside. "Too many memories. Hard to get at them all anymore."

He was too young to imagine that, but willing to take her word for it. As he helped her into the warmth of his still-running truck, he realized he was glad she had spoken of memories, not intuition. He felt a little better about what he was doing here.

If Winona actually remembered, then the dangers of giving Jenn misinformation were slim to none.

And even just a little real information might help Jenn settle. Damn, he hoped so.

But fear rode with him alongside Winona. It was entirely possible that whatever she knew could take Jenn away from here.

Like it or not, he was beginning to think he couldn't stand losing her.

Braden helped Winona over the snow and ice to Jenn's door. Lights from within told him the power had been restored. That much was good, but right now he was more worried about the reception he was going to receive after having pushed this situation on her. He hadn't listened to her objections, and he frankly wouldn't have been surprised if she slammed the door in their faces. That woman had enough tigers on her tail that he couldn't blame her for wanting to avoid him.

But everything froze as if in crystal when Jenn opened the door hesitantly. For several seconds, none of them moved. Jenn stood looking like a frightened deer as she saw Winona. Winona, however, experienced no such qualms.

"I suspected it," she said. "You're Jennifer MacCallum."

Chapter Ten

Jenn froze in shock. She hadn't expected such a blunt statement, and while the name Jennifer clearly resonated with her, MacCallum didn't.

Winona wasn't deterred. She pushed her way through the door. "Damn cold out there. A body could freeze between one breath and the next. Let an old woman in and give me some coffee if you have it."

The words galvanized Jenn. Something to do. A need to fill. She didn't know what to make of the rest, but she supposed she was now going to find out whether she wanted to or not. Braden helped Winona out of her coat, then the woman eased herself into an armchair and took the coffee from Jenn.

"Sit down, girl," she said. "I don't know what you're doing hanging around here pretending to be someone else, but you got family that hunted for you for years and are now grieving for you because they think you're dead. That's pretty sad for all of you."

Jenn didn't know how to react. She wasn't pretending anything, but she could hardly tell this woman it wasn't sad.

"Why are you calling yourself Julie Smith?"

Silence hung in the air. Jenn could barely breathe. The crackling of the fire seemed loud. She felt Braden come to stand behind her, placing his hand on her shoulder. That touch gave her strength.

Jenn gathered herself, finally reaching a decision. Braden had accepted her amnesia, and so could everyone else. She was tired of all the tiptoeing, all the evasions. Let the chips fall. "Frankly," Jenn said defiantly, "I have amnesia. I don't remember who I used to be."

"Ahh." Winona nodded, then spent a few minutes sipping coffee. As the seconds ticked by, Jenn felt as if she were being stretched on a rack. Finally, Winona spoke. "Then you need to know."

A spark of fear-fueled anger. "Maybe I don't want to know."

Winona arched a thin white eyebrow at her. "Then what are you doing here? What we want and what we need isn't always the same thing."

Too true, Jenn thought. She was caught between fear and need, virtually paralyzed except for the butterflies in her stomach with her blood hammering in fear, on the edge of fighting or fleeing.

Braden spoke. "Take it easy on her, Winona. She's had a long, hard struggle to get this far."

Winona nodded and settled back. "The girl's had a lot of hard life. Guess that hasn't changed. But good life, too, between the bad. Maybe it's time to answer all the questions and deal with all the bad, and get herself settled."

"I'm still here," Jenn said between her teeth. "Quit talking about me like I'm not."

"Part of you is here. Part of you is lost. Homer recognized you, too. Took me a while longer."

Braden spoke again. "You want to explain that?"

"Maybe I'll get to it. I got my own ways of telling a story. First off, like I said, you're Jennifer MacCallum. You have family grieving you. But no, you took a notion to run off and you never came back, and they couldn't find you. How far did you run?"

"Why do you need to know?"

"Because your folks scoured three states for you and couldn't find any trace. Finally, they got around to believing you were dead."

"For all practical purposes, I was." Jenn wished the woman would get to the point, would spare her the inquisition. Wished her heart rate would settle, and the tension seep away. She wondered if she would ever live without it again.

"Nice fire," Winona remarked. Then she drew a breath.

"Jennifer MacCallum, like I said. That's you. Born in Whitehorn."

"Whitehorn!" Braden seemed surprised.

"Where's that?" Jenn asked.

"Not all that far from here, but far enough you probably wouldn't trip into it."

"So I got close?" Jenn asked.

"You got close," he reassured her.

"Like a little homing pigeon with a glitch in the route," Winona agreed. "Guess you were trying to get home somehow."

Jenn didn't answer. She supposed she had been in her search for her past, but she still didn't feel as if she had a home, not even with a name attached to it. Whitehorn? The name didn't even ring a distant bell for her. Some of her tension was easing, however. Maybe it was Braden's hand on her shoulder, squeezing gently. Home, she realized, or as close as she could get, had become this man.

"I haven't got all night," Winona said as if they were

holding her up when she was taking her own good time about all of this. "Best get to it."

"Jennifer MacCallum." Jenn prodded her.

"That's right. Had a busy life for such a little one. Kidnapped at three…"

"Kidnapped?" Jenn stopped her. "What happened?"

"Mary Jo Kincaid ran off with you, carried you over the mountains when she took you from Whitehorn to North Dakota."

Jenn looked at Braden. "Maybe that's why I recognized the mountain."

"What mountain?" Winona asked.

"Fall Mountain," Braden answered.

Winona nodded. "That would be the one. So you recognized it?"

"It seemed familiar. But who was Mary Jo Kincaid?"

Winona rocked a little, as if she were used to sitting in a rocking chair. "You got a tangled story, Jenny. Really tangled. You want it all?"

Jenn hesitated only briefly. "Yes. All of it." Better all of it than more questions.

"Your mama ran away. Her name was Maria March. Don't know where she got off to, but your daddy was a Kincaid. Jeremiah Kincaid. The MacCallums took you as a foster child and made you their own. Must be why Mary Jo thought she should grab you from the MacCallums, you being a Kincaid and all. Jeremiah sure didn't want you much, and he was getting up there. Might as well have been a little ragamuffin except for Sterling and Jessica MacCallum. They adopted you when they got you back and brought you up."

Jenn tried to absorb this. So her birth mother hadn't wanted her, her real father hadn't been interested, and somehow she had become adopted. She was afraid to ask more about it, though, because she didn't want to distract Winona, who was at last telling her the story.

"Anyway, you grew up fine with just a few hitches. A lot of spunk, folks said. Spunk got you into trouble."

"How?"

"You ran away."

"Why? Why did I do that?"

"You got an inheritance from Jeremiah Kincaid on your twenty-first birthday. You didn't like it. You made no bones about not wanting the money because Jeremiah had been thieving it from the local Native Americans. Made himself a wealthy man that way. Now I suppose there were lots of ways you could have dealt with that. Could have given it all away, I guess. But you were hotheaded, and your parents wanted you to invest it so you'd be okay no matter what. I heard there was a big fight between you. Even told them they weren't your real parents and had no right to tell you anything."

Jennifer felt her heart sink. She had wondered if she would like the person she used to be, and right now she wasn't sure she did. Telling her adoptive parents, the people who had raised her by choice, that they weren't her real parents? She wanted to shudder. "But they did love me?"

"Enough to tear three states apart looking for you."

Jenn let that sink in, and while she couldn't recall her adoptive parents, she felt awful for acting that way. Even though it was like listening to a story about someone else, Jenn's heart squeezed, and she drew a ragged breath. She didn't like that girl, not at all. "God," she whispered brokenly.

Braden's hand squeezed her shoulder. "You were young."

"Not much older now," Winona observed. "But maybe a bit wiser?"

Jenn didn't know. How could she know? Her fingers lifted to her necklace. "What about this?"

"Guess that's the only part of your inheritance you took. I remember Maria wearing it for a while, but it was Jeremiah's, from *his* father. Reckon you didn't think it was dirty like the money."

"Maybe." The blank wall remained even as the details were filled in.

Winona held out her coffee cup. Before Jenn could move, Braden went to refill it.

Finally, Jenn asked a question that seemed suddenly important. "What about my family? Who are they?"

"Good people, fairly young when they took you on right after Maria left. Sterling MacCallum is a police detective. Jessica, his wife, is a social worker. Sterling tried like hell to find you, but somehow you skipped without leaving any trace behind. They kept waiting for you to come home, sure you'd get over it, but you never did. They've been grieving over you for a long time now. Think you could find it in your heart to ease their sorrow, girl?"

"But I don't even remember them! How could I help them?"

"Seeing you and knowing you're alive would do most of the work. I can see you're a kind woman, and it might ease your heart some just to know them now. You need your own heart eased, too. You've been through a lot." Winona finished her coffee quickly then stood up. "These old bones need their bed."

Braden hurried to help her on with her coat. Winona paused at the door and looked back. "You think about it,

Jenny MacCallum. Even if you don't remember, you'll find something you need."

"I'll be back," Braden said as he followed her to the door.

She was still alone and without a real past. Rejected, kidnapped, adopted and a runaway. It was a hell of a résumé.

She wondered if she should just find a rock to crawl under. Because she really, really didn't want to be that girl. Unwanted. Then turning cruelly on those who had raised her.

No, she didn't like that person at all.

When Braden returned, to her surprise, he didn't say one thing about Winona's revelations. Instead, he swept her into her bed and made love to her, driving everything else from her mind.

But later, much later, she lay awake. The languor of lovemaking had long since departed. The arms around her felt good, but they didn't answer the fears that had plagued her and now plagued her even more.

She watched the faint movements of the firelight on the ceiling, trying to settle the revelations in her mind and heart.

But her heart didn't answer them. She might as well have read about Jennifer MacCallum in a novel. Hell, maybe she'd have connected more with a fictional character.

None of it felt as if it belonged to her, except the name Jennifer, a mountain, a Christmas pageant barely remembered. The world was probably full of Jennifers, though, so how could she be sure she was this one?

Her past gave her no answers. Her heart held no connections. They had been severed as if by a guillotine.

She needed to move. Nerves began to trouble her anew. Her fears had come to life, and now she had to deal with all this somehow.

And she really didn't want to be that selfish girl who had turned on and then run away from the people who had raised her. Who loved her.

Braden stirred then turned to gaze at her in the dim light. "Need to talk? Need to get up? You've become as stiff as a board."

She rose without a word and climbed into her warmest fleece sweatshirt and pants. Jamming her feet into quilted slippers, she walked over to the stove. But its warmth wouldn't reach her heart—she felt cold all the way through.

Braden joined her wearing only his jeans. He squatted to throw another log onto the fire then stepped back and faced her. "Want some coffee? Lights?"

"Coffee, please. No lights." She felt like a deck of cards that had been thrown into a fan, although the truth was, she'd felt that way before.

He started the coffee then sat at her feet, facing her. "Tough night," he remarked.

"Yeah." It had been, every bit of it. She just wished she knew how to deal with this, wish she didn't feel like shattered glass that she couldn't quite glue together.

"How did it make you feel?" he asked.

"Like I don't want to be that girl. That was my whole reaction. I don't remember any more than I did before, and I don't like that Jennifer MacCallum."

He nodded, but didn't say anything. Reaching up, he placed his hands on her curled-up legs and rubbed gently. When at long last he finally spoke, he said, "I think what matters is what Jennifer MacCallum does now. She was a young girl, really."

"I'm not much older."

"Maybe not in years, but certainly in experience."

She shook her head. "How can you like someone who turned on her adoptive parents that way? Who ran away? And since I can't remember a damn thing, how can I be sure I've learned anything at all?"

"Because you lost everything," he said simply. "Because you know better than anyone the price of running away, the cost of having no family, no roots."

"Yeah," she said almost bitterly. "I did the ultimate in running away."

"Not by choice, I suspect."

She shook her head a little, but despite her resistance, his words were rippling through her. Had she really learned something by her constant struggle to find her past? God, she hoped so.

He rose and poured coffee for both of them before settling again on the floor at her feet.

"You need sleep," she argued, trying to think of someone besides herself. "You must have a lot to do tomorrow."

"I've survived on short sleep before. I'm more worried about you."

"I'll be fine," she protested, although she wasn't really sure. Shattered glass, no way to put it back together again. Somehow she had to absorb all this and accept it.

"You've been fine on your own for some time now. Well, you're not alone anymore. You have friends and you have me. We're here for you."

It was a touching statement, but she wasn't quite ready to believe it. "What do *you* think of a girl who'd do that to her family?"

"You know, I was twenty-one not so long ago. I remember being pigheaded, stupid and very stubborn once

I'd made up my mind. I had the answers to everything. It's a wonder my family could put up with me. I went toe-to-toe with my father more than once. Hell, I can't even remember some of the things we fought about, but we fought. And my mother would always say, 'Bob, he's growing up. Trying to find his place. He'll settle down.'"

He shrugged. "I think I gave my folks a harder time than all my brothers combined. Or maybe I was worse because I had all those older brothers. Sometimes I think I was kicking and screaming my way to maturity, or at least to getting them all to accept I wasn't just the baby anymore."

"It must have been hard." Not that she could really imagine it. She didn't have the experience from which to guess what it had been like. "But it sounds normal. What I did isn't."

"I don't know," he said. "Lots of young people run away from home. Unfortunately, too many of them never make it back."

She shook her head. "I was pretty old to pull that one."

"Not really. When the pressure gets to be too much, for whatever reason, any of us could decide to take a hike. Hell, Sutter moved to Seattle because of a big fight. It happens."

"But he didn't lose touch, and he came back."

A quiet sound escaped him. "You didn't *choose* to lose touch, remember? For all anyone knows, you might have been getting ready to head home when you were injured. Might have been only hours away from making a phone call. From the sound of it, you got your amnesia only a short time after you left."

"That's a pretty light to put it in."

"Well, it may be true. No way to know now."

Silence fell again, punctuated only by the faint crackling of the fire. Shadows danced on the walls, making it feel almost as if there were spirits in the room with them.

There was certainly a lot in the room with them. Whole bunches of unanswered questions, decisions to be made, a broken life that only seemed more broken now.

Finally, she put her coffee cup down on the table. "We both need some sleep."

"What are you going to do? Will you look for the MacCallums?"

"I don't know." She put her feet on the floor, and he stood. "I just don't know, Braden. They're strangers. I don't remember them. I feel no pull in that direction. What good would it do them to have a daughter who might as well be dead?"

"It might give them hope."

But he didn't say another word as he guided her back to the bed. This time they didn't make love. He pulled her back against him, spooning with her, holding her close as if he could keep everything at bay.

If only it were that easy.

Christmas was drawing close, and excitement filled the air. Most of it left Jenn untouched, but Vanessa was positively bubbling over about the opening of Maverick Manor, and telling everyone they were going to be amazed by the mural she had painted around the lobby, but she wouldn't share a single detail. "It's a surprise for everyone!" Jonah Dalton, her fiancé, merely smiled at her excitement but kept mum.

The whole town seemed to bustle with new life, and whether or not Jenn was as excited as everyone else didn't matter. She enjoyed watching the enthusiasm build, enjoyed watching the shoppers running around with secret treasures in their bags. She started spending more time at the donut shop, having coffee with her friends, or just sitting and watching life through the window.

She no longer felt such a strong need to be alone. She even, finally, confided to her friends about her amnesia.

They were sitting around the table at Callie Kennedy and Nate Crawford's place, jabbering about nothing consequential, when she dropped the bomb. She didn't know what kind of reaction she expected, but after a silence, she was suddenly awash in sympathy and questions. She felt surrounded by loving concern and hugs as the women promised to help her in any way they could. Then came the questions, mercifully truncated by Cecelia, whether she meant to or not.

"God, that must be awful," Mallory said. "How can you stand it?"

"Like she has any choice?" Callie remarked.

Vanessa remained silent longer than the rest. Finally, "Did you come here for a reason?"

"I've been trying to find something familiar," Jenn admitted. "Snow and mountains seemed to draw me."

"Well, you sure as hell found them," Cecelia said bluntly. "Seems like you found a cowboy, too."

Jenn flushed. "What do you mean?"

"Only that some folks have noticed that a certain Triple-T truck seems to make its way out to your place a lot."

The others giggled, seeming more interested by that than by the amnesia. While their reaction to her amnesia was a welcome relief, their interest in her relationship with Braden was not. Jenn smiled weakly, mainly because that truck hadn't been making its way to her very often. Braden called at least once a day, and they talked for hours sometimes, but he was buried in work, both the problems left by the storm, and his mother's insistence that it was time to deck out the Triple-T for the holidays. Apparently, she went whole hog.

Jenn thought of volunteering to help, but she was still feeling uncertain in so many ways. She didn't want to push herself on Braden and his family. Even without a memory, she understood that holidays to a great extent were purely a family affair. She wasn't part of the Traub family, even remotely. And she still didn't want to find a way to get in touch with the MacCallums. But she was missing Braden, and often wondered if he were trying to put distance between them. The excuses sounded real enough, and he *did* call a lot, but there was no escaping the sense that he didn't have a whole lot of time for her.

She told herself to buck up. He'd warned her he'd be busy at times. She couldn't expect him to show up every single day. But it was still hard to accept when she wanted him there all the time.

Five days before Christmas, Braden showed up at her place with a tree and all the trimmings.

"No home should be without one," he said as he edged through the door with cardboard boxes. "Now it's small, so it won't push you out, and it's artificial so you don't have to worry about dry needles, and do you need another wood delivery?"

"I was supposed to get a couple of cords last week. I don't know what happened."

"Well, that can wait until we put up this little old tree."

For the first time, the magic of the season began to really reach her. There was something about having her own tree, thanks to Braden, about setting it up and stringing the miniature lights, about opening the boxes of small but exquisite ornaments, that began to make her feel truly happy. Excited, even, almost like a kid. As if she could remember.

She brushed that thought away like an annoying gnat, and joined Braden's good humor as they worked on the tree. He often stood back to guide her as she went to hang an ornament, telling her whether to move it to the right or left.

"Are you an ornament perfectionist?" she finally demanded.

"You could say I was raised to be one. Not until the day we take the trees down will my mother stop adjusting them."

"Trees? Plural?"

"Sure. One for the family room, one for the living room, one for the dining room. She even has one in her and Dad's bedroom, but she doesn't let anyone else touch it."

"She must love Christmas."

"No question. It means having everyone home, a house full of family."

Jenn felt a pang of guilt as his words reminded her of a family that was missing all that because she had run away.

"Hey." Braden touched her chin and lifted her head. "No getting down. We were having fun."

The tree went into the corner between her sleep nook and the stove, protected from the heat of the woodstove by the dogleg in the wall. Braden moved the two armchairs a little so that they could sit and admire it.

"It's beautiful," she said. "I thought I could do without it, but I'm so glad it's here. Thank you."

"My pleasure." He paused. "I guess not having a bunch of good Christmas memories makes this a little meaningless to you."

"I'm enjoying everyone's excitement. People seem so happy. And I do have one Christmas memory, I think."

She told him about what had happened at the pageant, how she could feel herself dressed as an angel like Lily, and looking out into a sea of faces trying to see her parents. "I couldn't see them, though. At least not in my flashback."

"Well, that's something. Not much, I admit, but something. Maybe you'll get other flashes with time."

"Maybe." But now she wasn't sure she wanted them. Not given what she had done.

"Have you decided when you'll call them?" He didn't have to say who he meant. The MacCallums were hanging over her head like the Sword of Damocles.

"Not yet," she said, trying to sound firm. "I'm not ready yet."

"Ready for what?" he asked. "That they might be thrilled to see you and glad you're still alive?"

The tension came to a shrieking head then. "You can't know that! I don't know that. I did a terrible thing to them. What if they can't forgive me? Besides, they're strangers to me. God, wouldn't it be weird to have them call me their daughter when I don't even know who they are? What if I don't like them? What if they don't like me?"

"I somehow suspect they aren't like that. Winona said they looked everywhere for you. That they grieved."

"That doesn't mean anything. I was rejected before."

"What?" He rose to his feet, and the next thing she knew they were standing toe-to-toe, about to really get into it. A fight. Their first fight? Or their last one?

"My birth parents didn't want me, not either of them."

"But these people chose to adopt you!" His brow was lowering.

"And then I treated them like dirt. Why in the hell would they want anything to do with me ever again?"

"God!" he said exasperatedly. He ran his fingers through his hair. "Maybe you've forgotten the most important thing of all, Jenn."

"What's that?" she demanded.

"Love. What it really is." He swore and grabbed for his jacket. "Think about that, why don't you? You're judging people you can't remember, but what are you basing that judgment on? I thought you were braver than this."

"Braden…"

But he was already out the door, leaving ashes in his wake. Her mouth turned sour, and she felt as if her heart had been cleaved in two.

Maybe she *did* know something about love, because he had just cut her to ribbons.

Braden told himself to let go of it. It wasn't his problem, it was hers. She had to make the decision whether to reach out to her family. He reminded himself of her fear of the past, a fear that was probably even greater than her desire to know. He reminded himself that she didn't like the girl who had run away from her family. Why the hell would she want to know any more?

Of course he didn't think she was being fair to herself, but given her loss of memory, how could she even compare her actions to the actions of others her age? Hell, he'd even told her about Sutter, but that hadn't seemed to ease her guilt any.

It had been a really big deal when Sutter moved so far away after the blowup. Ellie had cried quite a bit, and Bob had got all stern-jawed. But Sutter hadn't stayed away. Once he'd found a way to make peace with the family— especially Forrest—he'd started coming home to visit. The important thing was, Sutter had not been lost forever.

Remembering his parting words to Jenn, however, he

felt pretty small. That had been a terribly cutting thing to say, yet it went to the heart of his own fear: that she might not be capable of really forming a relationship. No past, no memories—it would be easy to imagine her turning into a rolling stone, always looking for something that would never be there.

Of course that concerned him, because he had come to care about her a whole lot. His inability to imagine life without Jenn had grown by leaps and bounds until he was cussing the demands of his own life, demands he had always welcomed until they kept him from seeing Jenn as often as he would have liked.

It seemed the bug had bit him, and it had bit him with no guarantees of any kind.

Then, finally, he realized he'd had enough. This had to be settled somehow. If Jenn hated him forever, then so be it. At least he'd understand where he stood with her.

Not his business? Hell, yeah, it was his business because he was involved. And it really bothered him that she wouldn't make one blessed phone call to put some peoples' minds and hearts to rest.

Maybe it would turn out bad. Maybe nothing would come of it, but there were a couple of parents who had a right to know that their daughter wasn't dead.

Remembering all too well his mother's grief after Sutter had left, he knew something about that end of it. As for Jenn, she needed the closure of knowing, whether she wanted to admit it or not.

That night, instead of calling Jenn, he hunted for a phone number in Whitehorn. To his relief, the MacCallums were still listed there.

A short while later, a woman's voice answered the phone.

"Hello?"

"Jessica MacCallum?"

"Yes."

"You don't know me, Mrs. MacCallum. My name is Braden Traub. I'm a rancher over in Rust Creek Falls."

"I recognize the Traub name," she said warmly. "Would you rather talk to my husband? At least, I'm assuming this is business of some kind."

"I can talk to you, but you'd better sit down."

"Why?"

"Because I know your daughter Jennifer. She's alive, and she has amnesia."

When he hung up the phone a half hour later, he wondered if he'd go to hell forever.

Chapter Eleven

The Maverick Manor's grand opening hovered only one day away. Vanessa was in a flutter, nerves and excitement keeping her high. All her work in decorating the place was going to be on display, and she both feared and craved the reactions. She must have called Jenn a dozen times, and probably called their other girlfriends, as well.

The entire town had been invited for the grand opening Christmas party, which promised plenty of food and drink from the Traub family's own relative, Thunder Canyon cousin DJ Traub and his popular barbecue restaurant, DJ's Rib Shack, as well as the first peek at the work that had been going on for months. It would be a milestone for the town, especially after the flood had taken so much.

During one excited call, Vanessa reminded her, "Don't forget to dress up. An excuse to dress up is rare enough around here."

"I bought a dress," Jenn assured her. "Just for this." It had seemed like a terrible extravagance, but important anyway. She just hoped her legs wouldn't freeze, because even though the weather had remained clear since the blizzard, it didn't seem to have warmed much.

Braden said he'd meet her there. He hadn't come by since their fight, and he hadn't come over, or even suggested it. Now he wasn't even going to take her to the grand opening, but rather meet her there. That sounded entirely too casual to soothe her aching heart.

She missed him. She missed him intensely, and feared she'd driven him away forever. Why couldn't he understand the tangle of feelings she had over the MacCallums? It wasn't as if she could remember them. Just thinking about reaching out to them made her throat lock up and her mouth grow dry with fear. She didn't know which would be worse, being rejected by them for her behavior—behavior she couldn't even remember but sounded pretty bad to her—or being welcomed like the prodigal daughter. Either way, they were strangers, and she couldn't imagine how she would handle it.

Well, she told herself, she had time to think about it. First she had a party to get ready for.

In the late afternoon, the day before the big bash, the phone rang again. Jenn expected it to be Vanessa once more. Even Jonah's calming words weren't helping much with her friend's nerves. Busy as she was with last-minute details, she seemed to need frequent breaks on the phone for reassurance.

Smiling, Jenn answered, glad that she could provide even some small comfort to Vanessa.

Instead, for only the second time since he'd brought the Christmas tree, she heard Braden's voice.

"Hi, Jenn," he said quietly.

"I thought you were mad at me."

"I wasn't, not really. Just a little disturbed. I'm sorry. I've been thinking of you constantly."

"I have, too," she admitted. Even though it had only been two days, they had been the longest two days of her life, feeling like forever.

"Would you mind if I came over?"

"Of course not." She was past playing hard to get, if she'd ever been capable of it.

"Would it be all right if I bring a couple of friends?"

She looked around the cabin. "I'm not exactly set up for entertaining."

"They want to meet you. I'd like that, too. Don't worry, we'll manage. Just put the coffee on."

Wondering what the heck he was doing, she started the coffee and looked around for where she had left the coffee cake she had bought that morning at the bakery. The whole darn town looked so festive right now that she kept having urges to splurge a little on something special.

At least she had clean dishes. Between phone calls from Vanessa, she'd spent a whole lot of needless time tidying this space up, trying to keep busy and ease her anxiety over, well, over everything. Braden's parting shot, what it meant, the unknown family hanging over her head. Her lack of a past. Everything seemed to be coming to a head at once. Maybe if she were honest, she'd admit she was almost as nervous as Vanessa, Nate and Jonah were, though her fears weren't as imminent. So much depended on the success of the Manor.

But Braden's call, the fact that he was coming over to see her again, leavened her mood and eased her doubts. Maybe one thing in her life would work right. Maybe Braden wouldn't abandon her.

Although in honest moments she couldn't imagine why he'd want to hang around someone as messed up as she was.

At last she heard the sound of his truck and another vehicle. The idea of meeting some of his friends made her hold back rather than race to the door. She didn't want to appear too eager in front of strangers.

She heard voices outside. One of them sounded like

a woman. She couldn't explain why that surprised her. When he'd said friends, for some reason she had assumed it would be a couple of guys.

Then Braden threw the door open without knocking, and an attractive, middle-aged couple stepped in. She wondered if they were his relatives from out of town or something. The woman appeared to be in her late forties or early fifties, with dark hair that was beginning to silver. The man could only have been a couple of years older, but gray had totally taken over his temples. Their gazes swept the cabin swiftly, then fell on her.

In the next instant, Jenn's world turned upside down.

"Oh, my God," said the woman. "Jenny!" Tears started rolling down her face. The man with her quickly put his arm around her shoulders, but his eyes remained on Jenn, seeming to devour her. "Jennifer," he said, echoing the woman.

Jenn looked at Braden, even though she somehow already knew. Her legs began to feel like rubber bands, and it was a good thing the chair was right beside her. She collapsed on it, unable to speak. Part of her tried to summon some fury that he'd done this to her, but the fury wouldn't come. She sat trembling, looking at a weeping woman and a man with a kind, worn face.

"Jenn," Braden said, clearing his throat. "I'd like you to meet Jessica and Sterling MacCallum."

Braden took over. Jenn was incapable of moving, of responding. She didn't recognize these people, and her heart felt almost crushed that she couldn't. Strangers who were not strangers. This wasn't right. Everything was out of kilter, off balance.

But Braden ushered Jessica to the other armchair then brought the chairs from the dinette for himself and Sterling. Nobody seemed to know what to say for several minutes, but the tears kept rolling down Jessica's face.

Braden brought coffee that no one even touched. Then he sat waiting, as they were all waiting for whatever might come.

It was Jessica, finally, who broke the silence. "I know," she said brokenly, "that you don't remember us. Braden told us about your amnesia. I don't want to overwhelm you in any way, but sweet Lord, I am so happy to see you alive!"

Faced with these people, Jenn took her courage into her hands and asked the question that had been terrifying her since Winona had told her the truth. "You don't hate me?"

"Why in the world would we do that?" Sterling asked, his voice gravelly with emotion.

"I hear I was awful to you before I left."

He waved a hand. "We've been worried, we've been scared, and finally we thought we'd lost you for good. That you were dead. We didn't even have a grave to put flowers on. All we wanted in this world was to have our daughter back."

Something inside Jenn began to thaw. The wall that fear had built began to melt away. "I'm sorry I don't remember you. I'm sorry I ran away like that."

Jessica pulled a wad of tissues from her purse and wiped at her tears. "None of that matters. We'll deal with it. The important thing is that you're still alive. If you never remember us, at least we have that. You're alive."

Jenn looked at Braden, as if he might have some answer to this strange situation, but he was simply smiling faintly, silent and staying out of this. He'd made it happen. Surely he should have something to say for himself. But he didn't.

Which left her. The MacCallums seemed uncertain how to proceed. Well, of course they would. She didn't remember them. They were probably on tenterhooks, too.

Jenn struggled for something positive to say, something encouraging, but she kept coming up against her inability to remember these people. Her parents, it seemed.

So she fell back on the only thing she knew for certain. "I was trying to get back home," she said slowly. "I know that much. It's been driving me for four years. But I feel so bad that I can't remember you. I admit I was afraid, too. Afraid of not knowing you and the kind of people you are, afraid of how you'd react to me. And honestly, I don't like the few things I learned about myself from Winona. So I was afraid of the things I'd learn about myself. I guess I said terrible things to you, and I can't even really apologize because I don't remember!"

Sterling leaned forward, resting his elbows on his knees. "Forget what Winona told you. That old busybody has only part of the story."

"Yes," Jessica said. Her tears had begun to dry, but she couldn't drag her gaze from Jenn. "She couldn't possibly know it all. We made some mistakes, too."

Jenn looked between the MacCallums wishing she could feel even the faintest spark of recognition. Just one little quiver. "You made mistakes?"

"We've had plenty of time to think about it," Sterling said. "You were a young woman, and instead of pressing you to accept an inheritance you felt was filthy, we should have let you decide. You weren't our little girl anymore. Sure, we wanted you to have a secure future, but really, it wasn't our decision. So instead of letting you do as you chose, we fought with you. I'm not surprised you felt you had to get away."

Jenn felt a stirring of warmth toward him. He was apologizing to her. Whether it was justified, she didn't know, but he was trying to mend the fence from his side.

"I don't remember," she said finally. It was her only answer.

Jessica surprised her by rising from her chair and coming to drop a kiss on her head. "You don't have to remember. We'll fill in the gaps for you. Show you all the photos. Tell you how much we've always loved you. And you still don't have to remember. Just share your future with us as much as you comfortably can. We couldn't bear to lose you again."

Jessica returned to her seat. Jenn felt all jumbled up inside. Her fear was gone for the first time in forever, and she knew she should be feeling happy to have found her place, if not her memory. But the lack of memory had never been starker than it was right now. She was sitting and talking with her parents, and they might as well have been strangers. Nice strangers, but still.

She glanced at Braden and wondered what he was thinking, but still nothing showed on his face except a faint smile. She supposed she should be angry with him for overriding her desire to wait, but she couldn't manage it. He had saved her days, weeks or even months of agonizing over whether to call these people. For good or ill, it was done.

"I'm sorry," she said again, looking at Jessica and then Sterling. "I wish I could remember you. I feel awful that I can't."

Sterling shook his head. "Let go of that. We're just glad to see you again. It's time to start building bridges.

You might never remember, but the important thing is what we do now. We want you to come home with us."

Braden stood. That was his cue, he supposed. He had seen the fear leak out of Jenn, but he couldn't do anything about the rest of it. She would have to deal with this however she could, as best she could. Going home with her parents seemed like the right thing to do, even though it would take her away from him. He wouldn't deny her the opportunity to build a relationship with them, perhaps have her memory jarred a bit so that she could remember some of her past. Not for anything would he deny her the chance, even if it meant he would never see her again.

Watching the fear go, watching Jessica and Sterling reach out to her, watching the dawn of small hopes in her expression…that was all he needed.

"I need to run," he said, when Sterling and Jessica paused in the midst of recalling Jenn's childhood, recollections that were making Jenn smile and relax even more. "Still some stuff to do tonight."

He wouldn't have been surprised if Jenn had merely nodded and let him go with a simple good-night. He was well aware that she had every right to be mad at him for taking charge and putting her in this position without warning.

But instead, she followed him to the door, and after he pulled his jacket on, she laid her hand on his arm.

He looked at her, sensing she wanted to say something, but he couldn't tell what it was, and this might not even be the right time. Not with the MacCallums here. If she wanted to rake him over the coals, best she did it when they weren't around to be hurt.

He bent, and tried to speak volumes with a necessarily brief and chaste kiss. "Tomorrow night?" he asked. "Meet at the shindig?"

She nodded. "Absolutely." Then she smiled.

He carried that smile away with him, tucked in his heart. After tomorrow night, he might not see it again for a long while. She might well transplant herself permanently to Whitehorn, and construct her life there where at least she would have the MacCallums' support.

He stepped out into the night, closing the door behind him, and sucked in deep drafts of icy air. He might have just closed a huge door, he realized. A much more important one than the door of her cabin. He might have just helped Jenn leave for good.

The thought squeezed his heart like a giant fist, telling him how much and how rapidly he had come to care for this young woman. He'd closed doors like this one before, but it had never hurt so much.

Damn!

Small comfort that he believed he had done what was right for Jenn. A lot of her questions could now be answered. Even if she never got her memory back, she'd have answers for those questions she was always trying to evade. She'd have that sense of continuity that had been interrupted, even though he supposed it might never be the same for her as for everyone else.

The drive home was at once contradictorily long and too short. He wasn't ready to join the holiday cheer, and while his whole family was gathered in the main house, sleeping in their old bedrooms with their wives and fiancees, kids sprawled in sleeping bags in the family room, reliving past holidays and good memories while building new ones, he just didn't have the heart for it tonight.

Instead, he drove past the house out to his own little place, an unnecessary house, given that he'd always have room with his parents, except that a few years ago he'd felt a need to have his own space, his own place.

Which he guessed wasn't so very different with Jenn. He'd built a house. Now she would build a past of sorts. A place of her own in a world that had been too blank for long.

He ought to be celebrating for her. Instead, once he was inside, he built a fire and poured himself a whiskey. Sitting there alone, away from everyone he cared about, he had some small sense of the isolation Jenn had endured, except hers hadn't been by choice.

He'd built this place partly with an eye to a future that would include a wife and maybe a couple of kids. A place of their own.

Not likely he could deprive Jenn of her family. He could only wonder at himself. The unsnaggable bachelor who had broken off every relationship early. For good reasons, or so he had thought when he did it. Jenn was different. He couldn't understand it any other way. Some ineffable quality of hers had drawn him and snared his heart.

Just in time for him to wave it all goodbye.

Hell, he thought, and poured another whiskey. He'd done it to himself this time.

Jenn walked through the next day in a daze. She met her parents for breakfast in town, and they'd talked for hours. Well, Jessica and Sterling had. She'd mostly listened, drinking it in, trying to create associations in the empty places of her memory.

More than once, they pressed her to come home with them. More than once she simply said, "Not yet."

"But we want you for Christmas," Jessica finally said. Jenn was almost appalled at herself when she answered, "Not until after Christmas. Please understand. The people I know, my friends, they're here. I want to be with them. After Christmas, okay?"

They looked saddened, but they accepted it. Eventually, Jessica brightened. "We'll have a late Christmas with you. Big dinner and all of that. Better late than…"

She didn't say the word never. Of course she couldn't since she and Sterling had concluded a while back that Jennifer must be dead.

Sterling surprised her by clasping her hand warmly. "Call us when you're ready. We'll be waiting. As long as you want."

Jenn waved them on their way then headed back to her cabin. Hard to believe it was after noon already, and the big shindig started at five. She needed to wash her hair, maybe style it a bit if she could remember how. Ponytails didn't seem right for tonight.

And then, of course, there were Vanessa's calls. Her nervousness practically shrieked over the phone. Jenn lost track of how many times she said, "It's going to be great! It's going to be perfect!"

Five o'clock seemed to roll around awfully fast for Jenn. Wearing her new dress, a deep blue velvet with threads of gold in it, her hair styled up into some kind of bun, her tarnished necklace around her neck, she headed for the lodge just outside town.

The parking lot was full of cars, the elaborately redesigned entryway full of people. It seemed everyone from Rust Creek Falls, Thunder Canyon and even as far as Kalispell wanted to be here tonight. Jenn had some trouble finding a place to park, then she joined the moving throngs all headed for the Maverick Manor.

She hadn't been here for the Great Flood, but she had

already learned that this opening was a milestone event in most minds. While there was still plenty of recovery underway, this was a big one. It meant there would be tourist business, or so everyone hoped.

She wasn't sure how much good that would do for this small, rustic town in the long run, but folks were happy, and she wished Nate Crawford well in his enterprise. He seemed like an okay guy. And then there was Vanessa, who had been pouring her heart and soul into the mural that would be revealed tonight, and Jonah who must be tied up in knots because he'd helped with some of the redesign of the place.

She barely got in the door before Vanessa grabbed her. "Tell me it's okay."

"I haven't had a chance to see it yet," Jenn protested, amused. "Do you want me to just say yes, or would you rather I look first and tell you the truth?"

Vanessa rolled her eyes. "Don't do this to me."

"Let me walk around. Give me a few minutes to look. I'm sure it's perfect."

It was not at all what Jenn expected, though. She began to move through the growing crowd and look at the huge walls. Vanessa seemed to have painted the history of the area, of the ranchers of Whitehorn and Rumor, the Queen of Hearts Mine of Thunder Canyon—and even a tip of the hat to Lily Divine, the once-notorious "Shady Lady" of that still-booming mountain town. The mural also portrayed the more recent history of Rust Creek Falls. As she began to recognize some of the families portrayed up there, from the Crawfords, Daltons, Traubs and others, shown doing what they did for a living, she felt her amazement grow.

Over there, tucked in a corner, she saw the Newcomers Club, all those smiling faces of people who had become her friends. She could even pick out her own face, though it was in the background. As if Vanessa had sensed she was hiding.

She loved it. She turned again and again and realized that Vanessa had given this town a beautiful gift: she had given it its memory. It was enough to make her eyes prickle.

"Well?" Vanessa said impatiently from behind her.

Jenn whirled and threw her arms around her. "Fabulous. Perfect. Maybe it means more to me, I don't know."

Vanessa stepped back, raising a brow. "Why would it mean more to you?"

"Because this is the town's continuity," Jenn said, waving her arm. "Its history. Its memory. Maybe most people don't know how much that means."

But the comments from everywhere were approving, and Jenn could hear them as Vanessa grabbed her again for another hug. "I love you, girl."

"Hey," said a deep male voice, "that's my line."

Jenn's heart stopped. Turning from Vanessa, she saw Braden, all duded up in a suit and string tie. She wanted to throw herself at him but held back because it was possible he was trying to ease her out of his life. He smiled at her, but it was an awkward smile, only raising her fears.

"I have only one criticism," he said to Vanessa.

"What's that, cowboy?"

"You put the Traubs and Crawfords too close together."

Vanessa started laughing. "Work it out, you bunch of stubborn idiots." Then, still grinning, she let Jonah draw her away to the groaning buffet tables.

Braden stepped closer. "How are you?"

"Never better," Jenn answered not quite truthfully. The one thing that could have made her feel better was if Braden had at least hugged her. Even given her a little hello kiss.

"So you're not mad at me over the MacCallums?"

"No. I guess I could have been, but I'm just so glad to be over that hump. They're wonderful people." She looked around. "Is your family here?"

"Everyone's here, but finding someone in this crush is almost impossible. So are you going home with the MacCallums?"

Jenn turned her gaze back to him. "Not until after Christmas."

"I'm surprised."

"Why?"

"I figured now that you had a family, you'd want to go with them. Find your old life. No reason to commit to hanging around here anymore."

Jenn's jaw dropped. "Braden?"

He threw up a hand. "I'm making a hash out of this, and I can hardly hear myself think. Want something to eat?"

"No!" Frustration surged in her. "Are you telling me to get lost?"

His eyes widened, then a change came over him. His jaw set, and he grabbed her elbow. "Did I tell you how beautiful you look tonight?"

"You overlooked that part," she said acidly.

"Well, you do. Where in the hell is your coat?"

"Checked at the coat check with a million others. What…"

"Hell," he said. He'd been headed for the lobby doors but took a sudden sharp turn toward a closed door near the front of the lobby.

"Where are you quit dragging me?"

"I'm trying to find a quiet place."

"Good luck."

But somehow he managed it. Leading her through a door labeled "Employees Only" they entered a silent hall-way with empty open offices on either side. He pulled her into one of them and closed the door.

"What's going on?" she demanded.

"I'm acting like a caveman."

"I can see that. But why?"

"Because…because I've spent the past two days think-ing about you going to Whitehorn. And you're going. It's not exactly a hop-skip away. You'll be there, and I'll be here, and I won't get to see you very often."

"I'm not going forever," she protested. It was nice, though, to know he cared that she'd be leaving. She'd begun to wonder. But she just didn't know how to reas-sure him. If he even wanted reassurance.

"Maybe you don't think you're going forever," he said. "Maybe you don't intend to. But that could change. You might find everything you want there."

Not him, she thought. She wouldn't find Braden there. A terrible heaviness began to settle in her heart.

"Anyway," he continued before she could respond, "I've got to face facts. You've got a future waiting for you, one that gives you at least some of your past. I don't want to stand in your way, and I sure as hell can't ask you for any kind of commitment. Not under these cir-cumstances."

She'd been in pretty much of a daze since the arrival of the MacCallums, with an overload of things to ab-sorb. But all of a sudden matters began to clear up. She focused intently on one word as her heart began to race. "Commitment? What kind of commitment?"

"This isn't very romantic, is it."

A flare of annoyance sparked in her. "Will you stop being so evasive? What exactly do you mean?"

He sighed then released her arm and took her hands. "I don't have any practice at this. I've never said anything like this before. But I want to be fair to you."

"So be fair by telling me what you're driving at." Hope and fear warred within her, familiar even now, but different. This wasn't about amnesia. This was about what she truly wanted *now*.

"I love you," he said finally. "I can't escape it, and since I brought the MacCallums into your life, I've been staring down a bleak road without you. I know that you need to go, but I don't want to let you go. Selfish, but there it is. I want you in my life forever. I want you to marry me. But you can't make that decision now."

Surprise filled her, even as joy began to wash away the fear. "I can't? Who says I can't? Nothing has affected my ability to know how I feel."

He squeezed her hand, and the expression of hope on his face was almost painful. "Do you think…you can love me?"

Her heart cracked wide open. "Braden, I already do. With my whole being. I thought you were trying to say goodbye to me."

"Never!" His eyes blazed, and he pulled her into his arms, holding her so tightly she could barely breathe, kissing her as if she were the breath of life itself. When he dragged his mouth from hers, he said raggedly, "You don't have to promise anything. Not yet. Your family…"

"They're nice people. I want to get to know them better. I'm going to visit them, but it's just a visit, because there's only one place on earth I want to be. With you."

He hugged her for a long, long time, his face pressed to her neck. She hugged her back, never wanting to let go.

But finally he eased his hold. "We're being rude to our friends, I guess. Time to get out there and ooh and aah appropriately. Later?"

"Yes, later."

It was likely, she thought as they returned to the lobby hand in hand, that anyone who looked at them would know the truth. That only made her smile wider.

Braden loved her. Who needed more than that?

Epilogue

Christmas morning dawned clear, bright and cold. Jenn stood at the window, squinting out at the winter beauty, wrapped in her warmest robe and slippers.

Strong arms closed around her from behind. "These have been the best two days of my life," Braden said.

"I'm pretty sure I can say the same." She turned within the circle of his arms, smiling, to look at him.

"Merry Christmas, love."

"Merry Christmas," she answered. "I'm sorry I don't have a gift for you, but time got away from me." She didn't mention the uncertainty that had nearly paralyzed her. That now seemed like part of a distant past. Braden had made sure that she knew how much he wanted her.

"You're the only gift I want. I'd love to be giving you an engagement ring this morning, but I want you to pick it out."

"Oh, Braden…" She leaned against him, pressing her cheek to his shoulder, filled with inexpressible gratitude. She had lost a lot, but she had found the most priceless gift of all. "So little seems to matter anymore except that we're together. I love you with my whole heart."

"I love you, too, sweetheart. I'm bursting with it." Then he sighed. "Unfortunately, it's time to head out to the Triple-T."

She lifted her head. "Already?"

"Big brunch to be followed by huge dinner later." He tipped her chin a little higher and searched her eyes. "Are you ready for this? The whole clan can be overwhelming, but I promise not to leave your side."

Her fear of large groups hadn't entirely abandoned her, but she figured she needed to do this, needed to overcome her resistance.

"We don't have to go," he said. "If you want, I'll give them a call and…"

"No." She pressed her fingertips to his lips. "I've been invited to join the Traub family for Christmas. That's not an invitation I want to turn down. Ever."

He smiled softly, his eyes filled with warmth. "You are so brave. Have I told you that?"

"Once or twice, I think."

"Well, I'll keep telling you. Brave. Resourceful. Smart. Beautiful. An incredible lover. A marvelous companion…"

"Oh, stop," she interrupted, her cheeks flaming. "I'm not perfect."

"In every way that counts." Then he lifted her off her feet and swung her in a circle. "Welcome to my life, Jennifer MacCallum. There's been a place waiting for you in my heart since I was born."

Love had rescued her, and now joy swept her into a whole new world, a world with family, friends, and everything she had ever lacked.

Her search for her memory had brought her a future brighter than any she had ever dreamed. Who would have believed she could be so lucky?

A couple of hours later, when she stood amidst the warm and welcoming Traub family, and applause greeted

Braden's announcement of their engagement, followed by more hugs than she could count, she knew she had truly found her home. She belonged at last.

* * * * *

MILLS & BOON®

Exciting new titles
coming next month

With over 100 new titles available every month,
find out what exciting romances
lie ahead next month.

Visit
www.millsandboon.co.uk/comingsoon
to find out more!